OUTSTANDING PRAISE FOR
IN THE SHADOW OF THE LION:

"A fast-paced new spy thriller . . . Combines a little of Robert Ludlum, a lot of Helen MacInnes, and even a dash of Ken Follett." —*Detroit Monthly*

"Treachery galore . . . Lots of intrigue and excitement." —New York *Daily News*

"The pacing is excellent. The portrayal of an innocent hurled into a labyrinth of murder and deceit is utterly convincing. I devoured this thriller at a single sitting. S.K. Wolf knows the trade." —Robert Moss, author of *The Spike* and *Carnival of Spies*

"The action is well-plotted and Wolf's research is good." —*Chicago Tribune*

"Wolf pulls this one off handsomely . . . It holds one to the end." —*Boston Globe*

"Entertaining . . . Realistic, spine-chilling, hard to put down . . . full of rich characters and plenty of action all the way to the end." —*Drood Review of Mystery*

IN THE
SHADOW
OF THE
LION

(published in hardcover as
MacKinnon's Machine)

S.K.WOLF

ST. MARTIN'S PAPERBACKS

This book is a work of fiction. Names, characters, places and incidents are either the product of the author's imagination or are used fictitiously. Any resemblance to actual events or locales or persons, living or dead, is entirely coincidental.

In the Shadow of the Lion was previously published in hardcover under the title *MacKinnon's Machine.*

Published by arrangement with Simon & Schuster

IN THE SHADOW OF THE LION

Library of Congress Catalog Card Number: 90-28353

ISBN: 0-312-95077-2

Printed in the United States of America

St. Martin's Press hardcover edition published 1991
St. Martin's Paperbacks edition/June 1994

St. Martin's Paperbacks are published by St. Martin's Press, 175 Fifth Avenue, New York, N.Y. 10010.

10 9 8 7 6 5 4 3 2 1

FOR J.N.,
WHO MADE ME WRITE IT,
AND S.C.,
WHO MADE ME WANT TO

ACKNOWLEDGMENTS

I wish to extend thanks to the many people who helped with the research on this book. In particular, I would like to thank Jim Mackie, formerly of the U.S. Army Rangers; Police Inspector David Varlow of Folkestone, Kent, UK; Coroner's Officer Graham Coombs of Kent County Constabulary, UK; as well as Pat and Doug Smith, Patty and Eugene Wank, and Lee Zombory, for their willingness to respond to some very unusual questions.

1

YAHAD SETTLEMENT, ISRAEL

Daniel Gideon stood in the shadow of an outcropping of rock and gazed across the valley below. Occasional clouds slid before the moon, but for the most part he could see well enough. A few piles of rocks still dotted the edge of the valley, but the bulk of them had already been removed, taken to the far hillside where they were being used to build the community center. The school had already been built— the first priority. After the center would come the living quarters. Until then, tents would suffice. But the work was coming along well—only a few weeks more and the center would be completed. By midsummer, if things went well, half the settlers would be out of the tents and into permanent homes. The valley floor had been carefully prepared, the trellises set in place, and the grape slips tenderly planted. There would be a few lean years until the grapes could be harvested, and in the meantime the settlement would have to live off its sheep and goats and the truck gardens planted at the near end of the valley. Gideon leaned against the rock and smiled into the night. It's one of the many things that make us different from them, he was thinking. We plan ahead and then work toward the goal. We'll sacrifice everything, working toward the goal—which is what makes us the intellectuals, the scientists, and the musicians of the world. And they will never be anything more than nomads, never thinking beyond today, or tomorrow at best. And that's why they kept this place a desert—or maybe even let it get that way in the first place—and now we're turning it into a garden.

He thought about cigarettes and wished he had one. He looked at the moon and then at the lighted digits of his watch. Two twenty-seven. An hour and a half left. Everything was still. He hitched the strap of the Uzi higher on his shoulder and thought he heard a noise. He listened, but there was nothing. He rubbed his right thumb against the Uzi's grip and shook his head, grinning at himself in the night. Hearing things. Maybe just the back of his jacket brushing against the rock. Or a desert salamander slithering across the scarp. A bare kilometer inside the border—a person could get paranoid.

Gideon had lived in Israel for seven years now, the first four in Tel Aviv, where he'd taught in a secondary school, and the last three in the West Bank. He'd come to Yahad Settlement eight months ago, when the valley was still strewn with rocks and brush, and had worked at the clearing, had built the grape trellises, had planted the cuttings by hand, and was now doing the masonry of the new buildings. Those were the things he did by day. By night he took his turn standing guard. His duty was midnight to four, every other night. At four, when his relief came, he would hand over the Uzi and head for the tent where he would find Ariela already asleep. He'd slip in beside her, slide a hand around her waist, and she would stir. He'd cup her breast in his hand and she would turn toward him then and kiss him, her tongue sliding across his teeth. He would wind his hand in her loose hair and hold her close, and she would slip her hand between his legs. . . . It was a long way from West Hartford and the investment business that his father had intended him to join, but he had never felt so alive.

Above Gideon, and slightly to his left, a shadow moved soundlessly across the rock. A man, hardly larger than a child, bent and watched the guard below. He grinned into the night and shook his head. You think you are safe. You think because you stand with your back to the rock and a nearly sheer cliff above you that your back is covered. But you have not had to be a goat like me, living in the hills, climbing the rocks, eating whatever comes your way. The money that pours in from America supports you, and you fool yourself into thinking that you have done it on your own. If we had had the money you have, we could have done wonders, too. He crouched lower and leveled the gun at the guard below. It was a handgun; a larger weapon would have been in the way as he climbed, and he would have been in constant fear that it would brush against an outcrop of rock, unseen in the dark. A handgun was safer, could tuck into a holster at the small of his back. It didn't matter that it meant he would have to come closer. In the dark, the closer the better.

The man felt gingerly at his feet for a loose stone, found one, and held it in his hand for a moment. He looked at the lighted digits of his watch. Just after two thirty. The ideal time—between two and three—when the body is at its most sluggish, the responses the slowest. He flung the stone out to the side and waited a half breath until he heard it scudder down the edge of the rocks below. The man beneath him leaned forward, looking carefully, trying not to betray his position, and above him the silenced gun spat a sound like a puff of air.

At almost the same moment that Daniel Gideon would have heard the sound, the bullet crashed into his brain, and he crumpled to the rock at his feet. Above him, the other man was already clambering down. He reached the body quickly, and without stopping to contemplate what he had done, he lifted the guard's torso and yanked the Uzi out from under him, then let the body fall back against the rock. Without pause he moved on down, his footing just as sure as if he had spent a lifetime clambering over this very hillside. As he moved, his eyes scanned the valley and the surrounding hills, taking in all the dark silent shapes but always returning to the rendezvous point. Eight guards, eight Uzis. It was all that was needed, but to take only the guns would be a dead giveaway. The group would kill everyone in the entire place, and maybe they would be rewarded by even more guns. The theft of the guns would appear as only a small detail of the whole picture—an entire settlement wiped out while it slept. No one would think anything about the guns. No one would realize. And he grinned to himself at the irony of it. As if it were necessary to steal guns. As if the men couldn't pay for all the guns they wanted. But these would be Uzis—clean, traceable to Israel

—and that was what was important. That was what was being paid for.

He was still grinning as he ran across the valley now, heading for the big olive tree that was the rendezvous. All you had to do was think it out, plan, work toward a goal. And even if the goal seemed impossible to reach, even if each action seemed unrelated to the whole, it was the final outcome that mattered. And, as always, he had that final outcome clearly in mind.

LONDON

"A. C. MacKinnon." The name hung in the air, as if floating on the speaker's cigar smoke that drifted gently toward the ceiling.

Raymond Morse shifted in his chair and brushed a piece of lint from his gray flannels. "MacKinnon," he said, frowning.

"I had him with me on that Iranian thing," Glover said.

Morse gazed at him, saying nothing.

"He's a Brit, like you. Former SAS. Oh, yes, I know—you Brits get all misty-eyed over your Special Air Services. The whole country could go to hell in a hand basket, but as long as your vaunted SAS hangs on, you think you've got something to be proud about. Well, when it comes to men like MacKinnon, you're right on the money. He did a few for-hires when he came out. I know you've run across him."

"Yes, I know him," Morse said, looking away. "Not personally, of course, but by his rep. He's a drunk, they say."

"Drunk or sober, he's the best fucking sergeant major in the world. If you want the best, he's it."

Morse gazed at Glover again, wishing he would sit down, wishing he would put out the bloody cigar. "Drunks are trouble, Ken; you know that. We can't have trouble on this." He glanced to his right as if seeking support.

Sitting behind the massive mahogany desk, Kherman Shahabad said nothing. He dipped his head until his cigarette touched the lighter, then he snapped the lighter shut and pocketed it before looking from one man to the other.

He inhaled and the smoke came out with his words. "It is your choice. You two must decide," he said at last.

"Get someone else," Morse said.

"I hear he's on the wagon. And there is no one else with his qualifications. Not only is he the best, he also knows the place. He was down there in seventy-seven."

"What good does that do?" Morse snapped. "You can't be thinking of telling him to train for it. And anyway, it doesn't matter whether they say he's reformed or not, a drunk is a drunk."

Glover let out another belch of smoke. "He can know that it's going to be desert, that the terrain is like what it was in the Sinai without his having to know what it's about." He spoke with enforced patience, as if explaining to an uncomprehending child. "He's the one, Ray. Wait until you see him at work. It's hard enough finding good men these days. I'm not making excuses ahead of time; I'm just telling you how it is. With what they'll have to go up against . . ." He stepped over to the desk and knocked a three-quarter-inch ash into the pristine ashtray.

Shahabad's eyes followed the movement.

"I'll get the best guys I can get," Glover went on, "but if you want them turned into the best fucking unit in the world, it'll take someone like MacKinnon. And if you want my opinion, there isn't anyone else like him. When they go, they'll be the best machine they can be. Guaranteed."

"Extremely high praise, I'd say." Morse turned again toward Shahabad, who was gazing silently at the smoke as it hung in a shaft of light sifting through the damask-covered window. "But I still don't like it," Morse said. "He's a drunk, and even if you don't tell him ahead of time, he'll recognize the place when he gets there and then he'll balk."

"Not if we don't take him."

Morse stared as if he hadn't understood.

Glover grinned and nodded. "Yes. We don't need him after he's done the training. When they're ready they'll run by themselves, like a Swiss clock. We don't need him down there."

"No loose ends, Ken; that's already been established. When it happens, he'll know."

"No, he won't."

"It'd be pretty damn hard for him not to."

"Not at all." Glover took the cigar out of his mouth. His right eye almost closed into a wink, and then he reached over to the ashtray and rolled the end of the cigar against it. "Give you odds on it, in fact." He was grinning.

"I wouldn't have expected to hear that from you," Morse said quietly.

Glover raised his eyebrows. "You wouldn't? What's it matter? They're all going to be dead afterwards, anyway."

Morse shrugged. "That's different."

Glover shook his head. "There's no difference, and you know it. That's the way it is on an exercise like this. In the end it doesn't make a shit's worth of difference whether you're the first fatality or the last."

Raymond Morse uncrossed his long legs. He'd never particularly cared for Glover. The man represented everything he most disliked about Americans: so sure of himself, so sure that his way was the only way. No taste, no class; and the bloody cigars smelled like rotten rope. No sensitivity, no finesse. The only thing was, he was very good at what he did. Glover had been his own idea, in fact. He'd seen the man run enough operations that he respected his ability, even though he despised him personally. Inwardly, Morse sighed. *You puts up with what you have to*, his mum used to say. He'd known back then what she'd meant, but he understood even better now. It was a very select world in which he ran, and one came to know nearly all the players, by reputation if in no other way. Glover would put together a good group, of that he was sure. And the line on MacKinnon had always been impeccable, though God knew what the man had been doing over the past several years. "I haven't heard of MacKinnon in years," he said. "Do you even know where he is?"

"Yes, I know," Glover said. "It took some doing, but I know."

2

COVINGTON STATION, SOUTH ISLAND, NEW ZEALAND

The house sat on the crest of a small grassy hill, with the outbuildings arranged below, on the north incline. The whole works was enclosed by well-tended board fences, forming a series of small paddocks that reached as far as the stream at the bottom of the hill.

Kenneth Glover pulled the hired Toyota into the drive and sat behind the wheel for a moment. He'd had all the way from Dunedin to plan what he'd say—all the way from London, as a matter of fact. But he knew he'd have only the one chance. He would have to make it good. He would have to present something so tempting that there was no way Mac could refuse. It was not exactly Glover's strong suit; he was better with actions than he was with words. Right now he'd make the odds little better than even on Mac's acceptance.

The house was a rambling one-story place, painted white. Beyond were a couple of higher hills and then more mountains. A few small oaks sheltered the house, and an apple tree stood alone in a corner of the fence. On the hillsides occasional trees mottled the landscape, but mostly it was only green grass. In the distance, Glover could make out white dots against the green. Sheep. He nodded to himself and got out of the car.

A woman stepped onto the porch, watching him come. The wind blew her hair into her face, and she brushed it away, then held her hand above her eyes to shade the sun. She looked to be in her mid-forties, and she smiled broadly as Glover approached.

"Would you be Mrs. Tyson?" Glover asked with his foot on the first step.

"I would. Martha Tyson. Welcome," she said, extending her hand.

"My name is Glover. Kenneth Glover. I'm looking for a man by the name of MacKinnon. I understand he works for you."

"Yes, he does." Then she frowned. "Is there a problem?"

"No, not at all. He's an old friend, and I thought I'd look him up."

"Come in, come in," she said, opening the door and leading the way. "How long can you stay?"

He followed her into a sun-filled parlor with yellow and white wallpaper and a yellow tile fireplace.

"It's always the first question we ask," she said almost apologetically, "how long can you stay." She was tanned, and her skin had been weathered by sun and wind. Close up, she looked older than she'd seemed at a distance, but he guessed that she wasn't.

"Well, I'm looking for Mac—"

"Yes, he works here, but he's out with a mob just now. He's moving them down from the far ridge."

"Sheep?"

"Oh, yes. I'm sorry. You're a Yank, aren't you?"

"When do you expect him back?"

"Ordinarily not for a couple of days. Can I get you a cup of tea?" She was moving toward the hall before he even responded.

He followed her into a large kitchen with blue-painted cupboards running along two walls. "Is there any way I can get out there?"

She lifted a tea cosy from a squat blue teapot and, with the tips of her fingers, touched the side of the pot to judge its warmth. "My husband could take you in the plane if you're in a hurry," she said.

"It's just that I don't have a lot of time."

"What are you doing in New Zealand, if I may ask?" She handed him a cup of tea and took her own to the kitchen table, motioning him to join her.

"Business." From a glass bowl on the table he took two

cubes of sugar and dropped them into his tea. "How soon could your husband take me?"

"He'll be back shortly. He's fertilizing right now—we do that by plane here. When he comes back for another load he'll see your car and come down to the house. What kind of business are you in that brings you all the way from the States?"

"Personnel. I do advising on personnel issues."

"Rather a long way to come. One would think they could find someone closer to home."

He grinned at her. "Sometimes it can be a rather specialized field. Do you and your husband own this whole ranch?"

"Yes, we do. But in New Zealand, Mr. Glover, we call it a station. You're a friend of Mac's?"

"Long ago. A longtime friend. I haven't seen him in a number of years."

"You'll forgive me if I'm curious." She dipped her head for a sip of tea. "Mac seems such a loner. He never receives mail, never sends any, never talks about family. I gather he was married once. And . . . I gather . . ." She hesitated.

"He was once a drunk? But I understand he's clear of that now."

She laughed. "No easy task in this country, I'll tell you." Then, more thoughtfully, "He's not an easy person to get to know, but I think it's done him good to be here. He may surprise you; he's very fit and sharp as a tack. Caring for sheep will do one thing or the other for a person—all this space, all that time alone with one's thoughts. It'll either sharpen you up, or else hopelessly dull you. I'd say it's been good for him."

"I'd wondered if by now he mightn't have gotten himself a family."

She smiled slowly. "No. Just us."

"How much help does your husband have?"

"Mac's the stock manager. Between the two of them—and the dogs—they handle it pretty well. And Jesse, our son, who's fifteen."

"An operation like this must require a pretty hefty start-up price."

"This station belonged to my husband's father before him. I would think it'd be very hard to start from nothing now."

He heard feet scraping on the porch as she spoke, and then the door banged open. The man who appeared in the doorway was tall and red-haired, and his face broke naturally into a smile. "I saw the car," he said, moving forward and extending his hand. "Phil Tyson."

"Kenneth Glover." He shook Tyson's hand and found it as callused as he would have expected.

"Mr. Glover's come to see Mac; he's an old friend of Mac's," Martha Tyson said.

"Are you really, now?" Tyson chuckled. "I would almost have guessed that Mac hadn't any old friends."

"I'd guess he has one or two."

"I told him you'd be able to drop him off up there with Mac. Mr. Glover seems to be pressed for time."

Tyson chuckled again. "In this place there is no such thing as being pressed for time."

"I had business in Auckland; my plane flies out day after tomorrow," Glover said.

"I'd be glad to take you up there, give you a few hours with him, and then pick you up again before dark. That suit you?"

"You can plan to spend the night here," Martha Tyson said, "and then leave first thing in the morning. It should get you back in time."

"I wouldn't want to impose on you like that."

"It's nothing," she said. "In fact, Phil, why couldn't Mac just leave the mob up there overnight and come back, too? With the plane empty, you could fit another body in there, and it would give him more time with his friend." She turned back to Glover. "You must stay. We so seldom have guests here, it's a real treat when we do. And Mac is like part of the family."

Tyson rolled his eyes and shook his head. "Don't try arguing with her. When Martha has a chance for a party, the devil himself couldn't sway her. Come along. I'll load up the plane and we'll be on our way."

Outside, Glover looked around. He almost asked about the plane but then he saw it, an old Fletcher, sitting on a hill beyond the house. He frowned. "Where's the runway?"

Tyson laughed. "You can see the hills. We take one of 'em, level it out a bit, and that does for the runway."

"How much does that one give you, anyway?"

"Enough. You'll see." Tyson strode down a small gully at the back of the house, then up the side of the hill.

Glover, who had thought he was in good shape, puffed along beside him. He could see the hilltop now, knocked off by a bulldozer or a backhoe, and then the grass had come back sparsely, showing two parallel tracks. The surface rose slightly and looked to be just over two hundred yards long. "It's pretty damn short," he said.

Tyson shook his head. "No problem." The plane sat next to a thousand-gallon polyethylene tank set on a trailer. Tyson reached for the hose, attached near the bottom of the tank's side, and swung it into position above the hopper set into the plane's fuselage. He pulled a lever and waited while the fertilizer fed into the hopper.

"You fertilize the pastures?" Glover had to shout to be heard over the rush of the liquid pouring into the tank.

"Have to. Sheep'll eat everything in a paddock except the fence. We rotate them every month or so, and the grass comes back pretty fast if we fertilize it."

Glover watched with growing disquiet as the plane hunkered down with its mounting load. He looked again at the runway. The two of them hadn't even gotten into the plane yet. There was no way they were going to make it.

Tyson shoved a lever and removed the hose, shaking out the last dribbles. "All right," he said, "let's do it."

Glover took one more look down the runway. "You're sure this'll make it?"

Tyson clapped him on the back. "Just watch. I've never had a wreck yet. You ever fly in anything besides a commercial jet?"

"Some." He climbed aboard. Everything in the cockpit

was dusted with a fine layer of super-phosphate, except the controls. Years of hard use had given them a dull silver burnish.

"You a pilot by any chance?" Tyson asked.

"No." Over the years he'd found it was better to lie than to risk the questions that might come next. He had logged more than a dozen missions in fixed wings and helos in Central America and nearly a hundred in Southeast Asia.

"Too bad. If you were, I might have asked if you wanted a hand on the throttle. Though it's probably best if you didn't." He was buckling himself into his seat. "Ever fly in mountains?"

"Some." Glover buckled his seat belt and wished for a shoulder harness.

"It's a little different kind of flying," Tyson shouted. He was revving the engine, checking the gauges. "You have to get used to the air currents over landscape like this. On the other hand, it's the only kind of flying I've ever done." He began his taxi back to the far end of the runway. "You get used to it mighty fast. On a good day I'll land and take off two or three dozen times."

The plane bumped over the grass to the end of the runway, where Tyson turned it around. He revved the engine twice, then turned to Glover. "All set?"

Glover nodded. His eyes were on the end of the runway. There's no way, his mind was telling him; this plane's going to be as maneuverable as a pregnant cow. They were moving now, picking up speed. Glover didn't need to look at the gauges; he could estimate the speed by the ground moving beneath him, but his eyes were on the end of the runway. *There's no way.* They had gone halfway, three-quarters, and the plane was still solidly on the ground; even the bumps gave it no lift. The end was approaching them, under them, and Glover felt the back of his throat close off in horror as the plane dropped off the runway, dipped twelve or fifteen feet, and then, with a strain of engine, leveled off.

Tyson turned to him, grinning. "The first time's always the worst."

But Glover was still staring ahead, this time at a hillside

that was fast approaching. Barely looking, Tyson banked hard left, still climbing, and missed the hill by less than twenty yards. Glover let out the breath he hadn't even known he was holding. Two or three dozen times a day. The man could probably do it in his sleep.

They were still climbing and still dodging the higher hills when Tyson pointed off to the left. "See there, the mob on that far hillside? That'll be Mac."

"How much do you own?"

"Over to that rounded hill; on the other side, to the ridge there. Just over two thousand acres."

"Must cost a pretty penny if a person were to get started."

"Well, you don't need quite as much as I have."

"How much would it take?"

"You could get by on something close to half that size. Not get rich, not support a big family, maybe, but make it at least."

"And how much per acre?"

Tyson looked at him in surprise. "You thinking of getting yourself a station?"

Glover looked down. They were flying over the herd now, and Tyson dipped a wing to the man on the ground.

"I'll have to let you off about a quarter of a mile away; the walk's not too bad. I'll make a few runs before coming back for the two of you. Same place. Mac'll know. Give me a half hour, forty-five minutes." He'd already let the throttle forward in order to land.

"How much does land around here cost?" Glover asked again.

"You really are thinking about it, aren't you? Just don't take my stock man away from me. Costs less than it used to, I can tell you that. Wool's a depressed market these days, so four hundred dollars an acre ought to do it." He was bringing the plane in on another flattened hill. "It'll be an empty load coming back, just the three of us. No problem at all."

This time Glover believed it.

Before Glover had walked ten yards, Tyson had turned the plane around and was taxiing back. Glover watched the plane take off again, bumping across the grass runway. It dipped out of sight momentarily at the end of the hilltop and then rose, turning right, threading its way between two ragged hills.

When he turned toward Mac, he was doing the calculations in his mind.

Mac, a dog at his heel, watched him come. Glover put up a hand to wave, though he knew there was no way Mac could know or guess who he was at this distance.

He could tell when Mac recognized him: his jaw dropped open for just a moment, then he closed it again. He didn't step forward and he didn't wave, he just stared. I'd give a million bucks to know what you're thinking right now, Glover thought. He waved again, and Mac nodded, not raising his hand.

"Mac." Glover extended his hand as he approached.

"Ken." Mac took it in a firm grip, shook it hard once, and let go. "I didn't exactly expect you."

"I'm sure of that." Glover looked around. "Looks like you've got yourself a pretty good life here." He didn't say "considering," but he thought it.

"I do," Mac said simply. "What brings you here?"

Glover shrugged. "A little business, a little pleasure. You look fit. I haven't seen you in . . . seven years? Eight?"

"Ten. Iran." Mac turned and gave a command to the dog, and the dog ran off. "You want to tell me what you're here for?"

"You can probably guess."

"I probably can." His eyes had narrowed. His face was tan under the stubble of beard and there were flecks of gray in the black hair, but there was not a pound of extra flesh on him. Walking these hills had made him hard and tough. He was as good as ever.

"I'm putting together an operation," Glover said. "I'd like you for sergeant major."

"I'm out of that now. Not interested in the least."

"Listen before you decide. I'm offering you just one more time. It's good money, Mac, and your involvement is minimal."

MacKinnon's eyes shifted to the right, and he looked across the hills. "What makes you think I'd want to leave a place like this to go do those kinds of things?"

"Because it's your kind of work." He paused. "I might add that we wouldn't need you to go. We only want you for the training, to build us an A-1 fighting machine, that's all. We'll give you whatever you want. The budget is major on this. The men'll be the best we can find: snake-eaters—your kind of guys. Won't take more than five weeks of your life."

"Five weeks."

"Plenty of time, the way I see it. It'll be a tough exercise but not complicated. We've got a good training site, good approximation of the target. And, as I say, you train, that's all you do. And you advise on the hardware list. If you have any good men in mind, we'll contact them."

"Who's doing this?"

"You come in and you'll find out all you need to know. But not until then—it's too sensitive."

"Who?" Mac asked again.

Glover allowed himself a small grin. "The training site is a former military base in the States—in the desert." He paused, letting Mac absorb that and what it should mean.

Whatever Mac was thinking, he gave no indication. He said nothing.

"Okay," Glover said, speaking more slowly now, "think of the guy who's the longest-running threat in the Middle East, the man who funds half the terrorists in the world. He's going to be in seclusion seven weeks from tomorrow, for five days. Absolute certainty. It's a chance to take him out, and we're going to do it. You can be part of it if you want, and pick up a pretty good piece of change for your trouble."

MacKinnon stared at him for a moment. "How much?"

Glover congratulated himself. He hadn't lost his touch. "How much would it take to bring you in?"

"Don't play games with me, Ken. That's not the way it works, and you know it."

"Okay. A hundred thousand, American. In cash. Half when you arrive at training, the other half when you leave."

Before Glover had even finished speaking, MacKinnon was laughing softly. "What is this? Five weeks of work and I'm not even going along? What are you paying the men who are going? A quarter of a million? Don't make me laugh."

"I told you the budget was major. If I judge that it'd take that much to get you into it, that's what you'll get. We could have dickered here for the next half hour and arrived at it, or I could offer it to you straight out. It's not my money."

MacKinnon lowered himself to a crouch and flicked at the grass with his hand. He didn't look up. "That's an unconscionable amount of money. How much do the rest get?"

"Same. Fifty up front, fifty after."

"If they live to collect. It wouldn't sit well with them if I didn't go in."

"They don't have to know how much you're getting."

"Why don't you want me to go?"

"We don't need you, simple as that. You don't fly—I do. A squad doesn't need more than one leader."

MacKinnon looked up at him. "You're flying in, then."

Glover nodded and grinned. "Helo. Yeah, we'll be flying down in the grass. All that radar isn't going to mean a damn thing." He crouched to the same level as MacKinnon. "I won't shit you, Mac. It's going to be a tough exercise. I like you too much to bring you along if you don't really have to go. Maybe I should say I respect you too much. Take the money and run, Mac. Somebody's going to do the training. For that kind of money, it might as well be you."

MacKinnon looked away. "War's always dangerous, but that doesn't mean that soldiering was ever a good paying job."

"All the more reason, then."

"Why? That's what I'm wondering. Why would they pay so much?"

"The personnel on this is everything," Glover said quietly. "And their weapons. A small, elite group, fifteen men, tops, plus me. We'll have to get them into a very remote, probably highly guarded area to do a very neat, quick, surgical operation. The thinking is a million and a half for the men; that'll be the major cost. Weapons'll be entirely hand-carried—assault rifles and grenades, maybe sidearms. It's a small compound. Getting the guys in and out is going to be the only other expense. They can afford to go heavy on the personnel costs. To make it work, they'll pay what they have to. A few mil is not such a bad price to get rid of this guy, you have to admit."

MacKinnon gazed away, saying nothing.

Glover spoke again. "There are a lot of folks—on both sides of the Atlantic—who would like to see him dead and who are willing to pay, as long as they've got deniability."

MacKinnon stood, and Glover followed suit, his thighs and calves aching, though he tried not to show it. "If you say yes, a round-trip ticket to the States'll be in the mail for you the next day."

"We already got the mail for this week."

"Next week's mail'll be soon enough. You get the ticket next week, and the first installment when we pick you up at the airport. Seven weeks from today you can be a wealthy man."

"A hundred thousand dollars does not necessarily make a man wealthy."

"It's not a bad down payment on your own station."

"You've done your homework."

"Always."

"You didn't come all the way down here to make an offer you could have made to someone else who's half as far away."

"I told you it was a combination trip."

MacKinnon said nothing.

"All right," Glover conceded. "I didn't. It's because you can do it better than anybody else. There are mighty few names that come up anymore when you're talking about this kind of operation, and yours is at the top of the list. They want the best, and they'll pay for it. They don't want another Desert One-type fuckup."

MacKinnon shook his head. "There's something else. What aren't you telling me?"

"Why do you think that? Why should there be?"

"This station may be far from the rest of the world, but I'm not that out of touch. I don't care what you say about budgets and how many people want this guy out of the way, a hundred thousand is still more money than anyone ever pays for something like this. With that kind of money, you're looking for more than what you've said so far."

Maybe he'd gone too far. "Would it make you feel better if I offered you only twenty grand? I can do that if you like; I can offer you less."

MacKinnon smiled. "I was thinking of going the other way. If the budget is so big on this, how about two hundred thousand?"

Glover chuckled. "You may be the best, Mac, but you're not God."

"I'm not even John Wayne."

"What do you say?" Glover wondered if he was wrong to press, but once Tyson came back with the plane, he'd be unlikely to have any time alone with MacKinnon.

MacKinnon shoved his hands into his pockets and turned away. He whistled at one of the dogs, and she turned on her heel and bounded up the hillside, disappearing over the top. "How soon do you have to know?" he asked.

Inwardly, Glover sighed with relief. "Tyson's coming back with the plane to pick me up, and he suggests you come along, too. I'm spending the night here."

"How did you know where I was?"

Glover nodded. "It took some doing. I have to leave in the morning. I'd like to know by then."

"Is there anything else you're going to tell me?"

"I already told you what it is."

"Then there's no point in my going back to the house. When do you fly back?"

"Day after tomorrow."

"Tell me the name of your hotel. I'll call you tomorrow night if I decide to do it."

"What's the difference? You might as well decide now."

"The difference is a day. I hear the plane; you'd better head back over there." He tilted his head toward the next hilltop.

Glover stood silent for a few moments; then he, too, could hear it. "Living out here hasn't hurt your hearing any," he said.

"Among other things." MacKinnon held out his hand.

Glover took it. "I'll be seeing you."

"Maybe," MacKinnon said as Glover started away.

The plane was coming closer, and Glover walked toward it, reviewing the conversation as he went. At least he hadn't said no. Which meant he was probably going to say yes. The odds had definitely become better than even. Shit, for a hundred thousand dollars, paid under the table, a man would do just about anything. Just about. He grinned to himself. Hell, it was a good investment.

Behind him, MacKinnon watched him go for a few moments before turning away and whistling for the dogs. An airline ticket to the States. A hundred thousand dollars and an airline ticket to the States.

BUR SUDAN, SUDAN

The craft was a Sikorsky S-61R, called the "Jolly Green Giant" in Vietnam. Officially it was an amphibious rescue helicopter, but in reality it had been used there for all-around transport as well as for rescue. After this particular one had seen six years of service in Vietnam, it was sent, along with eleven others, to Turkey as part of United States military aid to a friendly country. That had been before the Turks had shown they could outfight the Greeks in Cyprus. The Greeks had yelled bloody murder to Washington because the Turks were using American-supplied arms against them, even though Athens had been assured it wouldn't happen. So the Americans had cut back their aid, but the Turks still had their armaments. By the time the Turks got around to wanting the Sikorskys upgraded, Cyprus had been forgotten in crisis-driven Washington. By then the concern had become the fighting between Iran and Iraq, on Turkey's eastern border, and it seemed like a good idea in Washington to make sure the Turks were still, or again, solidly in the American camp.

As a result, newer model aircraft were sent to Ankara in

an even trade for the old models, which the Americans didn't exactly want back but did want given to some of their less fortunate (read: lower priority) clients. So a half-dozen of the Sikorskys went to Venezuela, two to Senegal, one to Fiji, and one to the Sudan. That accounted for ten of the twelve that originally were sent to Turkey. The remaining two had crashed at mountain-ringed Cigli Air Base during winter storms in the intervening years.

Nine of the ten copters went directly into military service. But the Americans were wary of appearing partisan in the unsettled Sudan, one place in the world where they hadn't yet figured out which side they wanted to back. So before the Sikorsky even arrived, it was modified for civilian use: its military radios and radar replaced with civilian versions, its gun mounts and overhead tracks removed. As an additional gesture, its gasoline tanks were beefed up, giving the craft somewhat less capacity but an expanded range.

Then, with a certain amount of fanfare, the U.S. AID representative in Khartoum donated the craft to the Sudanese Red Crescent to ferry food to drought-stricken regions. Years of experience in Ethiopia had shown that trucks bringing food to the starving were only semi-helpful, especially in contested territory. Government troops and rebels alike held the trucks for ransom, or to keep supplies from getting to the other side. On the other hand, helicopters could fly over the scrapping troops on the ground, could land almost anywhere, and had the further advantage that they didn't require roads.

For the last three years the Sikorsky had flown such missions weekly, taking food into the remote areas and bringing out the worst of the still-curables. The only vestige of its previous life was its camouflage paint job. No one had bothered to spend the time or the money to repaint it.

For most of that time it had been piloted by Alexander Federenko, a burly Canadian from Saskatoon who had flown crop dusters in Saskatchewan, covert arms deals in Central America, a domestic airline out of Adelaide and another out of Jakarta, and was now biding his time until his itchy feet or a more interesting offer propelled him into another move. It had not escaped his notice that only one continent remained on which he had never worked.

Sandy Federenko stood now in the helicopter's rear bay, watching the truck back slowly toward him. The freighter had landed three days ago, and Federenko had had to cool his heels all this time until the promised truck showed up to transport the crates the two kilometers from the docks to the helipad. At this end it was a shitty job; no one was ever on time—not that he hadn't gotten used to that long before he'd found himself in the Sudan. In addition, half the time there'd be a crate or two missing; once a whole shipment disappeared in that two kilometers from the docks. Sometimes he wondered how many of the gold teeth in the truck driver's grin had been paid for by the kids at the other end who hadn't gotten a full ration of rice or, if they were far back in line, hadn't gotten anything at all.

It was the other end that made the thing worthwhile, if anything did. It had taken a couple of months to get over the uplifted faces, the sunken eyes, and the mouths, stretched tightly over starvation-stunted teeth, calling his name as the helicopter landed. With a range of just over a thousand kilometers he could reach two-thirds of the country, and the Sikorsky had come to be known throughout all of it. The people in the aid camps had told him that the children began calling his name when the craft was only a faint throb in the still desert air. They crowded around as soon as he landed, their fly-speckled faces lifted in eager anticipation. "Sandy! Sandy!" they chanted at him, some of their voices mere croaks of sound, the only sound they might make all day, talk being a wanton use of precious energy to the near-starving. Or they only mouthed the word: *Sandy*.

It had frightened him at first in a way that tracer bullets and rocket launchers in the Central American highlands never had. There, death reached out, but a clever pilot could believe that he was better than death. Here, hands reached out to touch him as if he were a magical thing—the bringer of food—and he knew that most of the children would be dead within a year, and some of them within a week.

The bearer had loaded the last of the crates. He grinned toothlessly at Federenko and touched his forehead, then he scampered down the loading ramp and jumped into the back of the truck. The driver shoved his papers into Federenko's face, and Federenko noted that this time by some miracle the number of crates on the manifest was the same as the number loaded into the helo. Maybe the kids would all have a chance for full stomachs this week. The driver touched the front of his cap and grinned at Federenko before climbing back into the cab. The bearer had already settled himself into a corner of the now-empty truck bed. You could let him ride in the cab, Federenko thought, but he said nothing. Even after nearly three years, there were things about this place that he found hard to understand.

His glance moved now to the two men who had been standing patiently. One was dressed in a suit of pale shark-skin fabric. It looked expensive to Federenko. Some fucking official checking things out. He claimed to be an Interior Ministry guy from India, and he certainly could have been; he was small and dark-skinned, though not as dark as most of the Indians Federenko had seen in Indonesia. The other one, nearly six feet tall and thin as a stick, was Italian, or so he claimed. He was in jeans and a faded blue shirt. An odd pair.

Federenko was used to ferrying strangers around—people wanting to get across the Sudan—and sometimes his Sikorsky was the fastest way. Certainly it was the cheapest. It never bothered him. He wasn't much for conversation, but he could hold up his end if the others wanted to talk. Sometimes they did and sometimes they didn't. He was more suspicious of the ones who didn't. It was his guess that nearly half of those who hitched rides with him were something other than what they said they were. These men even had some kind of official papers. Which didn't necessarily mean anything.

He nodded at them now, and they came forward. The tall one came aboard first and sat in the copilot's seat. The other one sat in the jump seat right behind the pilot.

"Glad you were ready. I don't like to waste time," Federenko said to the one in the suit, who seemed to be in charge. Federenko pressed a button and the ramp lifted, closing the loading bay.

"The least we could do is be ready when you must leave," the one in the suit said. He pronounced the words carefully, as if he were afraid that his English was not good enough or as if he were trying to control the impact of his accent. But there was a finality to his statement that Federenko recognized. These two would not be talkers.

He ran through the checks and talked with someone in the tower. Then the rotors started churning, and the Sikorsky shuddered on the ground with their mounting power. It was the moment he always enjoyed: pulling up the rod, feeling the power, the lift, the sudden freedom, watching the earth separate and fall away.

He wheeled the helicopter eastward and then south, following the ribbon of turquoise breakers and pale sand lying between the deeper blue of the sea and the brown of the foothills. He would follow the coast, avoiding the highest of the mountains before he turned inland. The first stop was a camp just this side of the Eritrean border. It was always the first stop; the string of refugees there was always the longest.

He cleared the city of Bur Sudan and the houses that straggled along beyond it. Now there was only white sand along the shore and a narrow strip of vegetation before the mountains rose. Beside him, the tall, thin Italian seemed engrossed in the gauges in front of him. "You a pilot?" Federenko asked.

The Italian looked back at the Indian as if wondering how to respond, but Federenko never heard the answer. Nor did he hear the man behind him withdraw a pistol from a holster at the small of his back, beneath his perfectly tailored suit jacket, nor the shot that followed shortly after.

Beside him, the Italian grabbed the controls. The Sikorsky dipped, half-turned, then righted and went on its way.

Three minutes later, now fully out of sight of any habitation on the ground, the Sikorsky wheeled left, dipping toward the sea; the bay doors opened, and three crates were shoved out. They would break on impact with the water, and pieces of them would eventually wash up on shore, finally providing an explanation for the fact that Sandy Federenko never made it to the camps that day. The remains of the Sikorsky and Sandy himself would be presumed to lie at the bottom of the Red Sea.

In the meantime, the helicopter turned eastward until it was out of sight of land. Then it headed on a near-zero-degree bearing. Four hours later the signal light was spotted, a hundred kilometers east-northeast of Al Wajh, Saudi Arabia. The chopper set down on a wide, windswept wadi, just long enough to refuel from the tanks that had been trucked there by two silent, rifle-toting Saudis. After the helicopter was refueled, the man in the suit gave the Italian a packet, and the Italian handed it over to the Saudis. Before they had even counted to make sure all the money was there, the helicopter was on its way again, this time heading northwest. It skirted the Israeli border, flying close over the rugged terrain of the central Sinai to avoid Egyptian radar detection. It passed more than fifty kilometers east of Ismailiya and out over the Mediterranean.

An hour later, with nothing in sight but the sea below them, they threw out the body of Alexander Federenko. They kept the rest of the crates. It would only raise questions if pieces from them, with their distinctive markings, happened to wash up on some Mediterranean shore. Besides, there might be something in them that could be used.

Less than three hours after the helicopter cleared the Sinai coast, it set down on the remote island of Aghios Giorgios, southwest of Cyprus. The Italian, who really was an Italian, unfastened his seat harness and opened the side door. He stepped outside to stretch before unloading the crates, but before he had turned back to the helicopter, the Indian, who was not really an Indian, shot him in the back.

After he had shot the pilot it occurred to Kherman Shahabad that he should have waited until the craft was unloaded. But it didn't matter; the guards could do it. There was plenty of time.

He stepped around the body and made his way over barren, rocky terrain to the water. The guards would be in the shed on the other side of the island, and the walking was better closer to the shore. They could take care of the body when they unloaded the crates.

3

Howard Kammer stood with his back to the wall, his hands clasped behind him. He tried not to think that this was what Phyllis called his "Howie pose." He tried not to think of the cartoon that the *Post* had reprinted from one of the Detroit papers just last evening, sending Phyllis into gales of laughter. It showed a chubby male figure in short pants, with the distinctive hairline and round glasses that the nation's cartoonists had immediately appropriated as their symbols of the man most of them considered too inexperienced and ineffectual to handle the tough job of secretary of state. The childish figure was tugging on the pant leg of a much taller figure—one everyone would recognize as John Calvin Rockwell, the President's National Security Advisor—and pointing at a street vendor whose helium-filled balloons were labeled with the names of the world's current hot spots. The cartoon's caption read: *Just one, sonny, is all you can handle.* It was clever, Howard had to admit, but it struck too close to home. That was no joke; the cartoonist's perception was incredibly close to reality. For all intents and purposes it was Rockwell who was running the nation's foreign affairs, and Howard Kammer had yet to wrest them away from him.

Kammer stood now, trying to look more mature than his apple-cheeked fifty-two years and trying to get the Prime Minister of the State of Israel to take him, the Secretary of State of the United States, seriously.

"I am sure you understand that things in the government are very delicate just now." Avram Gershon's English was nearly perfect, with just a trace of an accent.

"We can speak as one man to another, can't we?" Kammer asked, pausing to emphasize the word *man* in such a way that Gershon would realize he really meant another word.

Gershon nodded. "Of course."

"The United States has always been very supportive of the State of Israel, even when it seemed as if the Israelis were thumbing their noses at us—"

"I am sorry, I take exception to that," Gershon said brusquely.

"Need I mention the attack on the *Liberty*? Need I mention Jonathan Pollard?"

Gershon raised his eyebrows and flicked a hand to indicate his assessment of the importance of those cases.

"But even some of the most supportive groups"—Kammer paused for emphasis—"some of the most *supportive* groups are asking questions. They're beginning to ask why you won't at least talk. The Camp David accords were viewed by some of these people as a real step forward, but since then—nothing. They've led to nothing. There are some real moderates in the Arab camp now, and it's my assessment that they would be willing to sit down with your people and at least begin a dialogue. What would be the harm in it? I can almost guarantee I could get them to the table with no preconditions. How can you lose?"

"We are not monolithic, you know," Gershon said. "Not any more than you are. We have all sorts of opinions in Israel, just as you have here. Yes, there are those who would be delighted to go to the table with moderate Arabs and look for a good beginning. But there are others who will not, who never will—or at least so they say." Gershon glanced out the window for a moment and then looked back. "I assume you have heard of the attack on Yahad?" The question was entirely rhetorical; the attack had been front-page news in the United States the week before. A new settlement, close to the border, completely wiped out— men, women, and children. No group had laid claim to the atrocity, but everyone in Israel, everyone in the United States, for that matter, knew who had to be responsible. "There are those—and they have power in the government —who will never forget, forgive, overlook, or in any other way diminish the rancor they feel over such attacks. No, my friend, it may be fine for you to think about going to the table just to talk, but there are too many people in my country who would rather die than go to the table with people they consider barbarians and murderers. And they would rather kill me or anyone else in the government who might think there are reasonable Arabs than let any of us sit down to discussions with them, no matter how moderate those Arabs may seem. That is a political fact of life."

Gershon rose to leave, brushing the wrinkles from his navy chalk-striped suit. He was half a head shorter than Kammer but wiry and tanned, and he exuded a strength of purpose that gossipers conjectured was the source of his uncanny attractiveness to women. He was sixty-five but his gray eyes were still hard, and he still had a full head of black hair. Kammer had heard that Gershon only wore clothes from one particular Savile Row tailor, and looking at Gershon now, fussily picking a piece of lint from his sleeve, he believed it.

"If anything, Yahad proves it," Kammer said. "Reasonable men on both sides must begin talking with each other. You can no longer let the hotheads on either side drag you down with them."

Gershon shook his head sadly. "Would that things were so simple."

Kammer stepped forward and offered his hand, trying not to sound as bleak as he felt. "Perhaps at some future date. We have to keep trying, Avram."

Gershon took Kammer's hand in both of his. "Please keep in mind, my young friend, that while you are trying to make peace, we are trying to stay alive." He shook Kammer's hand then, and the two walked together toward the door. "There is no need for you to see me out; I can find my own way. I have been here a time or two, you know."

But Kammer shook his head and walked the Prime Minister all the way to the C Street entrance of the State Department Building. He tried not to think that this was one more failure, that this meeting, for which he had hoped so much, had come to nothing. Was it, he wondered for the hundredth time, because he really was as ineffective as the cartoonists seemed to think? Or was it because John Calvin Rockwell was so powerful that foreign representatives didn't even bother with Howard Kammer except for the required diplomatic niceties?

Gershon took one step out into the pale January sun and then turned. "I want you to know that I think it is very important that Israel has such a good friend in you, a man in your position." Then he turned and walked to the waiting limousine.

Was I that transparent, Kammer wondered. Did even he realize how ineffectual he made me feel?

Gershon stepped into the automobile and leaned back against its cushions. If only you knew, he thought. If only I could have told you.

BRUSSELS

Kenneth Glover ran across the cobbled street, seeking the lee side where the gray buildings offered some protection from the rain. He had been in Brussels three times before and never yet when the sun was shining. He had begun to think it never shone at all here.

He thought it was stupid to be meeting in Brussels anyway. He was en route to London, and Morse was based there. It would have made a lot more sense to meet in London, but he had worked with Morse before and he'd learned that sometimes the man did peculiar things. Maybe it was out of self-protection. Maybe it was some sense of secrecy that he liked. Maybe it was just a game that he played. No, he thought, not that. Morse was not a game player. No sense of adventure and as little risk as possible—that was Morse. Even in this business he played things as safe as he could.

Glover hurried down the narrow sidewalk now, his feet splashing puddled water, his hands jammed into the pockets of his raincoat. His face was turned away from the wind, his nearly bald head protected by a tweed Tyrolean hat. Despite the weather, he felt good. He'd arrived yesterday from Auckland, and the uneventful flight had given him time to schedule the next ten days. The meeting today shouldn't take long, and then he'd be on his way to London and, after one or two (he hoped) successful days there and in a couple of other English towns, he could be on his way to the States. Mac had given him some names; a couple he recognized, the others he didn't. He had told Mac he'd do what he could, and he had meant it. He'd always believed in treating the troops right. Whatever trouble it cost, you almost always got more than the value out of it. He was feeling upbeat about that. Mac had been the first hurdle, and it had been a success.

"I've been thinking about your offer," Mac had said, his voice coming faint and slow over the phone lines.

He had paused then, and Glover had held his breath. The whole exercise surely didn't depend on Mac's participation, but Glover had come to depend on Mac's agreement as a talisman of eventual success.

"I'm still not comfortable with training men for a dangerous mission they and I know I will not have to face myself," Mac had finally added.

"Would it make you feel better if you were paid less than they?" Glover had asked.

Mac had cleared his throat on that one. "I suppose it would make me feel better if they were paid more than I," he had said.

"We're already talking a great deal of money here," Glover had said.

"I have always treated my men well. And fairly," Mac had responded.

"I have, too. I'm not sure that's the point."

"If I am worth a hundred thousand dollars to you, then surely they are worth more."

"You know how things go," Glover had said. "You pay what you must to meet the market. We can assume not everyone's as happy with their current life as you are."

There had been a silence on the line.

"All right," Glover had said and then paused, as if figuring. "I can go fifty before and seventy-five after. But frankly, I'd rather the men and you didn't discuss money."

"Since when did soldiers not discuss money?"

Glover had laughed at that. "You drive a hard bargain. Does this mean you're in?"

Silence came over the line. Glover looked down at the receiver as if willing the answer. Then he heard MacKinnon's voice again. "You make it very difficult to refuse. . . . Yes," he'd added finally. "I'm in."

"The ticket will be in your next mail delivery. You'll be met at the airport."

"Will the . . . work begin immediately?"

"Almost. I'm giving you a day to account for jet lag and to take a look at the training site."

"I'd like a day or two on my own before, if that's possible."

"What do you mean, on your own?"

"I have some other business to attend to in the States."

"That'll have to wait until after. We're moving on a tight schedule."

"If I'd said no, you'd have had to spend the time to recruit someone else."

But there was no way Glover was going to give him that. "First things first, Mac. You get the training done, and after that your time is your own. I'll make your return ticket an open one—you can use it whenever you like. But your business is going to have to come after."

"Who will meet me?" MacKinnon had asked.

"Probably me."

MacKinnon had chewed on that one for a while. "All right," he'd said at last. "I'll be seeing you then." And that was the end of the conversation.

Glover grinned to himself now, despite the passing taxi that splashed water over his pant legs. That part done, the rest of the men should be cake.

He had reached the place now, and Glover shoved open the brass-trimmed oaken door. There was no nameplate on it and no sign attached to the building, just the simple numbers painted in solid block form on the wood of the door: 609. He started down an interior hallway but had gone only a few steps when the door at the end opened.

Raymond Morse stood in the opening until Glover reached it, and then he stepped aside. Glover had removed his hat and was shaking the water droplets from it. "Damned nasty weather," he muttered, coming into the room.

It was a small office, sparsely furnished with a desk bare except for a reading lamp and a pen stuck into a holder. Three straight chairs sat randomly beside a nearly empty bookcase.

"Shahabad's not here?" Glover asked, laying his coat across one of the chairs. Another coat hung on a single hook at the back of the door.

"He's not coming today. Neither of us thought it would be necessary," Morse said. He motioned toward one of the straight chairs and sat down in the other vacant one. "I got your message. It seems you've taken rather long to get the one man."

"He's the key. No matter what kind of experience the other men have, we still need someone who can turn them into a damned good fighting unit."

Morse leaned back in the chair. "You found him sober, I assume."

"I told you he was on the wagon. I got that confirmed before I even saw him." Glover reached into his pocket and pulled out a cigar. He examined both ends of it and then stuck it into his mouth.

"Please," Morse said, "not in here."

Glover looked at him briefly and then took the cigar out. He rotated it between his fingers for a moment before jamming it back between his teeth, but he didn't light it. "From here I go to London. A day or two more and I should be back in the States." He stepped to the chair and lowered himself into it. "I told him a hundred thousand, half when he arrives and the rest when he's done." He moved the cigar to the other side of his mouth, noticing that Morse hadn't reacted at all. "He thinks the others should be paid more than he since their lives are on the line and his isn't. I upped their ante to fifty before and seventy-five after. He likes his men well taken care of."

"*His* men," Morse repeated.

"Yeah, his. That's how things work in the services. You train the men, and they're yours forever after. It's another reason why he's going to have to be shopped. Even if he didn't recognize the place."

Morse exhaled deeply. "I really don't see why he's so important. Already he's more trouble than he's worth. Nobody's that good. And it's going to be—what?—fifteen times fifty we're going to throw away on this."

Glover took the cigar out of his mouth and leaned his head back. "I can't believe you're saying that. It's peanuts. Less than a mil. Your money men spend that before breakfast. Cash, did I say that?"

Morse looked beyond Glover's shoulder. "Fifteen men—are you going to have them in time?"

"Signed, sealed, and delivered. What about the weapons? Is there a problem? Is that why Shahabad isn't here?"

"No, there's no problem," Morse responded. "You know about the Uzis, I assume."

Glover shook his head impatiently. "Those Uzis are throwaways. I'm talking about the real stuff."

Morse cleared his throat and shifted in his chair. "I'm not sure how much of this you really need to know."

"Look, MacKinnon's not the only one who treats his people right. I want to know going in that you're getting what I've asked for."

"AK47s traceable to South Yemen. He's arranging it now. And the MP5s. A crate was stolen from a Hamburg police armory three years ago, and we're getting four of them." Morse lowered his head until his eyes were level with Glover's. "You can't be serious about treating your people right."

"No one ever said I didn't think my men were worth the best, and they aren't going to say it now. What about the grenades?"

Morse nodded. "RGD5s, coming out of Southeast Asia, maybe leftovers from Nam. Otherwise I suppose they're newer—China's making them now. And of course there are the sidearms as well." He ran his finger down the crease of a pant leg. "Tell me about it, Ken. What's the bloody point of all that, anyway? Frankly, Shahabad's wondering about those sidearms, and so am I."

"We'll need them, and he should know it."

"*Why* do you need them?"

"Don't be stupid," Glover countered. "You want this to look right or not? What kind of arms connections does Shahabad have, anyway, if he doesn't even realize that?"

"And the rocket-propelled grenades? Doesn't that seem like overkill?"

"Those are insurance."

"Then why don't they just use the grenade launchers in the first place? Certainly it would be easier—blow the place to pieces."

"Grenades aren't the weapons of choice here. You want every man dead, and the RPGs aren't that precise. It would be like trying to kill a rat by bombing your house—you'd reduce your house to rubble, but you still wouldn't be able to tell for sure if you'd killed the rat or not. On the other hand, if nothing else works, if there's way more defense than we've been led to expect . . ." Glover shrugged. "Shahabad should know all this even if you don't."

"Don't worry about Shahabad."

"I worry about him because I don't know him."

Morse raised an eyebrow. "What is that supposed to mean?"

"Who is he, anyway? Who does he represent?"

"You don't need to know that. He's getting what you asked for, that's all you need to worry about."

"And I'm getting what you need, right? A crack surgical strike group, right? And you even know me—we have some history together. But you still worry that I don't know what I'm doing. Why shouldn't I wonder about him? Kherman Shahabad—what kind of name is that, anyway? It ought to be Persian, Iranian, something like that, but he doesn't have a Farsi accent. And he looks like he could be East Indian, or maybe he's only a small, dark South American. What the hell is he?"

"He's a man who knows his business. One doesn't ask

him anything more than that." Morse spoke rapidly, as if to dismiss the subject, and he stood as he spoke. "That's it, then, isn't it?"

But Glover wasn't willing to let it go. "Is that all you know about him? You don't even wonder what kind of man you're dealing with? That's not like you."

Morse looked at him straight on, with cold, hard blue eyes. "Look them up in an atlas if you like—Kherman and Shahabad, two cities in Iran. Of course it's not his real name, and of course he looks as if he could come from half the countries in the world. That's his security. He'll give us what we want, and then he'll disappear into the woodwork again until someone else needs him, until someone else is willing to pay the very high salary he commands to do what no one else in the world can do as well."

"Which is what?" Glover persisted.

"You know perfectly well. He delivers arms. No questions asked, all clean and with documentation running back to whatever country you want it to run back to."

"And does he also deliver men?"

"You're delivering the men, Glover."

"This time. For this one. But does he deliver men if they're needed?"

Morse cleared his throat and reached for the raincoat hanging on the back of the door. "He delivers whatever is needed. To wherever it's needed. He doesn't ask questions, and he doesn't answer any."

"And what about you?" Glover pressed.

Without pausing, Morse put his arms through the sleeves. "I am a businessman, pure and simple, as you are a soldier. And I think," he went on, his words more measured, "that both of us would profit from not asking any more questions than we need to. You knew what this was when you came in. You're no innocent."

Glover nodded slowly. No, he was not. He had known from the start what it was, and who was the banker and who was the arms supplier. And it would not have taken much thought for him to figure out what was behind it. Whenever he became uncomfortable about that, he had only to think of the five hundred thousand that had already been deposited for him and the other five hundred thousand when it was all over. After all, as it turned out, even MacKinnon had his price.

4

COVINGTON STATION, SOUTH ISLAND, NEW ZEALAND

A. C. MacKinnon stood in the kitchen in his stockinged feet, the ticket in his hand. Martha Tyson was at the sink, silent, her back to him, an intended rebuke. "I didn't know you had anyone in the States," she had said when he'd told them. Phil hadn't said anything, and that had made it even more difficult. "It's coming on fall," he'd said to Phil. "I thought you could manage without me." Phil had nodded then. "I understand," he'd said. It was Martha who had asked what Phil never would have: "Will you be coming back?" There had been a silence while MacKinnon wondered what to say, and Phil had nodded again. Martha had sighed and turned away. MacKinnon had looked down at his hands. "I could never tell you how much all this has meant—" But that hadn't been at all what he'd wanted to say. I found my life here, he should have said, I became a man again here. But even that wouldn't have told them what they had no way of knowing. Finally he had just turned away and gone to his room. Did you think I was going to stay here forever? he'd wanted to ask them, but that would have been unfair. Until Ken Glover came, he himself might have thought that he would stay forever.

That was four days ago. He told them the day after he had called Glover, giving himself that long to get used to the idea, that long to ponder how he was going to tell them. Even then, when he had done it, he did a mighty poor job. There was an awkwardness with Martha, as if she thought she had a right to tell him not to go, but wouldn't. And there was a strangely jovial offhandedness from Phil, who was trying to make it easy and only succeeded in making it harder. He'd been waiting for the mail ever since.

He saw the letter on the kitchen table as soon as he came in this evening, and he knew what it was by the return address, an Auckland travel agency. Martha said nothing as he retrieved the letter, slit it open, and read the ticket. She was washing baking pans, banging them against the sink. She'd been baking up a storm for the last four days. He knew what she was doing, but the only recognition of it was to tell her again what a fine cook she was.

The ticket in his hands at last, he felt a sudden heaviness within, a fearful loss of all light and warmth. When he came to New Zealand seven years ago, it had been in desperation. He'd known then that it was going to be the last chance for him to make his way, and that had been disquieting; but he'd also known it was necessary, there was no choice about it. He could either make his way or end up dead. But this time there was a choice, and the brass ring he was reaching for could turn to dust and then there would be no coming back. Even if Phil would take him back, and he probably would, there would be no returning; it would all have changed. Covington Station would be the same, Phil and Martha and Jesse would be the same, but he knew that he, A. C. MacKinnon, would not.

He looked at the ticket again, and the dates. Depart Auckland, January 18; arrive Los Angeles, January 18; and then an almost immediate flight to San Diego. January 18. Six days. Glover had said that he could tend to his business afterward, but Glover hadn't known. There was no way he could come this close and then wait another five weeks. And there was no reason to wait here, either; he was only going through the motions here. It would be better for all if he left as soon as he could.

"It looks as if this'll be my last night here," he said to Martha.

She turned then, her hands soapy and her eyes cloudy. "I haven't made it any easier for you, have I?" she asked, her voice flat.

"If it makes you feel better, it isn't easy for me, either."

"What is it he wants you to do?"

MacKinnon shrugged. "A job."

"Should we have paid you more?"

"You know better. You pay me as well as any—better than many, in fact. It isn't the pay."

"What is it, then?"

"It's nothing to do with you or the job. It's something to do with me."

She looked at him, her hands dripping soap on the floor, and he was afraid she was going to ask him if he hadn't been happy here, but she didn't. He answered her anyway. "You and Phil and Jesse—I might almost have become a part of that, but never completely. If I don't want to be on the outside all my life, this is something I have to try."

"What is there for you? I thought . . ."

He smiled wanly. "Maybe nothing. After all this time, maybe nothing."

"I'd always felt you hadn't any family. Was I wrong? Do you have someone?"

He walked over and kissed her lightly on the forehead, and it felt cool to his lips. He had lived in her house, eaten her meals, worn the clothes she washed and ironed and mended, and this was the first time he had purposely touched her. "You would think that, wouldn't you, Martha?" he said, looking down at her, managing another smile. "It is so like you to think it must be that. No, it's just what I said, a job—but a job unlike anything I could do here. When a person flies halfway around the world to ask you to do something he and you both know you can do as well as anyone on earth—well, it's more than flattering. You want to do it, if only to prove that you still can."

"I thought you'd been in the army. What is it you do so well? Kill people?" She spoke to his retreating back; he was already walking away from her.

"No." He chuckled, not looking back. "You might say I inspire them." It was all he said as he left the room. It was the truth, at least part of the truth, and if he refused to tell her the whole of it, that was his own concern. Those were the last words he spoke to her except good-bye the next morning just before he and Phil headed out for the plane. He would be in Christchurch before noon, and from there, if he was lucky, he could get the ticket changed to an earlier date.

IRAKLION, CRETE

The man called Kherman Shahabad strolled slowly along the *limani*, admiring the boats tied to rusted iron rings driven into the cement that lined the harbor. It was late afternoon, but the westering sun still shone brightly. He wore dark sunglasses, confident in the knowledge that his eyes could not be seen. In his black serge suit and white shirt open at the neck, there was nothing in particular to distinguish him from any of the other men who walked along the seafront. Ahead, the blue-painted tables of a coffeehouse spilled out onto the pavement, and from behind the dark glasses his eyes scanned the tables. They came to rest at last on a corpulent man, close to sixty years of age, with close-cropped gray hair and a flushed face. His collar was frayed at the neck, and he held an outsized handkerchief with which he continually dabbed at his temples. Shahabad watched him for a few moments, betraying no expression, then let his eyes slide again over the rest of the tables. Satisfied, he continued walking until he had passed the coffeehouse. At the far end of the port he turned and headed back, still strolling casually, still admiring the boats.

When he came to the coffeehouse the second time, he looked up as if aroused from his reverie and searched the tables once again. Most were occupied—men in groups, engaged in desultory conversation; men alone, flipping worry beads through their fingers; women and men together, bent in whispered conversation over cups of Turkish coffee. He paused and changed direction so that his path now took him to the doorway of the coffeehouse. He stopped there to read the menu posted on the blue-painted doorjamb. Then he shrugged, turned away from the door, and made his way to the fat man's table.

"Do you mind if I share the table with you?" he asked in English. "The view from here is exceptional."

The fat man grunted assent and moved a newspaper,

placing it on the ground near his chair. He glanced around casually. "Did you think you were followed?"

Shahabad tapped his cigarette ash to the ground before answering. "I never think I am being followed. I always assume that I might be."

The fat man shrugged and looked away. It annoyed him that Shahabad, or whatever he was calling himself now, refused to remove his sunglasses. "Everything you requested has been accomplished," he said without looking back.

"Good."

"In a locker at the San Diego airport in four days."

"You're bringing them in by plane?"

"Of course not. But an airport is a very good place for carrying baggage in and out."

Shahabad nodded. A waiter came and took his order for a coffee. The fat man pointed to his empty tea glass, and the waiter smiled acknowledgment. When the waiter had gone, Shahabad spoke again. "It will not all fit in one locker."

"Of course," the fat man agreed. "There will be additional keys in the locker. And the rest will be done in the same way. In Naples, in five weeks."

"Everything? Even the *plastique?*"

The fat man looked at him then. "I said everything." He shoved his tea glass toward the center of the table and leaned his hands heavily on the worn surface. "Your part is all arranged, then?"

"The men are being hired now."

"And what are they being told?"

Shahabad chuckled. "That they will be assassinating Moammar Qaddafy. We will have no problem getting them. It will be easy to think that the western nations are funding a strike force to do what none of them dares to do openly."

The fat man grinned. "And how do you propose to get rid of them afterward?"

"Why did you think I wanted the *plastique* ? Don't worry; none of them will be left when it's all over."

"And has the money been forthcoming?"

"There has been no problem with the money. Raymond

Morse has done all that one could ask and more as far as that's concerned."

The fat man leaned back in his chair. "Good. When it's over, who will be left that knows?"

"Morse. And you. And I. And whoever your people are."

The fat man took a cube of sugar from his tea saucer, looked at it for a moment, and then popped it into his mouth. "No one else?"

"No one."

"What about your recruiter?"

"He'll go with the rest of them."

"I assume he doesn't suspect."

Shahabad's eyes narrowed. "Most people fool themselves that they are too important to be victims of a double cross. Only the wise ones protect themselves."

The fat man's eyebrows rose. "Is that supposed to mean something?"

A slow smile spread across Shahabad's face. "I plan to live a long life."

The fat man looked into Shahabad's glasses. "And so do I, my friend."

"One more thing," Shahabad said. "What if there's a change in plans?"

"You will be informed in the usual way."

"Can you be certain you will know of a change in plans, even at the last minute?"

"Absolutely. I can be absolutely certain."

"Then it looks as if everything can proceed."

The waiter brought the drinks, and Shahabad made a move for the money in his pants pocket.

"Thank you, my friend," the fat man said, raising his glass.

Shahabad nodded, noting that his companion had not even tried to pay. It was petty, he realized; he was being paid handsomely and could well afford the price of a couple of drinks.

The fat man popped another cube of sugar into his mouth and pushed himself up from the table. "I shall be in contact. You will know of any changes in plans."

Shahabad watched the fat man waddle away. Then he picked up the newspaper, still lying on the ground. He opened it as if to scan the headlines and saw the key taped to the front page. Without reacting he folded the paper again, as if he had changed his mind, and tucked it under his arm as he rose to leave.

WASHINGTON, D.C.

Secretary of State Howard Kammer heard the soft buzz of the telephone and looked up from the report he was scanning. He punched the button on the telephone console. "Yes," he said. His eyes were still moving down the printed sheets on the desk in front of him.

"Sir, Tel Aviv finally got back to me."

Kammer recognized the voice of Jonathan Driscoll, his aide for Middle Eastern affairs, and he looked up from the report. "And?" he asked, wishing that he didn't have to sound so desperate for hope.

"Sorry, sir. The Prime Minister is unavailable during that time period. They'll be glad to schedule a meeting for you with him later, however."

"He's completely booked? I find that hard to believe."

"They sounded very apologetic, if that's any help."

"They can sound apologetic as hell, but he still won't meet with me, right?"

"That's right."

"You told them about my schedule?"

"I did."

Kammer let out a deep breath. When he last saw the Prime Minister, Gershon had exuded grace, and now the man refused to see him? Were they stonewalling him? And if so, what for? It had to be something important. With all the aid the United States gave to Israel, it was rather hard to countenance a refusal to met with the American Secretary of State. And that's what it amounted to, a refusal. It was inconceivable that the Israeli Prime Minister could really be tied up so completely. Unless. Unless even the Israelis had given up on him. Unless even they were beginning to deal only with the President's National Security Advisor.

Ah, Kissinger, what have you done to us? He'd asked himself that plenty of times before. The National Security Advisor was answerable only to the President and was not even confirmable by the Congress, as was the Secretary of State, which made the man who held that position potentially the second most powerful man in the country. If he chose to use the power. And it was becoming perfectly clear that John Calvin Rockwell was choosing to use the power. All right, he thought to himself, if I can't even keep the Israelis talking to me, what the hell can I do? It had to be Rockwell. There was no conceivable way that the Israelis would refuse to meet with him otherwise.

Unavailable, my ass, he thought; unwilling is more like it.

5

LONDON

Raymond Morse opened his eyes, and immediately his mind clicked into gear. He was used to travel, and he never had trouble remembering where he was when he awoke. He lay on his back, contemplating the ceiling, planning his day. Beside him, Angela still slept; he could hear her breathing, soft and regular as a heartbeat. He turned and gazed at her, at the pale shoulder that showed where the sheet had slipped down, at the mass of ash-blond hair that lay on the pillow. He lifted the sheet gently and studied the soft contours of her back, the gentle rise of her hip, the crease of her buttocks. She stirred slightly, and he let the sheet fall back. Angela. He wondered if it was her real name. He wondered where Pauline found girls like Angela, all of whom deserved names like that—Angela. Lithe, long-limbed girls with cascades of blond or russet or jet hair that shone in the candlelight, girls who wore silk and lace against their skin, who spoke in soft, educated voices, whom a man could take to the theater or a concert and then, at the end of the evening, take in his arms with equal assurance, knowing she was safe, clean—knowing, even, that she was discreet. Angela. He would remember the name. The next time he was in London he would ask for her particularly.

He eased himself out of bed, trying not to wake her, and padded across the rose-colored carpet. He shoved open the door to the bathroom, catching a glimpse of himself in the floor-to-ceiling mirror that ran the length of one wall. He smiled at his reflection: he would be forty in two months, but there was still not an ounce of fat on him. His stomach was lean and hard, his chest, arms, and legs solid with the long muscles that come from swimming. His one indulgence: he swam nearly every day, no matter where he was.

When a man was rich enough, he could always find a place to do laps. And that thought broadened the smile. His goal had been a million pounds by thirty-five, and he'd made it with a year to spare. If he hadn't been handicapped from the beginning, he could probably have made it by thirty. As it was, a millionaire by thirty-five was no mean accomplishment for the illegitimate son of an East End prostitute. And now, two months from forty, he was working on his tenth million. As his ma used to say, "Them what has . . ."

He turned on the shower and let the water run until it was hot enough. Then he stepped in and closed the curtain, the water pelting against it like driving rain. He stood under the water, letting it plaster his hair, letting it steam against his skin, and then he picked up the soap and slowly began to lather.

He saw the form, indistinct, through the wet curtain, and then the curtain was drawn back and she stood before him. He saw that she had taken the time to brush her hair, and he knew that if he took her in his arms, if she stepped under the shower with him, she would smell again of asphodel. She had the small, secretive smile that had amused him last night, and the nipples on her full breasts were high and tight. He felt the heat beginning in his loins. It would be so easy, her hands on him, working his body, his mouth on her small, shallow navel, her pale, silky mound beneath his hands.

"No," he said, taking the curtain from her and closing it again. "Not this morning, I'm afraid." He turned and let the water dissolve the soap, running it down his legs in streams. He let the water steam him until all thoughts of her body had left, until he knew he would concentrate on the work ahead. Then he turned off the shower and reached for a towel.

When he emerged from the bathroom, she was still nude, standing before the window, looking off toward Westminster. She heard the soft sounds of footsteps on the carpet and turned. "It's a beautiful view," she said, "don't you think?"

He didn't answer. He pulled on his undershorts and

reached for his pants. "I'll be back in a couple of months. I'll ask for you." He looked at her then, and she nodded. He drew two hundred-pound notes from his wallet and let them fall onto the bed. "These are between you and me," he said. "Don't let it get around. I wouldn't want to start a precedent."

She remained by the window while he pulled on his shirt. She would wait until he had left before she took the money. They always did that. He always said the same thing, and they always waited until he was gone. He supposed it was part of the training. Pauline would have attended to even the least detail. He liked the smell of asphodel; it made one think of children running through the grass. The last one had smelled of camellias.

He walked out of the hotel room at three minutes after ten. At eleven minutes after ten he entered the London branch of the Swiss Cantonbank. Twenty-three minutes later he walked out, one and a half million dollars in used American bills in his attaché case.

CONESVILLE, IOWA

Kenneth Glover stepped out of the rented car and looked across the sidewalk at the white-painted building. Faded red paint above the door bore the words EL CHARRO. Somehow it seemed incongruous—the only place to eat in an Iowa town barely large enough to have a name was a Mexican restaurant.

He stepped over a dirty mound of melting snow at the curb and walked into the place. It was dim, the air fairly vibrating with sounds emanating from a jukebox in the corner; he would not have dignified the sounds by calling them music. A few patrons sat at tables ranged carelessly around the one large cement-floored room. To the right of the door was the bar, and leaning against the bar, his shirt sleeves rolled up to the elbows, was Bo Sullivan. Even in the dim light, even after all the years, he had no trouble recognizing Bo.

Glover walked over to the bar and put his hand out.

"Bo," he said, as if the last time they'd met had been just yesterday.

"Ken?" Sullivan said, taking half a step back. Then his face broke into a wide smile, his unshaven cheeks folding at the edges, his eyes crinkling. "Ken Glover! By God! It really is you!" He grabbed Glover's outstretched hand in his own large paws and pumped it up and down. "You old fart! What the hell are you doing here?"

Glover withdrew his hand while it was still in one piece and said, poker-faced, "Came in for a drink."

"The fuck you did! What the hell are you doing in Conesville, Iowa, for God's sake?"

"If you give me the drink, I might tell you."

"What'll you drink, then? If it isn't beer, you'd better not be too choosy."

"Beer's fine. Whatever's on tap."

Sullivan took a long look at Glover before turning to draw the beer. "How long's it been? Eight years?" He turned back and shoved the mug across the bar.

Glover nodded. "Eight years, that's right."

"God," Sullivan said, shaking his head. He let out a deep breath. "Hard to believe it's been that long."

"Life been treating you okay?"

Sullivan looked around. "I'm livin'. Guess I can't complain."

Glover swigged the beer and wiped his mouth with the back of his hand. "A person can always complain."

Sullivan leaned both hands on the bar. "What the hell are you doing here?" he asked again.

"I have a little proposition if you're interested."

Sullivan leaned forward, his elbows on the bar. "Shoot."

"What time do you get off?"

Sullivan looked at his watch. "Five. That's when Mike comes in. He owns the place. I work days and weekend nights. He works the rest."

Glover looked at his own watch and then at the clock above the bar. His watch said three fifteen. The clock said two minutes after nine. "You really serve Mexican food in this place?"

"Try it. You'll be amazed. Best Mex food north of Texas."

"I'll have a couple of tacos, then."

"Same old Glover, aren't you? Playing it safe. You gonna tell me anything more about this proposition?"

"When you're off. When we can talk by ourselves."

Sullivan leaned over the bar, his face only inches from Glover's. "Is it legal?"

Glover leaned back and laughed. "So legal it's squeaky."

"Something military? You can tell me that much."

Glover nodded. "A special op. I'm just recruiting Ranger types. Wait'll you hear."

Sullivan grinned again. It seemed as if he couldn't stop smiling. "You're really gonna make me wait, aren't you, you son of a bitch?"

"How about those tacos?"

"I'm just the barkeep. You sit at the table, and the girl'll come out and wait on you." Sullivan chuckled. "I guess two of us can play this waiting thing."

Glover turned away from the bar and walked to a table, grinning to himself. Sullivan was so hungry for it he could taste it.

LA JOLLA, CALIFORNIA

The University of California at San Diego spreads along North Torrey Pines Road, only a short distance back from the Pacific. The students looked younger than MacKinnon had expected, fresher faced and, given what he'd seen at the L.A. airport, more neatly dressed.

He'd arrived the evening before. He hadn't bothered to count the hours involved in the trip, but he did take notice of the odd fact that although he left Auckland at eight forty-five in the evening, he arrived in Los Angeles at three thirty in the afternoon of the same day. Theoretically, a trip like that ought to make a person feel younger, but in reality it had made him feel ten years older. Living in the back country had slowed him down; he was no longer used to major changes, and that was a bad sign for what lay ahead. Perhaps, after all, it was a good thing that he was only going to do the training.

He'd come to the States without a plan but knowing that this was going to be his best chance. He'd considered stopping off in Los Angeles, since the flight debarked there anyway, but he'd been in that city once before, and once was enough. It was a bad place to be even if you knew what you were doing; in this case it would have been impossible. So he came on down to San Diego, where Glover was to pick him up—a smaller city, not yet quite so dependent on its freeways, not so intimidating to the stranger.

When he hadn't been able to get a flight as soon as he'd hoped, he'd rented a car and driven down. It had given him a chance to shake the lethargy of the long flight. He hadn't known for sure how he'd approach the search, but he had two days before Glover would be expecting him. In those two days perhaps he could at least get started, though how one traced a person in the States was beyond his imagination.

He would need help, that much he knew, and as he drove toward San Diego, he saw the signs for the university, and something clicked in his mind. She would be the right age; it made sense to start on a college campus.

Not that he ever expected to find her in San Diego, but it seemed reasonable to think that there could be lists of college students somewhere. It was a place to start, at least. As he strolled through the campus, he noticed that most of the students walked quickly, as if hurrying to classes. But occasionally he saw one or more lounging on the wooden benches that were scattered about. He finally approached one such group, three young men surrounding a single girl, and he asked them if it was possible to find a list of college students somewhere. They considered that, and debated whether the best place would be the administrative offices or the library, and then finally pointed him toward the library.

The library might have been the strangest building he had ever seen. Situated in a grove of tall eucalyptus trees, it resembled a tree itself, an enormous eight-story tree lifted into the air on concrete pylons that reached up and out, its middle floors stretching wider than the top and bottom ones, just as the middle branches of a tree stretch out the farthest. When he walked in, he stopped to orient himself. RESERVES and CIRCULATION, the signs immediately in front of him said. Beyond, and to the left, another sign said REFERENCE.

"Do you have a register of college students?" he asked the woman at the reference desk. She wore a name tag that said "Anne Rowen, Reference Librarian."

"Yes, I do." She reached behind the desk for a paper-covered book, the size of a telephone directory for a small city.

He looked at the cover. "No, what I meant was a register of college students for the whole country."

She shook her head slowly. "All the college students in the whole United States? No, I doubt if there is such a thing. Maybe we can get the information some other way. What is it you really need? Are you looking for someone in particular?"

"I'm looking for a girl. She'd be twenty years old. I figure she ought to be in college."

The woman nodded. "She'd be the right age, but of course not everybody goes to college. You know her name, I assume."

He nodded but didn't volunteer the name.

"You don't know where she lives?"

"If I knew where she lived, I wouldn't have to go about looking for her, would I?"

"It's a very large country. Why don't you go to a private investigator? They know how to do these things."

He looked away for a long moment. Then he turned back and cleared his throat. "I'm not in the habit of hiring other people to do my work for me," he said stiffly.

She smiled. "This may be very difficult if you try to do it yourself."

"But not impossible?"

She frowned, and her mouth formed a serious line while she thought. "I don't know, to be honest." Her face broke into a rueful smile. "Librarians are supposed to know everything, aren't they—or at least how to find out everything. But this—I hope you know more about her than her name."

"I do." But he bloody well wasn't going to tell her everything he knew.

"Why don't you just give me any information you have. Maybe something will ring a bell."

"She wasn't born in this country . . ."

"So there wouldn't be a birth certificate. But maybe she's become a citizen? Are there records of naturalized citizens? That's a possibility." She made a note on a slip of paper.

"I know her parents' names."

"Oh." She looked up at him, studying him, a slight frown creasing her forehead.

"Is there something wrong in that?"

"No." She shook her head quickly. "Nothing. What are their names?" The pencil was poised over the paper.

"Richard Barber," he said, leaning his hands on the counter that separated them. "Mr. and Mrs. Richard Barber. Richard and Marie." He said the words slowly, almost as if he relished the sounds they made, which he didn't. It was a way he had of proving to himself that it was true. "You wonder why I'm looking for her, don't you? A man my age, looking for a twenty-year-old girl."

She looked up at him with eyes the color of the winter sea. "I guess it's really none of my business, is it?"

"No," he said, standing straight again. "It bloody well isn't."

She looked down at the paper again. "Anything else you can tell me? You don't have her social security number, I suppose."

"No, I don't. That's all I can tell you."

She sighed. "It's not very much. A private investigator might save you a lot of time. It might turn out to be your only hope. I don't even know if—"

"I already told you: I'd rather do it on my own."

"Mmm-hmm. Except that I'm not sure how you're going to do it."

He looked at the paper on the desk in front of her. "She's my daughter," he said after a time.

"I wondered. Except that then you said—"

"My wife remarried. He'd be her stepfather. I don't even know if she uses his name or mine."

She glanced down at the paper. "I didn't get a name for her."

"It's Laurie. It might be Barber, or it might be . . . MacKinnon." He watched her write the name.

"I'll tell you what," she said, looking up at him again— she must have been forty years old, but she had freckles marching across her nose—"things are a little busy at this time of day, and I've probably given you more time than I should have." He half-turned and discovered three or four students waiting behind him. "If you could wait—or come back would be even better—maybe I could give this some thought, and we could work out something. Right now I have to admit that I'm stumped."

He nodded and stepped back. "I suppose you're really not supposed to be helping people who aren't students."

"No, no, that's all right. It's just that you can see some others are waiting . . ."

"Sure."

"Come back in a couple of hours. Let me give it some thought."

"Sure." He turned away, suddenly disheartened. For all those years he'd promised himself that someday . . . someday. And now he suddenly faced what he should have known all along: There were two hundred and fifty million people in the United States. How was he going to find a twenty-year-old girl when he didn't even know what name she was living under? He should have left it a dream. He should never have come.

He didn't go back that day, almost didn't go back the next, except that he spent the rest of the first day walking along the San Diego harbor, and he had a second day and didn't feel like going to the zoo. Twice he'd almost gone to private detectives, looking them up in the yellow pages of a telephone directory. Once he had gotten as far as the building itself before he changed his mind. It wasn't just what he'd told that librarian—that he'd rather not have any help. After all, he had asked her for help. But somehow private detectives had always meant shady business to him: spouses trying to get proof of infidelity, employers looking for proof of wrongdoing, ordinary people suspected of insurance fraud. Laurie was not shady business. He didn't want her tainted with such people.

And so the next day, more from hope than anything else, he ended up at the library again. But she wasn't at the desk when he returned, and that took him aback because he didn't want to start all over again, to explain it all to someone else. So when the person behind the desk said, "May I help you?" he stood there in silence, wondering what to say, and then the person narrowed her eyes. "You're not the one that Anne spoke with yesterday, are you? But of course! You must be. Just one minute." She reached for the phone and punched in a number.

He was not just disconcerted, he was angry. She had told them about him? Everyone in the bloody library knew that he was looking for his long-lost daughter? God in heaven. "Mr. MacKinnon." The voice came from behind him.

He turned, and her hand was outstretched as if to shake his. She wasn't wearing the name tag now, but he remembered the name: Anne Rowen.

He didn't take her hand, but she ignored the rudeness and extended it farther to touch his elbow and move him gently away from the desk. "I've been doing some thinking and a little asking around."

"That's obvious, I'd say."

She blinked at him. "Is that supposed to mean something?"

"I didn't intend when I came in yesterday that the whole library should know."

"Know what?"

"That a bloody fool would think it would be simple as pie to locate his daughter."

"Mr. MacKinnon, the reference staff knows that if a man answering your description comes in, I want to talk with him again. I didn't see any harm in that. I never told them what you're after." She was wearing a suit with a pale silk blouse; with her short, dark hair and earnest gray-green eyes, she looked as professional as she sounded. "I expected you to come back yesterday."

She was leading him back to an office. It was a large room separated by half-walls into small individual areas. There was a desk with a chair behind it and another chair in front. She sat behind the desk and motioned him into the other chair. "It may be that your best bet is Immigration and Naturalization. If you contact their local office—and I can give you their phone number and address—you can get a Freedom of Information form. With that form you can request information on the immigration and/or naturalization of your daughter—and of your ex-wife. If either of them became a naturalized citizen, you can find out in which city that happened. If you're lucky, they'll still live in the same area. At least then you'd have a narrower geographic area to search."

"And how long would all that take?"

She tilted her head. "I have no idea. A week? Maybe more."

"I don't have a week."

"You're looking for a needle in a haystack. It's going to take time."

He stood and walked restlessly to the edge of the partition. "And even then it might not mean anything," he said. "Richard Barber was in the American army. I imagine he was moved about. She could have been naturalized in one place years ago and be in quite another place by now." He turned away from her. He would go to a private detective. It was, after all, the most sensible thing to do. By the time he finished with Glover's little job, the detective might have an address.

"You should have told me that before, Mr. MacKinnon; it would have saved us some time."

Surprised, he wheeled around to face her. She was still sitting, but a smile had broken the professional reserve. "There are such things as service registers—lists of American servicemen. We have them here in this library. Your Richard Barber should be listed."

"Will it give an address for him?"

"I don't know. Let's go see."

They found it in the third book they tried, in pale, computer printout type, a list of names that went on for three hundred or more pages. His name was on the retired list. On the active, reserve, and retired lists, there was a total of four Richard Barbers, but by the birth date and grade, only one was possible. Richard Barber, MSg, a social security number, and the date retired. A Yank could retire after twenty years, he knew. Well, that made sense; Rich could easily have had twenty years in by now. He'd retired four years ago.

Whenever he thought of Rich Barber he thought of that grin and of Rich dancing that night at the NCO club with Marie, and he hadn't even realized anything was different until the next morning just before he left when Marie told him she wouldn't be there when he came back. Then it had dawned on him, but it was too late; the cab was already honking outside, and his kit was all packed and standing by the door. He'd walked into the bedroom they shared with the baby; the baby was still asleep in her crib, and he'd bent over and kissed her. Then he'd walked out without another word to Marie, not surprised but stunned nevertheless because it seemed she really meant it. When he came back seven months later, he returned to the apartment and knocked, but someone else answered the door, and then he knew that she had really meant it.

"I don't suppose it's going to be easy," the librarian said, and he realized that he had been staring at the name in the book for a very long time.

"No, it won't." He was not interested in sharing his thoughts with her.

"You might be able to trace him through his social security number. Or you could contact the U.S. Army Military Personnel Center."

"Um-hmm." He was staring at the name. Richard C. Barber.

She smiled thinly. "Even the most amicable divorce is

bound to be difficult. It's a failure, you end up feeling like a failure."

"You don't have to tell me how I should feel."

"I wasn't. I was telling you how I feel."

He looked at her and she nodded. "Two years ago. It still hurts. Sometimes it seems half the people I know are divorced, but that doesn't make it feel any better. You get up there when you're young and you make those promises, thinking you'll keep them, and then one of you doesn't."

He didn't really want to hear about her problems and was relieved when she didn't go on. She stood, brushing the creases from her skirt. "You can just leave the book on the table when you're done. And I imagine you can find your way out?"

"I imagine I can."

He watched her walk away. *You get up there when you're young and you make those promises, thinking you'll keep them, and then one of you doesn't.* Or neither of you does, he thought, because it's no kind of life for a woman who likes partying to be married to a trooper who only shows up every once in a while. He should have left things the way they were; he was nearly ten years in the Regiment before he got married. That was how he should have left it; a trooper had no business being married. He looked at the name once again and then closed the book, realizing for the first time that by now Marie might not be with Rich, either.

6

SAN DIEGO

A. C. MacKinnon was an hour and a half early when he walked through the doors of Lindbergh Airport, carrying the duffel he'd brought from New Zealand. It was the only luggage he'd taken there seven years ago and the only piece he'd left with as well. He'd never had much use for trinkets and remembrances. What a man was had always seemed more important that what he possessed. *Your most important tools are found at the end of your own arms and between your two ears*, Sergeant Major Hawk used to say. Those days at Hereford now seemed impossibly long ago. He could never have been that young, that keen for anything, that—yes—naive.

He grimaced. Like himself, the men he would face in the next weeks knew exactly what war was, knew what it could mean; and yet they would come, and it would be his job to make them as they had once been and were willing to be again: a fighting unit, pumped up and ready. He paused as an impossibly young man strode by in a U.S. Marine Corps uniform, hair shorn nearly to the skin, an airline ticket in one hand and the small hand of an adoring blonde in the other. His eyes followed after them as they walked the length of the hall until, nearly at the end, the youth and the girl embraced.

"It is for that that we do it," MacKinnon said softly, looking away, not willing to share the intimacy of the moment even at this distance. But he hadn't meant the infatuated look on the face of the girl. What he'd seen was the youth's face, which even now was turning away from the girl and shining with excitement and the flush of half-imagined daring. It was the face of all the good young men he had ever seen at Hereford, and it had been his own face once, fresh off the docks of Glasgow, or, before he knew better, newly arrived from the herds and foggy downs of Ardnamurchon in western Scotland.

MacKinnon walked through security, laying his duffel on the moving belt to be X-rayed, and picked it up on the other side. He doubted that Glover would come to the debarkation lounge. That would be too obvious a meeting. He guessed Glover would be playing the gray man, blending in, so inconspicuous that even a curious onlooker would fail to notice him. For that reason it was unlikely Glover would greet MacKinnon just off the plane. No, MacKinnon was almost certain where he'd be, but just in case, MacKinnon was at the debarkation lounge when the flight he should have been on landed. Its passengers spilled out of the jetway, and MacKinnon let himself be caught up by them; as he walked with them toward the baggage claim area, he allowed himself a self-satisfied grin. Glover's caution had turned into MacKinnon's cover, and it had worked very well. Glover would never know that he had already been here for two days.

There was no reason for Glover not to know, he supposed, but it was MacKinnon's habit, born both of personality and experience, not to volunteer more information than was required. He was going to do the job for Glover, and that was all Glover needed to know.

He caught sight of Ken standing beside a rotating baggage carousel. He was wearing a light gabardine jacket, his hands were thrust into his pants pockets, and his almost bald, bullet-shaped head was cast downward as he stared at the luggage gliding by. Any casual observer would assume that he was looking for his own bags.

MacKinnon walked slowly up to the carousel and set down his duffel bag. He rummaged in his pockets until he found his ticket and withdrew it, checked it, looked at the carousel, and looked at the small crowd of people standing around it. The two men's eyes never met; there was no acknowledgment between them. Glover continued watching the baggage flow by, then shrugged finally and turned to walk away. Half a minute later, MacKinnon pocketed his ticket and picked up his carry-on duffel bag and followed.

Glover was waiting for him in the parking lot, the trunk of the rented car already open. MacKinnon stowed his bag and slammed the trunk lid. It wasn't until they were both settled into the front seat of the car that Glover spoke.

"Good flight? Any problems?"

"Nothing that a short hike and a night's sleep can't cure."

Glover nodded. "Yeah. I know what you mean. That flight's a dog."

"I got off the plane at the refueling stop in Hawaii. Almost didn't get back on."

Glover glanced at him, checking to see if he was serious.

"It's a hell of a long way to bring what amounts to a drill sergeant," MacKinnon added. "It still seems to me you could have found someone closer."

"If it makes you feel any better, that's just what the organizers of this exercise thought."

They were driving along the shore. Yesterday MacKinnon had walked it; now as they drove by he watched boats riding at anchor in the harbor. The sun was fading behind a cloud bank over the Pacific.

Glover spoke again. "I told them I wanted you, and if we couldn't get you, they could get someone to replace me. I want the damn operation to work."

MacKinnon leaned his head back against the headrest and closed his eyes as if he were tired. "A surgical strike. Assassinate Qaddafy. And you don't even want me to come along. But you're going to be with them?"

"I'm the officer in charge. I told you I'm going."

"And I should go, too."

Glover shook his head, though MacKinnon couldn't have seen it with his eyes closed. "We've already been through this. I have to go; you don't. We need you for the training but not to go along."

"I'd think with a job like that you'd want as many as you could get."

"You don't think that at all. The trick is going to be to get close enough to do the job. You don't take a battalion in for a job like that; you take just as few as you need."

"How many guards will there be?"

"The information we have is that the place will be well guarded. Well guarded but not overloaded. We have a model at the training base. You can see what we think the guard placement will be."

MacKinnon opened his eyes and turned his head, still leaning against the headrest, toward Glover. "What's he going to be doing at this place, anyway?"

"It's the beginning of Ramadan. He's going into the desert to fast and pray. He'll be there for up to a week."

"I didn't know he was such a holy bugger."

Glover laughed. "We catch him at his prayers, and he'll probably go straight to heaven, or whatever the ragheads call it. We'll be doing him a favor."

"Paradise."

"What's that?"

"Paradise, that's what they call it."

"Yeah." Glover was maneuvering through the rush-hour traffic.

"How much time do we have?" MacKinnon asked.

"Five weeks from tomorrow we take off. That'll be the end of the job for you."

"I get the rest of my money then?"

"Cash. Yup. Fifty thousand, American."

"I get the first half of it when?"

"As soon as we get out there if you want it. Or I can keep it in the safe for you until you're ready to leave. Whatever you'd rather."

MacKinnon didn't like the implication. In a small operation like this appeared to be, each man's life depended on each of the others. He'd always thought that if you can't trust your money to a fellow soldier, then you had no business trusting your life to him. On the other hand, he had lost Marie that way. Rich Barber, U.S. Army. Stationed in Hereford for training with British SAS. A fellow trooper, a buddy. Or so MacKinnon had thought. One night the two of them at the sergeants' mess; another night at the American NCO club. And sometimes Marie went along. But he never thought Rich had stolen her. She was grown; she'd gone of her own free will.

"I'll take the money tonight," he said. There were bound to be places to hide it, and after all, the others were getting their half-shares as well. He looked to his right at the navy boats in the harbor. "It still seems a little steep for a mercenary activity."

Glover gave him a quick look. "This is not a mercenary activity. Mercenaries are people who love the blood and exhilaration of battle. They're undisciplined rogues who fight for whoever pays the most, or pays at all, for that matter. Soldiers, on the other hand—"

"Save me the guff, Glover. A mercenary is a man who fights for pay, and when it's all said and done, so is a soldier."

"You think they're doing it just for the money? You think they would've come in no matter what we were doing—if it were to kill the President of the United States, for instance? No way, MacKinnon, and you wouldn't have, either. Or even to kill a dictator of some half-assed African so-called republic. You wouldn't've come for that, would you? But for a man like Qaddafy, I could've had guys lining up at my door. No way, Mac. A mercenary and a soldier are two different things."

MacKinnon closed his eyes again. "Have it your way," he said. The car was accelerating now, moving rapidly past the far edges of the southeastern suburbs, toward the darkening eastern sky.

COACANTICO WELLS, CALIFORNIA

Coacantico Wells is not even a dusty crossroads village. It is dusty, though, with a pale alkaline powder that coats the occasional car driving through, just as it coats the roof of the place's one building—a once-painted general store and bar which leans slightly with the desert winds and most of whose windows have been replaced with plywood. The dust makes the roof look powdered with snow and coats the face and clothing of anyone foolish enough to stop at Coacantico

Wells and get out of his car. But no one lives there, and no one has for nearly twenty years. The store and bar once served a small army base that took its name from the town but was closed at the end of the forties. Whatever had been done at Coacantico Army Base could be done just as well at one or more of the dozen other military bases within a radius of a hundred miles. Almost twenty years after its closing, the base became, briefly, a home for a scraggly band of hippies who lived there for a while as squatters with visions of a marijuana plantation, but who eventually discovered that marijuana likes, among other things, water. After the ersatz farmers were routed from the army base, they moved into the store/bar combination a few miles down the road and lived there until they got tired of sleeping on the floor. Then they moved on, loading their sparse possessions into a battered blue van and driving off toward the relatively greener pastures of Indio.

MacKinnon leaned forward in the car seat and surveyed what he could see of the rock-strewn desert in the sweep of the headlights. He had not expected the place to look like this, and it had taken him by surprise. Glover, behind the wheel, said nothing, as if waiting for MacKinnon's reaction. They'd spoken little for most of the trip. In the fading light Glover had taken Interstate 8 out of San Diego as far as Ocotillo, then a state route to just beyond Plaster City. It was fully dark long before they turned north on a road that was hardly more than a path through the desert. As they passed the single building of Coacantico Wells, it was only a ghostly shape at the side of the road, lighted briefly in the car's headlights and then slipping past on the left. Ten minutes beyond the building, Glover slowed and pulled off to the right. In the headlights MacKinnon could not even see a track, and he wondered how Glover had known where to turn. Half a mile later Glover slowed, then stopped. "You want to get the gate?" he said, and he handed over a key.

A three-barred metal gate stretched across whatever road they were on. MacKinnon stepped out, and he could see barbed-wire fencing rising six feet from the ground and running from both sides of the gate into the darkness. He unlocked the padlock and swung the gate open, then closed it again after Glover drove through, locking the gate as before.

"What is this place?" he asked, getting back into the car.

"Old army base," Glover said without further explanation.

He drove on for some time before MacKinnon was able to make out in the sweep of the headlights a barracks on the right and an emptiness on the left that could be the parade grounds. Dim lights shone from one of the buildings. The place was set back far enough, MacKinnon noticed, so the lights could not be seen from the road. Almost certainly the buildings couldn't be seen from the road either, even in broad daylight. It was a good place to train for a secret mission: remote enough, yet not all that far from major transportation, not only land and air but also sea. He wondered who had made this place available to them. It was an intriguing question. In his experience neither recruitment nor training for a military operation took place in any country in the world without at least that country's tacit complicity. It made sense: Glover had been an Army Ranger and the United States would be only too happy to have Qaddafy put away. They might not be able to do it themselves, but they could certainly look the other way if someone else tried. And they might even help as long as deniability was maintained.

Glover had been tight-lipped about who was funding the strike, but MacKinnon had guessed it anyway. He was pleased now to see it apparently confirmed. From what he had seen there were very few activities the U.S. government wouldn't at least clandestinely approve. And whatever those might be, he was not sure that he would be comfortable involved in them, either.

"Who's here now?" MacKinnon asked.

"Nobody, just you and me. The rest are coming tomorrow."

"How many did you finally get?"

"Fifteen, including one or two that you suggested. The rest were men I knew, or who came with the highest recommendations. I'll be going back to San Diego tomorrow afternoon to round 'em all up. You'll have tomorrow morning to look over the training area, and the model, and the mockups. We'll go over the plan; I'd be interested in your opinions. After I leave, you can check out what I have on them. I think you'll be impressed." He stopped the car beside the lighted building and turned off the ignition, then he leaned closer to MacKinnon in the darkness. "What even you would call soldiers, Mac."

MacKinnon got out of the car. A breeze blew gently from the northeast. He looked up. It never ceased to amaze him how brilliant the stars were in the desert. He'd almost forgotten that. Even more brilliant than in New Zealand. He smiled, still gazing upward, lingering even though Glover had gone into the building. Ursa Major was in the northeastern sky. At Covington Station it never rose high enough above the horizon to see.

In daylight the place showed its years of neglect. Two buildings had been put hastily in order: one a barracks for the men, the other, he assumed, quarters for the officers, though as far as he knew, Glover would be the only officer. But Glover had seemed to indicate that there would be others arriving, though he hadn't mentioned what their roles might be. Maybe representatives of whatever governments were backing this, MacKinnon thought. It would be interesting to see who they turned out to be. He was quartered in the sergeant's room of the enlisted men's barrack. Glover was staying in the other building. It stood to reason; Glover, after all, had been a colonel.

He walked around the grounds at sunup. They would do. He could assume that the men would need toughening up; that would be the easy part. In addition to that, they'd have to become a unit. They'd have to learn to trust themselves. In a strike like this, you never knew what was going to happen; they were going to have to learn that the unit could successfully deal with the unexpected.

In daylight he could tell why this place had been chosen; it was the same kind of desert as could be expected in southeastern Libya: a gray desert of gravel and rock and dust. Except for a few stunted sage and salt grass bushes, there was nothing green within a half mile in any direction.

Glover showed him the model and it came as a mild surprise. He'd expected the typical bedouin camp of tents—Qaddafy was famous for staying in bedouin-type camps. But this place would have permanent buildings. It looked like a one-time army outpost—reminding him vaguely of the Sinai, of a place there where he'd spent some time back in the old days. God, that was a long time ago. It was no wonder he got out. It was no wonder Glover didn't want to take him along. He remembered that place—the dust, the stones. People who'd never been in a desert always fantasized that deserts were like big beaches—miles and miles of fine sand dunes, blowing into ever-new and ever-intriguing combinations of ridges and valleys, fit for art photographers. Most deserts he'd seen were rock-strewn wastelands.

The mock-ups were another half mile beyond the buildings, even more remote from the road, and MacKinnon was impressed. They were a fair representation of the model. Glover wanted to go in with assault weapons and grenades, using rocket-propelled grenades as back-up. Sounded reasonable. They'd discuss it more when the rest came.

An old Mexican woman showed up around lunchtime and heated up a couple of cans of soup, and MacKinnon and Glover ate mostly in silence. They discussed the plan, and MacKinnon asked questions. Now he was digesting the answers. Someone else arrived before they finished, and the woman threw in another can of soup. Glover introduced the man as Raymond Morse. The name meant nothing to MacKinnon, but the man wore what looked like a new khaki outfit that a place like Harrod's would sell, and MacKinnon could hear an edge of the East End under the City accent. The man said little and went straight across to the officers' quarters as soon as he finished his soup.

Afterward, Glover brought him a slim file folder, dropping it on the table beside MacKinnon's soup bowl. "What we have on the men. Thought you'd want to get to know it. Other than that, you've got the afternoon to yourself. You might want to sleep; your body clock probably hasn't adjusted yet. Tonight, after I get back, you and Morse and I will get together. Tomorrow morning, crack of dawn, training begins."

"All right." MacKinnon nodded, opening the folder. He glanced through it, then closed it to take to his quarters.

Glover started to leave, then turned back. "Of course, it doesn't all have to be sweat," he said.

MacKinnon frowned.

"I mean, maybe some evenings we could get up some games of football. Get in shape and have fun at the same time."

"I'm not familiar with that kind of training," MacKinnon said stiffly.

"Loosen up, Mac," Glover said. "Don't tell me you never had any fun in the Regiment. Never played any football—soccer—whatever."

"We don't have regimental football," MacKinnon replied. "We climb mountains for fun. We jump out of planes."

Glover turned and left the building. In a few moments MacKinnon heard the car's engine start up.

MacKinnon wandered back to the enlisted men's quarters and studied the folder's contents for a while. He smiled approval at one or two of the names and read each man's dossier carefully. Glover had been right; he'd chosen good men. Then MacKinnon laid the folder down on the small table at the side of the bed and stepped out of his room. He spent the next two hours walking the perimeter of the camp.

BISKRA, ALGERIA

The man sat at a table, sheets of meticulously recorded figures before him. He had been there for more than two hours, carefully checking each figure. He had a penchant for detail; he carried the minutiae of the Organization in his mind. But now his mind was wandering. By temperament he was not much given to reflection, but in the last few years he had become more and more introspective. It was a sign of age, he assumed; he also was aware that it could be a sign of fatigue or even of depression.

Outside, in an alleyway nearby, a cat let out a single snarl. His mind drifted to the sound, and he could imagine a stray cat—in Biskra all the cats were strays—cornered by a dog, also a stray, and he smiled, wondering how the confrontation would come out. Or maybe this time the cat was the predator, stalking a rat hidden amid a pile of garbage. Sometimes the prey, sometimes the predator. He smiled, nodding, and an errant breath of air drifted through the closed shutters and ruffled the papers on the desk.

He didn't like planning too far ahead; one could get caught much too easily that way, and he had built his life in the last few years on living unpredictably. It had kept him from assassination more than a few times, but he was well aware that sometimes planning was necessary. He had not become an engineer by refusing to plan. He had not become the man he was without a great deal of careful planning. And this would take planning, too. There was hardly anyone he could trust on this. One man, anyway, was all he could bring. No problem in that; he was used to traveling light. If Nidal, *if anybody*, ever found out . . . he could kiss it all good-bye. But he still had to do it. He had held it together as long as he could, but the Organization had never been so fragile. There was too much factionalism; there were too many who would no longer wait, too many who were taking to the streets and joining splinter groups. If it was ever going to be done—if *he* was going to be the one to do it—it would have to be this time and this way. If he didn't do it this time, everything could come unraveled, and then they would lose for sure.

From below, in the alley, came a clatter, and he wondered about the cat. He put a hand to his fleshy stubbled chin and thought about the cat. The other thing had been put out of his mind, compartmented. When the time for it came, he would do what he had known all along he would do. He would go and he would deal as best he could, and if an agreement came out of it, those who chose to villify him would be the ones who were content to see the children die.

COACANTICO WELLS, CALIFORNIA

MacKinnon stood facing the men. All were at attention, all were dressed in the khakis they'd been issued on arrival. Glover stood to the side of the double rank of men; he would go through the drills with them. They had discussed that last night, he and Glover and Morse. A colonel doesn't lead a platoon, MacKinnon had insisted. This isn't war, Mac, Glover had replied; we don't have to follow service rules in an exercise like this. You let your men know that and you're in big trouble, MacKinnon had shot back. They weren't trained to be troopers, most of them. What they know is the military way; you have to unlearn those things when you become a trooper. Glover had stared at him for a long moment before he spoke. Your SAS may be good, Mac, he'd said, but it doesn't have a patent on intelligent men. It's possible to find them in the other services, too.

Morse had looked on during all that, picking imaginary lint from his pristine khakis. MacKinnon wasn't sure yet what Morse's function was, but he had an idea. Any military strike had to be funded. Even if the money originated from a government, it still had to be channeled through someone. Morse had the look of a money man.

Glover's insistence had given MacKinnon the cue to his own approach. He'd been worried about how it was going to look to the men when they found out that he wasn't going along. He hadn't liked it from the first, but Glover was not to be moved on that one. Now MacKinnon knew how he could use it. They were experienced soldiers, but in some ways he would treat them as if they were raw recruits. To mold them into a unit, to forge trust among them, he would present them with the one element a successful army needs: a common enemy.

With his eyes MacKinnon skimmed the tops of the men's heads. Right to left across the rank of men, then back, left to right. Then back again, right to left, and again, left to right, never looking directly at any of them. They stood at attention, their eyes on him, and his eyes roved just above their heads, and the sun rose imperceptibly in the eastern sky.

"My name is MacKinnon," he called out finally. "A."—

he began a right to left sweep—"C."—his eyes paused
briefly and then moved back toward the right—"Mac-Kinnon." He pronounced each syllable as a separate word. His
eyes took another sweep. "As far as you are concerned my
name is 'Yes, sir.' " Another sweep. "Got that?"

The men's voices called out in a ragged chorus: "*Yes, sir!*"
Even Glover called back the response.

MacKinnon's implacable face stared back at them. His
eyes roamed across their heads for another two minutes
while they stared at him in silence.

"Some of you may think you know me," MacKinnon
barked finally. "*May think.*" He paused and his eyes moved
across them again. "Well, you don't. . . . But I know you,
all of you." He paused again for almost a whole minute. "I
stand before you to tell you that you do not know me. Not
now. But you will. You will. And by the time I am done with
you, nothing will surprise you. Nothing. *Got that?*"

"*Yes, sir!*" came back at him like a wall of sound.

His eyes ranged across them again. "You have all served in
special forces," he said. "I don't know how success was defined in the units in which you served. Maybe it was getting
out with your skin. But I'll tell you how it will be defined
here. . . . Success"—his eyes moved from right to left—
"success is a matter of not engaging the enemy in battle. At
all. Success is stealth. Success is surprise. Success is getting
off the first shot, and the last, and all the ones in between,
and then getting away. Success is catching the buggers in
their underwear. In the kind of strike you are going to carry
out, combat means that something has gone wrong. Remember that. What you will be trained for here is success.
Not failure. Is that understood?"

"*Yes, sir!*"

"With that clear," he barked back at them, "we will begin." His voice accelerated now. "Ahead right, march twenty
paces, double march twenty paces, run twenty paces, fall
down, roll over, get up in double time, turn left, and repeat
until I order you to stop. *NOW!*"

As one, the men turned and began the drill, and MacKinnon watched, still at attention. But his eyes were on the men

themselves now, watching them, searching for a hint of
weakness, seeing who was first and who was last to fall, to
roll over, to get up again. They knew his eyes were on them
and what he was looking for, and they were determined not
to let him find it.

In the mornings they drilled. After lunch they had half an
hour of strategy sessions and then double-timed the perimeter of the camp. Twice. After that they worked on hand-to-
hand, knife-to-hand, knife-to-knife. They crawled under
and over and through barricades MacKinnon had con-
structed. Blindfolded, they made their ways through, in, and
around the mock-ups of the camp, with MacKinnon arm-
locking them by surprise or jamming a knife at their sides or
clasping their necks so tightly that they fought back with the
fury and fear of the truly endangered.

Nearly all former Rangers, they knew most of the drills,
but they were rusty. Sullivan had a gut that evidenced too
many beers and tacos; Kozlewski was lazy and sloughed off
if he thought no one was looking; Halstead, on the other
hand, had kept himself in shape and liked to show off.
Thomasson, long and lanky, had gone to the Rangers from
the farm and had gone back to the farm afterward; he was
tanned and strong, his movements as slow and easy as his
drawl. Seipke was dark and short, with an intense concen-
tration and a quick wit. MacKinnon teamed them together
and watched as flint struck wood until each adjusted to the
other. He had known Lawrence, the single Brit, from training at Hereford, but he never showed it. The Yanks would
look for signs of favoritism. If anything, he pushed Lawrence harder, or else ignored him altogether.

Raymond Morse stayed around longer than he had
planned, watching in fascination. Shahabad arrived and
nodded approval. Glover dragged himself around with the
rest of the men, older than most, more out of shape than
any, but determined not to quit. As MacKinnon's superior
in rank, he could have quit, or he could have pulled rank
and demanded easier going for all the men, but he didn't.
The men knew he could have and didn't, and they respected
him for it. "Old Ken," they called him back in their quar-

ters. "The bastard" was one of the nicer things they called MacKinnon.

MacKinnon spent his nights alone in his room, the sound of the men's grumbles and snores coming through the thin walls.

Occasionally he met with Glover in Glover's quarters; sometimes Morse and Shahabad were there, and sometimes they weren't. Shahabad was even more of a riddle than Morse, who, MacKinnon had decided by now, was almost certainly the money man. Shahabad was introduced to MacKinnon, but that was all. He was younger than Morse or Glover, perhaps only in his thirties, MacKinnon noted as he caught the name and wondered. It didn't sound like a name a man would really have—Kherman Shahabad. It seemed more like a name a man would choose for himself, to hide something. Or maybe to express something. Or maybe just to confuse.

In that strange setting, MacKinnon felt the odd man out, not part of the troops to go, not part of the planning team. Sometimes at night he picked a direction by the stars and walked for an hour or more. He'd gotten used to the solitude at Covington Station; it didn't bother him anymore. If there was anything about the setup that bothered him, it was Shahabad himself. It was the way the man looked at you and didn't see you, or at least didn't seem to be seeing another human being.

The sun was not yet over the horizon when A. C. MacKinnon strode into the barracks room. "All out! All out!" he barked as he walked down the rows of bunks, dragging a wooden box on a makeshift dolly. Onto each bed he threw a gun. The quicker of the men caught theirs in midair on their way out from under the sheets. The slower ones ducked, then recovered when they realized what their new bed partner was.

"AK47," MacKinnon said. "The real thing, straight from the U.S.S.R. Not some cheap East bloc knockoff. Effective." My God, man, he'd said to Glover when he'd seen the weapons, what're you trying to do?

Glover had nodded. I know, I know, Mac, he'd said.

You promised me the best, MacKinnon had said. The best in these terms is for every man to have the gun he knows the best. Not, for bloody God's sake, a gun *none* of them knows best. We have five weeks, man, and none of these buggers is in the shape he should be. And now you want them to learn the weapons as well?

He'd stormed out of the officers' quarters, and Glover had come running after him. Mac, it's the way it has to be. Listen—

You listen, he'd said. You told me the best. You told me whatever I thought they should have. I told you before, they should have their choice of weapons. Every special operations group grants that—

You're wrong, Glover had said. You're wrong and you know it. You didn't take a Sterling into Iran that time, you took a Skorpion, and you know why. Sometimes the cover demands it.

He'd stood there and stared at Glover, knowing Glover was right and hating him for it. A man depends on his weapon; it should be something he knows as well as the feel of his own mouth. The men should have been given their choice, not have weapons shoved at them that they might not have seen in years. What else? he'd asked. And Glover had told him: H & Ks, Soviet-made grenade launchers, perhaps a few Uzis. It was clear what they were trying to do, whoever was behind this show. The H & Ks would have been stolen, the Uzis too, no doubt. Whatever weapons were left behind would lead nowhere. Cover upon cover upon cover. It would have been a good idea if it hadn't been done at the expense of the men themselves.

He stood now in the barrack room with them, each man handling a gun. "AK47s," he repeated. "Effective, reliable, powerful. Learn them. You know where the range is. Tomorrow, this time, we take up the RPGs." He started out the door, then paused and turned back. "When Kozlewski can break his down and put it back in less than two minutes, you can eat breakfast." Then he was out the door, leaving

Kozlewski smiling sheepishly and turning the gun over in his hands.

Even though it was only February, the sun burned down on A. C. MacKinnon's back, and the sweat marks showed on his shirt a ragged dark splotch down the center of his back and wide half circles under his arms. His eyes were creased against the brightness of the sun as he watched the men, barking out orders at them. In response to his commands they double-timed in close order to the mock-up of a desert camp. They had been under and over and through these buildings until they knew them by heart, and still he took them back, as if the place were the center of their lives, as if it were their only rightful place in the world. They marched to it again today, and the men must have been wondering what new torture MacKinnon could think up for them.

Kherman Shahabad watched their retreating backs through a dusty window, nodding to himself. He had a good two hours. He could depend on MacKinnon to keep the men occupied at least that long. He turned around and surveyed the large room before him, beds neatly made as if a drill sergeant would be coming to inspect them, foot lockers closed and locked.

He began with the first bed, deftly running his hands across the light blanket. Then he felt beneath the mattress and across the top and bottom of the flat pillow. Quickly he moved to the foot locker; one practiced turn of the tool from his pocket opened the lock. He lifted the extra clothes, the shoes. He opened a Dopp kit and laid out its contents, trying the razor to make sure it was real, checking the toothpaste tube and the shaving cream can. He riffled through the identity papers, picked up a picture of a young man— too old to be a son; a brother, perhaps, maybe even a lover. He compartmentalized the information with the name on the inside of the locker. One never knew what could be used later; memory, Shahabad had always known, is one of man's greatest gifts. He closed the locker, set the lock, and moved on to the next bed.

In just over an hour he had finished the room, running

his hands along the bare wood ledge where the ceiling met the walls of the room, finding little there but dust. One never knew. He had not survived this long by leaving anything to chance or by trusting anyone.

Finished in the large barrack room, he moved on to the small room at the end of the building. He paused in the doorway for a moment. He had always had an uncanny sense of other people, as if each person's being could speak to him separately from its body. Born under other circumstances, he might have called himself a mystic or a guru or even a channeler. He felt MacKinnon now in the room, could see him asleep on the neat bed, could see his boots laid in soldierly fashion at the foot of the bed. There had been something about MacKinnon when they had first met, something more than he seemed, and it had bothered Shahabad. More slowly than with the rest, he examined the bed, pulled the pillow out of its case and felt it, looking at the seams for an edge of new stitching. He replaced the bedclothes and opened the locker. MacKinnon's civvies lay neatly piled atop the folded duffel bag with which he'd come. Shahabad unfolded the shirt, examined the cuffs, the collar, the pocket, then refolded it exactly the way it had been. He drew out the pants and examined them just as carefully. Then he withdrew the jacket and felt the lining and the pockets. In one pocket was a pen and a half sheet of buff-colored paper. He unfolded the paper quickly. *University of California, San Diego* was printed at the top of the page. Beneath that and to the left were the words *from the desk of Anne Rowen.* Someone had written on the paper: *Service Registers.* Below that, another hand had written out a name: Richard Barber. And a number. Shahabad was not certain what the number meant; it was nine digits, not the right length for an American telephone number. He turned the paper over but found nothing on the reverse. Then he refolded it and returned it to the jacket pocket. In another pocket he found MacKinnon's airline ticket and his British passport. He paged through the passport, reading the entry and exit stamps. MacKinnon had not been out of New Zealand for seven years. He had left there on January 18 and arrived on the same date in the States. Shahabad smiled to himself. One never knew what one was going to learn. Glover had gone to meet MacKinnon's flight on January 20, two days after MacKinnon had really come.

Shahabad looked at the ticket and noted that the dates corresponded with the passport stamps. Then he replaced the ticket and the passport and folded the jacket the way it had been. Closing the locker, he looked more carefully about the room. Before he left it forty-five minutes later, he had examined everything in the room and taken apart everything that would come apart. Crawling under the bed, he had seen a space between the worn floorboards that didn't look right. Gently he pried at the board and was not surprised when it came away easily. Beneath it were five stacks of bills. He knew each would contain a hundred hundred-dollar bills. He hefted one in his hand, thought a minute, and then put it back. All in good time, he told himself.

A. C. MacKinnon lay in bed in the dark, muffled sounds of sleep seeping through the wooden walls from the barrack room on the other side. He rose, flipped on the light, and looked at his watch. One seventeen. He turned off the light and walked to the window. High clouds had rolled in, obliterating the stars and leaving only a pale glow where the moon should be. He dressed quickly in the dark and ran his fingers through his hair as if to comb it. Then he opened the door and strode into the barrack room.

"*All out! All out!*" he called, flicking on lights as he went. "Dressed and outside in two minutes." At the outer door he paused and turned. "Lawrence, alert your commanding officer." Then he stepped outside.

Three minutes later they formed a ragged circle around him, Glover at the edge of it, panting and still shoving his shirt into the waist of his pants. "Two miles due north— zero-degree bearing," MacKinnon ordered. "All speed and all stealth. Two miles ninety degrees. Return on a two-twenty-five bearing. Give me five minutes." Without further comment he slipped around the corner of the building into the dark and was gone.

"Shit," Kozlewski whispered.

"Form up and let's go," Ken Glover said quietly.

"He said five minutes," Halstead whispered.

"Yeah," Glover said, grinning in the dark. "All's fair, as they say. Let's move it." He took a bearing and pointed north, and the men moved out, walking in the slow, rolling motion that assured total silence. They all knew that Mac-Kinnon was out there somewhere, waiting. The darkness was meant to confuse, but it protected as well. They knew silence; sixteen men walked across a graveled desert soundlessly. And they had taken a jump on the time. With luck, they would pass him in the dark, and he would never know they were there.

With luck. He had taught them about luck. "There's no such thing as luck," he had told them. "You make your own breaks. Your mind, that's your luck. Your brains. Think, men, think!" As one, they were thinking now: he tells us five minutes, and we wait half a minute instead. Yeah, making our own luck. Yeah, MacKinnon, that's how we do it.

They moved silently through the darkness in close order, signaling one another by touch: a growth of salt grass, an escarpment, a faintly heard sound. Their heads were clear now, sleep the furthest thing from their minds. There was only one thought: beat MacKinnon. Beat him at his own game.

At the two-mile point they found the token: a white handkerchief tied around a rock. Thomasson, in the lead, picked it up and held it aloft in triumph. As one, the body turned ninety degrees and headed eastward. Yeah, MacKinnon, watch us do it.

A single shot whistled not six inches above his head, and Thomasson, without a second thought, hit the ground. Behind him, the others went down. Silence. Seipke put his head up to listen, and it was nearly blown off as automatic rifle fire raked across the group. "Jesus H. Christ," Sullivan whispered to the man whose ear was practically in his mouth, "that's live ammo he's got."

More silence. They lay there, their faces digging into the sand and stones, waiting for the next volley, and they were greeted with silence. Halstead made a mental check of each of his body parts. Kozlewski had a sudden, unbearable urge to pee. Archie Lawrence gazed at what would have been the horizon if he'd been able to see it. Fucking bloody bastard, he thought. Hasn't changed an inch. Train you or kill you.

Ken Glover moved his arm cautiously until he could see the lighted digits of his watch. Give you five minutes, he thought. Okay, man, this time we'll give it to you. He watched the seconds blink by in utter silence and then allowed two more minutes. Then one more. "He's gone," he whispered finally.

"You wanna be the first one up?" came a whisper close at hand.

Glover listened again and heard nothing. Slowly he raised his head off the ground, then his shoulders, then his torso. Finally he stood. Around him, one by one, the others stood. "He's definitely gone," Sullivan whispered to Kozlewski, who nodded agreement in the dark. Chastened, the group started off again. It was still fully dark. How had he seen them? If it were possible to be quieter than silent, they were, as they moved eastward. Thomasson still held the handkerchief-covered rock in his hand, a talisman against failure.

Behind them and to their right, MacKinnon followed, a shadow slipping through the surrounding darkness, unseen, unheard.

In the last week of the training, in an evening meeting with Shahabad, Morse, and Glover, MacKinnon pronounced the men ready. Shahabad stared at him, his eyes blank as usual. Morse turned in his chair. "What do you think, Ken? Are they?"

A smile broke Glover's sun-darkened face, and he nodded vigorously. "They are, in spades, and goddamn, I am, too!" He laughed. "Didn't I say he would do it? Didn't I say he'd build the best fucking strike force that could be done? This exercise is going to run like a Swiss clock, just as I said." He grinned across the room at MacKinnon. "Do we give 'em a break tomorrow? Let 'em sleep in an extra half hour?"

MacKinnon looked quizzical. "What you should be asking, Ken, is if we should get them up a half hour earlier. They have the rest of their lives to sleep in."

His words sobered Glover more than MacKinnon would have thought. "Of course. You're right, Mac. Right now we've got 'em on the edge. We might as well keep 'em there until the exercise is over."

MacKinnon's eyes flashed back at Glover. "Exercise? Goddamn, Ken, *exercise?* You've been calling it that since you brought me in, and it's about time you stopped. This is no bloody 'exercise'! This is not one of your *games!* Some of these men are going to die in that desert, and don't you forget that. No matter how hard we train, no matter how good they are, do you think they're all coming back? It's bad enough to fool them into thinking they'll all make it; don't fool yourself, man. This is no fucking simple *exercise*. They're going in to kill or be killed, and so are you!"

Glover, astonished at the sudden outburst, stared wordlessly. Morse smiled and set his drink down. Even Shahabad turned and seemed to be seeing MacKinnon for the first time.

"You're right, of course," Glover said, recovered. "It's easy enough to forget those things sometimes."

"Well," MacKinnon growled, "see that you don't forget." He nodded curtly then and left. Outside, he looked up at the stars and headed out briskly to the northeast. Two more days, he was thinking.

Inside, Glover repeated himself to the other two men: "Didn't I tell you he would do it?"

"He got you to quit the bloody cigars," Morse said. "That's enough to praise him for right there."

Shahabad said nothing. He was standing at the window, watching MacKinnon walk off into the darkness.

"You guys can stay up," Glover said, rising. "You don't have to be on that parade ground at six in the morning."

"Two more days," Shahabad said from across the room. "That's all that you're going to have to do it."

"Don't I know it!" Glover's voice trailed after him as he made his way down the hall to his quarters at the opposite end of the building.

"Everything ready?" Morse asked.

"You already asked me," Shahabad responded.

"And you guarantee that it'll work right?"

Shahabad stared at him for a long moment. "I wasn't hired to make it work wrong. There won't even be enough pieces to put back together to figure out how many there were."

7

CAIRO

Hussein Bakr, President of the Republic of Egypt, strode rapidly down the wide steps of Qasr el Gumhuriya without even looking at the security guards that lined the way. Ever since Sadat's assassination, Egyptian presidents had been more wary of appearing in public, even if it was only to leave one government building for another. There was an undercurrent of angry disapproval these days from the fundamentalist militants, and no one knew precisely how strong they were or when or in what way they would strike next. Since taking office Bakr had been outspoken about his refusal to be intimidated. He still stood for moderation in the Arab world, and he was not going to let what he considered a band of crazy fanatics run the country with a campaign of terror. But that did not mean he had to be foolhardy. Though he did not respect the fanatics, he knew what they could do. He had been at that bloodied parade ground in 1981.

Bakr stepped into the waiting limousine, and a bodyguard closed the door behind him, walked around the car, and slid into the front seat beside the driver. Bakr nodded imperceptibly, and the driver caught the movement in the rearview mirror and eased away from the curb. Bakr breathed deeply, a trick he'd learned to calm his nerves. He would take one man with him, an aide, but no bodyguard. That had been the agreement. If the others could do it, there was no reason why he shouldn't. After all, he was only the host, only the catalyst.

The breathing exercise had relaxed him as it was meant to do. He smiled to himself, pressing further back into the seat. What had happened at Camp David had been a step, and it had been important at the time, but what might happen at Bir el Khadim could be astonishing.

The limousine threaded its way through the perpetually congested traffic of Cairo until it reached the airport road. Even there the traffic was horrendous: camel caravans competing for space with dangerously overloaded buses, private automobile horns honking at slow-moving donkeys, and the dust that was inherent in Cairo hanging thickly in the air like a brown mist. The limousine moved in a motorcade led by an armored police car, and the various vehicles and animals that crowded the road moved off to let it pass. The people could see nothing through the dark glass of the limousine, but they knew who it must be. That was one of Bakr's regrets: in a world of fanatics and terrorists a head of state hardly dared to let his person be seen, and it had become impossible for him to mix with the people, to walk along the broad sidewalks of Qasr el Nil, to sit in the coffeeshops and listen to the gossip, to eat *taamiyya* at the stand that had once been his favorite. That was one of the things the terrorists had done: they had separated a leader from his people.

In the ensuing days the word would be spread that the President was on a quiet skiing holiday in Switzerland; a few would believe it, but most of Cairo would wag its head knowingly and gossip that he was once again ensconced in the twenty-second-floor penthouse apartment where he had installed his latest mistress. And the fanatics would cry aloud once again for a leader who enjoyed simpler pleasures, a leader who had not forgotten the people.

WASHINGTON, D. C.

Howard Kammer cut himself. He stared into the bathroom mirror and silently swore as the blood began to ooze from the cut. Of all days. He tore off a corner of toilet paper and pressed it against the blood. Then he jerked open the medicine cabinet and rummaged through it. Didn't there used to be something that you put on the wound when you cut yourself shaving?—What was it called? Styptic pencil, something like that? How come he didn't have one anymore? Did things like that just disappear off the shelves? Could you even buy one anymore? "Phyllis!" he yelled. "Phyllis!"

From below he could hear her response.

"*Goddamn it!*" he muttered, ripping the toilet paper fragment off and putting on a fresh one. He walked into the hall and called down over the banister, "I cut myself shaving. What've we got to stop the bleeding?"

He could hear her footsteps below, and then she appeared around the corner of the dining room. She looked up at him and shook her head. "Why don't you use your electric razor?" Her voice was maddeningly calm.

He patted his chin to make sure the toilet paper was still on it. "Just tell me what we have."

"Or you could change blades more than once every six months. I think we can afford it."

"Are you going to tell me, or would you like me to bleed to death?"

"What is it that's supposed to work?" she said, frowning, turning away, no longer looking up at him. "Cream of tartar? Powdered alum?" she asked herself, moving away now toward the kitchen.

From above, he could see the gray hairs at the crown of her head. She was taller than he, and he didn't get this view of her often. She pulled out the gray that she could see—her only vanity. He wondered if she realized how much gray she couldn't see.

He walked back into the bathroom and ran the cold water, wet a washcloth, and dabbed at his face with it. Just what he needed. If he were superstitious, he'd think this was a sign. In fact, he'd probably think this was the sign that became the last straw. Neither the Prime Minister nor the Foreign Minister available in Israel. President Bakr unavailable in Egypt. At least he would be able to meet with the President of Syria and King Hussein in Jordan, as well as the Foreign Minister in Egypt, though he would have preferred to meet with Bakr. It wasn't going to be a wasted trip, but there was no way it was going to be as productive as he had hoped. He'd even thought briefly of canceling it, but there were no victories to be won by staying in Washington. If anybody was watching Howard Kammer these days, a canceled trip would be only further proof of the erosion of his power.

He heard the muffled sounds as Phyllis ran up the carpeted stairs, and he could imagine what she was thinking. "Here," she said to him, rounding the corner and coming into sight at the doorway, "try this."

He reached for the box she held out to him and drew the washcloth away from the cut. He looked at his reflection for a moment, holding his breath. "Never mind," he said at last. "It's stopped."

"Must not have been that major a wound," she said, stepping around to examine his chin firsthand.

He looked at her reflection, and her eyes lifted and caught his in the mirror. He had been right about what she'd been thinking. Her hand went to his back, patting it as one comforts a child. "It'll be all right," she said. "You ready for breakfast soon?"

"Five minutes."

Her hand slipped down to his waist. Even after all these years he winced inwardly when she did that, knowing that she would surely feel the flab. She gave him a quick squeeze. "Love ya," she said, and then she was gone.

And she did, which was the amazing thing. She had been first in her class at Brandeis. She'd been visiting a school friend in New Rochelle that summer and had met him in a bookstore. He was reaching for Keynes, and she had just spied a Galbraith. He made a condescending remark, and she spit one back just as fast. They argued economics for over an hour in the aisles of the bookstore before discovering that they had lived three blocks apart in Boston for the last two years. He asked her out, and five weeks later they were married. The Oxford fellowship that had been waiting for her that fall went unfilled as they moved into a tiny one-room efficiency in Roxbury and he returned to grad school. She became pregnant two weeks after the wedding but supported them until her ninth month by clerking at Filene's.

Twenty-seven years and five children later, she had never looked back. She had her garden with every form of daisy known to modern man; she had her children, now mostly grown, with only two still in college; and she still had the sharp mind and the wicked sense of humor. She would laugh with abandon at the Howie jokes—and there was always at least one circulating in Washington. She cut out the cartoons that mocked him and sent them to his sister in Larchmont or one of the kids at college, usually with added comments of her own penned in the margins. But she had lived with him for twenty-seven years; she fixed him breakfast every morning and waited up for him every night; she argued politics and economics with him; and when they made love, he forgot that he was fifty pounds overweight because she made him feel like the most exciting man on earth.

COACANTICO WELLS, CALIFORNIA

A last quarter moon shone dully in the southern sky, barely outlining the small cluster of building shapes against the desert. On the north side of the compound all was in shadow as the figures of four men crept silently, keeping close to the walls for protection. They paused, scarcely able to see one another in the dark, and there was no communication among then. Each knew his job, each had his responsibilities clearly in mind. One man, Eric Halstead, had broken with the group and was slipping around the building from the opposite direction. Charlie Kozlewski was the first man of the remaining three, and when he reached a corner of the building, he paused, making a peculiar series of motions with his hands. Almost immediately Jack Thomasson moved past, slipping around the corner of the wall. Now in partial light, he edged quickly along the wall toward the next corner. Just around it, he knew, was the door.

Meanwhile, Halstead was coming toward the same door from the opposite side of the building. Since this side faced the interior of the compound, reason suggested that it would be less carefully guarded. Still, Halstead paused, sensing something. But there was no sound. Nerves, he thought, and moved on. He was almost to the corner when he was hit from behind. Simultaneously a hand clamped over his mouth and nose, and a voice whispered close to his ear: "Knife in the back. You're dead, man."

At a sound in the dark, Jack Thomasson stopped, held himself flat against the wall, and listened. Then he moved toward the corner again, slipped around it, and took a quick deep breath. In front of him was a closed door; he lifted his AK47, his finger lightly curled around the trigger. Without looking behind him, he knew that Gordon Seipke, RGD5 grenades in hand, would be ready as soon as he swung himself out of the way.

At exactly the same moment, two more groups of four were making similar moves at the remaining three buildings. And in a wide imaginary circle enclosing all the buildings, three men stood at equal distances from one another, each holding an RPG7 portable rocket launcher. All three were under identical orders: Rockets were to be fired in response to any strong resistance, and the men inside the perimeter would get the hell out.

In the darkness a single man let himself into one of the buildings through a narrow cut in its side. He paused, listening. Over the years he had become used to soft, barely heard sounds, and he listened now with that heightened awareness born of the silent waiting just before the rush of adrenaline. He heard a soft slurry of sound against the outside wall—a sleeve or pant leg brushing against rough wood. Then silence. But he could feel the presence now, just outside the door, and he moved forward toward it with the same assurance in the dark that he would have had in daylight.

His hand crept to the door and stayed, the palm against bare wood. He felt the soft vibration as whoever stood outside tried the latch—a chance in a million, perhaps, but one never knew when a door might be left unlocked. And then the vibration was gone, and with one quick motion of his left hand he released the bar and pulled the door open. His right hand, closed around a H & K MP5, was already stretching out as he jerked the door open.

"You're dead," he whispered to Thomasson, standing in the open doorway. Then, seeing Seipke just behind Thomasson, he added, "And you're throwing your grenades, but I'll be out of here before they explode, and if I'm good enough, I can get out of this place. *No survivors. Remember that: no survivors!*"

From the perimeter, Archie Lawrence's voice called out, *"There! Building C! You're in my scope!"* Jack Thomasson leaned against the wall of the building and grinned laconically. Gordon Seipke punched Thomasson lightly in a gesture of victory.

MacKinnon jerked his head slightly to the right. "You lost one back there."

"How?" Thomasson asked, straightening.

"Took him out with a knife."

Seipke made a quick move as if he'd taken it literally, then recovered. "Then how'd you get in the building? The only door is here, and we would've seen you." .

At that moment Halstead came around the corner. "It was the only door this morning. Since we were last here, the bastard cut another hole in it. Took me out and then slipped in."

MacKinnon folded his arms across his chest. "Take nothing for granted. The best intelligence is always faulty. Nothing is ever exactly the way it seems. You depend on anything other than your own eyes and ears, and you risk losing the fight."

"You knew we were coming," Halstead said. "You did have that advantage. They aren't going to be prepared like that. If you hadn't known that, you're the one who would have been dead."

"You think that way, and you're dead meat for sure, Halstead. That's the whole job of a guard, to be expecting someone." The rest had come up closer now, faces blackened against the night. It had taken him by surprise the first day —how young they looked. Only Ken Glover, who had been one of the ones on perimeter duty and who stood now at the outer edge of the group, was a contemporary. Too long out of it; he really was getting old. They crowded around him now, like school kids, like a football team around the coach, and he knew what they wanted to hear. "You can all keep that in mind," he said, his voice only slightly raised. "No matter how few guards there might be, their whole job will be to expect someone. You. Each one of you is the one they're going to expect, and you're the one they're going to kill, just like I would have killed Halstead if I'd really had a knife, and Thomasson if I'd had bullets in this thing. And probably would have killed Seipke as well." He let the silence hang over them for a moment, then he nodded at Glover. "They're all yours, Colonel."

If they got back when it was all over, then they would know they'd done a good job; he wasn't going to ruin them by saying it now.

In his quarters MacKinnon packed up his few things. Glover had told him earlier that he wanted one last meeting afterward and that someone would be taking him back tomorrow. He supposed it wouldn't be Glover; Glover would be too busy with the men. It would probably be Morse, the money man—they still owed him the other fifty thousand.

Glover would want to be assured tonight that they were ready, and they were. He had brought them to exactly where he wanted them this last night, an almost success. They all knew that Thomasson and Seipke were two of the best; if they could get caught, they'd all have to think again. The next time they did it—the only time that really counted—they'd all be on the edge, determined to do it without a hitch. He straightened, leaving the bag unzipped. In the morning he'd only have to shave and zip up the bag. And take out his money. Maybe he wouldn't even shave. He wanted to get an early start; he wanted to be gone by the time the men were up because that was the best way to avoid the awkwardness.

He stepped outside and looked up at the sky. He kicked at a stone, and it scuttled away into the dark. He started away from the barrack, heading south, putting even more distance between himself and the mock-up of the desert camp. Training site. Whatever it was. He supposed there was a similarity to such places; after all, there were only so many ways you could arrange four to a half-dozen buildings. He continued south, using Sirius in the southern sky as his guide. After a while he came to the fence and turned west, walking along it. He paused, thinking he heard something, and then, after listening to the silence, moved on.

He made one last perimeter and then headed for the officers' quarters. Glover ought to be back by now. He hoped Glover hadn't congratulated the men too much. He'd warned Ken about that, but Glover had seemed preoccupied. He knew that feeling and almost missed not having it now. But seeing those faces had brought it home in a way that nothing else could have. He was too old for those things now; he supposed that was why Glover had maneuvered him into not going along. Take the money and run, Glover had said, and that was just what he was going to do. He smiled wryly at himself in the dark: a soldier grown too old to soldier anymore. At least he'd had the luck to find something else. The world already had too many soldiers grown too old. He walked into the room and squinted at the light for an instant. Glover was just knocking off the cap from a beer, talking as he did it. "Mac!" Glover interrupted himself. "I was just saying— Shit, they did one hell of a job. That is going to be one hell of an operation. Those pricks aren't even gonna know what hit 'em. Have a drink, Mac. Didn't you think they were great?"

Despite himself, MacKinnon grinned. "They're going to be good enough—"

"Good enough! My God, good enough?" Glover turned to the others for confirmation. "Didn't I tell you? This asshole has got those buggers so fuckin' hungry to do it, and to do it right, they probably can't even piss straight. God, MacKinnon—" He shoved a beer across the table at MacKinnon.

MacKinnon shook his head.

"Celebrate with us, MacKinnon," Morse said. He leaned against a file cabinet, one of the things that had been left forty years ago when the army pulled out. It was battered and dinged; it looked as if the hippies had used it for target practice with beer bottles. The Mexican woman had washed it up on the first day, as she had washed everything else, washable or not, in the two buildings in use.

"I don't drink," MacKinnon said.

"One won't hurt," Glover responded, shoving the bottle closer.

"I'm going back in the morning, isn't that correct?" MacKinnon asked.

Glover nodded. "No one's asking you to get drunk, you know."

"I'm not worrying about the hangover. I'm wondering when I get the rest of the pay."

"In the morning, when he takes you back," Glover said, nodding his head at Morse.

"You didn't come cheap," Morse said. "But from what I've seen—and what Ken says—you've earned it in spades. When will you be ready to leave?"

"Before light, if possible. Before the men wake."

Morse's eyes narrowed. He leaned down for a moment, as if inspecting his shoes. "You don't like those men very much, do you?"

"You've never been in the service," MacKinnon said.

"Can't say that I've had the pleasure."

Glover set his bottle down and walked closer to MacKinnon. "I guess I might not see you after tonight. Well, I guess maybe sometime . . . But I meant it, Mac, you did one hell of a job."

MacKinnon took his hand and shook it warmly. "I didn't really expect you to go through the whole thing, Ken. I admire you for that. They couldn't have better leadership."

Glover held his hand a moment longer than MacKinnon would have expected, but he said nothing more.

"Sure you won't have a beer?" Morse asked.

"Thank you, no." Then, because he just thought of it, he added, "Are you making that trip specially for me?"

"No." Morse shook his head. "I have to be moving out myself. You wanted to leave early—how would six be? We can pick up some breakfast on the way or when we get to San Diego. You're certainly tired enough of Mamacita's idea of food to be ready to eat something more palatable, I should think."

"I'd hoped for earlier than that, but that'll do," MacKinnon said.

"You have a plane to catch? What's the hurry?"

"Just that I want to get going."

"Don't worry about the men. They'll be sleeping in tomorrow, I should think. They have the day off, haven't they?" Morse asked Glover.

"Except for packing their gear," Glover answered.

"There can't be much of that. After getting up with the sun for the past five weeks, MacKinnon, don't worry, they'll be dead to the world when we leave at six," Morse said.

"All right, then, six," MacKinnon said, turning to the door. He walked out into the night again, wondering about Shahabad, who had lounged in a corner the whole time but hadn't said a word.

He woke long before six. Through the wall he could hear occasional grunts and snores—the unmistakable sounds of men sleeping. He stretched his legs in the bed, and its old metal frame creaked. He'd been dreaming, and that was rare. He almost never dreamed, or at least almost never remembered dreams when he awoke. He was with Marie at some cheap Kilmory hotel, eating dinner in the dining room, which didn't even have tablecloths or a view of the water. His eye was caught by a man who walked into the room—Rich Barber, and on his arm was a girl who was young enough to be his daughter. Marie saw them too, and called them over, and motioned them to sit down at the same table. She was flirting audaciously with Rich, but MacKinnon didn't even notice because he was suddenly certain that the girl, whom he had never seen before, was Laurie.

The dream dissolved before he spoke to her or she to him, and the snores from the next room rose to his consciousness. He was long past blaming himself, and he was certainly long past blaming Marie. Or Rich. People did things, he knew, that seemed best at the time, or at least most comfortable, or, if nothing else, least uncomfortable. She could have avoided telling him altogether; she could have just let him come home that next time and found them gone. And he could have let the taxi go, could have stayed instead of reporting back, could have tracked them down later, insisted on his rights as a father. He could have contested the divorce. Could at least have helped support Laurie. Now, all these years later, maybe he didn't even have any rights left. Maybe she didn't even want to see him; maybe she didn't even know Rich wasn't her real father. Real father. Biological father. He had read that phrase in a newspaper article once, and he'd known what it meant. Real father was something else.

He arose finally and dressed. He didn't shave. He dug under the floor for his money, and then zipped the last of his things in the worn duffel bag and hoisted it and walked out the door without even going into the big room one more time. Outside he lay the bag down and urinated against the side of the building. He hadn't wanted to risk going into the head even for that.

He lifted his duffel and walked briskly toward the other building. Morning was just beginning to lighten the sky, drawing a pale band behind the eastern mountains.

The car's engine was already running; he checked his watch—five fifty. He opened the back door and threw his duffel in, then got into the front. "Ready to go," he said, turning. With a sudden jolt as if from an unexpected blow, he saw that the man behind the wheel was Kherman Shahabad.

Shahabad smiled at him, and in the light from the dashboard his small, even, yellowed teeth showed in his mouth. It was the first time MacKinnon had seen him smile.

"I thought it was going to be Morse."

"He couldn't make it. I had to leave now anyway." Shahabad put the car in reverse.

"Wait a minute. What about my pay?"

"You'll get it."

MacKinnon's hand darted out to grab the ignition keys, but Shahabad's reaction time was quick, and his hand on the steering wheel was closer. His hand reached the keys first. "I said you'll get it."

MacKinnon's larger hand closed around Shahabad's and squeezed. It was the same hand he had used for the past seven years to subdue and control two-hundred-pound cantankerous bucks at shearing time. "Now," MacKinnon said.

Shahabad's hand went limp inside MacKinnon's "Let go of my hand," he said, and he was no longer smiling.

"I want my money now," MacKinnon repeated, his hand still on Shahabad's.

"Let go of my hand and I'll give it to you." Shahabad was smiling again, a thin, cold smile that showed little of the yellow teeth.

"Slowly," MacKinnon said and released his grip.

"What do you think?" Shahabad asked, his hand moving slowly to a pocket of his jacket. "That I was going to pull a gun on you?" He smiled ironically, and when his hand appeared again, it held two thick stacks of bills. "Five hundred hundred-dollar bills. That's correct, isn't it?"

MacKinnon took the money and riffled the edges of the packs.

"Did you want to take the time to count it?" Shahabad asked.

"Why didn't you just give it to me when I asked for it in the first place?"

The yellow teeth flashed again briefly. "Raymond told me to give it to you when I dropped you off in San Diego." He started the car again, turning the wheel so that they were headed toward the gate. "I was just following orders."

"What is it you do, besides follow orders?"

Shahabad shook his head. "That is exactly what I do; I follow orders."

"Morse is the money man. Glover got the men, and he'll lead them. I trained them. What is it that you really do, Shahabad?" But he was already thinking what was left: weapons.

Shahabad kept his eyes on the track ahead; even in daylight it was almost invisible. MacKinnon stared at him, and he must have known that, for after a while he spoke again.

"To make a strike like this work right, there are countless
details which must be dealt with. That is my job. Someone
points out a detail that must be taken care of, and I take care
of it. Like driving you to San Diego. Like arranging transport for the men. Like I say, a thousand little details."

MacKinnon continued staring at him. Like arranging
transport for the men. Like bribing the official at some out-
of-the-way European airport to look the other way while
sixteen men with assault weapons take off for some obscure
island in the Mediterranean. Like finding Coacantico base,
remote yet convenient to major transportation. Like bringing in the matériel without arousing suspicion. Like keeping
the whole strike under wraps.

And making sure it stays that way.

He looked away from Shahabad and stretched his legs. He
leaned his head back against the headrest. "Mind if I catch a
few more winks while it's still dark?"

"As you wish," Shahabad responded. "As soon as you get
the gate up here."

MacKinnon opened his eyes, his head still back against
the headrest. The perimeter fence was coming up; he could
see the gate clearly now in the car's headlights. "Sure," he
grunted, straightening. He took two deep, quiet breaths and
felt his heartbeat slow.

Shahabad braked the car ten feet in front of the gate and
handed the key to MacKinnon. MacKinnon stepped out.
Shahabad would wait, he figured, until the gate was open;
no point in doing work you didn't have to, even if your job
really was to take care of details. MacKinnon bent to the
lock and inserted the key, his back a broad target, but he
knew that professionals could make a target of anything; it
was the timing that counted. He unlocked the gate and
shoved it open, pressing down imperceptibly on the far end
as he swung it wide. It grated on an angle into the dirt,
caught finally, and jammed. He grinned sheepishly into the
headlights, pushed the gate partway back, and tried swinging it again, but it jammed again at the same place, half
open. He looked up, frustrated, into the headlights and motioned Shahabad on through the half-open gate. Shahabad,

taken by surprise, hesitated a moment and then veered to the right and drove slowly through the opening. As soon as he was through, MacKinnon rammed the gate closed and bent as if to lock it, but at the moment the silenced gun spat he was already rolling away, getting the car between himself and Shahabad.

Shahabad had stepped out of the car to get a better angle for the first shot. Now he swung around and reached in, slamming his hand against the light switch, and the headlights went out. Shahabad knew better than to let himself be a target. He had the advantage; he knew MacKinnon was unarmed. All he had to do was stalk him in the dark, or wait until there was enough light in the eastern sky to see him.

MacKinnon lay on the ground at the back of the far side of the car. The moon, a slim crescent in the southern sky, gave no light. He rolled silently under the car and waited. For a long time there was no sound, and finally MacKinnon was able to make out Shahabad's legs in the dark. The man was still standing on the driver's side of the car, but he had moved back a step. There was no way that MacKinnon could reach out from under the car and pull his legs from under him. Shahabad was crouched, just waiting, and MacKinnon knew what he was waiting for. The sky was rosy now in the east. MacKinnon rolled back out from under the car; on the hard-packed desert floor he was able to move soundlessly. He removed his shoes, placing one just beside the back tire of the car. The other he placed three inches beyond it. Then he picked up a rock and threw it fifteen feet, letting it scudder against a steel fence post. At the same time he moved quickly forward, away from the fence. He had gone beyond the shelter of the car now, but he was headed west, into the thicker darkness. Shahabad would not be fooled by the stone, even for a moment; it was the sound MacKinnon was after, using it to distract Shahabad as he ran away from the car. With the stars as a guide he made a wide circle, coming back in just over five minutes to where he could see the car again in the gathering light. But now he was on the same side as Shahabad, who was still just a dark shadow against the car. And he did not have to remind himself that the shadow still had a gun.

As the eastern sky lightened, Shahabad remained motionless, confident because he was on the dark side of the car. MacKinnon stayed where he was, waiting until he could see what he needed to see. Finally he was able to see it, and he picked up another stone and threw it, aiming again at the fence post closest to the car. He missed, but the stone landed with a firm *clunk!* just on the far side of the fence. Shahabad ducked, looked under the car, and then he saw it, too. In the faint light a single shoe could be seen jutting out beyond the edge of the car's right rear tire. Shahabad, aware of the direction in which the shoe was facing, began moving silently in the opposite direction. Twenty feet beyond, to the west, in fuller darkness, MacKinnon rose and began moving with him. By the time Shahabad rounded the left front fender, MacKinnon had halved the distance. By the time Shahabad reached the right front fender, MacKinnon was three feet behind him and already stretching his arms. Before Shahabad was able to see along the right side of the car, MacKinnon had thrown his right arm around Shahabad's neck.

The man was a good six inches shorter, and he reached around his body with his right hand, still holding the gun, but MacKinnon was ready for the move and grabbed Shahabad's wrist in his left hand, twisting hard and quick, the way he would twist the neck wool of a recalcitrant buck at shearing, not fearing to break his neck because of the protection the wool provided. But Shahabad's wrist was not so protected, and he got off one wild shot before the bone snapped and his hand went limp. The gun fell at their feet, and Shahabad kicked it away into the darkness.

Shahabad's body relaxed, his arms hanging slack at his sides for a moment, but then he bent suddenly, throwing MacKinnon off balance and pulling away from MacKinnon's grip. Drawing a knife from his pants pocket with his good hand, Shahabad crouched and wheeled to face MacKinnon, and the knife blade snapped into place. MacKinnon took a half step back, just out of range of the blade.

Shahabad's right hand hung useless at his side. MacKinnon outweighed him by at least fifty pounds, but he still had no weapon. He concentrated on Shahabad's arm. He knew the man's eyes would tell him nothing; Shahabad would know better than that. The two began a slow circling. MacKinnon was aware that the man's wrist had to be painful, but he also knew that help was more likely to come for Shahabad than it was for him. He kept his eyes on Shahabad's left arm: the first movement would come from there. But Shahabad only had to hold him off. The attack would have to come from MacKinnon. He continued circling, his feet moving constantly, like a boxer's, and then, finally, he lunged.

He misjudged Shahabad's reaction by a hair, just catching the man's right shoulder as Shahabad countered the lunge. The knife snaked forward and caught MacKinnon on the forearm, slicing the length of his sleeve and drawing a quick line of blood from the elbow to the wrist before MacKinnon was able to pull away. As he dodged the knife blade again, he grabbed Shahabad's useless hand and turned the wrist again. Shahabad jerked with the pain but didn't cry out, and the knife came again. This time MacKinnon was closer and ready for it. He seized Shahabad's left hand in both of his and brought the man's forearm down hard against his upraised knee. Shahabad gasped but still didn't cry out and didn't release the knife. Still holding the man's left hand in his, MacKinnon swung back his right and delivered a smashing blow to Shahabad's face and a second quick one to his now-exposed neck.

Shahabad went down hard, still clutching the knife. MacKinnon wrenched it from his hand and turned, searching the ground for the gun. He could see it now, ten feet away, and he scrambled for it, aware that Shahabad had half-risen and was about to come after him again. He snatched up the gun and made for the car, slamming the door shut and turning the key, still in the ignition. The car started immediately, and MacKinnon floored the gas pedal. He didn't even turn to look at Shahabad as he sped away. He was halfway to the abandoned general store before it dawned on him that he had left his shoes behind.

8

COACANTICO WELLS, CALIFORNIA

Kherman Shahabad watched the car disappear toward the western darkness. He was half on the ground, propped up by his good left arm. His right arm throbbed with pain, but he could ignore that. He'd had bones broken before, been shot before, felt pain worse than this before. It was not the pain that angered him as the car sped out of sight, it was the fact that MacKinnon had outsmarted him.

Since the age of six, Kherman Shahabad had lived by his wits. That was the year he had left his mother, or the woman he had always thought of as his mother though he had never been quite sure. She'd always had a half dozen children around, and they were too close in age for all of them to have been her own. But she harbored them, and whenever one disappeared, she soon found another to take its place. She preferred girls because girls were more profitable, but if a boy came her way, she made do, though she always demanded more from the boys.

When they were infants, she carried them herself, wrapped in rags. She stalked the fashionable streets of Beirut, her face set in a piteous mask, her voice murmuring pathetically of sickness and hunger and poverty. The youngest children trailed after her, clinging to her scruffy skirts, their hair uncombed, their faces unwashed. She never let them eat in the morning so that their eyes would show the proper longing, and if she slapped them around beforehand, it was even better because then there would be tear stains running down their dusty cheeks.

She called him Asad, which meant *lion*, and by the time he was four he was on the streets by himself. She had already taught him to differentiate between Christians and Moslems. When one approached Moslems, one kept one's eyes downcast. It was one of the pillars of the faith to give alms to the poor, but rich Moslems liked their poor to be suitably forlorn. If a Moslem had nothing or for some reason chose to give nothing, he always at least said, "Allah will bless you," and it was meant as a blessing, not an excuse. And it did indeed seem to bring luck; within an hour of such a blessing the beggar would usually receive unexpectedly large alms. Christians, on the other hand, were driven by guilt. As a child he had once peered into a Christian church and was astonished to see that what they seemed to be worshiping was a gigantic statue of a man in obviously great pain. Whether they worshiped the pain or the man was unclear to him, but what he had learned was true: with Christians, you looked them straight in the eye, and they felt so guilty they usually gave you something just to get rid of you.

Once he was on his own he learned even more tricks. For a couple of francs he could buy bracelets thinly plated with silver. A child, if he was engaging enough, could put two or three such bracelets on his arm and then head for the Corniche, where the tourists stayed. He would walk right up to some lady and politely say, "Hello, my name is Asad," and extend his right hand. If he didn't look too dirty, she would take his hand because she would be too polite not to, and then with a practiced flip he would slide the bracelet down his arm, across their joined hands, and onto her arm. Before she could react, he would release her hand and raise his open palm. "Ten francs, please," he would say, stretching the grin across his face. Usually she would pay because such a thing had never happened to her before, and she wouldn't know what else to do, and anyway, ten francs was not such a bad price for a silver bracelet. He learned the phrases to deal with tourists in English, French, German, and Swedish.

If one hung around the Corniche, one found all sorts of ways to make money. Tourists negligently hung cameras on the backs of their chairs as they sipped coffee or cognac at sidewalk cafes. They cashed traveler's checks at stores, and after producing their passports to identify themselves, laid the passports carelessly on the counter as they signed the checks. In a congested store or on a busy street, a small child could insinuate himself into the crowd, grab the valuable, and disappear before the tourist even realized anything was gone. Tourists always worried about their traveler's checks being stolen. Passports were more valuable and easier to market.

As time passed, the boy called Asad became more and more resentful at the cut the woman took of his earnings, so one day he just didn't return to her mud-brick hut with the corrugated tin roof on the eastern edge of the city. She was probably not his real mother anyway. She had probably gotten him from some woman who already had too many mouths to feed, or some prostitute, or some young girl who had been made pregnant and was still hoping to pass herself off as a virgin in order to find a husband. In the polyglot of nationalities that was Beirut, he had no idea whether he was Arab or not, but it hardly mattered. He kept the name Asad for a while and then changed it to Renard, which is French for fox, because he liked the sound of it, and the implications.

When he was sixteen he could still pass for twelve, but he was too ambitious to spend his life as a street beggar or even as a petty thief. It was 1973, the year of the three thousandth anniversary of Persia, and he changed his name again, taking a last name for the first time in his life. He looked at a map of Persia and named himself after two cities in the ancient north, and he almost convinced himself that his real mother had been a wealthy Persian woman who had perhaps borne him by a lover and whose husband would have been enraged when the child didn't resemble him at all.

As Kherman Shahabad he ran petty cons in Beirut until he had saved enough to buy himself the proper papers, and then he was ready to move on. Beirut was crumbling anyway, the victim of an impossible government and the pressures of the PLO, which had made it their home. By then he was almost eighteen years old, and Beirut had become too small a pond for him to play in.

One reason that he had taken a Persian name was that he disdained the Arabs, despised the Jews, and hated the Christians. Persians were none of those. When the Ayatollah took power in Tehran, he hardly cared; he thought of himself as Persian, not Iranian. He had no loyalties except to himself; he had no family, no ties, no formal education, no friends. All that he had was wrapped in one package that could pass for any of a dozen different nationalities, and the wits that had been sharpened by a lifetime on the streets.

And that was why he was furious now. MacKinnon had fooled him, and since the time when he was twenty years old and took a fall for a Bulgarian arms dealer, no man had successfully outwitted Kherman Shahabad. It was enough to make a dead man of A. C. MacKinnon, if his death hadn't already been sealed the moment he agreed to train the force.

Shahabad rose to his feet and began walking back toward the camp. There was another car there besides the bus that Glover would use to transport the men. Morse would just have to ride the bus back to the city and get his fancy clothes dirty for a change. Shahabad felt vindicated in at least one respect: he had insisted on two days' leeway "just in case." He had convinced Glover of the need for those days by pointing out that the men could use some time on the other side of the Atlantic to adjust to the time change and recoup their mental and physical agility after the long flight. Two days at the staging area on Aghios Giorgios was entirely reasonable. He would meet them there. He would use those two days now to find MacKinnon and kill him.

In the meantime he didn't even have to wonder where he would begin his search. *Richard Barber* and a number. Whatever that meant, he could start with Anne Rowen, University of California at San Diego Libraries. She was the connection, either to Barber or to MacKinnon or to both.

MacKinnon had half-dozed much of the way out, but he had a strong sense of direction. He knew they had traveled mostly south out of San Diego, then turned more eastward, and finally straight north into the desert. He remembered some of the place-names.

He had stopped when he was a good ten miles away and pulled his boots from the duffel in the backseat, and then he'd gone on. At the very least he had fifteen to twenty minutes on Shahabad, and that ought to be enough. In Shahabad's condition it would take at least that long to make it back to the camp and the other cars, even if he tried running. Even given a faster car, it was too much of a head start for Shahabad to catch up, and there was no way that Shahabad could trace him.

He drove now partly by instinct and partly by memory, with no map to guide him. By the time he hit Plaster City it was fully light. He remembered that name, a strange name for a town, he'd thought. Route 8 came shortly after, and the signs pointed east to El Centro and Yuma and west to San Diego. He knew nothing about El Centro or Yuma, and he turned west, toward San Diego.

He had thought that by this time he'd be on his way to finding Laurie, but now that would have to wait. He'd taken all this time, a few more days could hardly make a difference. There were far more urgent matters now.

He needed to figure out what Shahabad's actions meant. He stared straight ahead, forcing his mind to go blank. He knew the imperatives for something like this: there could be no givens, no assumptions. Shahabad had tried to kill him, that was the only certain thing.

The road stretched out ahead of him, winding uphill through a shallow pass. As he moved westward the occasional growth along the roadside became more frequent— sage and salt grass again, creosote plants now and, rarely, mesquites, their anguished-looking limbs twisted and bent from their hardscrabble existence. But mostly it was just earth—hard-packed and dusty and scattered with rocks.

The moon was a pale sliver, and the sun was still low in the east, but he could tell it was going to be another hot day. Only February. He could not imagine what it must be like in the summer. Yes, he could, though he had not been there in years. It would be like Egypt. Like the Sinai, like Bir el Khadim. The sun beating down, its heat reflecting off the rocky shale and baked earth.

Why would Shahabad want to kill him? "*I take care of details*," Shahabad had said, and MacKinnon had looked at him and thought: weapons. Weapons, perhaps, but what else?

Shahabad. He knew next to nothing about the man except that Shahabad had tried to kill him. *"That is exactly what I do,"* Shahabad had said. *"I follow orders."*

Whose orders, MacKinnon wondered.

He played the scenes again in his mind. Shahabad had rarely said two words. It was Ken who always did the talking, and occasionally Morse. Last night Ken had been the voluble one, the excited one, as if pleased that he'd been vindicated. *"Didn't I tell you?"* he had said and looked from Morse to Shahabad, as if waiting for their confirmation that he'd been right in choosing MacKinnon. As well he might have; a hundred thousand dollars, MacKinnon had said from the first, was an unconscionable amount to pay.

He looked down at the speedometer and let up slightly on the gas.

Unless, of course, they had never intended to pay it.

He realized his headlights were still on, and he pressed the button to turn them off.

It was clear that Ken Glover was not in charge of the operation. Above MacKinnon, for sure, but not in charge. From what he had seen, both Raymond Morse and Kherman Shahabad were above Glover. Unless even that appearance had been deceiving. No, he was certain of it. Whatever Shahabad was, he was more important than Glover, and the implications of that were interesting. If Shahabad was that much closer to the source, then it stood to reason he wouldn't have had to kill MacKinnon just for the money. Unless he was some sort of pathological killer. Or even a pathological thief. But MacKinnon was just one pawn. There were fifteen snake-eaters, all getting the same pay. No, even more, Glover had promised—and the weapons and the helicopter. Against all that, MacKinnon's hundred thousand was too paltry a sum to have killed for. What was he? What *was* Shahabad anyway?

A car pulled around to pass him on the left, and MacKinnon jumped in surprise. He had not been watching out the rearview mirror, had not even seen that car approaching. He looked over and felt relieved that it was a kid in a white sports car, a cigarette hanging from his lip. It could not have been Shahabad, he told himself; there was no way Shahabad could have caught up to him. But he knew better than to take anything for granted. Certainly not Shahabad, but also not Raymond Morse . . . or even Ken Glover. Or anything else.

His mind went back to the beginning. "*A quick strike*," Glover had told him. Quick in and quick out. Assassinate Qaddafy. In retreat for Ramadan for five days. The clandestine support of half the nations of the western world. Weapons, training, everything you need. And very good pay. And you don't even have to go along. Just train, that's all. And he had believed it because he'd had no reason not to, but once one started distrusting, it was hard to tell where the distrust should end. How much of it was true? Or was any of it? And how was he going to find out? Because if Shahabad was not killing him for the money—if it had been part of the plan all along—then he was going to have to find out, if for no other reason than to know who else might be after him.

He drove up a long, curving hill, and now both sides of the road were covered with piles of rocks, mountains of boulders, as far as the eye could see. For God's own earth, who would live in such a place? He could not imagine how he could find out how much of Glover's story had been true, but if Glover was going along, then certainly he knew the truth. He thought about that, about getting to Glover and forcing the truth from him. But the men were all leaving today, taking off for the staging area, and MacKinnon didn't even know where that was. It hadn't seemed important to ask, and no one had volunteered. He could not go back into that. He had no way of knowing how many of them wanted to kill him. Maybe all of them by now. He certainly hadn't ingratiated himself with the men. That had been the whole plan: they were Glover's troops. They would follow Glover into hell itself by now. And they hated MacKinnon's guts. Oh, yes, he'd done a very good job with them. Glover could do exactly what he wanted with them.

The only question was: what was it they were going to do? If not assassinate Qaddafy, then what?

He would leave it alone. It was none of his bloody business. He had done what he'd contracted to do and had been paid handsomely. He could go back to New Zealand and buy his own station and the rest be damned.

Except that he could not. If they had lied to him about the mission, then it could only have been for one reason: if they had told him the truth, he wouldn't have done it. And the rest of the men the same. There was no way he could allow that. Whatever it was that he wouldn't have done, he would be as responsible for it as if he had done it himself, knowingly. They were not going to use him like that. He had not come out of New Zealand to be given an unconscionable amount of money and be used like that. A. C. MacKinnon had never been used, and he was not about to start now.

He glared at the roadway ahead. The blacktop slid under his wheels as the car sped westward. He had no idea how one could find out what was really being planned. He had no experience in those kinds of things, but he knew of one person in San Diego who seemed to know how to find things out, and she was the only person in the United States he knew how to locate. It might at least be a place to start. He remembered the name: Anne Rowen.

DAMASCUS, SYRIA

A black limousine with smoked windows rolled slowly around the circular drive and stopped at a guarded walk at its far end. A man stepped out of the front passenger side, looked quickly about, opened the back door, and then moved out of the way as another man, short and balding, emerged. Howard Kammer carried a briefcase in one hand as he walked away from the car. It was five o'clock in the afternoon, and the sun shone obliquely on the west-facing portico before him. A Syrian army general who had been standing on the walk saluted and then fell into step beside Kammer. The aide who had opened the door and another one who had appeared from the other side of the limo walked briskly just behind them. There were two guards at the near end of the walk and another two at the far end, just before the building's portico. But President Hatoum was nowhere in sight. Kammer had not really expected him to be. President Hatoum was maintaining a cool attitude toward Washington these days, and it would not do for him to be seen greeting an American envoy, even in the relatively private surroundings of the Syrian President's official residence.

The doors of the residence opened, and Howard Kammer stepped inside. The foyer was relatively small, its inlaid marble floor set in geometric designs. The walls were stone and plaster, carved in intricate curled and looping patterns. Wordlessly but with a flourish of his hand, the general indicated a long, broad hallway. At the end, nearly thirty yards away, stood an enormous man wearing a white robe that almost swept the floor. Kammer imagined that he must be some sort of elite household guard, though it occurred to him that he might just as easily be a servant.

Halfway down the hall the general paused at an open door, and Kammer stopped as well. Inside the room, in front of a pair of tall windows, was a desk made of carved cedar. The man sitting behind it looked up and blinked once at Kammer, who had stopped at the threshold. Then Ismail Hatoum rose from his chair, letting a smile break across his face. "Mr. Secretary," he said, coming out from behind his desk, his hand extended.

He had for all the world the demeanor of a busy man caught by surprise at the arrival of an unexpected visitor. Howard Kammer wondered for whom this little charade was being played, and then it occurred to him that it was probably for Kammer himself, to show him just how little value Hatoum placed on the visit of the American Secretary of State. Kammer did not bother to wonder whether the disdain grew from the fact that he represented the United States or whether it was for himself personally. Though Hatoum could hurl condemnation on the United States publicly, he had no choice privately but to deal with the country, and both he and Kammer knew it. On the other hand, he could show almost open scorn for Howard Kammer and leave unsaid whether that scorn sprung from Kammer's Jewishness, his emasculated position, or simply the fact that Hatoum had made a career out of opposing the United States and its emissaries.

"President Hatoum," Howard Kammer said as their hands touched.

The President gave his hand one light shake and withdrew, motioning Kammer to a chair in a wide sweep of his arm. "Welcome to Damascus. You have brought the sun, I see. We have had clouds for almost two weeks straight." His accent was very slight, his English almost perfect, the result of six years of undergraduate and graduate study in the United States. Kammer recalled that Hatoum had an American wife, though the President kept her well out of public view. In Washington she was considered by many to be the main chink in Hatoum's armor, though the Ambassador, who had briefed Kammer last night, had warned him that the woman was thought to be completely Arabacized. No one in the American diplomatic community had even seen her.

Kammer took a seat on a small settee covered with gold-embroidered damask. Hatoum sat opposite him in a straight-backed wooden chair with a crimson silk cushion. Kammer's aides, Driscoll and Schaeffer, took wooden chairs a discreet distance away.

"May I ask how your flight was?" Hatoum said.

Kammer nodded. "Fine." There was no point in mentioning that he hated flying, that even the comforts of Air Force 2 could not alleviate the white-knuckled fear he felt at fifty thousand feet, with nothing below him but miles of space above further miles of ocean.

Hatoum cleared his throat.

"Mr. President," Kammer hurriedly began, "there are a number of issues about which my country is concerned and about which your country, I should think, ought also to be concerned."

"Yes?" Hatoum's eyes, behind black-rimmed glasses, disclosed nothing.

"But most of all," Kammer went on, wondering now if what he was about to say would drive a crack into that heavy facade of disinterest, "I am here with what my government considers a major new initiative for peace in the Middle East, and I have come to you first because we feel that this is a proposal that you and your country can—in fact will be happy to—live with."

There was no change in Hatoum's eyes. The President sat back in his chair. "I am ready to hear whatever you propose."

Kammer leaned forward, his eyes fairly dancing. He was not a good poker player, and he knew it. He was about to make a proposal that ought to stun the socks off the Syrian President, and he did not want to miss an eyeblink of the reaction.

LA JOLLA, CALIFORNIA

The Central University Library of the University of California at San Diego opens at eight each weekday morning, and the first thing Anne Rowen generally did when she came in was check her mailbox. On this day she found three routing copies of professional journals, a couple of publishers' announcements of new books, the agenda for today's reference staff meeting, and a note from a professor requesting the purchase of four books. She put the journals aside; she would take them home to read in the evening. She skimmed through the publishers' announcements, circling three titles in red and throwing the rest of the information away.

Darlene Grace leaned around the modular divider. "Going to the concert tonight? The Chieftains?"

Anne screwed up her face. "Didn't get tickets before they sold out."

Darlene grinned. "Just happen to have an extra. Still want to go?"

"Are you serious? I'd love it! Are you and Danny going?"

"I wouldn't miss it. But Danny's out of town—some system up by Portland they're thinking of buying and he's up there checking it out. He says there's no way he can get back."

"You're sure?"

"If he says there's no way, there's no way."

"Want to make a night of it? Dinner at my house first?"

Darlene waved a hand lazily. "Twist my arm."

"Margaritas at six. Can you get a sitter that early?"

"No problem, but with the Chieftains, don't you think you ought to have something more . . . more . . ."

Anne grinned. "Like Irish whisky, I suppose? No, it's going to be margaritas, and it's going to be two for you and no more. I'm not going to *carry* you into that concert."

"Okay, then. Irish coffee after. And then we'll go down by the marina and cru-u-u-uise." She smiled wickedly, flapped her arms like a bird, and was gone.

Anne looked at her watch. Twenty minutes until the reference staff meeting. She initialed the professor's note and placed it in campus mail for Book Purchasing.

A. C. MacKinnon walked into the library, well aware that his boots were as dusty as the desert where they'd spent their last five weeks. He had no other choice; they were the only shoes he had left. The rest of his clothes were the ones he'd worn on the plane coming to the States. He spoke to the woman standing behind the reference desk. "I'd like to see Anne Rowen, if you please."

"I'm sorry, she's in a staff meeting. Could I help you?"

He paused, then shook his head. "I guess not. When do you suppose she'd be available?"

"Anytime. They ought to be breaking up soon, I would think. You could wait for her."

"I suppose I could." It was probably a mistake. How on earth could she help him, anyway? "Perhaps it's not that important," he said, backing away.

"I'm sure she'll be available in just a few moments. Maybe you'd like to browse until then? We have recent books just over there," she said, pointing to MacKinnon's left, "and we have newspapers and periodicals straight across on the other side of the building."

MacKinnon turned around and looked where she pointed. Newspapers? Perhaps there would be something about Qaddafy going into seclusion, something telling where or when . . . "I'll just spend some time with the newspapers, then," he said to her.

He found the day's *New York Times* lying on a table where someone had left it. He bent over the table and turned the pages slowly, scanning them. Nothing about Qaddafy. He hadn't really expected it; that would have been too easy. On the third page he saw a picture of Secretary of State Howard Kammer boarding Air Force 2 for a trip to the Middle East. He read the accompanying article, headlined "Kammer Tries to Revive Flagging Role." He had not kept up with the intricacies of international politics in the last few years; back home, at the station, it had seemed easy to forget that there was a world out there. He knew nothing about what the *Times* article seemed to be hinting: that the American Secretary of State was little regarded at home or abroad. Kammer would be traveling to Damascus, Amman, Jerusalem, and Cairo, trying to sell some new proposal to Middle Eastern leaders. The article speculated that new developments were unlikely, that Kammer's proposals were just a rehash of old initiatives already rejected. MacKinnon shook his head; they were still going around on that and would probably continue to do so as long as there was Arab and Israeli breath left. Some things never changed.

"Mr. MacKinnon."

He turned at the sound of the voice.

"It *is* you. I wondered who was asking for me. Did you find your daughter?"

"Ah, no." He should have left; he should have gone. What was he going to tell her? How was he going to explain to her when he didn't understand much of it himself?

"I'm sorry I wasn't able to help more," she said, "but it has to be like looking—"

"I haven't come about that," he interrupted. "In fact," he said more slowly, "I'm not sure why I did come."

She looked at him for a long moment. "Is there anything I can help you with?"

"Is there a way," he began slowly, unsure of what he needed to know or how to ask it, "of finding out where someone is at any given moment—someone famous, like Moammar Qaddafy, for example? If it's not in the papers, is there any way of knowing?"

"I guess it depends on the person. American officials usually make schedules available to the press. Is it Qaddafy you're really interested in?"

"I'm not sure."

She cocked her head and frowned.

"That's not much of an answer, is it? Okay, let's say, just for an example, that I heard that Qaddafy is going into seclusion in the Libyan desert for a number of days. Could I verify that? Do you know a way?"

She looked at the newspaper lying open on the table. "Well, it looks as if you've made a start. How many papers have you looked at?"

"Just the one, but . . ."

"One of the problems is, is it newsworthy? Would the papers even report it?" She paused and glanced away, then looked back at him. "Even if they did, this is the slow way to find out. Do you really want to find out about Qaddafy, or do you just want to know if it's possible to do it?"

"Yes. Both." If not Qaddafy, then who? Surely not Kammer, who seemed to be heading only for Middle Eastern capitals. Whoever was going to be assassinated, it was going to be in a desert, in a remote camp. That didn't sound like any of Kammer's destinations.

"Mr. MacKinnon, there are such things as computerized indexes and databases, which are much quicker for looking up the kind of information you're looking for . . ."

She went on talking, explaining the differences to him, explaining how one used them and what purposes they served. He tried paying attention, but his mind kept slipping away. Since Shahabad had attempted to kill him, everything had changed. There was nothing he could take for granted anymore. Except that there was going to be a strike, and someone was going to be killed. And if it wasn't going to be Qaddafy, then it almost certainly was someone none of them would knowingly have been willing to kill. And it was going to happen in a desert, in a remote spot; they would not have gone to all the trouble at Coacantico base for nothing. And it was probably going to be in the Middle East.

He thought for a long time before he formulated the next idea. There was no one he could trust. He looked at the woman standing in front of him: half a head smaller than he was, short dark hair, gray-green eyes. She knew how to find things out. There was no way Glover and his friends could have gotten to her, but still . . .

You put your life in the hands of your mates, Sergeant Hawk used to say.

Trust no one, his gut told him.

9

LA JOLLA, CALIFORNIA

A pale haze drifted far offshore, blurring the line between sea and sky. They sat on a wooden bench on a cliff high above the water, watching the waves rolling onto the beach below, eating take-out hamburgers from waxed paper wrappers. The near-noon sun warmed their backs as they faced the water, and MacKinnon marveled. In the desert one expected the heat, but even here by the water it was warm. The temperature was close to eighty; it was warmer in southern California in the winter than it was on South Island in the summer.

She had taken an early lunch, and they'd come here, only a short drive from the campus. The water was so far below that he could not even hear the rush of waves. Only an occasional cry from a passing gull broke the silence—that, and her questions. He hadn't meant to tell her anything, but then he'd found himself steadily retreating from that position. He still hadn't told her everything, but he had come much closer than he'd originally planned. "What did you do before you became a librarian?" he asked. "Work for the police maybe?"

"Why on earth do you say that?" she responded.

"You don't learn interrogation like that in the library."

"As a matter of fact, you'd be surprised. People come in and ask a question that *maybe* comes within ten miles of what they really want to know. Someone might come to the desk and ask where the psychology periodicals are. Well, possibly the person just wants to know where they are, but usually he's looking for articles about something specific, and since he doesn't know anything about indexes, he assumes he'll have to leaf through a whole lot of periodicals until he finds an article that will help him. You can just let him do that, or you can take the time to find out what the person really needs. That's called a reference interview. And, yes, I guess it really is a kind of interrogation."

"And is part of the training that you don't react, no matter what you're told—or asked?" A hundred yards to their right, a man with hang gliding equipment walked to the edge of the precipice, hesitated only a moment, and then stepped off into the void. He dropped a half-dozen feet, and then an updraft caught and lifted him. MacKinnon had never seen such a thing, and he stared openmouthed as the craft hung in the air and the red of the wings shone in the sunlight. "Fantastic," he whispered.

She smiled slowly. "It must be like flying." She turned to him. "Have you ever flown a plane?"

"Once, when I had no choice. It's not ideal when one hasn't had the lessons."

She laughed. "I suppose not." Then, "Would you mind if I called you something other than Mr. MacKinnon?"

"I hadn't noticed you calling me anything."

"Right. Because I didn't know what else to call you. 'Mr. MacKinnon' seems so formal, so I haven't called you anything."

"My friends call me Mac."

"Mac? Sounds like something you'd call a cab driver, or he'd call you. Don't you have a first name?"

"A. C. are my initials, if you prefer."

"What does the A stand for?"

"As I said, my friends call me Mac."

She gazed thoughtfully at him. "It can't be that bad. What is it—Andrew . . . Abelard . . . Alfred?"

"You won't guess it, so don't bother trying. I was asking if you never react to anything."

She pushed her sunglasses farther up her nose. "The goal is not to be judgmental. Information ought to be free—and private. If someone comes in asking about AIDS research or abortions, I don't assume they have AIDS or are contemplating abortion. If someone comes in asking about information on building a bomb, I don't necessarily assume they're actually going to build one." A second hang glider had joined the first, and now both drifted gently on the air currents. "What made you think the government was involved?" she asked.

"I didn't say that."

"Knew about it, then. Acquiesced."

"The training was at a former U. S. Army base. The recruiting was done openly as far as I know—at least as openly as it ever is. Operations like that are monitored by governments. If it happens—training or recruiting—within their borders, you can almost be sure they know about it. They let happen what they want to happen."

"And they're never fooled?"

"Rarely. And I wouldn't want to count on it. The training didn't have to be in the States. It could have been anywhere. One has to assume that if it was here, it was because the CIA or the FBI or both knew and allowed it."

"Why even go through this whole charade?" she asked. "Surely there are mercenaries who'll kill anybody for cash. No questions asked. Why didn't they hire people like that in the first place?"

"There are mighty few people like that, as a matter of fact. And the good ones have gotten out. The drug business is no more dangerous and a great deal more profitable. So is the gun dealing business. Just about the only ones left in the killing business are the loners and the incompetents. And the legals."

"Legals?"

"A bloke in good standing can pick up a quick job now and then, even during his holidays. There's no flack as long as it's something his government wouldn't disapprove and as long as it's deniable. Sometimes his government is even a sponsor. There are ways of knowing. How the recruitment and training are done are two ways. There are others. That's why this thing looked legal."

She leaned against the back of the bench. "I wouldn't have pegged you for an assassin." She stared at him more closely. "A killer."

"And good old Annie tries to remain nonjudgmental, right? Must be quite difficult sometimes, right?"

She cleared her throat. "My friends call me Anne, not Annie."

"I only trained them. I wasn't going myself to do it, if that makes a difference." He paused and she said nothing. "That's what I did for a long time, you know. I trained soldiers, and I was a soldier myself. That's what soldiers do, if it comes to it. And policemen, I might add."

"With policemen there's a trial first, before the execution."

"Okay, Annie. You be on the jury for Qaddafy. Guilty or innocent?"

"It's not for me to say. Augustin."

"*Augustin?*"

She shrugged. "Or whatever."

He wasn't amused. "It's not for you to say?" he pressed. "No terrorists have ever touched you, have they? If they had, you wouldn't be so bloody soft-hearted, I'd wager."

"You're so sure of things. You don't even know what this is all about, and still you're so sure. It doesn't occur to you that you just might be wrong. That there might be things you don't know."

"So right. For starters, I don't know how many people out there want me dead. Think about that. But what I do know is, the only good terrorist is a dead one, and let's have no talk about terrorists being the same as revolutionaries. I've seen the difference. I've fought with revolutionaries as often as I have against terrorists and I'll tell you something, Annie: there's a difference. You'd know that if you've ever been in a terrorist's gunsight." He looked away from her. "What do you care what happens in the Middle East?" he asked softly. "Or on some blown-up airplane that you or your friends don't happen to be flying. You live here," he nodded toward the water, "where even the winters are lovely. As long as nothing touches you, why should you care?"

"That's not fair. You don't know where I stand on those things."

"Where, then? There is no trial for Qaddafy and no jury. And so even though we all know he finances half the world's terror, he's still safe, is that it? And if your government underwrites—in all kinds of ways—an operation to get rid of him, you don't want to know anything about it, isn't that it? Because if you did, you'd have to be against it, and yet—somewhere back there in your mind—you really wouldn't mind if he got knocked off, would you? So don't tell me about it, you want to say, just do your dirty work and don't tell me about it."

"Except that now you don't think it is Qaddafy. It might be someone else, and you're beginning to worry that even you might not approve."

He shook his head. "Approve?" he demanded. "Do you think they asked my approval when I was soldiering? Approval has nothing to do with it."

"Then why do you care?"

"Because, don't you see, if it is something else, they want to kill me because I can finger them. And I need to know what it is, because until I do I won't know who wants me dead, or how many they are. If it's just Shahabad, that's one thing. If it's the whole bleeding United States government, that's an entire other thing." And it was also the other, though he wouldn't tell her that. When he was soldiering, they owned him, they had a right to tell him what to do and whom to kill. But he was his own man now, and no one had that right anymore. Despite what she said, it didn't take a jury to tell him the difference between Moammar Qaddafy and Secretary of State Kammer. Or whomever.

"I hardly think the whole United States government is gunning for Mr. A. C. MacKinnon. *Whatever* the *A* stands for."

"Maybe, maybe not. But your computers could help us figure out who it is. Or at least who that strike force is going to kill."

"Us?"

His eyes caught hers. "They're your computers. I don't know how to run them. Oh yes, I forgot, you're the kind of person who doesn't like to get involved."

"You don't know anything about me."

"I know this: I need some information. You may know how to find it. I'm asking for your help."

He was still staring straight at her. He was not, she guessed, a man who was used to asking for help. It shouldn't have made a difference, but it did.

She looked at her watch. "I have to be on the reference desk at one. I suppose I could do some looking before that." She stood and began gathering up the remains of their lunch.

"I can pay, if it costs."

"You'll have to tell me exactly what it is we're looking for."

"I wish I knew."

"What you do know, at least. We'll be searching the wire services, among other things. Names of places, people, even dates, anything that might be mentioned together. We'll put your Shahabad's name in and see what we get, and the other two. And Qaddafy, just to make sure."

And Kammer, he thought, because he didn't feel right about that one. There was too much coincidence with him in the Middle East. And, it occurred to him, they might as well throw in the Old Man while they were at it.

He parked in a visitor lot, and they walked back to the library. She would let him stay with her while she searched, though she warned that it was not the usual procedure. They were supposed to do computer searches only for faculty and students, but the librarians didn't routinely ask for identification, and she would treat him as she would anyone else who appeared at the desk asking for a search. If someone called her on it later, she'd worry about it then. She had only until one, when she went on the desk. She could fudge maybe ten minutes past. That should give them enough time. She was committed at reference for two hours and then had a meeting with a faculty member at three fifteen. So if they didn't find anything before one, he'd have to wait until after four. He was uneasy with that; the men surely would have flown out by then, and he had no idea how much leeway had been given. Surely not more than a few days. More likely a lot less.

She had told him what they'd be looking for and what kind of information the printouts would give. It would be up to him to recognize gold when they struck it.

It was twelve fifteen when they walked into the building. "Anne!" someone called from behind the circulation desk as they entered. "A guy was asking for you."

"A guy?" She walked to the desk. "A student?"

"No . . . maybe. I doubt it." The girl brightened as if suddenly remembering. "He had an accent, but it wasn't Hispanic."

"Did he leave a message?" she asked.

"No. Just asked for you. You weren't in the offices so I checked your schedule and told him you'd be on the desk at one. Thought you were probably out to lunch."

She turned, but MacKinnon's eyes were locked on the girl behind the desk. "Small guy?" MacKinnon asked.

The girl nodded. "Five-six, maybe. Slight. Dark."

"Maybe thirty-five? Something wrong with his right arm? Did he favor it? Maybe even in a cast?"

She frowned. "It might have been."

He turned to Anne and saw the chill registering in her eyes. "God help us both, Annie," he whispered. "I don't know."

He was at least two hours behind MacKinnon. He had jogged back to the barracks, holding his right arm across his chest with his left hand, and taken the other car. That had wasted only about twenty minutes; it was the wait at Ocotillo that put him so far behind. He'd stopped at a clinic there to have the broken bone set. He could drive left-handed, but he knew it was borrowing trouble to go on with the arm the way it was. In a close situation it could make the difference, and he had enough respect for MacKinnon to know that there might be a close situation.

There were three men ahead of him at the clinic, casualties of some knife fight at an after-hours bar. Just as they were patched up, an ambulance drove in with a couple of car crash victims. Broken arms, it seemed, were low priority in Ocotillo. He would have left and driven on, but there was nothing sizable until he got to San Diego, and there was no telling how long he'd have to wait in a city hospital. At least with a broken arm there were no questions. "I fell getting out of bed," he said, looking them straight in the eye, and no one had the nerve to ask whose bed.

It was while the cast was being put on that he asked the doctor where the University of California at San Diego was.

"It's not in San Diego, actually; it's in La Jolla, to the north. Take Interstate 8 all the way to 5 and then go north. You can't miss it."

"Thanks," Shahabad said. It made up for at least part of the time he'd wasted waiting to be treated. He wouldn't have to spend time asking directions now.

He had trouble at first locating the library. He hadn't expected there to be more than one, but when a girl on the campus responded to his question by asking which library, he hesitated. "The Central Library?" she suggested; that was as good a guess as any, so he said yes. As it turned out, he had guessed right. So that was a little more time saved. He asked for Anne Rowen—unsure about the pronunciation of the last name—at the first desk he saw when he entered, and learned that she was gone but would be working at the reference desk at one. He looked at his watch: nearly an hour until one, but at least he'd found the right place. The reference desk, as pointed out by the helpful girl he'd asked, was in sight.

He glanced about, then wandered around the main floor. It was not as bad a layout as it might have been. He could linger in the bookshelves just beyond the reference desk, and that would give him not only a clear view of that spot but an almost unimpeded view of the front doors as well. If she had gone out of the building, as the girl at the circulation desk seemed to think, she would probably be coming in there. It was true that he had no idea of what she looked like, but there was always the chance that MacKinnon would be with her. MacKinnon was the prime target, after all. He could deal with the Rowen woman later, at his leisure.

He saw MacKinnon when they came in, and the woman with him. She was dark-haired and a good half foot shorter than MacKinnon. The girl behind the circulation desk called them over and spoke briefly. The woman glanced toward the reference desk, and Shahabad moved to his right, slipping behind a bookcase, but he could still see them between its shelves. He'd gotten a good look at the woman; he would recognize her again.

He saw MacKinnon scan the area now, and he knew what the man was looking for. Shahabad smiled. MacKinnon knew, but it didn't matter. This time it was going to be different.

MacKinnon saw nothing unusual. But he's watching, he thought; if not in here, then somewhere nearby. He felt the cold, impersonal sensation that had once been so familiar steal through his body. It was a quiet, busy library on a tree-strewn campus, and it was possible that it was about to become a battlefield. He shut off the question that begged for an answer—how did Shahabad know?—for the infinitely more important question: what to do now? He had brought her into it, and somehow even Shahabad knew about her. He had left the gun in the glove compartment of the car; it had never occurred to him that he would need it here.

Within seconds he weighed his options and knew what he would have to do. "The computers you use for the searching, are they out in public, or are they hidden away somewhere?"

"There are some that are not in a public area," she responded. "But I don't think—"

"This isn't a time to think. This is a time to act. If he's here, he's already seen us together; he'll have to assume the worst. You're in the soup now whether you like it or not." He could see the fear in her eyes, but she wasn't panicking, not yet. He took her by the elbow as if to guide her, though he had no idea where they were heading. "Let's go. This is the only time we're going to have." She began moving away from the desk. Chalk one up for her, he thought; she was scared, but she wasn't backing off.

"He's around here, isn't he?" she asked, closing the door to a small room with space for only three computers and the desks they sat on.

"It's a good guess, but don't ask me how he found out about you."

"Will he come in here?"

"Not likely. There are two closed doors between the public area and us. He has no way of knowing who else is in here, and he has reason to think I have a gun. He'll wait for a better chance."

"And do you have a gun?"

"Unfortunately, not on me."

"That means you'll kill him if you get the chance, doesn't it?"

"Call a spade a spade. He wants me dead, that's a fact. I actually don't care whether he's dead or not, as long as he leaves me alone. If I can get him to think he's killed me, that's just as good as if he'd really done it. But whether I kill him or not is irrelevant. The strike will go on without him, I'm sure of that, and stopping the strike is what I'm after." He ran a hand restlessly through his hair. "I should have killed him out there in the desert when I had the chance. Then we wouldn't be worrying about him now."

"Why didn't you?"

"At the time I thought he was after the money. I still thought then that Ken Glover had dealt with me square. One doesn't like to think badly of people who have been one's friends. It wasn't until I was on the highway a while that it dawned on me I could have been snookered. Shahabad here, looking for me, is proof of that unpleasant fact."

She took a deep breath. "Will he kill me?" Straight out. No mincing words.

"Not here. As long as you stay in the library, you're safe. He's the kind who likes to operate in shadows. Let's get into your computers. Maybe we can find something—"

"I can't stay here the rest of my life." An edge of panic had crept in.

"Are you going to help me find something or not?"

"Could you catch him? Could you get him to tell you what the force is about to do?"

"Could I catch him? I don't even know where he is. Or how many he has with him. No, Annie, I think you don't even know what you're asking. I had his arm in my hands and I twisted it until it broke, and he never let go of the gun until I had broken his arm. And then he pulled a knife. He never winced, he never backed off. Six inches shorter than me, lighter by fifty pounds at least, a broken arm, and he was still fighting. You can torture a man like that to death, and he still won't talk. We'd be more likely to get something out of your computers than from him."

"What about after you're gone from here?"

"After, we worry about after. Now, we worry about now. In the time we have we'll look, and if we don't find anything, then we'll worry about how to deal with Mr. Kherman Shahabad."

She sat down and pressed a switch, and the computer began to hum. "I'm not guaranteeing anything."

"I don't ask for guarantees. I ask you to try." He looked at her hands on the keys. "All I ask is for you to try. I know you're scared. You have a right to be. Give me this one thing, and then I'll lead him away from you. You're not going to be a target for him, I promise you that."

She pressed a few keys and then looked up at him. "There's no way you can promise that."

"Forget him out there. There's nothing you can do about him now. The thing you can do is right here, at this keyboard. Think about that. If you're good enough, maybe what you find will be the key to him as well."

She took a deep breath and turned back to the computer. "Okay." There was a silence, and her hands were motionless on the keyboard. Then, finally, she spoke, and her voice was professional, as if she were giving a demonstration.

"We'll be searching a database that contains articles in newspapers and news magazines, and wire service reports. First we'll look for any mention of Qaddafy at all in the last two weeks. If we don't find anything that looks likely, we'll widen the time span to three months and link Qaddafy's name with specific key words like 'desert,' 'seclusion,' maybe 'Ramadan,' and see what that gets us." She began keying in an access code.

He sat down in a chair beside her and shook his head. "I'm pretty sure it isn't Qaddafy."

"Yes, but let's just make sure we don't pull up anything. Just in case you're wrong. If we don't get any hits, it still won't be proof that it isn't Qaddafy, but if we do find out he's going into seclusion—wouldn't you want to know that?" And she began the commands.

As he had suspected, there was nothing on Qaddafy that would indicate the man was going into seclusion in the desert; in fact, most of the references related to a speech he had given the previous week in which he threatened American warships in the Mediterranean not to stray within his hundred-and-twenty-mile limit of Libya. There were also renewed reports that he was underwriting small arms for the IRA.

She tried Kammer's name then and found a multitude of references to his trip to Middle Eastern capitals, and she even managed to pull up the tentative schedule, but somehow it didn't seem to fit. The timing was right, but the places were wrong. It was the one reality he still clung to: the assault force he had trained was going on a desert mission, there was no doubt in his mind.

He had her try the Old Man's name, but there was little. He had been seen in Algeria this week and had been to a meeting of Palestinian exile leaders two weeks before. Beyond that, nothing.

She looked at her watch. "It's after one. I'm going to have to stop."

"What happens if you're late? Someone else stays until you come, right?"

"Right, but—"

"Keep going," he said.

"But it's not fair."

"Fair? This isn't a game we're playing. It's there. It has to be. Find it for me." Then, because she would expect it, he added, "Please."

She turned back. "Five more minutes."

She tried going further afield, searching on the names of other Middle Eastern leaders: the President of Egypt, the Jordanian King, the Saudi Prince, the Prime Minister of Israel. And still there was nothing. They tried Soviet names linked to Middle Eastern places, European names. Nothing fit. They moved further afield to other desert places: the Australian outback, the Gobi in China, southern Asia, even the United States and Mexico, but again nothing fit.

They were out of time and frustrated. "I'm sorry, but I really have to end it now," she said.

He was tearing through the pile of printouts once again, hoping to make a connection.

"Why don't you call the government? If it's Kammer, after all, they'll want to know."

"It's not Kammer," he insisted. "Can't you see, it's all wrong for him—none of the places are right."

"Call them anyway. There's no way you can do it on your own."

"No? And will you guarantee that your precious government isn't behind it?"

"It doesn't sound like a covert operation to me. You're not even American."

He bent over, his face not six inches from hers. "Let me tell you something, Annie. It may not sound like a covert operation to you, but it sounds exactly like one to me. When your CIA is up against something your Congress would scream bloody murder about, this is exactly what they would do. Iran-Contra was just one. I could name dozens. There are any number of former military men and former CIA men who work as so-called advisors, and this is the sort of thing they do all the time. The CIA isn't allowed to snuff someone? No problem; there's always somebody who'll do it for hire, no questions asked."

"Well, they certainly wouldn't be killing Kammer, would they?"

"God help you all if they are, but I never said I thought it was Kammer."

She took the printouts from his hands and refolded them.

"What are you going to do about the one out there?" she asked.

He let out a low whistle. "That's the next problem, isn't it?"

"You said you'd take care of him."

"I know what I said."

"I was counting on that, MacKinnon. I gave you what you wanted. It's not my fault there wasn't anything there."

He was staring at the wall in front of him.

"You're sure you can't get him to tell you?" she asked.

He had already started to turn away, but he suddenly wheeled around, facing her again. "Annie, my friend," he said softly, "just maybe I can. But you're going to have to help me."

"I already did everything I could."

"Help me get him off your back and maybe also tell us what it is."

She felt the steel of his eyes on her. "How?" she asked.

"That's the question, isn't it? You go and do your desk duty while I try to work out how."

"And I'm going to be out there where he can see me while you're back here in hiding? Not on your life!"

"Not at all. I'll go out first. He'll follow me out and leave the field clear for you."

"How do I know he'll follow you?"

"Think, woman. I'm the prize, not you. You're peripheral. He can come back for you anytime."

"Thanks a lot."

"Don't worry. He won't. How long did you say you had to be there?"

"Until three."

"Okay. So I keep him occupied until three. By then you'll be gone from view. Can you be at your desk in the back? Somewhere out of sight?"

She nodded. "And after that?"

"After that I spring the trap."

She still had the printouts in her hand. "If it's slow at reference, I'll look through these again. Maybe there's something we missed. Give me a call."

"Right." He nodded. "You can never tell."

She gave him the phone number, but it was evident that he didn't expect her to find anything. She didn't expect to, either, but it seemed better than nothing.

It would be after two thirty before she finally found it, and by that time she had no idea where MacKinnon was.

10

A. C. MacKinnon opened the door to the main part of the library and walked through, glancing around distractedly. From behind a bookcase Kherman Shahabad watched, secure in his position. MacKinnon hesitated a moment, as if thinking, or deciding on a course of action, then strode quickly toward the circulation desk. He asked one question, and the girl behind the desk pointed him toward a public telephone. Curious, Shahabad moved forward.

MacKinnon looked something up in the telephone directory but didn't use the phone; then he glanced about again, this time more carefully. Shahabad stepped back behind another bookcase and felt sure that MacKinnon had once more missed him. MacKinnon, moving quickly now, headed for the front doors. Shahabad slipped out from behind the bookcase and followed. He knew how to find the woman again, knew where she worked and her name—he could probably find her home address in the phone book—but if he lost MacKinnon this time, he might lose him forever.

MacKinnon, his hands shoved deeply into his pants pockets, started away from the library at a rapid pace, but soon his hands came out of his pockets and he increased his pace to a jog toward the parking lot nearest the library. Shahabad exited behind him, running up the asphalt path, trying to keep a screen of trees between himself and his target. He thought of pulling the gun from his pocket but changed his mind; there were dozens of students on the paths. It was not a good place; even the parking lot would be better, where at least there were cars one could dodge behind. He ran at an oblique angle to MacKinnon's, toward his own car in the same lot. He would need to get away as fast as he could afterward.

MacKinnon wasn't running fast but his legs were longer, and Shahabad didn't seem to be making up the distance between them. Shahabad could ignore the dull throb of his arm and there was no doubt he could still shoot a gun with that hand, but he couldn't be sure enough of the steadiness of his arm; he'd have to use both hands. It would mean he'd not be as quick. MacKinnon was too far ahead for a certain first shot, and Shahabad knew that he'd have no second chance. MacKinnon was running scared already. One shot would send him scrambling for cover like a startled snake. It would be wiser to wait.

MacKinnon reached his car, unlocked it, and slipped inside. Shahabad rejected the notion of running up behind and getting his one shot in before MacKinnon could drive away. It was too chancy, and if he missed, MacKinnon would be gone. His best course was to tail MacKinnon by car. Shahabad knew that behind the wheel he was at least MacKinnon's equal; the discrepancy in their sizes no longer counted. If he pushed the man hard enough, he could shoot out a tire and leave MacKinnon's car rolling over into oncoming traffic or, even better, off the edge of a cliff into the ocean. Or he could pull up alongside unexpectedly and with one well-aimed shot blow MacKinnon's head off. Or he could pull up behind and fire on the gas tank until it exploded and took the whole car with it. He smiled at that one. He reached his own car, thrust the key into the lock, and got in. MacKinnon was just pulling out of the parking lot. Shahabad already knew MacKinnon's car; he'd take his time until things were right. Whether or not MacKinnon knew that he'd been chased out of the library, Shahabad could hold back now and let MacKinnon think he'd lost him.

MacKinnon turned south toward San Diego, increasing his speed as he left the congested university area behind. Shahabad, gauging his speed by MacKinnon's, kept MacKinnon's car in view but remained back far enough that MacKinnon wouldn't realize he was being followed. Mac-

Kinnon clung to the right-hand lane, and Shahabad hunkered in behind him. A mile down the freeway MacKinnon suddenly pulled into another lane, passed three cars, and then veered back into the right lane. Shahabad watched and grinned. He would not be drawn into a duplicate maneuver that would reveal his presence. He could still see MacKinnon well enough. He knew MacKinnon was looking for a tail. Well, he could look all he wanted; he wasn't going to find one.

MacKinnon slowed down at the next exit, and Shahabad let up on the gas. By the time Shahabad followed him off the freeway, MacKinnon was almost out of sight. Shahabad stayed as far back as he dared, and MacKinnon drove straight on for a half mile before turning into a shopping center. Shahabad drove past the entrance MacKinnon used, keeping an eye on MacKinnon's car in the parking lot. He entered the lot at the next opening, but MacKinnon was already weaving his way through the lanes. Shahabad made a guess and hung back once again. Five minutes later MacKinnon drove out of the parking lanes and left the lot. Shahabad, stopped briefly in position near the entrance MacKinnon had used, pulled out of the spot, and grinned. MacKinnon was turning toward the freeway. Once again he had missed seeing the car that was following him.

MacKinnon drove normally now, moving with the speed of the early afternoon traffic toward downtown San Diego. As the cars became more numerous, Shahabad pulled closer. It was clear now that MacKinnon no longer worried about possible pursuers. He turned off onto a downtown street, turned left two blocks later, and found a parking spot near the corner. He got out and had just put money into the meter when Shahabad drove by slowly. Shahabad watched but made no move. The traffic was heavy. If he shot MacKinnon here, he'd have trouble getting away. Money in the meter meant that MacKinnon was returning. He pulled into a parking spot half a block away and settled down to wait. He had seen MacKinnon going into an army/navy surplus store. It occurred to Shahabad that MacKinnon was after more ammunition, but it didn't bother him. MacKinnon had been playing into his hands for the last half hour.

Seventeen minutes later MacKinnon emerged from the store carrying two plastic shopping bags. He opened the car door, tossed the bags into the passenger seat, and then got into the car himself. Ahead, Shahabad already had his engine running.

MacKinnon pulled slowly out of the parking spot. He drove two blocks, then turned right, and continued until he came to Harbor Drive. Shahabad was three cars behind him, well shielded but in good position in case MacKinnon should try an unexpected move. MacKinnon made a right turn onto Harbor Drive, picking up speed only slightly. Shahabad stayed well back, watching. He had the feeling that MacKinnon was looking for something, and he wanted to be ready for whatever that something was.

A marina was on the left, its long piers lined with boat slips. Most of the slips were occupied by sailboats, their masts rising bare against the clear sky, rocking back and forth in symphony with the ocean's swell. There was a strong offshore breeze, and the boats tugged at their moorings.

The marina slid by at last, replaced first by a bare shore of rock and then by a procession of metal buildings stretching out over the water on wooden pilings. A series of wharves took over, decked with signs offering boats for hire for whale watching, harbor tours, dinner cruises. The boats tied to the wharves were mostly small- to medium-sized motorboats, some open and some with covered decks. Men in plaid shirts and denim pants stood in some of the boats and loitered on the wharves in small clusters, waiting for passengers. An occasional sailboat bobbed among the motorboats, mainsail bound loosely around the boom. Cautiously Shahabad pulled closer to MacKinnon's car. He had an uneasy feeling about this place, and over the years he'd come to trust his instincts.

MacKinnon was driving as before, as if he were going somewhere specific, but Shahabad had no idea where that might be. He's very good, Shahabad thought to himself. Either that, or . . .

MacKinnon suddenly accelerated, and his car shot forward. Shahabad stepped on the pedal to keep up and then was surprised when MacKinnon's brake lights flashed and the car suddenly slowed, swung a wide right into the next lane, and then made a tight U-turn and headed back. He had timed his speed so as to pass Shahabad's vehicle now, going in the opposite direction, exactly in tandem with another car on the inside lane, preventing Shahabad from trying a shot across the lanes. Shahabad reacted automatically, making his own quick U-turn, but up ahead MacKinnon had already slammed on the brakes and was jumping out of the car. The movement was too fast for Shahabad, who was still turning, and he couldn't level his gun fast enough. MacKinnon had left his car in a small parking area and was running full-tilt toward the wharves. In his hand were a length of rope and a canvas supply pack. A knot of men in the middle of the wharf moved closer together as he ran by, as if to make room, and then MacKinnon leaped over the side and onto a sailboat that rocked gently in the water at the end of the dock. The men shouted at MacKinnon and started forward when they realized he was about to make off with the boat, but then they saw MacKinnon's pursuer.

Shahabad was already out of his car and running, no longer mindful of witnesses, just wanting to get MacKinnon before it was too late. He was on the wharf by the time MacKinnon had cast off, and halfway to the boat at the end before the boat slipped away from its mooring. MacKinnon had started the small outboard motor and was heading out. He was on the far side of the boat, pulling hard now on the halyard as the sail lifted toward the top of the mast. The sail ruffled in the wind, hiding all of MacKinnon except for a few inches of his legs that showed between the boom and the gunwale of the boat. With his left hand supporting his right arm, Shahabad aimed at what he guessed to be Mac-Kinnon's chest beyond the sail. Just then the sail caught the stiff breeze, the boat rocked sideways, and the shot went wild. Shahabad corrected his aim and tried again, and once more the shot went wild. Now the boat was moving faster away from shore. Shahabad was about to try one more time when the boat suddenly veered again and the boom came about and MacKinnon, sitting at the tiller, was fully exposed.

The boat was forty yards away by now and moving quickly, every second putting more distance between it and the shore, but the shot was a clear one, and Shahabad could not have missed. He braced his right hand with his left and took careful aim at the broad target of MacKinnon's back. Even at this distance it was a sure target, better at this range and with the uncertain motion of the boat than MacKinnon's head. This time there was no sudden movement of the boat. Shahabad got the shot off and watched as MacKinnon almost seemed to turn and then slowly fell backward into the water. Released from MacKinnon's restraining hold, the boom swung hard right and the boat tipped dangerously. The motor died, the wind fluttered the loosened sail, and then the boat half-righted itself.

Shahabad's eyes were fastened on the water where MacKinnon had gone down. There was no movement, and no arm reached out to grab the floundering boat. He took a step back and then another. He turned and saw that two of the men had already jumped into a motorboat and were casting off from the wharf. The others stared with frightened eyes as Shahabad stepped closer to them, gun still in hand. He watched their eyes and knew that as long as he held the gun they would remain frozen in place. He glanced back toward the boat, and there was still nothing in the water. A few moments more and MacKinnon was sure to be dead. A person could hold his breath only so long under water, and then he'd have to come up. Shahabad moved back slowly, still watching the water, still keeping the men on the wharf in the corner of his eye, but they weren't moving. The motorboat was almost to the sailboat now, and its engine cut back to slow the boat's motion. It was clear that the men were looking into the water, searching for MacKinnon, and it was also clear that they were finding nothing. They reached the sailboat, caught its gunwale with a boathook, and drew it alongside. Then they made a slow circuit of the sailboat, still finding nothing.

Shahabad moved to the back edge of the wharf, with the men still watching. He hurried to his car, got in, and saw that the motorboat was still circling the sailboat. Shahabad drove away slowly, trying to lose himself in the anonymity of the passing traffic. People on nearby wharves had heard or seen part of the incident and were watching the motorboat slowly circle the sailboat, but those in the cars driving by were oblivious.

Shahabad had put the gun down on the seat beside him and now he was breathing easier. Even with a broken arm he knew his aim was as good as ever; one had only to squeeze the trigger, after all, and his left arm had compensated for any weakness in his right. The boat had held steady, and he knew exactly where he had hit MacKinnon—just between the spine and the left shoulder blade. If the bullet hadn't made it into the heart, it had at least lodged in the left lung. No wounded man could stay under that long. Without doubt, MacKinnon was dead.

11

SAN DIEGO, CALIFORNIA

A professional can make a target of anything; it's the timing that counts. The mark of the amateur is impatience; the mark of the professional is patience. Sergeant Major John Hawk had pounded that into his head and into the heads of all the other SAS trainees that gray and drizzling winter. By that time he had already spent six months on the Glasgow boat docks, more than long enough to know that he didn't want to be there for the rest of his life. He'd thought at first that the city would mean bright lights and good times, a startling change from the lonely downs and ever-grazing sheep of Ardnamurchan in western Scotland.

His father had been a sheep farmer, a stern and dour man whose life mirrored the land from which he scraped a precarious living. His mother, who was Welsh, had come north to better herself from the press of the coal mines that had taken the lives of her father and uncles. She had met Robert MacKinnon at a country wedding—she'd been brought by the bride's sister, a lively girl whose red hair and gift for amusing chatter enlivened the shop in which they both worked. Robert MacKinnon had been dragged there because the groom was a cousin and it was only fitting that he come since he had no good excuse not to. Though the wedding was in November, the crush of bodies in the small farmhouse was enough to drive the Welsh girl, who knew only the bride's sister, outside where the temperature was more to her liking and where she didn't have to pretend to be jolly with people she didn't even know. She was surprised to see the tall and burly man already standing on the doorstep, his pipe in his mouth. She hadn't noticed him inside, though she might easily have missed him in the crush. He looked to be at least ten years older than she, with pale brown hair and the ruddy complexion of a man who spent his life outdoors.

"I thought I'd take a breath of fresh air," she said, because she was still young enough to think she owed a stranger an explanation.

He nodded and moved aside as she stepped down from the porch.

She looked off across the heath, watching the building clouds. It had been sunny earlier, but now the sky had turned to gray, and to the west black clouds were rolling in. "Will it rain, do you think?" There was silence behind her, and she thought perhaps she hadn't heard him go back inside.

She turned and found that he was still there, staring at her, the pipe still in his mouth. In that moment she realized she would marry this man whose name she didn't even know. Later she would ask him what he had seen in her that first day that had made him, after all those years of bachelorhood, decide to marry, but he never replied. Instead, he gathered her hair in both of his hands and buried his face in it. It was as good a response as any. She never cut that hair, black as the mines that had claimed her father's life, and with waves like the sea that pounded on the rocks below Robert MacKinnon's land. They had five children, three of whom lived to adulthood, and all of them had hair like their mother's. The oldest of the survivors, the only son, had eyes like hers as well—a blue as deep as the summer's sky. And when she died at the age of fifty-six, her hair was still as black and as long as the day Robert MacKinnon first saw her.

At the age of seventeen A. C. MacKinnon left home for the city, and the docks seemed a natural place to find work. He had grown up at the edge of the sea, had always had a skiff of some sort that he'd built himself or traded for his own labor. In the seasons when the work with the sheep was minimal, he'd hired himself out to the crews of fishermen who harvested the sea from the Outer Hebrides all the way to the Grand Banks. If there was one thing in the world he knew besides sheep, it was boats. But he soon came to realize that for a dockworker the city meant a kind of perpetual, cold drabness, a closed-in, citified, and therefore even worse, version of the life he had tried to leave behind.

He had thought of joining the navy because, after all, he knew about boats and the sea, but on his final night before joining up he spent the last of his dock pay and got so drunk that when he went the next morning, he couldn't even sign his name. Later, recovered, he was too embarrassed to go back to the same place, so he recruited himself into the Royal Artillery instead. He was barely eighteen. Four years later, having learned to make distinctions between the services, he volunteered for selection into what its troopers call the Regiment and what the rest of the world knows as the SAS, Special Air Service, perhaps the most effective commando unit in the world.

What he learned in those first months of training was a perspective and a discipline of behavior that had built on the life he already knew and proved their value in the years that came after. One never revealed more than one needed to. One proceeded with caution in any unknown situation. Once committed, one carried through. And one remembered, as Sergeant Major Hawk used to say, that the mark of the professional was patience. He'd counted on that, knowing that Shahabad was also a professional.

He clung now to the far side of a sloop anchored in the bay, and he was breathing heavily. He had known it would be difficult, but that had never deterred him before. He'd also known he was too old for this, but he hadn't realized how much too old until it was too late. The clothing weighed him down more than he had calculated. The boots were heavier and the bulletproof vest he'd bought and put on at the army/navy surplus store was heavier, too. Staying under had not been the problem; coming back up had been.

His calculations had been right on the mark; that was one place, at least, where he was still just as good. He had lulled Shahabad into believing that he thought he'd lost him on the highway, and he hadn't given Shahabad a good enough target until he was ready—until he was far enough out from shore that Shahabad would have to shoot for the back instead of the head. He had even fallen out of the boat believably.

He'd swum underwater then to the far side of the boat and come up, realizing that it had been too long since he'd practiced swimming and even longer since he'd had to swim fully dressed. He gave himself longer than he'd planned to catch his breath, but he could hear the motor of the rescue boat coming closer and finally he took off. He pulled the snorkel out from under his shirt where he'd hidden it, but the first mouthful of salt water showed him that the waves were too high to make much use of it. He had to go under water again almost all the way to the sloop. The vest kept pulling him down and his lungs felt as if they'd explode, but somehow he managed to go far enough that no one saw him when he surfaced again. At least the waves were good for hiding. He bobbed a few moments to catch his breath and then went under again. When he came up the next time, he was right beside the sloop, and no one had seen him. He worked his way to the back of the boat where he could cling to the propeller shaft and where he'd be out of sight, because the wind was offshore and was blowing the boat seaward of the anchor.

Treading water, he struggled out of his jacket, then pulled the inflatable life vest from its pocket and discarded the jacket. He unfastened and pulled off the bulletproof vest and dropped it to the bottom as well, a move that was like unfastening an anchor from around his chest. Still treading water but with much more ease than before, he put on the life vest and pulled the plunger on the gas capsule. Now there was no doubt: getting back to shore would be like taking a dip in a child's backyard swimming pool.

He looked at his watch and saw that it had stopped. Waterlogged for sure. He noted the time that it had stopped and calculated how much more to add. It would be close, but he had probably used up enough time. Annie would be gone from the reference desk before Shahabad could return. He looked toward the shore. He was farther out than he'd planned, and it was going to take him longer than he'd anticipated to swim back. He hung on for a while longer and then shoved off.

DAMASCUS, SYRIA

Howard Kammer hung up the telephone and walked over to the window. It was twelve thirty. Below the window the garden was dark, and beyond the garden wall the city of Damascus slept or watched flickering televisions or ate late dinner or—his imagination suggested—hatched secret plans in narrow alleys or shadowy streets. Damascus was the kind of city for such envisionings.

The telephone call hadn't made him feel any better. He hadn't been able to say the things he wanted to say because there was no way of knowing who might be listening, on both ends of the line. He had told Phyllis mostly hopeful things. If President Hatoum's men were listening, they would report that the offer was apparently genuine and that the United States was willing to back it up. If anyone listened on the other end, they would believe that Kammer had made progress with the Syrians. One down, three to go.

What he had really wanted was just to listen to Phyllis's voice and imagine that he was in bed with her, her warm breath against his chest as she told him about her day. Everything always seemed so sane with Phyllis. He wished he had brought her along.

He turned away from the window and pulled off his tie. Another early morning tomorrow—a briefing again with the Ambassador and another one with the CIA chief of station, and then the flight to Amman.

And then it would begin all over again.

SAN DIEGO, CALIFORNIA

Kherman Shahabad drove north, glancing around in satisfaction. Cars drove alongside him, oblivious. He was just one more person on the freeway, nothing else. The whole thing had been fairly clean. No one had had the presence of mind to chase him; he hadn't even seen anyone running after his car to get the license number. It was a rental car anyway, rented in who knew whose name; he could have ditched it if he needed to, but it looked as if he wouldn't need to. He suspected that the men in the motorboat had been more worried about retrieving the sailboat than about pulling any bodies out of the water, but nevertheless, they had apparently not found MacKinnon, and that was a good sign. He cautioned himself against premature self-congratulation; MacKinnon had shown himself to be resourceful before. But it seemed unlikely this time. This time, he felt sure, he had won; he sensed it with the instincts that he had come to trust. The ease of his getaway seemed an omen. Kherman Shahabad remained only a shadowy figure, moving in and out of cities and countries without anyone's noticing, and certainly without attracting undue attention. He had become so used to the life that it hardly occurred to him that someday he might fail.

He turned onto Torrey Pines Road and later turned off at a campus drive. This time he knew where he was going. He parked in the same lot and looked around carefully as he got out of the car. It was habit; he didn't really expect to see anything suspicious, but it was one of the things he'd become used to over the years, and it had always paid off. He walked briskly toward the library. He wasn't going to go right up to her; he knew better than to warn a person like that. No—he would just make sure she was still there, and then he would plan how to handle her.

But she wasn't there. Someone else was at the reference desk now, and that gave him pause. He would have to think this over. He was reluctant to ask for her again. He didn't want to warn her like that, but he might have to. And then he remembered the last thing MacKinnon had done before he left the library.

Kherman Shahabad walked over to the telephones and looked for Anne Rowen's name in the directory. He wrote down the address and the number and then left the library. She would never know he'd been there. He preferred the privacy of her home anyway.

A. C. MacKinnon pulled himself out of the water. He was on the far side of a dock, and no one seemed to notice. He struggled out of the life vest and then took off his soaking shirt. He left the life vest and the shirt on the dock and walked back a quarter mile to his car, which even at this distance he could see was still there. One stroke of luck, though: the whole episode had taken only a little over half an hour. He supposed people along here had better things to do than steal cars even if they were unlocked. He got into the car and sat for a moment, thinking, and then got out again. He lifted the hood and looked carefully under it, checking the wiring and running his hands along all the surfaces. He popped the trunk and checked it, and then examined the exhaust pipe. He bent down and rolled under the car, checking its underside with care. Finally satisfied, he rolled back out and got into the car. He figured that Shahabad would have been in too much of a hurry, but you never could tell. He opened one of the plastic shopping bags and pulled out a work shirt. He was almost dry now from the air, and he put the shirt on, buttoned it, and felt under the seat where he had tossed the ignition keys. Then he started the car and drove away. No one on the docks paid any attention.

He pulled into a gas station that displayed a telephone company sign, stepped out of the car, and walked to the phone. He drew his dripping wallet from his pants pocket and took from it a folded paper. The numbers written in ink were still visible. He dialed the number and waited impatiently until it rang, then breathed more easily when it was answered immediately.

"This is Angus," he said.

"Angus?" she asked, and he wondered if she hadn't recognized his voice.

"Augustin. Alfred. Whatever."

"Oh," she responded, and he imagined he could hear relief in her voice. "It was all right then?"

"Just hang in there. Everything is perfectly fine."

"I think I know who it is."

He waited for her to say more, and when she didn't, he asked, "Are you going to tell me?"

"It's complicated. It's a deduction, but I'll bet I'm right."

"Then it can wait," he said. He'd wait to see what her deductions were and what had led her to them. He wasn't ready to trust somebody else's guess on this one.

"Where's your car parked? What's the license number?"

"Why do you want to know?"

"Just tell me."

She hesitated and then told him. "And where will you be?" she asked.

"I'll be there."

"Where?"

"Where you need me."

"How do I know that?"

"Because I say I will." He answered stiffly, as if insulted that she should ask. "And I have something for you," he added. "I know how Shahabad found you."

"Oh? How?"

"That can wait, too. Everything is still on schedule." Except he was going to have to buy another watch.

"Okay. Angus," she said.

He replaced the receiver. He might as well get the money he'd stashed in an airport locker when he came in from the desert this morning. No telling when he'd be this close again. He shook his head and chuckled. *Angus.*

She hung up the telephone. *Everything is still on schedule.* The voice had been calm, assured. As if he *expected* that everything would still be on schedule. As if he wouldn't have accepted it if things had been any other way. Whatever the schedule was.

A man used to bossing other men around. A man so used to training other men to follow that it never occurred to him things wouldn't go his way. Infuriating.

She looked at the telephone. So why was she doing exactly what he told her to do? Because she was scared, that's why. Because he had brought a killer into her life, and it was his damn responsibility to get rid of him. Yes, she would cooperate, but only to get rid of this Shahabad. Whom she'd never even seen. Who maybe didn't even exist.

She turned that over in her mind and chuckled. An elaborate ploy, sure. Want to get old Anne in the sack, rape her, whatever? Make up a story about some guy trying to kill her, and she walks right into it. Sure, Anne. Sure, that really happens. About as often as being struck by lightning. About as often as winning the lottery. About as often as having a killer out in the stacks waiting for her to come out so that he can shoot her. Or whatever.

She held out her hands and looked at them. They weren't even shaking. This is not real, she thought. This sort of thing does not really happen. But she had sat with him in the computer room for forty minutes. She had felt his intensity. And even before that, over lunch. She had asked all those questions, and he'd had an answer for everything. He hadn't liked some of her questions, she was aware of that. But there was a logic to it all, a *sense* to it. *He'd* believed it; there was no way he could have been acting. Then why wasn't she scared?

She pulled a file folder across her desk and opened it. Inside was the course outline for History 532, and in—she looked at her watch—twelve minutes she would be meeting with the professor to discuss which books on the recommended reading list should be ordered in multiple copies and which might be added to the list from the library's holdings. So why wasn't she scared?

The truth was, she was. Just because she wasn't shaking didn't mean she wasn't scared. He had looked at her and told her that she didn't have to be scared now. As long as she stayed in her office she was going to be all right. After that, he'd said, you'll still be okay; trust me. But at least you'll have reason to be scared once you come out. You'll have reason because of what you don't know. If you knew what I know, you wouldn't be scared even then.

And what is it you know? she had asked. Because that's not how he would do it, he'd said, as calm as could be. As if he talked about those things all the time. As if there were even a logic to that.

God, she thought, is this real? Does this really happen? A

man walks in and asks how he can find his daughter. A strange enough request, though if one works at a library reference desk one hears stranger things than that every week. And—what?—five weeks later he comes back, and this time he has a killer after him. If it had been Darlene—oh, yes, Darlene would have loved it, just up her alley. What Darlene couldn't think of to get into wasn't worth talking about. Or Therese, who wouldn't have let him out of the building the first time without arranging to meet him afterward. She would have taken one look at him and begun thinking how she could get him into the sack.

Why her? Why cautious, ambivalent Anne, who never made a move without thinking it over six times? Who was always afraid of making the wrong decision. Who had always taken the safe route, the sensible one. Who had gone straight from her parents' home to marriage, and straight from marriage to work in the library. Sure, the library was safe—with a killer by the name of Shahabad, whom she had never even seen, probably waiting for her out there. Thanks, MacKinnon, she thought. Thanks a lot. Just what I needed in my life.

She opened the course outline and tried to concentrate on it. All I ask is for you to try, he had said. I know you're scared. She stood and walked over to the window and looked out. *All I ask is for you to try.* A breeze ruffled the slim leaves of the eucalyptus trees. As if it were a simple thing to ask. As if he had a right to ask her. She had thought for a long time that some of the smartest and most interesting people she knew were librarians. It was fun, challenging, hard work. But it was safe. And A. C. MacKinnon thought she could do more. He thought she could manage to have a killer in her life and be scared and yet not back off.

She turned and walked back to her desk. A. C. MacKinnon thought he could come into the library—into her life—and tell her what to do and she would do it, just as if she'd been waiting ever since Frank left for some new man to run her life. Well, A. C. MacKinnon could think again. She was not that desperate. She was managing by herself very well.

The only trouble was that A. C. MacKinnon, for all his infuriating self-assurance, actually believed she could do all those things, and now she was beginning to wonder if she really could.

12

TUNIS, TUNISIA

The Old Man laughed, his face creasing into folds of stubble around his mouth. Namir leaned closer and whispered again into his ear and was rewarded with another chuckle, though the Old Man's eye had already been distracted. He was gazing across the room, his attention apparently captured by the girl who was dancing slowly, her body moving provocatively to the taped music. Namir leaned over once again and whispered into his ear, but the Old Man didn't even react. He had grown bored with this place and this man, with his jokes, his hangers-on, his opulent tables of food, and his idea of entertainment.

We are all victims, the Old Man was thinking, victims of our history and our geography and, perhaps most especially, our own personas. He looked at his watch and sighed audibly. He supposed he would have to stay another hour. Namir seemed to count his support by the hour, and if he could manage to last out one more, perhaps Namir would remain solidly in his camp. "They're using us," he'd said to Namir earlier in the evening, and Namir had nodded and smiled but had said nothing in return.

They have used us for a long time, he thought, playing our own divisions against us. Sabri al-Banna growing stronger by the day. As-Saiqa, funded by a Syrian government that was itself not even able to stand without financial help. They are more intransigent than we are, but they pump us up, letting us confront the Israelis, letting us and our children die because they have never been willing to give anything but money. They let us destroy ourselves, pitting one group against another for their own benefit, letting us fight their wars, weakening the ties that bind us until they become too fragile to hold. And if I fail to hold us together, there are a half dozen waiting to take my place. They are waiting for a mistake. If they knew, if they could turn it to their own use, surely they would.

In the meantime, he thought, we struggle merely to survive. In earlier days it would never have occurred to him that he would have to waste his time on such men as Namir, petty men who bought and sold their support like merchants in the market. But then, in the earlier days, there was a lot that wouldn't have occurred to him.

LA JOLLA, CALIFORNIA

Anne Rowen walked out of the library at seven minutes after five. Looking neither to the right nor to the left, she hurried to her car in a faculty lot. She opened the door and almost got in before she realized someone was already there. She stepped back in surprise, then saw MacKinnon in the middle of the backseat, his body sprawled half on the seat and half on the floor, the top of his head below the level of the rear window. He was grinning at her.

"Get in," he said. "Don't act so bloody surprised. And don't change the rearview mirror. Arrange the side ones if you need to."

She glanced up and could see that he had adjusted the rearview mirror so that he could use it from his position, half on the seat and half on the floor.

"What makes you think I want to get any more involved in this?"

"You're already involved up to your teeth, Annie. He knows your name. He can look you up in the phone book. This is how we're going to get rid of him for you. Now drive and do just what I tell you."

"Where are we going?"

"Out of the campus and south."

She drove out of the lot, wound through the campus, and picked up Gilman going south. She looked into a side mirror and saw a gray car turn onto Gilman behind her. She forced herself not to think about it. It was just after five. There were cars exiting the campus all the time. La Jolla

Village Drive was just ahead. She glanced back at MacKinnon, and he nodded as if he knew what she was thinking.

"Turn east on it," he said.

She did as she was told and in the side mirror saw the gray car follow her move. "There's a car—" she started, but he cut her off.

"I saw it. Put your left-turn signal on and stay in the left lane." Then he added, "Where's the next left going to take you?"

"Back onto campus."

"Oh, shit." Then, "Turn off your signal."

"He'll think something's screwy."

"He'll think you don't know what you're doing. How much farther until you can turn left without going back onto campus?"

"Not much. I-5 is just ahead."

"Take it. Go north on it."

She watched the gray car fall back until she could no longer see it. "Maybe that wasn't him."

"Maybe it wasn't."

He was just saying that. He didn't really think it, and neither did she. "MacKinnon, I can't—"

"Just keep driving. You drive all the time. Every day back and forth to work. You don't think anything of it."

"This is different!"

"It's no different. It's your car; it's the place where you live and work. It's no different from any other day."

"He's following me! It *is* different." Panic had edged into her voice.

"Maybe it's not him," he said.

She gripped the steering wheel tighter. "You think it is." She was moving through the cloverleaf that would put her onto I-5.

"You're doing just fine. Don't look in the rearview mirror if it scares you. Take the first right you can. That shouldn't take us back onto campus, should it?"

"No."

"You okay?"

Okay? she thought. Somebody's following me, trying to

kill me, according to you. You walk into my life and say things no one in his right mind could possibly— She pressed herself against the back of the seat. "No, I'm not okay. All right? I'm not okay. I'm scared and I want this to be over."

"Make three successive right-hand turns, one after another. Don't look in the mirrors. I'll watch for him."

She slowed to make the first turn.

"You're okay," he said quietly. "Doing just fine." He watched the gray car follow into the turn. "Next turn, just the same. Don't worry about a thing. Just driving down the road. You do this every day, nothing different."

She hadn't watched on the first turn, but on the second her eyes went to the mirror. She was fifty yards from the corner when the gray car nosed around it. "He's there," she said.

"I see him. You're doing fine. One more turn. Let's make sure."

She turned one more time and looked into the mirror. She was almost at the next intersection when she allowed herself to believe it. "He's not there," she said.

"So I see."

"We lost him."

"Maybe."

"MacKinnon, he's not there! I can see he's not there!"

"Don't get excited. This is only the first half. Now we have to go to your house."

She pulled over and stopped the car. "I'm not going anywhere."

"I need you there."

"MacKinnon, I'm scared. You can't expect me—"

"Why are you scared? He wasn't even following us."

"My God, MacKinnon! Are you *human?* Why do you push?"

"Because you can do it. And I was here, wasn't I?"

"Why are you always so . . . so damn *certain* of everything?"

He didn't respond.

She let out a short exasperated breath. Until there was no

doubt Shahabad was really gone she was stuck with him; she knew that. "I might like you better if you weren't so cock-sure all the time," she said evenly.

"You don't train soldiers to like you; you train them to like themselves, to have all the self-respect their abilities deserve."

"I am not in training to be a soldier!"

"More's the pity. You'd make a bloody good one."

She sat with her back to him, refusing to look at him, but she couldn't keep the words out of her mind. How do I know you'll be there, she had asked, and he had answered, Because I say I will. *Because I say I will. All I ask is for you to try.* As if all she had to do was try. As if it wouldn't even matter if she couldn't or if she was scared or how vulnerable she was. And she knew how vulnerable she was, but by now she was almost used to it. He would be there. He had said he would, and he had been. She would have liked to weep in relief and fear, but he would take it for weakness. *All I ask is for you to try.*

"So now we know he didn't follow you," he said finally.

"And you think I was scared for nothing."

"Not for nothing. You learned you could deal with it." They always made the recruits do what they feared most. If they didn't succeed, that was the end for them. But if they did, they became nearly fearless.

"Okay," he said after a while, "drive somewhere, and we'll have a cup of tea to settle your nerves."

"*Tea?*"

He shrugged. "Coffee, if you prefer."

"He didn't follow you from work," MacKinnon said as she slid into the booth across from him. "That tells us something."

"The gray car might have been him."

"Might. Might not. At any rate, he didn't follow us all the way."

A waitress came by. "Ready to order?"

"Sorry," Anne said. "Give us a couple of minutes."

"Tea for me," MacKinnon said and looked at her.

"Two teas," she said, and the waitress left.

"So I expect he'll be at your house," MacKinnon said, "and he can bloody well wait."

"I don't like it. I don't like him coming to my house. I told you that before."

"I don't like it, either. What would you prefer, that I call him up and ask him to meet me on some street corner so that I can start following him? Think, Annie. How else do we get him to a specific place? And what bloody difference does it make anyway? He knows your name; you're in the phone book. He can find your house whenever he likes. We might as well take advantage of it, don't you think?"

She looked at him and gritted her teeth. Infuriating. And all the more so because it was perfectly logical. She pulled something from a slim briefcase, a long sheet of computer printout, which she unfolded. "Take a look at this."

He glanced at her. "Your deductions?"

She nodded.

He looked closely at the printout. He had gotten used to reading such printouts this afternoon. It was mostly a list of short citations, but there were two longer items, articles that had been printed out in full, and one of them was marked with red pen. "Kammer to Mideast Again," the headline read. There were three introductory paragraphs, then a schedule of the Secretary of State's visits in the Middle East, and finally a summary of the points he was expected to promote. MacKinnon read through the whole thing and then looked at her, shaking his head. "I thought we had already discussed this. It can't be Kammer. None of the places he's going are right. It's a dead horse, Annie. Quit beating it."

"It's not Kammer," she said, leaning closer. "Look at the schedule."

He pulled the printout closer, and just then the waitress came. He moved the printout to make room for the tea.

When the waitress had gone, Anne leaned over the table again. "Look at the schedule. Who is he meeting with?"

MacKinnon ran his eyes down the schedule. "The President of Syria . . . King Hussein of Jordan . . . the For-

eign Minister of Israel . . . the Foreign Minister of Egypt."
He raised his head and frowned. "Syria, Jordan, Israel, and
Egypt. Just what you'd expect, isn't it?"

"The *places* you'd expect but not the people. The President of Syria, yes. The King of Jordan, yes. But not the
Foreign Minister of Israel. He's not the one who holds the
reins these days, it's the Prime Minister—Avram Gershon.
He's the one Kammer ought to be meeting with. And he's
not meeting with President Bakr of Egypt, either; he's meeting with the Foreign Minister, who as far as I know is just a
mouthpiece for Bakr. Why isn't Kammer meeting with Gershon and Bakr?"

"Didn't I read that Kammer is practically a cipher? Maybe
they don't want to waste their time."

"What on earth is your name anyway?"

"I told you, you can call me Mac."

"I'm not going to call you Mac. You *do* have a name,
don't you?"

"MacKinnon, then. That's my name."

"*MacKinnon*, then," she said through clenched teeth.
"Howard Kammer is still Secretary of State of the United
States. They still meet with him. They may not have any
respect for him, but they still *meet* with him. At least the
Israeli Prime Minister does, if for no other reason than
form. If for no other reason than that if it weren't for the
United States, Israel would be bankrupt."

"So why aren't they meeting with him?"

"Sometime in the next few days, you said. In the next few
days Kammer is going to be in Jerusalem and in Cairo, and
the primary leaders of those countries, who *ought* to be
meeting with him, aren't. Why aren't they going to be meeting with him, Angus? Where are they going to be?"

MacKinnon began rummaging quickly through the
printout. "What did you find on the Old Man?" he asked.

"Nothing. But that's not strange. He never publicizes his
plans; he just turns up somewhere. The last I got on him
was Algeria."

MacKinnon was looking at her across the table.

"Let's just say the heads of state of Israel and Egypt and the only man who can speak for the PLO," she said.

"Do you believe that?" he asked.

"Why not? If it's ever going to happen, it will probably be exactly like this. Israel and the Palestinians brought together by someone, and probably the first time would be secret. Why not?"

And he knew she was right. She had guessed it, but he had better reason to know. Bir el Khadim. "Then why wouldn't Gershon just tell Kammer to rearrange his schedule?" he asked, because one never leaped to conclusions even when one knew they had to be right. "Why not meet with Kammer in a few days when it's all over?"

"Would he know how long it would last? What would he tell Kammer—that he had a very important meeting he couldn't postpone? Wouldn't the CIA be all over Gershon's tail to see what was going on?"

"It's pretty damn hard to believe." It was not hard to believe at all. Of all people, he should have known, should have guessed. Bir el Khadim. He had recognized it in the buildings at Coacantico. He should have recognized it in Glover. He should have seen it from the start. It had taken her, who knew none of it, to see it. She was good at what she did; she was sharp. And he had been too long away, was too rusty.

"Somebody none of you would have been willing to kill, Alphonse." Her eyes flicked to his, and then down to her tea.

"Then who's behind it?" he asked, ignoring the name.

"You tell me. You're the one who met them."

He shook his head. "No. They're only the intermediaries. The principals are back in the bushes somewhere."

"God knows there must be people who don't want peace to break out in the Middle East. Or who don't want the Palestinians to make even the least accommodation to the Israelis."

"Or who don't want the Israelis to make an accommodation to the Palestinians," he countered. He pulled the printout off the table and slowly folded it. "Which makes it all the more important that I follow our friend Shahabad. It's time for you to finish off your part of the charade, so that he'll get out of here and get on with it."

"What makes you so sure he'll be there?"

"If I were afraid of what you knew but didn't hang around your work to knock you off on your way home, where the hell do you imagine I'd be?"

"You can't be expecting me to just go home and wait for him to show up."

"I'd like nothing better, but I don't suppose you'd do that."

The chill showed in her eyes. "I don't suppose I would."

"Do you know how to shoot a gun? Handgun? Rifle? Anything?"

"No, and I'm not interested in learning."

"Let me tell you something, Annie. I never sent a recruit into anything he couldn't handle."

She stiffened. "Get something straight once and for all: I'm not one of your recruits."

"Still."

She reached for her briefcase. "I think I'm not interested in doing anything more."

He stood as she did. "What are you going to do? Where are you going to go? How long are you going to stay away from your house? How are you going to know when it's safe to go back?"

"You're saying I haven't any choice."

"You don't like that, but it's true. You haven't."

Infuriating. Infuriating, domineering, self-confident . . . and right. How would she know it was safe to go back? How long would she stay away? Who— Suddenly her eyes widened, and she clapped her hand to her mouth. "Oh, my God!"

"What is it?" he asked.

"A friend of mine was coming for dinner. What time is it? What time is it?" She grabbed frantically at her wrist, looking at her watch. "Oh, my God, it's three minutes to six and she's coming at six o'clock! What if he thinks she's me?"

"Oh, shit," he said.

"Oh, shit, is right!" She was almost hysterical. "It's practically dark by now. He won't be able to see her that well. What if he thinks she's me? What are we going to do? There's no way we can get there before she does!"

"For Christ's bloody sake, why didn't you think of this before?"

"I forgot, okay? I forgot! I don't have people walking into my life every day and turning it upside down. You got me thinking about all this, and I forgot."

"You chose a fucking lousy time to forget."

"Are you going to stand there and swear at me, or are you going to tell me what we do now?"

He took her by the elbow and started out of the restaurant with her. "We're going to do nothing, that's what we're going to do."

"We have to do something," she said.

Other customers were staring at them. MacKinnon slapped a couple of bills by the cash register on the way out. "The hell we do," he said when they had left the place.

"She's a friend of mine! She could get killed!" she hissed at him, trying not to attract any more attention.

"So could a prime minister and a president and the leader of the PLO, and if we spook Shahabad, I'm not going to have anybody to follow."

"We don't know for sure he's going to do that."

"You seemed pretty bloody sure of it a few minutes ago."

"And they're more important than she is, is that what you're saying? She has two little kids. To them she's more important than some guys in the Middle East they've never even heard of. And anyway, you have no way of knowing Shahabad would lead you to them. If he's smart, he's not going to go within five thousand miles of wherever it is."

"Oh, yes, he is. If I understand this thing right, he's going to have to."

"Well, all that's a maybe, but what's certain is that Darlene's going to be at my house any minute now, and there's no way I can let her walk into that."

"If we stop her now, it'll spook him. He'll run off, and then I'll never find him."

"Why? Why would he run? All I have to do is call a neighbor to watch for her."

"He'll see it. It won't look right. It won't feel right. It'll feel like a trap. He'll get out."

"It doesn't matter!" She was shaking her head. "I don't care!"

He grabbed both her arms hard and held her, his eyes staring at the wall behind her. He held her for a full minute like that, his hands gripping her so hard that they hurt.

"Okay," he said finally. "Go call a neighbor, then."

He released her arms, and she was immediately on her way to a phone booth. She hadn't needed him to give her permission to call. And Shahabad can just be damned, she thought.

When she had finished phoning, she turned to MacKinnon. "Now what?"

"Maybe he's not easily scared off. Maybe he's still there."

"And what if he isn't?"

He sighed and turned away, walking briskly toward the car. She hurried after him. "What if he isn't?" she asked again.

"Why don't you try hoping that he is?"

Kherman Shahabad stood in the deep shadow cast by a slim cypress tree, the only tree in the yard, and watched the house across the street. He had sat in his car a block away until it grew too dark to see at such a distance, and then he had moved in closer. While in the car he kept the motor running just in case. He hadn't liked being in the car; it was too obvious, too vulnerable. Now that it was dark, he felt more secure, even on foot. A watchful eye looks for movement in the dark. Through experience Shahabad had learned the art of remaining absolutely still for hours at a time, like a crocodile, waiting for prey.

The street was still now, the children who had been riding bicycles chased in by the dark or called home to dinner. An occasional car drove by, its tires whispering on the street as it passed. From some open window came the sound of a television news show.

A car came along, and even before it slowed and stopped in front of the Rowen woman's house, Shahabad knew that it would. A woman got out and slammed the door, then hurried up the walk. Shahabad remained still, watching. This didn't seem to be the woman he'd seen with MacKinnon at the library. This one was taller, and even in the dim light from the street lamp her hair seemed different.

He watched her at the doorway. She rang the bell and waited. Then she rang the bell again. Shahabad was sure now that this wasn't the Rowen woman. If it had been, she wouldn't have had to ring the bell. He stayed in the shadows, waiting to see what would happen.

An outside light came on at the house next door, and a woman opened the door and looked out. She called something to the other woman, but he couldn't make out the words. The other woman walked over toward the light, and in its glow Shahabad could see well enough to know it was definitely not the woman he had seen earlier with MacKinnon. The two women exchanged words for a few moments, and then the woman with the car turned and walked back toward the street. The woman on the porch stood in her doorway until the other one had gotten into her car and driven away. Then she closed the door behind her, and the light went out.

Shahabad stared at the darkness across the street, an old familiar feeling rising in his gut. Something was wrong. He wasn't sure yet what it was, but all his instincts told him to get out. MacKinnon in the boat, and then in the water—too easy? Maybe, but he might as well forget about that now. If MacKinnon had rigged that one, he'd be smart enough not to show himself again. MacKinnon was gone and now the Rowen woman was gone as well, and he was running out of time. He didn't like going off and leaving something unfinished, but he had given it all the time he could. Timing, as anyone in his business knew, was crucial; sometimes one had to cut one's losses.

He turned and made his way in the shadows back to his car, already putting MacKinnon and the woman out of his mind. They were only to keep things neat anyway; they had never been the most important part.

"Turn left here," she said.

"It would have worked beautifully," he said. "We'd have reconnoitered first, the two streets paralleling yours on each side, and the two that intersect with it. You'd have been looking for cars you didn't recognize, anything that didn't seem right. I'd have been looking for things that didn't *feel* right. That's important, you know, learning to feel that something's wrong. If your street was dark enough or if I thought we could get by with it, we'd even have driven by your house. Seen how things felt. Then, unless we already knew where he was by then, you'd have dropped me off—"

"Turn right at the corner," she interrupted.

"—and I would've sneaked in to a good spot, and you would've gone to the nearest public phone and called the police, fire brigade, whatever. The commotion would have sent him running, almost guaranteed. I'd have followed, and you would've been off the hook. Simple."

"Turn right up here, that's my street. The last house before the corner."

MacKinnon looked, but the car maintained the same speed. To have slowed down or speeded up even slightly would have meant something to a man like Shahabad. If he was still around. "Why don't I see any cars on the street?" he asked suddenly. "On any of these streets?"

Oh, God, she thought. I should have thought of that. "There's no overnight parking on the street in this neighborhood, so most people park in the driveway or the garage when they get home in the evening. The streets are so narrow, and besides, it doesn't look attractive. In La Jolla we're big on looking attractive. Also it keeps the tourists from blocking up the street."

"Why didn't you tell me that before?"

"I didn't think of it."

She braced herself for his reaction and was surprised when he only said, "That's interesting."

The house was dark, a small bungalow, its outlines vague

in the faint light of a streetlamp down the block. He drove straight through the intersection, maintaining speed, and then turned right at the second corner. He had sensed an empty feeling on the street, an undefinable perception that he'd come to trust when he was with the Regiment. *You'll know when you've gotten good at your job*, Sergeant Major Hawk used to say. *It's when your instincts do the sussing for you.* And MacKinnon had come to trust that second sense as much as he trusted his eyes or his ears. But he also knew that ears and eyes can be fooled; he had done it himself this afternoon. And he was not ready yet to trust someone else's life to what his instincts told him.

He turned right at the corner and again at the next corner, and then he pulled over to the curb. "Okay," he said. "We'll do it anyway, just to make sure. I don't think he's here, but we'll do it. Call whoever you want that'll come and make a commotion, bang on your door, even try to get in if they can. But listen, don't tell them who you are. Don't tell them it's your house. Got that?"

She nodded.

"I don't want you to have to be there. If by some odd chance Shahabad is still around, I don't want him to see you. Understand that? Stay away."

"What'll you do if he's not here for you to follow?"

He shrugged. "Go to the airport. Leave. What else?"

She looked at him, her face pale in the dull glow of the dashboard lights. "I'll come back for you. I'll wait right here."

"It's not necessary."

She looked away from him. "None of this has been necessary."

He didn't say anything.

"In for a dime, in for a dollar," she said after a while.

"You lock the doors, then," he said. He leaned over, opened the glove compartment, and pulled out Shahabad's CZ–75. "And you use the gun if you have to. And don't wait longer than an hour after you call them." He racked one into the chamber and held the gun out to her.

She shook her head. "I told you I've never shot a gun."

"It's easy. Just remember to press on the trigger gently, don't jerk the gun or you'll miss."

"I don't want it. You might need it."

"I'm not interested in shooting him. I want to follow him. If he's even around anymore." He laid the gun on the floor beside her feet. "I'm leaving it. Use it or not; it's up to you." He opened the car door and then turned toward her again. "Don't forget to lock the doors." He stepped out, shut the door, and was gone.

She sat in the passenger seat for a while before sliding over to the driver's seat and starting the car. Before she turned the corner at the end of the block, she locked the driver's door. The other door was already locked.

Anne Rowen switched on the interior light long enough to look at her watch. It was thirty-two minutes since she'd heard the first siren. She had called the fire department and told them she was a neighbor who had seen flames at the back of the house and who knew there was no one home. She knew that the fire trucks would come with their sirens howling, and she hoped that a police car or two would show up as well. They would hang around for a while until they made sure there wasn't any fire. That ought to be enough for MacKinnon.

The last truck had left a couple of minutes ago, the sound of its engine fading into the night. She leaned her head against the back of the seat. Everything in the neighborhood was back to normal. Except for MacKinnon prowling around. And maybe this Shahabad.

In for a dime, in for a dollar, she had said. Cautious Anne Rowen, she thought, what the hell are you doing sitting in the dark, locked in a car with a loaded gun? Darlene would never believe it, not in a thousand years. Neither would the kids. Their mother doing this? God, Mom, Michael would say. We leave home, and look what you get yourself into. She smiled.

Frank would laugh. He'd throw back his head and laugh outrageously at the thought that the wife he'd left because marriage didn't seem exciting anymore was maybe, just maybe, having a great deal more excitement than he had ever dreamed of having.

She chuckled. What's more exciting, Frank? Driving along Highway 101 with the top down and a blonde half your age on the seat beside you? Or digging into a computer until you figure out—finally—that a prime minister and a president and the leader of the PLO are going to be assassinated? She ran her finger halfway around the steering wheel. How about sitting in a car in the dark with a gun, waiting for a man who thinks he can do anything he sets his mind to and who thinks you can, too?

Nothing would ever be the same again. He was right. It's easy, living in a place like this, to think that life should be safe, to expect even that life should be safe.

Precious, she thought, but not necessarily safe.

13

LA JOLLA, CALIFORNIA

She saw him coming toward the car, half-running, outlined from behind by the streetlight at the corner. She leaned over and unlocked the passenger door, and he opened it and got in.

"Watch out for the gun," she said.

He looked down on the floor. "You didn't even move it. They don't bite, you know." He put it away again in the glove compartment.

"You didn't find him," she said, starting the engine.

He shook his head. "Poor chance of it. He's gone."

"What happens now?"

"Get rid of you first. I don't want you going back to that house—not for a while, at least. Got any friends you can stay with?"

She turned in the seat to look at him. "I suppose you do this kind of thing all the time."

"I used to do things but never quite like this. And that was a long time ago. Don't you have any friends you can stay with?"

"How long am I supposed to stay away?"

"Overnight would be fine, I should imagine."

"You think he might come back."

"No, he's gone. But you ought to have someone who knows about bombs take a look first before you go in. You never know. In the morning call the police. Tell them you've been threatened with a bomb. Make them come out and go over it."

"They won't believe it after the false alarm just now."

"They don't have a choice, even if they don't believe it. Don't worry, they'll come."

"Why didn't you just take a minute to check it out while

you were there?" she asked. He seemed to think he could do everything else.

He took the question seriously. "Didn't want to keep you waiting. Besides, they'll be keeping an eye on the place for a while. I'm not so anxious to be caught climbing in or out a window just now."

"What are you going to do after you drop me off?"

"Make some phone calls."

"Who are you going to call?"

"You're a bloody inquisitive woman."

"That's a fact. Are you going to tell me who?"

He took a deep breath. "I don't even know. Fact is, there's probably nobody I dare trust."

She turned toward him again. "Look, I'm sorry. If I hadn't insisted on warning Darlene, you probably could be following him by now."

"Might not have worked anyway."

"You don't have the least idea where this is going to be?"

The frightening thing was that he did. Like pieces of a puzzle, things fit together too closely to be coincidence. "I have an idea of the place. It would have been nice to have had Shahabad lead me there and confirm it. Are we going to your friend's?"

She nodded. "I said I was sorry."

"I know you did. What time is it in Washington?"

"A little after ten. You may have to wait until morning to reach anyone you'd want to talk to."

"I can't wait until morning," he said impatiently. "And that's another call. I've got to be out of here just as fast as I can."

She pulled into a narrow driveway, but there were no lights on in the house. "I don't think Rachel's home," she said.

"What about your Darlene?"

"She was going to a concert after dinner." She didn't say *we* were going.

"Don't you have any other friends?" he asked.

"I'll try to think of one," she remarked sarcastically. "But first we're going to a restaurant. I'm starved, and you must be, too. We haven't had anything but a cup of tea since eleven thirty this morning. At least I haven't."

"We haven't time."

"Seriously, Adrian or Anthony or whatever your name is, how do I know you're the good guy and Shahabad, or whoever he is, is the bad guy? I only know it from you. What if you're lying?"

"You don't. One lesson for you: Don't trust anything."

"The fact is, I've been trusting you all along."

"More's the pity for you." Then he said abruptly, "Turn into the petrol station." Before she had stopped the car he'd opened the door. He walked over to the phone, looked up a number in the yellow pages of the phone book that was, miraculously, intact and hanging on a chain, and made a call. When he came back to the car, he was almost smiling.

"Okay, Annie," he said, getting in, "let's get your dinner."

"You called the airlines? When are you leaving?"

"Not until six thirty in the morning. Lousy connections from here, I'll give you that."

"Where are you going?" she asked.

"Right now, to that restaurant you want so badly. It looks as if I've got all night. Maybe I can get something done." He wasn't about to tell her where he was going.

It was a small restaurant, north on I-5. She had suggested Mexican, thinking, rightly, that he'd never had it before, but he wasn't in the mood for experimentation. Then she had suggested Chinese, but he'd said that half the restaurants in New Zealand were Chinese, and what was wrong with plain American anyway, so she took him to a place that specialized in ribs.

The lighting was dim, and they sat in a booth near the back.

"You know where it is, don't you?" she said after they had ordered.

He moved his water glass in a small circle. "I have an idea."

"Then why was it so important to follow Shahabad?"

"If it were you, wouldn't you rather be sure than take a chance?"

"You seem very sure that Shahabad will be going there, but why would he need to? I thought the others—the ones you trained—were going to do it."

"And who is going to kill them when it's all over?"

She pressed herself against the black leatherette of the booth. "I suppose it's normal for soldiers to talk about killing like that."

His forearms rested on the table, and he hunched over them, his eyes searching her face. "And for librarians it certainly isn't, is it? Annie, I'm sorry I brought you into it. I don't imagine this is the way you would have preferred to spend the evening."

"You were going to tell me why he came looking for me."

"Oh, yes." He leaned back. "The paper you gave me the second time I came into the library—the one with the name of the Service Registers on it—it's your own stationery. 'Anne Rowen, University of California at San Diego Libraries,' it says, right at the top. He must have searched my kit; the paper was in my jacket pocket. He probably figured you could lead him to me, and actually we made it quite easy for him, didn't we?" He took a drink of water and set the glass down, moving it again in small circles on the table.

"I'm surprised you didn't order beer or something."

"I don't drink," he said curtly, not looking at her.

"Oh." Had there been something wrong in saying that? She'd only been trying to make conversation, after all. She wondered if she dared ask him about the daughter he had come looking for.

"Why did you leave him?" he asked suddenly.

"Leave who?"

"Your husband."

She frowned, trying to remember when she had told him about Frank, and she finally remembered. "I didn't leave him. He left me."

He didn't say anything, and she looked up at him. He was staring at her with blue eyes that revealed nothing.

"In this country we sometimes call it midlife crisis, and

most of the time we make jokes about it," she said as if she were obliged to explain. "He was forty years old, had a good job. The kids were growing up. He got restless. Life wasn't" —she gave a little shrug—"*exciting* anymore, I guess. Some men in that situation go out and get a sports car; he went out and got a new wife. She was twenty-six and blond and very good looking. It was obvious what he saw in her, but I'm not so sure what she saw in him. He's almost old enough to be her father."

"And he left you for her."

She looked away. "Um-hmm."

"And the children?"

"One on her own in Seattle—she's a nurse. One still in college up at Berkeley. What about you?" she asked. "Is the daughter you're looking for your only child?"

"You must have married very young," he said, as if she hadn't even asked the question.

"Probably," she admitted with a little smile. "Too young to know better."

"You married a fool," he said. He was still staring at her.

"And what about you?" she asked again.

He looked away then. "A trooper has no business being married. It's not fair to the wife, nor the children."

"Just the one child?" she asked. "Or were there more?"

"Just the one."

The waitress brought their food: a slab of ribs for each, glistening in barbecue sauce.

"It looks ungodly good," MacKinnon said.

"It is." She grinned at him. Their eyes caught for a moment, and then she looked away. "At least I hope you'll think so."

"What are the names of your children?"

"Jennifer and Michael. Michael's the one at Berkeley. He's big on computers."

"Like his mom." MacKinnon nodded.

Anne laughed. "Not at all like his mom. He *really* knows computers."

"You impressed me."

"What do we do now, Alex?" she asked. "Where do we go from here?"

"You go to some friend's place for the night." He licked the barbecue sauce from his fingers. "You're right—it's very good. If you can, maybe you should take a day or two off from work, though I'm sure by morning he'll be long gone."

"And you?"

"It's a puzzle, isn't it? There's been nothing in the papers about such a meeting if it's really to happen. Well, they'd have to keep it quiet, wouldn't they, or risk problems from both sides. So who does one contact?"

"Someone in the Israeli government? There's no hope of reaching anyone in the PLO, is there?"

He didn't respond. Meir, he was thinking, though even Meir might be a mistake.

"You're right," she went on. "It has to have been kept so quiet that no one who didn't need to know about it knows. Maybe only the ones who are meeting know about it. That's why you think you have to go there, isn't it? There's no way of knowing whom to contact that could warn them. Unless maybe someone in the Egyptian government? Where do you think it's going to be?"

Bir el Khadim. "In the desert for sure, maybe the Sinai," he said.

"You mentioned Washington. Who would you have called there?"

He placed a bone on the plate and carefully wiped his hands on a paper napkin. "You're a damned nosy woman."

"You bet I'm nosy. You dragged me into this. I have a right to ask a few questions."

He looked hard at her. He saw it in her eyes again, just as it had been this morning when they'd argued over killing Qaddafy. You always saw it in the eyes of the good ones—that determination, that gutsiness, that refusal to stand down. He wondered if she even realized how good she could really be. She was smart, feisty, and resourceful. He had every confidence that she could find a way to make direct contact with Kammer if she wanted to. The trick was to get her to want to.

"Secretary of State Kammer," he said. "Himself. No one else. But it's impossible."

"I wouldn't have expected you to say that. I thought the great MacKinnon knew how to do everything."

He chuckled softly and shook his head slowly. "Would that I did."

She toyed with her glass. "Kammer's out of the country, of course. That makes it harder."

"Makes it impossible. There's no one who could put me in direct contact with him. No one I would trust, at least."

"What would you tell him?"

"What I think. What I know. He could make the contacts if I could convince him."

"What if I helped you?"

He leaned back and smiled sardonically. "You're going to go into that place with me? You who didn't even want to take a pistol into her hands?"

"I'm talking about what you came to me for in the first place—information. Names of people in government. Telephone numbers. Maps. If it weren't for the information I already got you, you wouldn't even know—"

Suddenly she was offering more than he'd counted on.

"What kind of telephone numbers are you talking about?"

"Telephone listings for virtually all American cities—those are on microfiche. And telephone books for most of the major cities of the world. Numbers of government offices."

"Would you have a telephone directory for London?"

"I should think so."

"Athens? Tel Aviv?"

"I can't guarantee it, but I wouldn't be surprised."

"How late is that place open?"

"Until midnight at least."

"Finish your dinner," he said.

She showed him to the telephone fiches and books, and then she moved on to search government information: Kammer's assistants, the lines of responsibility below Gershon and

Bakr, office addresses and phone numbers. She imagined how difficult it would be to convince an assistant secretary of state over the phone that he had to put her in direct contact with Kammer. Impossible, probably, but anything less would be too slow, and it would be even worse with the Israelis and the Egyptians. MacKinnon seemed to have the idea that if they could only talk directly with Kammer, they could get him to make the proper connections in the Middle East. He was there; he would be believed. Maybe, she thought. But how does one manage immediate and direct contact with the Secretary of State?

She pored again over lists of government offices and responsibilities. Somewhere in Israel or Egypt there had to be someone who knew where the country's leader had gone. Who? And even if they found the name, would he believe them?

When MacKinnon had finished with the telephone books, she took him upstairs to the maps. She pulled out maps of North Africa and the Middle East, and he scanned them slowly. He asked for a map of Egypt and examined it with care, his finger tracing routes: Cairo eastward . . . Cairo south along the Nile to El Balyana and then west . . . Cairo east again and into the Sinai. Without his having to ask, she pulled out a detailed topographical map of the Sinai, and he leaned over it, hardly acknowledging her, as if he'd forgotten she was even there. Never actually touching the map, he moved his finger along the roads of the Sinai and traced its wadis, lost completely now in the recreation of the terrain that spread beneath his gaze. As she watched his fingers move, she became sure that he already knew those roads and trails and wadis, that he was only doing this to refresh his mind. Who are you, she thought. What makes you think you know where it will be? *You're a damned nosy woman,* he'd said. She was; and she was particularly curious about him. Who was A. C. MacKinnon anyway?

She watched the trails he followed: Suez and eastward, Ismailiya and southeastward. Wadis running on irregular diagonals. But always his finger returned to the same place, a barren flat land scored by wadis and lying between mountain ranges. Bir el Khadim, the map said. The name meant nothing to her.

He looked up at her suddenly. "What time is it now in Cairo?"

"I have no idea. We could look it up—"

"Cairo to London is two hours. Do you know what time it is in London?"

"Five hours ahead of New York, I think. And New York is three hours ahead of us."

"Ten hours, then," he said, and he looked at his watch. "Seven o'clock in the morning. Where can I make long-distance calls?"

She thought only a moment. "I know where we'll go."

JERUSALEM, ISRAEL

Avram Gershon adjusted the knot of his blue silk tie, then flicked a piece of lint from the oyster-colored lapel of his suit jacket. The suit was new this season, and he was very pleased with the way it looked. He would be the only one at the Cabinet meeting this morning wearing a suit-coat and tie, but that had never fazed him. He was who he was. He knew what they called him behind his back: the dandy. His political opponents had assumed that a man who took precise care of his appearance could never compete in the rough and tumble of Israeli politics, and that had been their error. He smiled into the mirror at himself. He was better than they were in every way: more perceptive to changes in public sentiment, more skilled at building a coalition, more farseeing, and as they had discovered, more ruthless. Which was why they also called him "the emperor." Even the always fractious Knesset had learned to give Prime Minister Avram Gershon his due. If they didn't agree with his policies, they always at least gave them—and him—respect. No one in Israel doubted that the Prime Minister's first goal was always the good of the State of Israel. He had never been called on that. When this emperor had new clothes, the new clothes were real.

There was a tap at the door.

Gershon looked at his watch. Five minutes after seven. He

liked an early start on the day. He would be in his office before seven thirty. By the time the Cabinet met, he'd have finished up all the last-minute details. He could leave right after the meeting.

"One minute," he said. He turned slowly and faced a blank wall, closing his eyes, and as he did so all peripheral thoughts drained from his mind. For a moment he focused his whole being on the objectives of the next few hours. Then he opened his eyes, and opened the door and walked into the hallway.

Just outside the front door a black Chrysler with darkened windows was waiting for him. The driver was standing beside the car, hand on the back door latch. As Gershon approached, the driver opened the door in a practiced movement that allowed Gershon to enter the car without pause.

Someone was already sitting in the backseat. Gershon turned in surprise, then his face relaxed and he showed a slight guarded smile. Isser Landau, dressed in civilian clothes, sat wedged into the corner of the backseat. Gershon's mind registered Landau's clothing and the fact that the man must have gotten into the car at the garage, and he knew what Landau must be about. The automobile would have been swept clean for bugs, Landau would have made sure there was no tail, and if his guesses were right, the driver would take an alternate route today. As if on cue, the driver turned right instead of left coming out of the drive.

"So," Gershon said. "We can talk."

"I have seen Comsat photos of the area for the last week. Between the Soviets, the Americans, and us, we have the place quite well covered. So far I'm satisfied with what I see."

"Did you expect not to be?"

"Of course. That's my job. But it's not what we see now that would worry me; it's what will be there in the next few days. My men will be keeping an eye on it, but once we're in there, it's not going to be the same."

"And what do your men know?" Gershon asked, his eyebrows raised.

"Nothing."

"We don't enlist men into the Mossad for their stupidity. What are they guessing?"

Landau smiled lazily at Gershon. "They think it's a rendezvous of PLO leaders with western intelligence operatives. I dropped a hint or two and let them carry it from there."

"PLO leaders meeting in the Sinai?" Gershon frowned. "They aren't going to believe that. And if they do, isn't it a little close for comfort?"

Landau chuckled. "You have yet to fully appreciate how the mind of an intelligence man works. The more improbable the proposition, the more likely it is to be true. Only a CIA operative would think to join ranks with drug smugglers to their mutual benefit; the American man on the street would never dream of doing such a thing. I needn't remind you of anything closer to home, need I?"

Gershon shook his head. Pretoria, he was thinking. "And what are they to be thinking about you?"

All expression drained from Landau's face, and he looked straight ahead. "We are almost there," he said.

Gershon continued staring at him until he spoke again.

"I am due for a vacation. I keep a woman in Marseilles— half French, half God knows what."

"Do you really, or is that just a cover?"

Landau turned slowly to face him, his countenance as unreadable and cold as a stone monolith.

The automobile stopped, and the driver got out and opened Gershon's door. Gershon nodded once and stepped out of the car. Colonel Landau neither acknowledged the nod nor turned away.

LA JOLLA, CALIFORNIA

The teenager who opened the door had long tawny hair in a thick braid that hung down her back almost to the waist.

"Lisa," Anne said. "I'm a friend of Darlene's—Anne Rowen. I think we've met once or twice before, haven't we?"

"Oh. Yeah," the girl said.

"I was supposed to go with Darlene to the concert tonight, but something came up. I thought I'd come over anyway and keep her company when she gets back tonight. I understand Dan's out of town."

"Uh-huh."

"So anyway, I finished with the business that delayed me and thought I'd just come on over here. I guess Darlene's not back yet."

"No."

"Well, she should be back fairly soon. There's no point in your staying any longer unless you especially want to." Anne opened her purse. "What's the going rate for baby-sitters these days?"

"Well, she usually gives me two dollars an hour. But I don't know—"

"You think you'd rather wait until she gets back?" Anne said over her open purse. "I guess I can understand that. You don't mind if I stay, though, do you? You do remember meeting me before, don't you? I mean, I wouldn't want you to feel uncomfortable with me here. I could come back later."

"No, I guess it's okay." She shrugged and turned for her jacket. "I guess I might as well leave."

"Do you have a car? If you don't, you'd better wait for Darlene. I wouldn't want you to walk home so late."

"No, I have my car." She pulled on the jacket and zipped up the front.

"You must have been here since before six, right?"

"Yeah."

Anne handed her a ten-dollar bill. "Are the kids okay?"

"Yeah. No problem."

"Good. I'll tell Darlene. Is school going okay for you, Lisa?"

The girl shrugged. "It's okay."

Anne stood in the doorway and watched the girl walk to her car and drive away. A moment later MacKinnon stepped out of the car, which was parked down the street, and came to the house.

"No problem?" he asked.

"No. It was Lisa, and she's seen me with Darlene before. Dan travels a lot, and Darlene's not one to sit home just because her husband's out of town." She closed the door behind him. "The phone is in the kitchen. I think there's another one in the study, if you prefer. Would you like some coffee?"

"I'd rather have tea. Strong."

"Strong tea coming up," she said and walked into the kitchen.

He followed her silently, watching as she ran the water, set the teakettle on the fire, and opened a cupboard door for the tea, moving in this other woman's kitchen as if it were her own. He had long been fascinated by the domesticity of women, by their ease with the elemental things: the preparing of food, the furnishing of homes, the cleaning and mending of clothes. Even—especially—the care of children. It was as if they had the secret of what life was, as opposed to men, who mostly ran around and played their games of power and war.

He probably should have gone into the study to make the calls, but something made him want to stay here where it was light and warm, where he was not alone. Where she was. He leaned against the refrigerator and lifted the telephone receiver. In his life there had been a number of things he should have done. And what did this one matter? She knew about it anyway; there was little he would say over a telephone line that she shouldn't hear.

He tried the Athens number first—it would be later there than in London—but there was no answer. Then he tried the London number.

After ten rings a woman's sleepy voice answered. "Hullo?" That would be Sophie, the woman Meir stayed with when he was in London.

"I'm calling for Mark Levkovsky," he said. It was the name Meir used when he was in London. He knew that much about him at least: Meir's name and the name of the woman he stayed with.

"He's not here. Who's calling?" Her voice was not so froggy now. He guessed that she had come alert when he'd asked for Mark.

He hesitated a moment. "The name is Mac," he said finally. "Is there a way I can reach him? It's urgent, and I don't have time to waste."

"Do you have a telephone number where he could reach you, Mac?" she asked.

He looked at the number on the phone and was wondering if he should give it, if he would be here long enough to receive a call, when she spoke again.

"Just a minute, please."

He smiled into the phone.

A moment later Meir came onto the line. "Mac?"

"Are you still in the import business?" MacKinnon asked.

"That's a bloody hard business to get out of," Meir responded.

MacKinnon hesitated again. He knew perfectly well there was no such thing as a secure line, and Meir knew it, too. With all the eavesdropping satellites circling the globe and receiving dishes pointed in all directions and ships lurking offshore bristling with antennas, there was no telling who might be listening.

"I have some rather disturbing news that involves the head of your firm. Not of your Institute, mind you; I'm talking about his superior, the one who runs the whole show. This is going to take you back to where we first met—in more ways than one."

"What do you propose?" Meir asked. He hadn't even missed a beat.

"If you have direct access, warn him to stay home. If you don't . . . I can't guarantee the safety of the message or the messenger." Meir would understand. "At eight thirty tomorrow night—tonight your time—a TWA flight departs JFK for Paris. There'll be a ticket in your name."

"Isn't that taking the long route?"

"We'll move carefully on this one."

"There's no way I can make that flight."

"There's always a way."

This time Meir hesitated. Then he said, "All right."

MacKinnon hung up the receiver.

LONDON

Without a word Meir Karoz rolled out of bed and began dressing. Sophie Blackmun turned over onto her side, pulled the quilt up over her shoulders, and watched with sleepy eyes. He was a couple of inches under six feet, and wiry. She liked seeing him dress.

"I'll be gone a few days," he said when he'd gotten his pants on.

"Um-hmmm," she answered.

He pulled his shirt on and buttoned it. Then he unzipped his pants, tucked in the shirttail, and zipped the pants up again. He pulled out a small duffel bag he kept ready in the back of the closet and took his jacket from the back of the chair. By the time he was down the stairs and had closed the front door, Sophie was asleep again.

He looked at his watch. Going on eight in Jerusalem. He walked the short distance to Paddington Station and took the tube to the third stop. There he got out and made a call from a public telephone box. He tried Landau's apartment first, but there was no answer. Then he called the duty officer; he'd have to leave a message. He waited a full three minutes before the call was answered.

"I have an urgent message," he said. "It's about Cockerel. Where is he? Do you have his schedule for the next few days?"

There was a pause and the sound of shuffling papers. "He has a Cabinet meeting this morning. After that, I'm not sure."

"I've gotten a tip," Meir said. "Get a message to him to cancel all plans, to stay home until I can communicate further. Ultra Red. Got that?"

"Yes."

"I'll be in touch as soon as I know more." He hung up the phone.

TEL AVIV, ISRAEL

Captain Yakov Singer replaced the receiver slowly. The two major Israeli intelligence agencies were once again at each other's throats, each vying for superiority, each looking for the other's weakness. It was the bane of the country, and for a nation so beset with enemies, the astonishing thing was that it was allowed to continue. Responsibility for the Prime Minister's safety related to internal security, and that was the province of Shin Bet. Furthermore, Mossad was currently in disfavor over the daring assassination attempt on the deputy PLO chief. It was widely believed that the Mossad had been responsible for that attack, but those within the inner workings of the Mossad knew better. They were getting the credit for the attempted assassination but also the blame for creating a serious and potentially dangerous new unbalance in the ranks of the PLO. Foreseeing that, the Mossad had at first issued denials, but no one had believed them. Later it had been decided at the highest levels to ignore the whole thing. Too adamant a protestation would only serve to cement the connection in the public's mind.

In addition, retribution from the PLO had been anticipated ever since the attempt. Security forces aboard El-Al flights and at El-Al airline terminal counters had been doubled, but nothing had happened yet. Now rumors had begun that the PLO had a more prominent—and personal—revenge in mind.

As a result, Singer found himself in a quandary. Security around the Prime Minister was unusually tight. Any message to the Prime Minister would have to be funneled through Shin Bet to make sure it got there at all. But Shin Bet, distrustful of the Mossad since the assassination attempt, was likely to discount or distrust the message. It would take a man of impeccable credentials to bull his way through the security net that Shin Bet had created around the Prime Minister.

And that meant one person: Isser Landau.

14

TEL AVIV, ISRAEL

It was just after eight in the morning when Yakov Singer called Isser Landau's office. Singer half-expected to be told that Landau hadn't come in yet, but he was in for a surprise.

"Colonel Landau is not expected in today," a female voice responded. That would be Lieutenant Ber, Singer realized, the brusque woman on whom Landau depended to keep the world at bay when he was busy and who at other times served Landau as both secretary and aide. Lieutenant Ber was still in her twenties, with a very average face but the most extraordinary pair of legs Singer had ever seen. He had wondered more than once if Landau fully appreciated what he had right in his office.

"Is he reachable somewhere else?" Singer asked.

"Colonel Landau is always reachable in case of emergency," came the cool response.

"Thank you," Singer said. Then he added a halfhearted "I'll get back to him later" and hung up. It was not really Landau's problem; it was just that Singer knew the colonel could get the message where it had to get with the least amount of stalling. Proper procedure was to turn the information over to Shin Bet and let them worry about threats to the Prime Minister, or whatever Karoz had meant by his cryptic message.

JERUSALEM, ISRAEL

Shimon Weiss, a former army lieutenant colonel now in the Protective Security Branch of Sherut Bitahon, the internal security service of the State of Israel commonly called Shin Bet, sat on a hard-backed chair in a hallway outside the Cabinet Room in a subsurface floor of the modernistic

Knesset building. A young man whom Weiss didn't know approached. "Shimon Weiss?" he asked.

Weiss nodded, wondering who this young precisionist might be.

"Eli Lascov, communications. I have a message for the Prime Minister," the young man said.

Weiss jerked his head back toward the closed doors at his right. "He's in a Cabinet meeting."

Weiss noticed now that Lascov held a folded slip of paper in his right hand between his thumb and forefinger. He was snapping the paper back and forth nervously with the ring finger of the same hand. "It's an urgent message," he said.

"They don't want to be disturbed. Can't it wait?"

Lascov paused a moment. When he had taken the message over the phone, he had assured the contact from Mossad that he would get word to the Prime Minister immediately. On the other hand, if the Prime Minister wasn't safe even in his own Cabinet meeting . . . Still, a threat was a threat, and it was his duty to deliver the message. "There's some kind of threat against his life." He'd expected Weiss to react, and he wasn't disappointed. What surprised him was how quickly Weiss recovered.

The muscles around Shimon Weiss's eyes tensed and then almost immediately relaxed. "Where do you think you are?" he asked, almost showing a smile. "Where have you been all your life? We all live under threat every day of our lives."

"I mean a specific threat."

Weiss looked at the paper and at the finger snapping it back and forth. "From where?"

"I don't know. We received a call from the Institute. One of their people in Europe called in with it."

"And?"

Lascov shrugged. "Just a threat. That's all they know so far. The Prime Minister is to be told to stay home until further notice."

Weiss had been sitting all this time; now he rose. "I'm supposed to believe the Mossad is just turning that over to us? Why would the Mossad call us with that, Lascov? Why wouldn't they handle it themselves?"

"Excuse me, sir, but I think they are. It's just that they wanted the Prime Minister to know."

"You said someone in Europe. Where? Who?"

"They didn't say."

"Who called you?"

"It was a Yakov Singer."

"You know him?"

"No."

"You have proof he's what he says he is?"

"He called on a secure line, sir."

"Is that the message?" He pointed to the folded paper.

"It's just my notes of the call."

"If I may." Weiss held out his hand.

Lascov gave him the paper, and he unfolded it, read the few words, and then refolded it and put it into his pocket. He looked toward the closed doors. "Do you agree that he's probably safe for the time being?"

"I would assume so, sir."

"Thank you, Lascov. I'll personally give the message to the Prime Minister immediately the meeting ends. If you receive any further information, I would appreciate your getting it to me as quickly as possible."

"Yes, sir." Lascov nodded brusquely and turned to leave.

Shimon Weiss watched him disappear around a corner, thinking it had been wise to have arranged to pull this duty this particular week. He could not leave this spot now—one never knew when a Cabinet meeting might finish or recess —but his mind was already working, trying to figure out where the nearest safe telephone was.

LA JOLLA, CALIFORNIA

There are only a few locations a bomb can be placed in a small house if the goal is not just to destroy the building but to kill any occupant. A man who knows what he's doing can vet such a house in less than half an hour. MacKinnon didn't think Shahabad had had the time or the inclination to plant a bomb at Anne Rowen's house, but he cleared it anyway, for a couple of reasons. For one, he needed the time to himself, to think. She asked too many questions, pressed too hard, and he was still sorting it out. He was already disgusted at himself for telling her so much. If he hung around her much longer, he'd probably, and unaccountably, end up telling her every bloody thing in his whole life. It was none of her damn business.

And that was another thing. He had brought her into it, the more fool he, and now he had to make sure she didn't end up dead because of it. He would bet his own life that Shahabad hadn't hung around long enough to leave any bombs, but he wasn't quite willing to bet hers. Still, he couldn't deny it, she was good, very good: tensile steel wrapped in cotton wool.

And there was another reason he'd wanted to come, which he didn't realize until he was halfway through her house. It smelled much like she did, clean and fresh and somehow like some kind of flowers. He was in her bedroom, and he paused at the dresser, looking at his own reflection in her mirror. He looked at the pictures tucked into the edges of the mirror—a dark-haired girl in a red blouse standing in the shade of a tree; a young man in bathing trunks on a beach. He touched the edge of the dresser, then moved his fingers lightly to the handle of a brush that lay on a pristine dresser scarf. He had not touched a woman from love in a very long time. There were women in Christchurch and Dunedin and even closer to the station, but that was entirely different. He moved away from the dresser then, his hands and eyes again doing the work almost automatically. When he had finished, he strode one more time through her house before walking out the door. And going to get her.

JERUSALEM, ISRAEL

The Cabinet meeting finished before noon. Shimon Weiss rose to his feet as the doors opened.

Avram Gershon was first out of the room, and Weiss fell into step behind him as he moved down the hall. Gershon turned to him and slowed just enough that Weiss caught up. "I'm going down to Beersheba to visit my sister for a few days," Gershon said. "Get away, catch up on some paperwork. I'll be leaving immediately, and I won't be needing

you for the rest of the week. Gleim will handle things here."
He nodded to his aide whose long legs easily matched Gershon's quick stride.

"Yes," Weiss said.

"I expect they'll find other work for you to do at Shin Bet," Gershon commented.

Weiss chuckled. "They manage to. Have a good rest."

"I expect to."

Shimon Weiss slowed his pace and finally stopped walking altogether. Ahead of him, Avram Gershon, his oyster-colored suit as smooth as it had been at seven that morning, continued down the hall.

Weiss turned around and walked hurriedly in the opposite direction. He ran up a staircase and out onto the street. In the next block he found a telephone booth where he dialed a long-distance number. Looking at his watch, he nodded to himself, satisfied.

"*Ja*," the voice in Zurich answered the phone.

"Your principal should know that an attempt has been made to warn one of the pigeons."

"Which one?"

"The one who shaves."

"An attempt . . . ?"

"The message was intercepted."

"Where did it originate?"

"Europe somewhere. That's all I know. I'll let you know when I hear more. This is no time to blow everything. You tell your principal that."

"He'll appreciate the warning, but there's nothing anyone can do until we know the source."

"We had assurances—"

"*Ja*. We all have assurances."

"There will never be another chance like this. Never."

"*Ja* . They know that. Don't worry. He probably gets such warnings all the time. It probably isn't even connected."

"It is." He could sense it, even if this stupid Zuricher couldn't.

"Then you must have more information than you've given so far."

"I don't yet, but I'll have it."

"And you'll pass it on, I presume."

"*Ja*," Weiss said sardonically. "And your people will take care of it."

"Of course. They always take care of everything."

Weiss hung up the phone. He could handle the odd messenger from the Institute or Shin Bet himself, but everything else had, of necessity, to be taken care of by someone else. There was just the one thin thread to Zurich, the one connection. They had all agreed it would be safer that way. Now he hoped it was going to be enough.

LA JOLLA, CALIFORNIA

He unlocked the door and stepped aside for her. She walked inside and looked around, almost as if the place were strange to her. It occurred to him that maybe it was, in a way.

"Everything's in place, nothing's different?" he asked.

"It looks like it."

She walked into the bedroom and stopped, taking the room in. He stood behind her and looked beyond her to the dresser. She walked into the hall, peered briefly into the bathroom and the other bedroom, then out again and into the dining room and, finally, the kitchen. "I don't see anything, but how can you be sure he's gone?"

"Someone has gone to a great deal of trouble and expense to create a dispensable force. Shahabad is the man who will do them in. He has to be with them. They left earlier today for the staging area, and in one or two days they'll be half a world away. It's going to take me a day and a half to get there, and it's going to take him some time, too. He doesn't have time to fool around with you. Me, he would come after because he knows I know things, but he thinks I'm dead. On the other hand, you've never even seen him."

"He doesn't know that."

"Don't be mistaken, he knows it. He also knows that without me to back it up, your story is going to sound as if you've been drinking too much. Or been out in the California sun too long. What does a woman like you—a librarian, for God's sake—know about surgical strikes, assault forces? You'd open your mouth and sound like a fool."

"Thank you very much."

He raised his hands as if in defense. "His thoughts, not mine."

She turned away from him and without even asking began running water into the teakettle. He shoved his hands into his pockets and watched her.

"How do you know all these things?" she asked finally.

"It was my job to know them. For all those years . . . to make the enemy think—something. To *let* the enemy think something. And whenever possible to know what the enemy was thinking. In special forces, that's what you do half the time—outthink the enemy. He does it, too, whatever his training might have been."

"Who's the enemy?"

"Terrorists. Hijackers, kidnappers, hostage-takers. Revolutionaries, or counterrevolutionaries, depending on the situation. It's low-level aggression, Annie—what they call low-intensity warfare. You read about an attack one day in your papers, on page eight maybe, and the next day you've forgotten about it, but it goes on all the time. We're the people—I was one of the people—who do something about it."

She turned around and looked at him for a long moment. "Why?"

He shoved his hands deeper into his pockets and laughed softly. "No one ever asked me that before."

"I'm asking."

"Someone has to do it." He turned away and looked out the kitchen window. Light from the kitchen spilled against the wall of the garage next door.

"Someone has to be the executioner, too, but that still isn't a reason."

It was past one in the morning; there were no lights on in the nearby houses. "It's exciting," he said at last. "When you're young, you want to do something exciting, you want every day that you live to be exciting. After a while you become accustomed to the rush of adrenaline—like a hit of heroin or coke, you become addicted. You want it, you feel most alive when you have it. If you can't be doing that, you'd rather not be doing anything at all."

"You make it sound terrible."

He turned to look at her, and she was peering into the teapot, checking the color of the tea. "Terrible? It's the most exhilarating thing you can imagine."

"Then why did you get out?"

Because I came to see what it was, he could have said to her. An addiction, just like the alcohol. If I wasn't having the one, I was having the other. That was my whole life. And someday I was going to mix them up and get somebody killed. What he said was: "It was time."

She poured the tea into cups with flowers on them, much like the ones Martha used at Covington Station.

"I'm very sorry I brought you into it," he said.

She took a sip of tea. "Don't be. It's been like a salt wind."

"I don't understand."

"You know how far from the water this house is. Still, now and then when the breeze is blowing right, if I open the windows, you can smell the sea. It blows the stuffiness out and brings in the smell of"—she looked down and chuckled at herself—"for me, too, excitement, maybe. The smell of something far away."

"Even the scared parts?" he asked.

"Fortunately, they didn't last too long."

He moved closer to her and touched the back of her upper arm. She took another sip of tea, deliberately, he thought, as if trying to work something out.

"If it had been me, I would never have left you," he said.

"What happened to the wife you had?"

"I told you, she left me."

Her eyes held his for a while, and then he looked away.

"I was younger then; I didn't know a lot of things. And anyway, she wasn't at all like you."

"You're going to be gone in a few hours." She set the teacup gently on the counter.

That was when he kissed her.

15

Yakov Singer walked into the bookstore and took a moment to let his eyes adjust to the sudden dim light. Then, catching sight of the signs above the racks, he meandered slowly toward the back of the store until he found the books about music. He stared at the volumes for a moment and then casually pulled out a biography of Rubinstein. He was not unused to such procedures, but it still seemed a rather melodramatic way to meet someone. Perhaps Shin Bet had an exaggerated view of the way Mossad worked. Perhaps the man who had called him had felt it necessary to prove himself, as if he believed a Mossad officer would be suspicious of any overtures from Internal Security.

Nearby, a man in tan slacks and shirt replaced an art book on the shelf and moved toward the center aisle. "Excuse me," he said as he passed Singer, and Singer glanced up, as if momentarily distracted from the book in his hand.

Four minutes later, having riffled the pages of the book three times, studied the chapter titles until he knew them by heart, and examined most of the photographs scattered throughout the text, Yakov Singer replaced the book and left the store. Ahead of him by half a block—he must have dawdled coming out of the store or spent time in front of a nearby shop window—was the man he had seen in the bookstore. Singer walked briskly; by the time he reached the second cross street, he'd come even with the man. When the man made a left turn, he followed, keeping pace.

"My name is Shimon Weiss." The man continued looking straight ahead and didn't offer his hand. "I am with Protective Security in Shin Bet, and currently my responsibility is the protection of Cockerel. I understand you are the one who received the message from an agent in Europe and transmitted it to our organization—to an Eli Lascov. Is that correct?"

He was establishing his *bona fides*, Singer knew, but he still wondered why it was necessary. In the Mossad, at least, men rarely stood on such formality. "That is correct," he responded.

"I have reason to think that this threat may be a serious one," Weiss said, "and also that in some way security may already have been compromised. I also have heard some things that I find somewhat disturbing, and therefore I am treating this with the utmost caution. Who has been told of this?"

"I called Lascov on a secure line. I have no idea whom he might have told."

Weiss nodded. "Don't worry about Lascov; he's a good man and tends to be overly cautious. I'm sure he's been correct in this. What I'm concerned about is your end. Who else knows? And what do they know?"

"As you may be aware, this is not an unusual situation. There are procedures for handling these things. I called Shin Bet—Lascov—and I made a report to Reuven Cohen, my superior."

"And that's all?"

"Yes, sir. That was according to procedure." He did not say that he had also tried circumventing Shin Bet entirely by going through Colonel Landau. There was no reason for a Shin Bet man to know that, and anyway it hadn't worked.

"Then the breach may have come in Europe. Where was the message from, what city?" He knew better than to ask which agent. No Mossad man worth his salt would have revealed that. Perhaps he didn't even know.

"I . . . I'm not sure I can tell you that," Singer said.

That was part of the answer. Singer did know then which city the message came from. "We are not dealing in neat espionage games here, Singer," Weiss said sternly. "We are concerned about the safety of the Prime Minister and, by extension, the safety of all Israel. There has been a security breach, or at least I have strong reason to believe that. The Prime Minister's safety is my concern, my primary concern.

If you continue playing this coy game, I'll have to speak with Reuven Cohen. I'm sure he will clear me for the information."

This last statement was made with a heavy note of sarcasm. Singer, suddenly disconcerted, was at a loss. He knew proper procedures, and they did not include an officer in Shin Bet demanding information in broad daylight on a public street in Jerusalem from a member of the Mossad. On the other hand, Karoz, calling from London, had seemed so sure and so agitated. *Get a message to him*, he'd said, and Shimon Weiss was responsible for the Prime Minister's security. And now Weiss was talking about a possible security breach in Europe. Maybe he knew more than he was letting on. If Weiss thought it was important to know the origin of the message, then surely he ought to tell. After all, he wasn't asking the name of the agent, only the city. "It came from London," he said. "I talked with him myself, but it was very brief. He said he'd gotten a tip and that I should get a message to the . . . to Cockerel to cancel all plans and stay home until we had further word. That was all."

Weiss walked for a number of paces, staring at the sidewalk. "Then you expect to hear from him again," he said at last.

"Yes. I hadn't expected to leave my post at all today, not until I heard from him again. I only came out because you—"

"Then you'd better get back there." Weiss paused, then pulled a notebook and a pencil stub from his pocket. "I'll give you a number. Call me there as soon as you hear more. Cockerel will be very interested in knowing what this is all about."

"I'm sure he will." Singer took the slip of paper and stuffed it into his shirt pocket.

"I'll be waiting for word," Weiss said, starting to walk away.

Singer neither shook his hand in farewell nor followed him; he didn't even watch him go but immediately turned and walked hurriedly in the opposite direction.

SAN DIEGO, CALIFORNIA

The plane was a DC-10—three seats on each side of a center aisle. MacKinnon found himself in a middle seat, jammed between an overweight businessman sitting in the aisle seat with his briefcase on his knees to use as a writing table, and an elderly woman by the window who had already taken out her knitting. He couldn't complain; he was lucky to have gotten a seat at all; but from the looks of things, it was going to be a long seven hours to New York.

The woman nodded at him. "Looks as if it's going to be another beautiful day in San Diego," she said.

"Um-hmm," he agreed. Through the window beside the woman he could see the sun just above the horizon in a cloudless sky.

"Do you live in San Diego?" she asked.

"No, I don't."

"Were you here long? I was visiting my daughter—two weeks and never even a cloudy day. It almost gets boring, that much good weather, don't you think?"

"It's been very nice," he said, trying not to encourage her, but she had caught his accent.

"Oh, you're not American! Where are you from? Let me guess. England?"

"Yes." It was easier than having to explain.

"I just love England. I was in London five days. Rained every day but one, but it didn't matter. So much to see and do! We rode the tube everywhere we went. That was in 1975, and I've been wanting to go back ever since. Are you from London, by any chance?"

"No, ma'm, I'm from the north." The FASTEN SEAT BELT sign came on, and he fastened his. The businessman fumbled and squirmed in his seat, trying to find the belt. The woman's belt had been fastened when MacKinnon sat down.

"I just love flying, don't you?" she asked. Without waiting for an answer, she went on. "Once a year to San Diego to visit my daughter—that's about all I can afford nowadays. But it makes a good break at the end of the winter, just when you think you can't stand it any longer. Were you here long?"

"A few weeks."

"Visiting friends?"

"Yes, ma'am." He shifted in his seat as much as the seat belt would allow. The plane had begun rolling down a service runway.

"Going back to England now?"

"Um-hmm." He closed his eyes.

"Say hello to London for me. Good heavens, what a wonderful city! One never knows what's around the next corner. We saw the Queen ride by in her limousine one day. We'd just been to see the changing of the guard and were on our way to Westminster Abbey, and suddenly there she was. Well, the windows were darkened, so you couldn't see her, but I asked a man who was walking along the sidewalk if it might be the Queen, and he said it probably was. Imagine! The Queen of England! Have you ever seen her?"

"As a matter of fact, I have."

"There you are! I'm from upstate New York and you're from northern England, and we have something in common: We've both seen the Queen. I always say, if you talk with someone long enough, you're bound to find something in common. My husband—he passed away eleven years ago in January—he always used to wonder whenever he was in a crowd of people if there was someone he knew. Always thought there might be a chance. Or if not, then maybe someone who knew someone he knew. He'd always look for that someone, always asked people where they were from and where they'd ever lived, hoping to find someone they knew in common. Sometimes it even happened. He was always so thrilled."

MacKinnon looked at her, and she was staring at her knitting needles, shaking her head in wonder and smiling fondly at the memory. "If you don't mind, ma'am, it's going to be a long flight for me, and I was up rather late last night—"

"Oh, of course. Don't mind me, just an old lady. I like the company. It's going to seem awfully lonely at home after being with those three grandchildren. . . ." She paused and he felt her turn in her seat, but his eyes were closed again. "Well," she went on, "maybe you'd like to see some pictures after you've napped."

"Um-hmm." The plane turned again and began moving forward, gathering speed. The engines were roaring now, and he felt the woman beside him stiffen slightly. Then there was the rush of take-off and the gradual lightness when gravity finally let go, and the wheel assembly bumped into place. He kept his eyes shut. He could imagine the ascent; he didn't need to see it.

Beside him, the woman relaxed slowly, and her knitting needles began clicking again. He had not heard that sound in years, and he'd forgotten how comforting it could be. His mother used to knit. Marie never did.

He saw Annie in his mind's eye, the way she'd been last night. She was sitting on the edge of the bed, and the lace of her slip was white against her skin. Her blouse was unbuttoned but still on, as was her skirt. She had taken her shoes off in the kitchen, even before he kissed her.

"Why is it that people feel they have to jump into bed with each other, before they even know each other?" She wasn't looking at him.

He sat down on the bed beside her. "You don't want to."

She shook her head, still not looking at him. "I do—or at least I want what it means."

He put his arm across her shoulders and gently pulled her close, understanding what she meant. Her head was on his shoulder then, and she looked at him at last, her eyes roaming his face.

"Do you think that sounds stupid?" she asked.

"Not at all." He kissed her on the mouth.

Her hand came up the length of his back. He took his arm from her shoulders and lay back on the bed. "Button your shirt," he said.

She looked down at her blouse as if in surprise and then at him, and she began fastening the buttons. He watched her as he lay on his back beside her. "There are two things that separate the boys from the men," he said finally. "As soon as a boy has a gun in his hand and the enemy in view, he wants to shoot. He wants to get the first shot off, as if that enemy in his sights will disappear if he's not quick enough. You have to train that out of him, make him learn to wait until the time is right. Sometimes it's minutes, sometimes it's hours. In special forces it can be days or even weeks. Patience. That's one of the hardest bloody things to learn. Even politicians—especially politicians. They want to jump in and win the battle fast, and in doing so they sometimes lose the war. It's the same thing with women."

She turned and looked at him full face. "What an odd thing to say."

"Can't take credit for that. It comes from John Hawk, best sergeant major the world has ever seen."

"I thought you were that. I thought that was why they brought you over."

"John Hawk is probably dead. Buried. Gone to his reward long ago. He's the man who trained me, Annie, along with dozens of others, and that was nearly thirty years ago." He sat up beside her again. "And I don't think I ever said I was the best."

"You didn't have to. They didn't bring you all the way from New Zealand because you were only average."

He kissed her again, and her arms went around him. "Tell me about John Hawk," she said into his ear.

But he closed his eyes and held her close for a long time because he knew what she was really asking.

BIR EL KHADIM, THE SINAI

The Old Man stepped out of the helicopter just as the sun faded behind the mountaintops in a violet haze. Dust in the air, a *hamseen*, he thought. It was the season. Behind him Ali Rawad stepped out, and the two ducked under the rotors and ran forward toward Hussein Bakr, waiting at the edge of the compound.

Bakr stepped forward and placed his hands on the Old Man's shoulders, touching cheeks with the new arrival in greeting. The Old Man endured the ceremony though he had never cared for Bakr. In addition, his diffidence would be a signal to Ali Rawad, who had expressed skepticism over the whole proposal and was here only because the Old Man had insisted. At least Ali Rawad wouldn't be able to accuse him of falling completely overboard. And if the offers still appeared genuine after discussion and confrontation, and if they could hammer out something workable . . . well, in the end it would probably be Ali Rawad who would have to make it stick. So there was all the reason in the world to let Ali Rawad understand that at this point nothing had been given away. In the next few days they would all have to be won over, or this meeting would have been for nothing. No, he thought, smiling to himself, not for nothing. For the next few days I will sit across the table from the Prime Minister of Israel, and that is something I have been battling for for a very long time.

"Your quarters are this way," Bakr said, placing a guiding hand on the Old Man's elbow. "We will be having the evening meal together in an hour or so. In the meantime, if you care to freshen up . . ."

The Old Man shook Bakr's hand from his elbow. "I will eat in my room. Tomorrow is plenty of time to meet with them."

Bakr didn't react except to say, "As you like." The Old Man wondered if he had expected such a move. On his other side, Ali Rawad brushed his hands together as if to shake off the dust of the trip, but the Old Man had been around him long enough to know the sign. He was satisfied with the response, and unaccountably that relieved the Old Man, as if satisfying Ali Rawad was now one of his major priorities.

LA JOLLA, CALIFORNIA

Anne Rowen sat in front of the computer, her elbows on the desk in front of her and her hands cradling her face. She had looked everywhere, tried a few calls, and come up blank. This was a wild shot, but it was just about all there was left. She keyed in the codes and waited for the keyword command. When it came up, she keyed in KAMMER: FAMILY. If there was no way to reach him through official channels, perhaps there was an unofficial route: country club memberships, civic organizations, place of worship. She was looking for anything that would be a key to reaching the man without going through official intermediaries. There had to be a way; it was always there, you just had to find it.

Two titles came up. One was apparently a women's magazine puff piece titled "The Woman Behind Howard Kammer." The other, from a weekly newsmagazine, looked slightly more substantial: "What Keeps Howard Going: The Public and Private Faces of Howard Kammer." She ran off citations for both and exited the database.

Next to her, at another computer, Rebecca Phillips leaned back and sighed. "No good, no good," she grumbled.

"What's the problem?"

"The Women's Studies Program wants a historical bibliography of federal laws impacting women specifically. There ought to be something like that, but I just can't find it."

Anne frowned. "I saw one, believe it or not, just lately. Now where was that?"

"If you can find it, Anne, it'd be a godsend. I'd owe you one, in spades."

She looked away, trying to remember where she saw it. "Wait a minute. In . . . um . . . in— Oh, shoot, I'll think of it." Then suddenly she turned back. "Rebecca, you know more about government documents than I do. There must be some kind of list of British government publications."

"Sure: *British Official Publications*, it's called. It ought to be at the reference desk in Government Docs."

Anne stood and pulled her printout from the printer. "Thanks. I'll get back to you about that bibliography."

She took the elevator to the sixth floor, walked straight to the Government Documents department, and asked for *British Official Publications*. She ran her finger down the index until she found what she was looking for, then turned to the page. And smiled. When she read the last line of the five-line entry under *Army List*, her smile broadened. "Part II is the 'Retired List,' " it read.

"Do we have a copy of the British *Army List* here?" she asked the student behind the desk.

"Just a minute, I'll see." The young woman keyed into a computer, read the citation, keyed more in, and looked up a code in a code list. Then she turned back to Anne. "We don't have it here. The closest one is at Stanford."

"Thanks," Anne said. She turned and almost ran back toward the elevators.

Three quarters of an hour later she was back at her desk reading the second of the magazine articles about Secretary of State Howard Kammer. On her desk, between a pile of books to review and a stack of mail to go through, was a single sheet of paper, a copy of a page from the British *Army List* that a colleague at Stanford had faxed at her request.

JERUSALEM, ISRAEL

Shimon Weiss looked at his watch. Six fifteen. Almost seven hours since Lascov had come to him on the lower level of the Knesset with the message for the Prime Minister. More than five hours since he had talked with Singer on the street and Singer had promised to call as soon as he received further word. The Prime Minister and his faithful watchdog Landau would surely have left by now. That part was still secure, but the message from Europe still nagged. Who had called in to Mossad? Who was their man in London, and what had he heard?

Weiss hadn't wasted the last five hours. Mossad guarded the security of its agents with the tenacity of a Doberman guarding its territory, so he'd had to move cautiously. He'd looked into files, into the rare joint operations, but in those reports code names were used almost exclusively. Operatives in the field were in contact only with their controls. No one else knew who they were. It was no wonder Singer hadn't been able to tell him; it probably wasn't just a matter of security, most likely he really didn't know the man's identity. In a society in a persistent state of seige, such security precautions were as necessary as breathing.

He had called the contact in Zurich again, not a good idea even in the best of circumstances, but the man still knew nothing and still had not had contact with his principal. Soon, he had said, soon.

Weiss closed his eyes and tried to breathe deeply. Soon was not soon enough. The pigeons were getting into position. One could not expect a chance like this to occur again in one's lifetime. And beyond that was the unspoken fear of what might happen if the meeting actually took place uninterrupted.

His hand went for the telephone, and then he slowly withdrew it. He couldn't call Singer. Any further move on his part in that direction would only serve to incriminate him in the end. In that respect, no further communication from Europe was a good thing. So far he'd be able to say that he had warned the Prime Minister, but Gershon had only taken it to be another of the many threats he had experienced. They would be forced to take his word for it because Gershon himself would be dead. If Gershon had refused to take Weiss seriously, that was hardly Weiss's fault. If more specific information had come in on time . . . And that was the hook on which he was caught. His own skin could still be saved, but the very thing that could save it —lack of further information—could cost the failure of the operation. He had always believed that the goals of the Movement were more important than anything, including any one person's life. He had always assumed he'd be willing to sacrifice himself for success—all of them did. He still believed that, but he realized now that he believed something else as well: a live patriot could still work toward the goal; a dead one was worthless except as a role model for those who came after.

Even so, he had worked for years to get himself where he was—in Shin Bet where he would be in a position to know, in time to avert them, the threats to the accomplishment of the Israel they dreamed of. And they had all waited for this moment when the majority party could be unmasked for what it was: men grown soft with the illusion of the strength of Israel, men who had forgotten the battle that had brought Israel into being, men who believed that there could be any accommodation to the enemy, men who had given up or never believed the premise that Israel was for Jews alone, men who believed that peace was more valuable than principles.

He ran his hand through a thick mass of graying hair. Somewhere, somewhere in the files or in his notes there were pieces that would fit together. The training wasn't even in Europe, and the cover for it had been superb. The American government believed the principals were training a force to stage simulated guerrilla attacks on nuclear installations as a test of nuclear security. He had thought that up himself and had passed it on, and as he'd known it would, the American government swallowed the thing whole. That had been the little deception that allowed the bigger one: all the men in the force believed the U.S. government was behind, maybe even bankrolling, the operation simply because the training had been allowed on U.S. government property. If there was one other thing that that obscene Hitler had taught the world besides the fact that Jews had better stand up for themselves because no one else would, it was that a big enough lie told boldly enough is unlikely ever to be questioned. He smiled grimly at the irony of that. The lesson that would save Israel from the weaknesses within had been taught by Hitler himself.

He turned his attention back to the files on his desk with renewed vigor. In London, who might be Mossad with a link to someone within the strike force? He pored through the files and the names again. This would not have been a casual link. Whoever contacted London contacted someone he believed he could trust. Who on the strike force had ever had contact with a possible Mossad operative in London? As he pored over the papers, possible links forged and then dissolved. He guessed what he was looking for now: special forces operations in which Israeli and western units cooperated or were present together. It was hard going because in recent years it had become common for special forces units to send observers to watch each other in action. This was a new style of warfare—fighting against terrorists, hijackers, and the like—and each operation was unique. To be viable a force had to build not only on its own experience but on the experiences of all the others, and therefore whenever the opportunity allowed, observers from half a dozen friendlies could be found taking notes, possibly offering suggestions, even sometimes photographing the action.

It was as good a guess as any for the link, but he still found nothing. Not until he had worked himself back as far as 1977, and then he found it at Bir el Khadim itself. But instead of being pleased, he was disgusted with himself because he knew he should have realized it from the start. When one is a Jew, one learns a certain sense of irony.

NEW YORK CITY

The plane was, unbelievably, five minutes early, which was no consolation, MacKinnon realized, because he already had four hours to kick his heels until it was time for the flight to Paris. It was unlikely that Meir would manage to get to JFK that early, and even if he did, it was unlikely that their paths would cross until they boarded the plane. He had handled Meir's reservation himself, making sure their seats were adjacent. To casual observers, if there were any, they would appear accidental seatmates.

He found a public telephone and dialed the number. She had promised to be there. He remembered that desk from when he first went there with her; he had not even known her then, just a librarian helping him find his daughter. It could have been a hundred years ago. He hadn't been back to her desk since, but he could remember that it was one of several, each separated by those half-wall things that are supposed to give one a feeling of privacy but only turn the room into something more like a rabbit warren. He hadn't much hope that she would manage to find a direct route to Kammer. He had warned her not to try doing it herself, just to find a route if she could. He wasn't quite comfortable with her trying to make the actual contact. He still had no idea who was behind it, and there was no point in dragging her any further into it. He had warned her of that, but she'd almost seemed to ignore him. Bloody hardheaded woman she was.

"Hello," she said.

"It's New York, checking in."

"How was the flight?"

"I slept through most of it, thank God."

"You probably needed it. Feel okay now?"

"You're damn right I needed it. Some old lady wittering on beside me. I had to sleep in self-defense; it was the only way to keep her quiet."

"Watch what you say. Someday you may be old."

"God willing."

"I called Washington, and you were right, of course. I probably wouldn't have been able to talk to Kammer even if he'd been there, but it was clear they weren't about to put me in touch with him halfway—"

"I thought as much. It's a crazy story, Annie, no matter how you slice it."

"Well, if you think you can refrain from interrupting me, I'll tell you how I managed it anyway. There's more than one way to skin a cat, you know."

"Don't tell me you got in touch with him." How? In God's name, how?

"Not yet, but it's beginning to look promising. Through his daughter, believe it or not. After striking out on the phone to Washington, I got the idea to go through unofficial channels, so I pulled together everything I had about his private life. I thought maybe a country club, something like that. And that's where I saw that his daughter goes to college. And we know all about colleges, don't we, Alvin?" She paused as if to laugh, but no laughter came over the lines. "I called her school and asked if she was listed in the student directory. She was, so it was just a matter of dialing her dorm—"

"She was listed?"

"Yes, she was. And she was also asleep. I woke her up, and she wasn't too thrilled about that, but after she calmed down a little, I managed to talk her into calling her mother. Her parents are close—so say all the articles about his private life anyway—and it's a good bet they're in communication. At the very least his wife would know how to reach him."

"So what did you tell his wife?"

"She hasn't called back yet. Maybe she's out or something."

"Maybe she thinks you're a crank."

"Maybe."

"Annie, even with his wife, be careful."

"You're the one who has to be careful. I'm just sitting here at my desk and talking on the phone."

"In that event I'd better hang up in case she's trying to reach you. I'll call again just before my flight. That'll be in about three hours. Maybe you'll have heard from her by then."

"All right. Take care."

"Always do." He hung up the phone. She had said that when he'd left: *Take care*. And he had walked down the sidewalk away from her. *And come back* , she had whispered as he went, so quietly that he'd barely heard it. Or maybe he only hoped she'd said it.

MEXICO CITY

A half hour after he had seen the woman arrive at Anne Rowen's house and be sent away by a neighbor, and just over four hours after he had shot MacKinnon out of the boat in San Diego Bay, Kherman Shahabad was at Lindbergh Airport. He'd managed to get on an evening flight to Mexico City. Whatever had happened with Anne Rowen, he decided that he wasn't going to worry about that. MacKinnon could not have told her enough to incriminate anyone, and he had been in much tighter spots before. The important thing now was to get back in time to fly out with the men. After everything was over, he could return and take care of the Rowen woman. The way things had been set up for Bir el Khadim, he probably had eighteen to twenty-four hours before word of the attack got out, and that would be plenty of time to tie up that one loose end.

He had arrived in Mexico City too late for the last flight to Caracas, so he had to stay overnight in a hotel near the airport. He could have gotten a flight direct from Mexico City, or even from San Diego, but it was one of his inflexible rules that there should always be at least two airports between his departure and his destination. He lived by those rules, talismans for his safety and anonymity. Always at least two airports and at least one change of passport. His continued survival was proof of the efficacy of those rules.

He took a room on the third floor of the hotel. He preferred third-floor rooms and, while never making a real issue of it, always tried to manipulate the concierge into giving him one. A third-floor room, while too high for an easy break-in, was still low enough for a relatively easy escape out a window. He had only a small bag and he'd shaken off the porter who was hanging hopefully around the front desk. Once in the room he turned on the light, locked the door securely, set the bag down, and pulled back the covers on the bed. He looked at the sheet for a moment and then walked into the bathroom and ran a half glass of water from the tap. Walking back to the bed, he poured most of the water onto the sheet. Then he dialed the front desk.

"Excuse me," he said when the concierge answered. As at the desk downstairs, he spoke in English and, as always, politely. "This is room three-twenty. I'm afraid I've spilled something on the bed. Would you be so kind as to send a maid to change the sheets? Can that be done immediately?"

"Of course, sir. Is there anything else?"

"Please also have room service send up a plate of fried shrimp and bowl of fresh fruit. To be delivered half an hour after the maid has finished with the bed. Is that possible?"

"Of course it's possible, sir. Anything else?"

"I think not, thank you." He replaced the receiver, picked up his bag, and went into the bathroom. He had no idea how soon "immediately" would be. In German hotels it was always less than five minutes. Once in Athens he had waited in the bathroom for an hour and a half, and finally had to come out and make a second call.

He turned on the shower and waited. It was almost twenty minutes before he heard, above the sound of the shower, the maid's light knock, then a louder rap; finally the key turned in the door, and she must have entered. He stood beside the closed bathroom door and imagined her movements as she stripped the bed and remade it with pristine sheets. He'd seen pictures in magazines, advertisements perhaps, of beds with flowered sheets or stripes or other kinds of patterns. But the sheets in hotels were usually white, his preference, and if one asked to have them changed, one could always be sure they were clean. When he had started out, he always just asked for clean sheets to be put on the bed; in the hotels he'd had to use in those days, one could never be sure of clean sheets unless one asked for them. And there was always the inevitable hassle when concierges and hotel maids insisted the sheets on the bed were already clean. But he knew better. Then he had discovered a much simpler way of getting the sheets changed; no hassles, no arguments. He didn't even have to see—or be seen by—the maid; she would think he was taking a shower.

He imagined now the sheets against his skin—cool, unsullied, the precise creases of their folds still showing. He imagined the maid bending over the bed now, pulling the sheet tight and tucking it under the mattress, an almost sensuous gesture of care and provision. If he had ever thought of Paradise at all, it would have been a place where unseen women constantly made the beds with fresh new sheets, and unseen hands prepared buffets overflowing with flawless fruit and fish just taken from the sea.

He heard the door close and then the silent sound of emptiness from the adjoining room. He took off his shoes and stepped into the shower. He stood under the streaming water for a good five minutes, letting it wash away the dirt of a long day, a day that had started in the southern California desert. The cast beneath his sleeve reminded him of the way the day had started; but that had been long hours ago, and MacKinnon had finally gotten what he deserved.

When all of his clothes were fully soaked, he took them off one by one, unbuttoning the shirt and pulling the sleeve over the cast of his right arm. The doctor had told him to keep it dry, but he'd also told him to keep it clean, and Shahabad knew which was more important. Anyway, one could always get a new cast. He unfastened his pants and pulled them from his slim legs, then took off each of his socks; finally, he pulled off his undershirt and undershorts. Nude, he wrung out the clothes and laid them on the floor outside the shower. He took the soap and slowly began to cleanse himself. He always washed and rinsed three times before he was satisfied, and sometimes, if the day had been particularly strenuous, he would do even more. On this occasion there were five washings and rinsings.

When he had finally finished his ablutions, he wrapped a towel around his waist and wrung out the clothes once again, hanging them in the closet. If they were dry by the time he left in the morning, he would pack them in his bag clean. If not, he would discard them in an anonymous place the first opportunity he got. In this way he was never forced to pack dirty clothes in his bag.

The food came more than an hour after the maid had left. Still wrapped in the towel, he took the tray at the door and set it down on a small table. He turned out the lights. Drawing back the curtain, he looked for a few moments at the lights of the airport in the distance before he pulled the curtain almost closed again, leaving the opening just wide enough for a dim haze of light to reach into the room. Then he dropped the towel from his waist onto the floor.

He sat down in a chair and pulled the table a few inches closer. With a fruit knife he carefully peeled a grape and then placed it in his mouth, rolling his tongue around it, sucking on it for a few moments. He ate two of the shrimp. He cut open an orange, smiling at the sweet sharp scent of it as he peeled back the skin. When he pulled off a segment, a drop of juice sprayed out and landed on his chest. He wiped it off with a forefinger, licking the finger and savoring the orange and the clean fresh taste of his own skin. Another drop fell on his bare thigh, and he rubbed it into his skin. He was very fond of the smell of oranges. He squeezed a segment of the orange on his other thigh and rubbed the juice slowly into the skin. He ate the rest of the segments slowly, biting each in two, the pure fresh taste of each bite cleansing his palate anew. By the time he had finished the orange, he knew he was ready. He took a banana and slowly unpeeled it, then rolled the pale fruit between his hands until it softened. The scent of banana on his hands came to his nostrils, and he leaned back, his eyes closed, his hands still massaging the fruit. When the time was right, he dropped the banana to the floor and his hands, softened and lotioned now, found the place between his legs. He leaned his head against the back of the chair and began slowly stroking himself, taking his time, reveling in the fruity smell that surrounded him and the touch of his own skin.

When he had finished, he walked in the dark to the bathroom and took another shower. Then he stood naked in the room until he was dry, eating more fruit and shrimp. Finally he went to bed, pulling the fresh sheets over his cleansed body. No thoughts passed through his mind, no concerns pressed against him; he was asleep almost immediately with the deep, untroubled rest of the innocent.

The next morning, while MacKinnon was at the San Diego airport catching the plane for New York, Shahabad managed to get on an early plane for Caracas, and from there he took a flight to Lisbon. At the Lisbon airport he called the contact in Zurich. It was only to be a routine call; he knew the men were to leave later the same day for the final staging area, and he had planned all along to be with them on that trip. But the Zurich contact changed all that for him.

"There's been a hitch," the Zuricher said. "You have some kind of leak."

"What are you talking about?" Shahabad demanded. There couldn't have been any leak. The Rowen woman? She was a cipher, wasn't she? Just a woman working in a library. Maybe MacKinnon had slept with her, but surely that was all she was. Surely he hadn't misjudged her.

"A warning came to Mossad. Fortunately it was intercepted. The Jerusalem contact is working on it now. We know who the warning came from, and the man is in London, but that's all I have now. Get to London and call me back."

"It can't be. It's some mistake."

"It's no mistake."

"I have to be—"

"You have to be in London. That is a direct order from the Movement. I will have further information when you contact me from there."

Shahabad hung up the receiver slowly. In his mind's eye he saw MacKinnon once again, falling out of the boat. He couldn't have been mistaken about MacKinnon twice. In all his experience that had never happened. It had not happened this time either; he had seen it with his own eyes. But even as he turned away from the telephone, he knew that one can be fooled in what one sees with one's own eyes or hears with one's own ears.

On the plane to London he sat next to a girl with hair the color of the sand along the Corniche, or at least the way it used to be when the sun shone on it and before it had been blasted again and again with bombs and grenades. As she swung her hair across her shoulders, he could tell it would have the texture of silk. She smiled at him and asked if he was staying long in London, but he didn't respond. He hadn't had sex with a girl since he was seventeen, and he wasn't about to start again now. He hadn't had sex with a man since he was twenty-three. If one wanted to keep oneself clean and free of disease, there was only one way. And for him there was the added advantage: he was never forced to make himself vulnerable to another human being.

AMMAN, JORDAN

Fatigue hit Howard Kammer like a wall. He'd taken nothing before the flight over, not even his usual Dramamine. He hadn't wanted to risk the least amount of grogginess on this most important trip. It would take all his intellect and argumentative ability to pull this proposal off, and he knew that if this one failed, he might as well hang up his hat and call it quits.

He hadn't slept on the way over, still hyped by the last-minute briefings with his aides and advisors. The first day he'd run on sheer guts and will, and the adrenaline that flowed from the knowledge that this could very well be his last good chance.

Even today, the second day, meeting with King Hussein,

he'd still been running on that edge, fueled by the frustration of not getting a firm commitment from President Hatoum in Damascus. Hussein had been cagey, noncommittal, still wanting to sit on the fence, or maybe more afraid than he needed to be, Kammer thought, of the Palestinian reaction. Kammer had spent long hours over this proposal, and it was based on what he believed to be more realistic, though certainly still tentative, signals coming from both major sides of the question. But he had been able to get nothing firm from Prime Minister Gershon in Washington, and that had not augured well. Now Hussein was equivocating, and Kammer was almost at the end of his rope. Gershon was not even available, and neither was Bakr in Egypt. He knew perfectly well that underlings were worthless in a matter like this.

For that reason discouragement had begun to close in, one door after another shutting in his face until there was virtually nothing left. And with the discouragement came an immense fatigue. He had pushed as far as he could, and now, standing in yet another embassy in yet another country, he felt the end of his short-lived career closing in as well.

He wanted more than anything to be with Phyllis, to forget all this. He knew he could probably go back to what he once was—a Harvard professor of political science—and certainly Cambridge would seem infinitely more sane than what he had been doing for the last two years, but there was still that last vestige of ego that would not quite let go, that would push him one more day, or maybe even one more day after that, in search of the solution that had evaded the Middle East all these years.

And so he would not call Phyllis tonight. If he called and talked with her, listened to her voice, even though she would be all encouragement, he would only yearn to go back to the safe womb of her arms. He would sleep tonight—he was tired enough to be sure of it—and tomorrow, God willing, tomorrow he would press on.

16

NEW YORK CITY

He put the money in and listened to the echo as it fell through the equipment, then he dialed the number. It was just eight o'clock, five o'clock her time.

She answered almost immediately: "Hello."

"It's me again."

"Hi. I talked with his wife. She seemed almost convinced —she sounds like a nice person. She says he phones her nearly every night. It was about an hour ago that I talked with her, and she was expecting a call from him. But it's quite late there now; it would be about three in the morning, I think. He's supposed to be in Amman. She said sometimes it's late by the time he calls, so I guess he could still do it. I told her if he didn't call her, she'd better start trying to reach him, but I'm not sure she really will."

"How much did you tell her?"

"That there was a major assassination attempt planned. That he might be the only one who could stop it."

"Did she believe you?"

"I—" She hesitated. "I'm not sure."

"Goddamn it, Annie, she *has* to believe it." There was silence at the other end of the line. "I'm sorry. I guess I didn't get as much sleep as I should have," he said lamely.

"I guess neither of us did. Have you met your friend?"

"Not yet." In fact he'd spent the whole time in the airport waiting for Meir to appear, and even now was watching for him as he spoke with her. Another thing not fitting together right. "He might have been hard-pressed. He has half an hour yet."

"Call me when you get to the next place. Maybe I'll have some good news by then."

"It was good news already. A possible contact is a good piece of work, Annie. Better than I could think to do."

"Take care, MacKinnon."

"You, too." He cradled the receiver. *MacKinnon.* Somehow he'd liked it better when she'd called him the A names. Surely she hadn't run out of them so soon.

Meir Karoz was the last one on board. He came walking down the aisle looking like death warmed over, as well he might—rousted out of bed and sent across the Atlantic just to take another flight back the way he had come. His dark hair curled at his temples and at the nape of his neck. Needs a cut, MacKinnon thought. The beard needed trimming, too. MacKinnon watched Meir walk toward him as one would casually watch any fellow passenger. There was no hint of recognition between the two men, not even a momentary meeting of the eyes.

Meir stowed his rucksack in the overhead compartment and then rechecked his boarding pass. "Excuse me," he said to MacKinnon. "I think you're sitting in my seat."

"So I am," MacKinnon replied, not even looking at his own pass. Reluctantly he rose from the aisle seat and moved over into the empty one that was unarguably his. So it hadn't worked, and now he'd be stuck in a middle seat for another long flight. And he was not likely to get any sleep on this one. Nevertheless, he couldn't have arranged better positioning. Two blue-haired ladies were to his left, both talking so fast and at the same time that it was hard to comprehend how they could hear each other. Meir Karoz was to his right, on the aisle seat. In front was a woman traveling alone with a toddler and an infant. The baby was already crying. With luck, it would keep it up all the way. The whole row behind was a group of young people, shaggy unwashed hair, dirty jeans, sleeveless sweatshirts, even at this time of year. They were noisy, and one of them even had a guitar.

Meir rummaged in the seat pocket in front of him, pulled out an in-flight magazine, and began to thumb through it. MacKinnon reached up and switched off the light above his own seat. Meir glanced at the movement and then went back to his magazine. MacKinnon leaned back and closed his eyes. No one could have traced him to Karoz, of that he felt sure. He'd told no one, not even Anne, what plane he was taking or where he was going, and he knew that Meir would have been just as careful.

Twenty minutes after they took off, MacKinnon heard the flight attendants coming down the aisle serving drinks. He opened his eyes and watched lazily as they worked their way toward the back of the plane. The women on his left were still at it; the baby in front had settled into a whimper. Meir, on his right, seemed engrossed in an article on the Costa del Sol.

When the flight attendant reached them, Meir ordered a whiskey neat. MacKinnon asked for 7-Up.

"Have you ever been to that place?" MacKinnon asked, nodding at the magazine in Meir's lap. By rights, the initial approach was his to make.

"Not for a long time," Meir responded.

"Nor I." MacKinnon took a sip of his drink, and Meir watched him. MacKinnon could imagine what Meir was thinking. "A place like that changes over time, I suppose, just like people do. I wonder how those high rises built in the fifties and sixties are showing their age by now."

Meir shrugged and took a long drink of whiskey.

"I was at a little place in the late seventies, a dusty, dry place in the desert—in the Sinai as a matter of fact."

Meir nodded and set his drink down carefully.

"There were only a very few of us there," MacKinnon went on, "a couple of Brits—myself included—a couple of Americans. I don't even know what happened to the other Brit or one of the Americans. A few Egyptians—their desert, after all. And, surprisingly enough, also a few Israelis." He paused and took another sip of 7-Up. "What if I were to tell you," he said in a lowered voice, "that another meeting, in some ways similar and in some ways very different, is about to take place in the same spot?"

"I would ask how you knew."

"Did you get the message to your man?" MacKinnon asked softly.

"I relayed it. I assume—"

"You assume?" MacKinnon whispered angrily. "You assume? I told you that both the message and the messenger were jeopardized. Doesn't that mean anything to you?" He stared straight ahead. The baby was working up a second wind. As if to counter it, the guitarist behind was working seriously on some undefinable tune, and his friends were humming along.

"You call me out of the blue," Karoz whispered. "You give me no explanation, no justification. The whole Institute is supposed to turn itself upside down for that? If you'll pardon me for being totally candid, Mac, the last time I saw you, you were not exactly what one would call completely reliable. And you can keep in mind that I did fly halfway around the world to meet you."

"London to New York is hardly halfway around the world."

"It's not a bad piece of it."

"So why did you come?"

Meir Karoz looked at him for a long moment. "Because, rightly or wrongly, I have a great deal of respect for you."

MacKinnon let out a long breath. "When Sadat and Begin met secretly in Bir el Khadim, both of them were taking a chance. Both countries were not only officially at war, but Egypt had sworn never to rest until Israel was destroyed. Am I correct?" Instead of looking to Meir for a response, MacKinnon glanced around him. "I have reason to think that your Prime Minister is to be meeting for the next few days at the same spot with an even more recalcitrant enemy —the most persistent enemy your country has."

"My country has always refused to deal with—"

"Which is why this meeting has to have utmost secrecy."

Meir's face still revealed no emotion. "If you don't mind my asking, where have you been for the last several years? Certainly not anywhere that I've been."

"In New Zealand, as a matter of fact, but that's hardly—"

"And how does one hear of such supersecret meetings in the New Zealand outback or whatever they call it?"

MacKinnon took another sip of his 7-Up and said finally, "From the people who intend to assassinate everyone at the meeting."

Meir's eyes turned cold; otherwise his expression didn't change. "You met them in some bar, I suppose, and as you got drunk with them, they told you this?"

"This is how you show respect?"

"Respect enough to be honest. That was your line, wasn't it?"

"I don't drink anymore," MacKinnon said stiffly. "And apparently I still have a good enough reputation. Ken Glover —remember him?—Colonel Ken Glover of the United States Army Rangers, who was there with us in Bir el Khadim as an American observer, looked me up and asked me to train a strike force."

"To assassinate Gershon and Arafat. And you agreed?"

"To assassinate Moammar Qaddafy. And, yes, I agreed."

"You've lost me. I thought we were talking about Israelis and the PLO."

"Come on, Meir. One doesn't try putting together a task force to kill those two if one seriously expects to get any recruits. Every soldier is bound to favor one or the other and to resist killing them both."

"There have been plenty of men—in Africa especially— who didn't give a damn which side they were killing, just as long as they got paid," Meir said.

"There have been," MacKinnon said. "Past tense, and you know that as well as I do. The days of mercenaries like that are over. The work is too dangerous and the pay too poor. Nowadays there are much easier ways to make money. Yesterday's mercenary has become today's arms dealer or cocaine runner—at least the good ones have. The bad ones you wouldn't want anyway, and I hear that the only problem those new entrepreneurs have is keeping up with their Swiss bank accounts. No, my friend, despite what you would like to think, I am neither under the influence of anything nor am I mistaken. I trained a team of fifteen men plus

Glover to go into a compound too much like the one at Bir el Khadim for coincidence and wipe out every living thing within it. By my calculations it will happen within the next few days unless somebody stops it. And if your Prime Minister didn't get the message, he'll be right there along with the others."

An argument had ensued between the guitar player and a couple of men behind him over the volume of the music. The argument was at a decibel level twice what the music had been, and two flight attendants were hurrying back to mediate.

"Others? Who?"

"The President of Egypt, I assume. And probably a few security people. We were told to count on as many as ten or a dozen, though quite probably fewer."

"And they think they will be killing Qaddafy." Meir spoke slowly, as if still digesting the implications.

"Yes. He's supposedly on a religious retreat, this being Ramadan."

"And they are supposed to believe that Qaddafy would be in the Sinai?"

"If you're flown in, Bir el Khadim could just as easily be in Libya, or for that matter, lots of other places in the Middle East."

"Surely the men would realize," Meir argued.

"Why would they realize? Desert is desert, isn't it? To a bunch of Americans and Brits, an Arab country is an Arab country, isn't it? Only the pilot would need to know. One aircraft is all you need for that many men even if you planned to use a helicopter."

"And Ken Glover would be the pilot."

"Exactly, as well as their commander. That much, at least, they were honest about."

"And you were just to train them? Why wouldn't they have taken you? They couldn't afford to leave a loose end like you around, could they?"

One of the flight attendants was hurrying toward the front of the cabin. MacKinnon followed her absently with his eyes.

"I would have recognized the place the minute we touched down, and then I would have balked. They could have counted on that. But the others will go in shooting. And yes, I am a loose end, which is why they tried to kill me when the training was over. Twice, Meir, as a matter of fact. The second time I fooled them into thinking they succeeded. That's what gave me the first clue."

Meir Karoz drained his whiskey before turning to MacKinnon. "All right," he said, "start from the top."

LONDON

Kherman Shahabad entered England on a Brazilian passport that identified him as Immanuel Marquez Blasser, an exporter of raw lumber. From the airport he called Zurich again, but there was no further information.

He took a taxi from Heathrow to an address on Moorgate Street, walked the few blocks to Cheapside, and then hailed another taxi for Brixton. He walked four blocks from where this second taxi let him off to a tawdry semidetached house with a postage stamp-sized front yard where limp weeds left over from last year and bits of broken glass competed in a vain effort to cover the hard-packed dirt. As he came up the walk he noted with satisfaction that the poor plastic imitation of orange day lilies still held a place of honor in the parlor window and that they were still flanked by the same faded curtains.

He knocked four times on the paintless front door before it was finally opened by an elderly woman who shaded her eyes and squinted up at him as if the sun were shining brightly instead of hiding behind thick cloud cover and a fine drizzle.

"I've come to pick up a few things," Shahabad said.

"Oh, it's you. I couldn't imagine who it could be so early in the morning." She stepped back to let him in and then closed and locked the door behind him.

Paying her no further attention, he mounted the stairs that clung to one side of the narrow hall. At the top of the steps was a single room crouching beneath the eaves of the narrow house. With a key from his pocket Shahabad opened three locks in sequence, first the lower one, then the upper one, then the one in the middle. The same key opened locks on doors to similar rooms in Frankfurt, Paris, and Naples. Some years ago it had occurred to him that he could save himself time and trouble if he kept a *pied-à-terre* in more than one country, just some little out-of-the-way place where he could store materials that could not easily be moved through customs. In London, Mrs. Bradbury was only too happy to allow the man she believed to be Juan Gomez, a Spanish businessman, a place to store his clothes and other odds and ends in exchange for payment of fifty pounds every six months. She couldn't use the room anyway since she could no longer manage the steps, and he never asked her to clean it, which was a good thing because even if she had been able to climb the steps, her eyesight had gotten so bad that she wouldn't have been able to see the dirt. And he had been kind enough to present her with the lovely artificial flowers as a sort of seal on their agreement.

It was a good arrangement for Shahabad as well, though it was clear it would only last as long as the woman lived. One day he would come along and she would be dead, he knew, but in the meantime he could tell she was still in the house the moment he saw into the front window—no one else would keep those awful flowers longer than five minutes. And in case curiosity drove anyone to investigate his belongings while he was gone, he had prepared the locks: if they were jimmied or opened out of sequence, there would be an automatic detonation of enough plastique to blow the whole house, as well as the curious intruder, to smithereens.

He closed the door behind him and threw the latch. Then he opened the door of a wardrobe. From the floor of the wardrobe he took one of several neatly folded pieces of cotton fabric. He turned to the stack of boxes in the corner. One contained used kitchen equipment that he had bought at an auction in Surrey. One long box held two black umbrellas, some miscellaneous lengths of plastic pipe and boards, and, at the bottom, a Heckler & Koch MP5 submachine gun. The rest of the boxes appeared to contain books. Shahabad opened one of these, identified on the side with the words *Shakespeare and Michener.*

From the box he withdrew a Beretta .22, wrapped in an oiled cloth and encased in plastic, and a four-inch silencer. Using the cloth he'd taken from the wardrobe, he carefully wiped down the gun. Then he stuffed the cloth into the plastic bag, folded it over, and replaced the bag in the box. Once he shoved the box back with the others in the corner he was all set. It had not taken him any more time than it would have taken to make arrangements to acquire a gun of this quality illegally—the only way such a gun would be available to him in England—and he wouldn't have to risk dealing with someone who, for a bigger payoff, might betray him to the police. What Mrs. Bradbury didn't know wouldn't hurt her, and it certainly made life simpler for Kherman Shahabad.

From Mrs. Bradbury's house Shahabad walked to the Brixton station where he took the underground to Paddington. Once there, he walked the few blocks to the address he was seeking, a neat four-story block of flats. At the front, by the door, he checked the directory. As he had suspected, there was no Mark Levkovsky listed. *He lives with a woman named Sophie—that's all I have, I don't know a last name,* he'd been told. There were no first names on the register, not even initials. He pressed the buzzer beside the word "Porter."

"Yes," a tinny female voice responded.

"I'm looking for a friend, Mark Levkovsky. He lives here, but I don't find him on the register."

"Just a minute, love."

She came a few minutes later, dressed in a faded cotton dress that looked more like a sack, with a man's gray cardigan buttoned over her ample middle and her feet thrust into well-worn black loafers. She half-opened the door but stood in the way. "Who is it you're asking after, love?"

"Mark Levkovsky. He lives with a woman named Sophie. I don't know her last name."

"Oh, yes, Sophie's friend. Well, you'll be lucky enough if you find him at home. Mostly he's gone, you know."

"Is he gone now?"

"Now would I be knowing that? But like as not he is; I'm saying he's gone most of the time, it seems."

"Is Sophie home? Would you know that?"

She let the door fall closed a couple of inches. "Not likely I'd know that, is it, unless I'd keep my eyes to the window all day. No, a woman's work is surely never done, least of all one whose good-for-nothing husband claims to manage a block of flats, he who can hardly raise himself from the sofa."

Shahabad pulled a ten-pound note from his pocket and thrust it through the door at the woman.

She hesitated only a moment and then took it. "I honestly haven't the faintest notion whether or not Sophie Blackmun is at home. If you want to know, you're going to have to ring her yourself, love." She closed the door, making sure it latched, and then walked away.

Shahabad turned to the register and pressed the button beside the name Blackmun. There was no answer, so he pressed it again. After four tries he turned back to the door. Taking a close look at the lock, he selected a key from a small ring and inserted it. The lock held for a moment before yielding, and Shahabad walked into the building. He took the stairs to his right. *Blackmun*, the register had said, *apt. 401.*

He knocked on the door, and again there was no response, so he used the same key to let himself in. He walked quietly through the apartment, his eyes and mind taking everything in, his head shaking in disgust. A pair of red socks lay discarded beside the sofa, a sofa pillow was wadded up against the leg of a chair. A plant that had died days ago from lack of sunlight and water sat in wilted state in a red clay pot on an end table. In the kitchen, the remains of breakfast still lay on the table, egg hardening onto a plate, and the remains of making breakfast—fat congealed in a frying pan—sat on a stove that looked as if it had never been cleaned. One plate and one coffee cup, he noted: one person. In the bathroom, nylon pantyhose were draped over the curtain rod, and the sink was splattered with toothpaste.

He heard a sudden soft noise—a thud. Reaching for his gun, he whipped around to face the door just as a lanky gray cat appeared on the threshold. It gazed at him, then rubbed its back against the doorjamb and meowed. He walked past it and into the bedroom.

A half-dozen shoes were scattered on the bedroom floor, the bed was unmade, and dustballs the size of kittens lay under the bed. He glanced at the bed. The sheets were grayed and wrinkled, and he guessed they hadn't been changed in weeks. Two pillows seemed equally used. The cat had followed him into the bedroom, meowing persistently, but he ignored it.

The door to the closet stood half-closed; he opened it further and peered inside: a few men's things, mostly women's. He brushed the clothes aside to look at the floor of the closet but saw only a few more shoes lying in no particular order. One thing about a place like this: one needn't worry about disturbing anything. In this confusion who would notice? Sweaters in disarray covered the closet shelf to the thickness of six inches. He moved to the dresser and opened the drawers one at a time. Three of them had women's things; one had a man's. The woman downstairs had been telling the truth: the apartment was Sophie's much more than it was Mark's. His eye caught on a photograph tucked into the mirror above the dresser. It had been ripped in two and then carefully mended. It showed a short blond girl, slightly overweight, in pants and a shirt. Shahabad guessed her to be in her late twenties. Next to her, his arm proprietarily around her shoulders, was a man with longish curly dark hair and a short cropped beard. Levkovsky and Sophie, Shahabad guessed. Levkovsky was perhaps as much as ten years older than the girl.

There was no sign as to where either had gone or how soon they would be back. Shahabad had nothing but their names and this address. He could canvass the neighborhood, but if Levkovsky had any suspicious friends, it would only serve to warn him. He had already taken a chance with the woman below.

He looked at his watch. It was just after ten in the morning. The girl could be out shopping. The woman downstairs hadn't indicated that the girl went anywhere regularly, to a job or to classes, so it was possible that she would be back soon. For the sake of the kitchen, Shahabad thought grimly, she'd better be.

He considered his options. It was less than an hour since he had called Zurich, and that made it rather soon to check back. Besides, he'd have to leave to make the call from an untraceable public booth, and he was in the place now. There was no point in running the risk that someone would see him going out or in. Right now he would sit tight and wait. Still meowing, the cat rubbed against his legs.

Sophie Blackmun shifted the plastic bag to her left hand and opened the book. She skimmed the first chapter and smiled to herself when she neared the end.

She flipped to the front cover and looked at the price: £9.95, and that made it too dear. In a couple of months if she was lucky, she could get it at the lending library.

She glanced through a few more books, then stepped over to the sale table, but still saw nothing affordable. She should get back; the flat would be silent with Mark gone, and it was high time she put herself to work again. She hadn't written anything worth pursuing in more than two weeks. She felt dry inside, as if there were no place from which the words, or even the ideas, could come. But she knew better than to depend on inspiration; inspiration, like lightning, rarely struck at the convenience of human beings. If Mark was gone as much as three days, she could write a complete short story. She switched the plastic bag to her right hand and turned toward the bookshop's door. On the other hand, she could spend a lovely day at the library catching up on the magazines and taking out a couple of books she'd been meaning to read. She could stop by Lady's and splurge on a bag of chocolate-covered nuts and indulge herself. Buoyed by the prospect, she quickened her step, turning right as she left the shop. Yes, a lovely few days of pure self-indulgence. She could spend the day at the library and then the whole evening wrapped in some other writer's imaginary world.

She caught a glimpse of herself in a shop window and quickly turned away. Then, forcing herself, she looked back. Short. Overweight by thirty pounds. The window was no mirror, so it didn't show her bad complexion, but she knew that was there, too. Her pace slowed as one of her recurrent anxieties surfaced. One day Mark wouldn't come back. He would just go, with his little bag, and she would never see him again. Though she had never said it to him, she had always been certain that that was how it would end.

It was a convenience for him—someone to do the washing and the shopping. He cooked as well and as much as she did, but with two together, each had to do it half as often. And she always did the cleaning up, what there was of it. It was a convenience on both sides: he paid for the flat, and she paid for the food. And during the times she didn't make any money, as recently, he paid for that, too. And they each had the other to sleep with, a comfortable if not particularly erotic arrangement.

And if someday he didn't come back—she corrected herself—on the day when he didn't come back, she would have to give up the flat. She would have to find someone else to move in with or get a job that paid better than writing. She turned around and headed in the opposite direction. She would go back now and hit the flat like a tornado. She'd clean up everything, wash the stove and the sink, and clean out the fridge. She would clean the bathroom and take the dirty clothes to the launderette. The frenzy of cleaning would stimulate her mind, and by the time she was finished, she'd be ready to get to work. She would stay away from peanut butter and sweets until she had lost at least ten pounds, no matter how long it took, and maybe by then she would feel so good about herself that she'd lose even more. She would live on carrots and lettuce and apples. She would stop at the greengrocer's on the way home.

She fitted her key into the lock, turned it, and tugged the outside door open. The door to her immediate left popped open, and Mrs. Wyman appeared, pink plastic curlers in her hair.

"Some fellow looking for you, love. Looking for your friend Mark, he was, actually. Some foreign fellow."

"What did you tell him?"

Mrs. Wyman smiled broadly. "Why, that I didn't know whether you were in or not. I can't keep track of all the tenants, you know."

"A foreigner?"

"Yes. Dark, like a wog. And he had an accent."

"Thank you, Mrs. Wyman."

"He may have gotten in and gone up to your apartment, though heaven knows I didn't let him in. Perhaps he rang another bell. The persistent ones do that, you know."

"Well, no harm, I suppose." Strangers occasionally came to see Mark, though usually it was telephone calls instead. Telephone calls, and then he'd make some kind of excuse and leave. Like the one yesterday morning. And God knew how long he'd be gone at any one time. She had always supposed it was one reason he shared an apartment—he could come and go at will, and there was always someone around to bring in the paper and the mail, and take messages, if there were any.

She climbed the stairs slowly, a plastic bag in each hand, and the apples were heavy. She had bought two oranges, too, because she loved them so. They came all the way from Israel. Mark had told her that once. Before that it had never occurred to her to wonder where the fruit she ate came from. He told her he'd been to Israel and to a few other places, some of which she'd heard of and some of which she hadn't. He didn't talk about his business, which was furniture importing, or at least that's what he said. He had a warehouse somewhere, but she'd never seen it. He passed off the calls as buyers in London for a few days or dealers wanting him to take a look at a shipment. Sometimes she believed that, and sometimes she imagined that he was involved in something else entirely. But it couldn't be drugs, she was sure of that. She used cannabis sometimes, but he didn't, and didn't drug dealers always use the stuff themselves? If he didn't even use cannabis, he probably didn't do any other kinds of drugs, either. She certainly never saw any signs of it. Sometimes she imagined he was with the IRA, but somehow he didn't seem the type. And besides, though he often dealt with men with accents, there had never been a Northern Irelander among them.

She set down a bag to open the door to the flat and then stepped inside. The place smelled musty and maybe like the cat box needed cleaning again. She had no idea when it had last been cleaned. Funny how one got used to the smells one lived with. It was only when coming in from outside that one noticed those kinds of things. And noticed things visually as well. She saw the red socks on the floor and the pillow farther over. Yes, the place definitely needed picking up.

The cat came wandering in from the bedroom, where he'd probably been sleeping on the bed. Well, she ought to change the sheets anyway. He meowed at her, looking up at her face as if he expected a reply. She set the bags down and knelt to him.

"You missed me, Cat?"

He rubbed his cheeks against the back of her hand, purring loud enough to be heard across the room.

"Don't have any food, do you? I had to go out and get you some. Wait till you see—a treat for the two of us. Sardines. You like sardines, don't you, Cat? Me, too."

She rose and walked into the kitchen. "C'mon, Cat, I'll open the sardines and give you some. All out of food, aren't you."

She unzipped her coat and shrugged it off, laying it over the back of a chair. Then she flicked on the radio; it was already tuned to a rock station. It was one of the few disagreements she and Mark had. He liked classical, she liked rock. Because he wasn't home now, she turned the volume higher.

She began unpacking the groceries on the table: the apples and the oranges and the lettuce. She was just starting into the second bag when she felt a presence behind her, or perhaps she heard a sound. She turned around, expecting to see Mark standing in the doorway, the way he sometimes did.

But it was someone else—a stranger. In his left hand he held a gun, and it was pointing at her, but it looked very odd. And then she realized it had a silencer on the end of it. She had never seen a silencer in real life, just in the movies, but she recognized what it was. His other hand was close to his side, and he seemed to hold it funny, as if there was something in it, but she couldn't be sure. Panicked, she stepped back, bumping into the table, forcing its legs to scrape against the kitchen floor with a sound that grated into the fear that was rising. The man said nothing. She opened her mouth to scream, but only silence came out. She stepped back again and knocked over a chair. "Please," she managed to say, more a whispered croak than a word.

"Nothing will happen to you," the man said. "Nothing at all, if you'll cooperate." His voice was quiet and almost gentle, as if they shared some terrible secret, as if he already knew the worst things about her, and had forgiven her for them.

She took another step backward and found the cold wall behind her.

"Why don't you sit down?" he said.

She looked dumbly at the chair she'd knocked over and then back at him.

"Yes," he said. "Sit down. Make yourself comfortable. I just want to ask you a few questions."

She bent for the chair, and when she had righted it, she sat on the edge of its seat. "Who are you?" she whispered.

"I'm a friend of Mark's."

She stared at him for a long time, trying to remember if she had ever seen him before. But most of Mark's people called; she had no idea what they looked like. This one did have an accent, as did many of them. "If you're a friend," she said, suddenly emboldened, "how come you have a gun?"

He looked down at it for an instant as if surprised to see it in his hand. When he faced her again, he was almost smiling. "It's nothing. It's just to let you know this is serious."

"It's not nothing to have a gun pointed at you."

He crossed his arms loosely, the gun now pointing away

from her, toward the floor, yet she knew that in an instant it could be pointed at her again.

"Is that better?" he asked.

She could see now that what his other hand held was the cord of her bathrobe. The panic rose in her throat like vomit. "Who are you?" she cried.

"Where is Mark?"

"I don't know."

"Who is he with?"

"*I don't know.*"

"When did he leave?"

She had been ready to give the same response, but now she stopped, her mouth hanging open. She knew the answer to this one.

"*When did he leave?*"

"I don't know," she whispered.

"You know," he said, unfolding his arms.

"No . . . no," she said, shaking her head faster. "I don't know." Who was this man? What was he to Mark? What did Mark do, really?

He stepped closer to her, the gun aimed at her belly. "When did he leave?" he asked gently.

Why did Mark leave her here for men like this to find? Was it drugs after all? She was still shaking her head, and now the tears were running down her face. "I don't know."

"You know. Why do you protect him?"

Why did she? What was Mark, really? And then the old panic rose to meet the new: was this the time that he wouldn't come back? "He left yesterday morning," she whispered.

"When?"

"Early. I don't know when." Seven o'clock? Eight? Did it matter if she told him?

"Where did he go?"

"I don't know. I told you before."

"You told me you didn't know when, too, but you did, didn't you?" He stepped closer, almost close enough now to touch, and the gun was still pointed at her belly.

"I don't know that. I never know where he goes."

"He got a phone call, didn't he?"

She looked at his feet, tried to concentrate on his feet. If she screamed, maybe someone would hear her, or maybe they would think it was only the radio. Or someone else's telly. Or maybe he would shoot her then.

The gun came forward and with the end of it he tilted her face upward toward him. The gun was now pointed at her neck. "He got a phone call, didn't he?"

"Yes," she whispered. "He always gets phone calls."

"And who called?"

The tears started again. "I don't know."

"You know."

"I *don't*."

"Who is he to you? Why do you protect him?"

She shook her head, the tears running freely down her face. Mark, she thought, where are you? *Come home!*

He moved the gun to his other hand and kicked the chair sideways so suddenly it almost threw her off. She half-fell against the edge of the table. On the other side was a knife, she saw now, but it was well out of reach. It might as well be in China for all the good it did.

He was behind her now and roughly, as if handling a rag doll that would feel no pain, he pulled her arms back and wrapped the cord around her wrists. She felt the cold of the gun touch her arms as he worked the cord, holding both cord and gun at the same time. He pulled the cord now, and her arms jerked back, hurting at the sockets. "Who called him?" he asked again.

"I don't know," she sobbed, her chin falling against her chest.

He pulled the cord again, and this time the pain seared through her upper arms.

"How would I know?" she wept. Why was she doing this? Why was she protecting him when he wasn't here to protect her?

She felt the movement of his hands, and even before she felt the pain this time, she began to talk, babbling the words between sobs. "He came in late. . . . He'd only had a few hours' sleep. The . . . phone rang, and I got up . . . to answer it, because . . . I thought he would want to sleep. . . ." Why had she done that? If she hadn't done that, then she really wouldn't have known who called, and then this person wouldn't have seen it in her eyes, or known somehow—"But it was for him. I told them he wasn't home . . . because I thought he would want to sleep. . . . But he'd told me always to take a message . . . and to get the name . . . and when I repeated the name, he rolled over in bed and . . . and said . . . and said he'd take it."

"Who was it?" His voice was close to her ear; she could feel the breath against the side of her neck.

" 'Mac' was all he said. He said to tell Mark that Mac called." She half-winced, expecting him to hit her or to twist her arms again, expecting him to want more of an answer than that. "That's all I know," she said, as if in apology.

There was a long silence behind her. She bent her head and went on weeping.

"You're sure it was Mac?" he asked, his voice cold.

"Mac. That's what he said. That's all I know, honest. God. Let me go. I've told you everything." Her body shook now, wracked with sobs.

"When will your Mark come back?"

She was crying so hard she couldn't even answer; the best she could manage was to shake her head.

He bent down close to her ear again. "Where did he go? He must have told you."

"No! Honest! He never tells me! What is it? Who are you? Is it drugs?"

The man behind her rose slowly, letting go of the cord as he did. She felt the cord loosen; she pulled on it, and it gave way, freeing her hands. She began to turn toward him, but then a whispered sound broke out, unheard except to her because it was just behind her ear, but there was no time to realize what it was. Her head fell forward, and blood began to ooze from the gaping hole behind her ear.

Kherman Shahabad moved the gun slightly downward and to the left and pressed the trigger again, and a second hole gaped, this one in her neck, just at the carotid artery. He stepped away from her then, watching the pulsing flow of blood as it ran down her side and soaked into her clothes.

He walked over to the radio and turned it off. Then he walked through the living room toward the door. The cat followed him halfway to the door, meowing, and then stopped in the middle of the room and watched silently as Shahabad left.

On his way downstairs, Kherman Shahabad remembered that the woman on the first floor had seen him, too, and he wondered if she was worth the trouble.

17

LONDON

Meir Karoz, having taken the Paris-London shuttle, landed at London City Airport almost exactly two hours after Kherman Shahabad arrived from Lisbon. He was close to being convinced of MacKinnon's story; it made sense in the obtuse, left-handed kind of way that he had become used to while working for the Institute. Events rarely happened in a straight line, and there was no such thing as coincidence. If the setup of the place was like Bir el Khadim, then it almost certainly was Bir el Khadim. If the target was indeed to be Qaddafy, then one had to wonder what the man was doing in the Sinai; and if it wasn't Qaddafy, then one could be reasonably sure that whoever the target was, it was someone the force would have been reluctant to kill. MacKinnon's logic was faultless as far as he could see, but he still had reservations. Perhaps MacKinnon, too, was only another layer of deception. He turned that thought over in his mind. *One peels back the layers like the leaves of an artichoke,* Isser Landau had told him once, *and it is not until one reaches the heart that one finds the real golden nugget.* He would call Isser from London to make sure of the Prime Minister's safety, but he would tell him nothing else. There were too many unanswered questions and no way of knowing where the golden nugget lay.

MacKinnon had been impatient with his insistence on going back to London, but he was too close to turning Litvatov to just drop everything unceremoniously now. Things within the Soviet Union were changing so fast, it was nearly impossible to keep up, and a Mossad agent inside the political section of the Soviet Embassy in London was nothing to take lightly. If he dropped out of sight at this point, everything could be lost. He had to make at least one more contact before going off to Egypt. He would call Isser Landau from a public phone, then go to the flat and take off these clothes he'd been wearing for more than twenty-four hours. He'd shower to wake up as much as possible, and he could easily be at the rendezvous with Litvatov by noon. MacKinnon hadn't liked it, but MacKinnon had to realize that he wasn't operating in a vacuum, that there were other things going on in the world.

It was not the way a Mossad officer was supposed to work, anyway—he'd told MacKinnon that. A London *katsa* flying off to Cairo on his own. This is completely outside normal channels, MacKinnon had said, and he'd understood the warning. How could he not? Still, he could catch hell for it. Or worse. A good Mossad agent was a team player, anybody knew that. But Isser Landau hadn't recruited Meir Karoz because Karoz was afraid to take chances. Karoz grinned at that thought and knew what he would do.

He still could be in Cairo before MacKinnon needed to leave for the Sinai. Furthermore, the thought fluttered through his mind, with Prime Minister Gershon safe, the rest was not so important. It might not be too bad if the Old Man were terminated. And who cared anything about the President of Egypt, anyway? The only bad thing: with Gershon warned off, it would look like an Israeli trap. He picked over that idea, not quite able to decide whether such a situation would be favorable or not.

He paid the taxi driver at Marylebone Road, walked into nearby Marylebone Station, and called Landau. The phone rang half a dozen times before it was finally answered. To Karoz's disappointment, it was a woman's voice—Lieutenant Ber.

"Colonel Landau is not available at the moment," she replied when he asked for Isser.

"How soon do you expect him?"

"Colonel Landau is . . . on holiday at the moment. Is there someone else—"

On holiday. "Where is he?"

"I'm not at liberty to say."

Which could mean anything, from the retreat in France that Landau was rumored to keep, to seclusion with the Prime Minister, to . . . "Switch me to Captain Singer, then, please."

"Singer?"

"Captain Yakov Singer."

"Just a moment."

He shifted weight on his feet and looked through the graffiti-covered glass of the telephone kiosk. Another pane was broken. He wondered once again if the British realized how ramshackle their country had become. He was still thinking about that and about the clean, clear streets of Tel Aviv when Singer came on the line.

"I called you yesterday about Cockerel," Karoz said.

"Yes. I relayed the message."

"Are you certain he got it?"

"Positive. I was even contacted by his security man; he wants to know as soon as I hear anything more."

"It looks real, and I can't get hold of the Director. You know where he is? Holiday, Ber says."

"That's what they're saying. You're supposed to think he's over in Marseilles with one of his women, but I doubt that."

"You think he's with Cockerel?"

"Could be."

"And where would that be?"

"Your message said not to go anywhere. The story is that he's with his sister in Beersheba for a few days, but I think that's all rumor, too."

"There's no way you can get a message to the Director? Lieutenant Ber is useless."

"You're telling me? When he wants security, he's secure. What's the message?"

Karoz hesitated. For some reason MacKinnon was convinced that the assassination plan had its origins within Israel, with dissident hard-liners who somehow had learned about the meeting and were bound to stop it no matter what the cost. Karoz hadn't believed it even though he knew there were at least three fundamentalist organizations that were prepared to stop at nothing to keep the territories. But when he'd asked MacKinnon why such groups, if they really were behind the plan, wouldn't just kill the meeting by publicizing it, MacKinnon had no response. No, it had to be something else; he didn't know what it was, but it was bound to be something. In the Middle East, it always was. Nevertheless, he was reluctant to tell more than he had to. He knew Singer, and there was no way that Singer would betray the Institute or the Prime Minister, but he also knew that men much smarter than he had been fooled before. "Yakov," he said finally, "do whatever you can, but make sure Cockerel is safe. Do you understand?"

"Of course." There was silence, as if Singer were waiting for him to say more, and when he didn't, Singer spoke again. "The men responsible for keeping him safe would appreciate knowing a little more than just that. Isn't there anything I can tell them?"

"Just that I've had reliable information that indicates he should go nowhere for the next week or so. He must stay home; that's crucial. Is that clear?"

"Yes," Singer responded, "it's clear enough, but if I may say so, they might not think it makes much sense."

"I'll explain it to the Director if I can, but not, I think, to anyone else."

Karoz felt the silence at the other end of the line as much as he heard it. *I don't trust you*, his words had implied, and Singer had taken the inference. Karoz turned that over for a moment. "It's not you," he said finally. "It's not anyone. It's just that I've stumbled into an iceberg. I can see what's visible, but it's what's hidden that'll run us aground." He knew the words were a fancy way of saying nothing, but he wanted to explain in some way to Singer.

"I understand," Singer said, and his voice was noncommittal.

Karoz wondered what it was that he understood, if anything. "Keep trying to reach the Director for me, will you? I'll call back when I can."

He replaced the receiver. Okay, the Prime Minister was safe. He had always trusted his instincts, had had to do so more often than he cared to remember. This time everything was telling him to move cautiously. The Prime Minister was out of circulation—unreachable—but at least he had been warned. Landau was heaven knew where, but again at least he should have been warned. He realized now that in the press of the conversation he had forgotten to ask Singer what Landau knew. Tired. God, he needed sleep. He looked at his watch. Eleven ten. No time even for a quick nap. He would hike over to the flat, shower, and change his clothes, and he should be in place in Hyde Park in plenty of time for Litvatov.

Using his key, Meir Karoz opened the outer door and took the stairs two at a time. He unlocked the apartment door and was mildly surprised by the silence that greeted him. Sophie always played the radio at full blast when he wasn't home and half the time when he was, unless he asked her not to. Now it was quiet; she must be out. Odd. Somehow he never thought of her as going out. She had no friends he was aware of, and that suited him just fine, though it must be terribly lonely for her.

The cat appeared in the kitchen doorway and meowed once, then began licking his paws. Karoz shut the door and strode into the bedroom. Everything looked just as it had when he'd left early yesterday morning. He threw his small rucksack, not even opened since he'd left, onto the unmade bed. Unbuttoning his shirt, he walked into the bathroom and yanked the pantyhose off the shower rod, draping them carelessly over Sophie's towel on the rack.

He unzipped his pants and urinated into the toilet. As he bent to flush, a thought struck him and he looked down. The toilet seat was up; he hadn't lifted it. A movement caught his eye just then and he jerked around, but it was only the cat, standing now in the doorway of the bathroom, staring at him. The cat meowed once. Karoz looked back at the toilet seat. A man had used it last, but it was more than twenty-four hours since he'd been here. He was beginning to feel more fully now the sensation that had been tickling his conscious mind since he'd walked into the flat. The silence. The smell—above the mustiness and the odor of old cooking and the smell of the cat had been an odor of . . . of old fear. It was the kind of smell one could detect in prisons beneath the stench of urine and sweat, but it was not an odor one expected to encounter in a flat. At least not usually.

The cat meowed again and moved forward, rubbing his back against Karoz's leg. Karoz watched, his senses fully alert now. The cat meowed some more and looked up at him. "Hungry?" Karoz asked, his voice breaking the silence.

The cat was meowing almost constantly now, still staring upward. She went out, Karoz thought, his mind trying to arrange the information into a meaningful context. She must have gone out soon after I left, and she hasn't come back. The last thing I did was use the loo, and she'd used it just before the phone rang, so she probably didn't have to again before she left. But gone twenty-four hours? Where? Unless—an accident in the street? And she'd had no identification, or they'd called and no one had answered?

The cat was still meowing. And you, he thought, suddenly looking down, nobody's fed you, I suppose. He brushed past the animal and walked quickly through the bedroom and the living room and had even taken two steps into the kitchen before he saw and comprehended and stopped.

She'd been sitting on the chair that was near but not next to the table. In death her head had fallen forward, pulling her shoulders with it, and their combined weight had finally slid her off the chair and onto the floor where she now lay, crumpled on her right side. The left side of her head was exposed, and he could see the two entry wounds even before he came close.

He knelt beside her and touched her arm. He lifted her left wrist and slowly passed his palm beneath hers. She couldn't have been dead for more than an hour or so. Her fingers still flexed, her skin was still nearly warm.

The cat came up behind him and meowed.

"Sophie," Karoz said softly. He leaned forward and put the back of his hand in front of her opened mouth, as if checking for breathing, though he had known the moment he saw her that she was dead. He touched her hair and her cheek. Gentle Sophie, who wouldn't hurt a flea. Who never questioned, never made demands; who took his absences with equanimity and his silences with patience. Whose gentle dimpled smile was worth all the suns of summer. Who was an island of peace and contentment—indeed, sometimes the only sanity left for him.

They hadn't even made love that last night. Nor the night before. Now, suddenly faced with her like this, he was having a hard time knowing when they had last made love. More than anything else, they were like old marrieds, each keeping his or her own counsel, each having his or her own interests, having sex when one or the other felt the urge but not having to prove anything. They didn't even like the same music. He touched her arm again. It had never occurred to him before, but now he realized that at some time he must have begun to love her. He had no idea how she had felt about him. It was something they had never discussed.

He stood. The toilet seat. Prints. She must have let him in. Witnesses? He started for the telephone and then stopped just as suddenly and walked slowly back. He bent over her again. Her arms had been back in an awkward position, he had noticed that before. Now he saw behind the chair the cord of her bathrobe, fallen into a heap on the floor just near the edge of a puddle of blood. He rocked back on his heels and imagined it: she sitting in the chair, her arms tied behind her, then the person loosening her hands and shooting her. It was no robbery. The place was in a mess, but it was the mess they lived with all the time, not the result of a ransacking. It was no rape, either. Sophie was still fully dressed, her pants still fastened at the waist.

He stood slowly then and saw the two plastic bags, one of them unpacked. Apples lay on the table, and two oranges and a bunch of lettuce. Her coat was thrown over a chair. She had come home from shopping, and he was waiting for her.

Why the cord? What was he doing?

He glanced back at the cord behind the chair where it had fallen when it was released, when whoever it was had freed her arms. Not tied, not tied at all. That wasn't what the cord had been used for. It was then that it dawned on him, though he still didn't want to believe it. He wracked his brain trying to remember what she knew. *Mac.* The name, she knew the name. *They think they killed me the second time*, Mac had said. Karoz shook his head. "Not anymore," he whispered. *Where next?* he wondered. But he hadn't finished with the first thing yet. They knew him. They had gotten to him. And that meant his calls to Tel Aviv were perhaps doing nothing, that the Prime Minister was, for all he knew, on his way to or already in Bir el Khadim right now.

That nothing had been stopped.

That MacKinnon had been right on the money.

JERUSALEM, ISRAEL

Yakov Singer sauntered along Ben Yehuda Street, the spring sun warm on his back. There was no need for the fancy bookstore stuff this time; each would recognize the other now. It seemed a little odd that they should have to meet at all since he'd already told Weiss everything he knew over the phone, but Weiss seemed to think it was important. *We'll go over it again*, Weiss had said, *every word, just as you remember it. Perhaps he told you more than he—and you—thought. What's the matter with him, anyway? Didn't he trust you?*

Singer had winced at that, but there was little he could do or say. Meir Karoz was on his way to becoming a legend in the Institute. Singer himself had seen very little of the intelligence Karoz sent back, but the quality of what he had seen was extremely high. Karoz worked in deep cover; Singer was not sure if they had ever met face to face—if they had, Karoz would have been using a different name, neither Karoz nor the cover identity he used in London—though they had talked on the telephone occasionally. Karoz dealt almost exclusively with Landau, who ran him like a hound after the foxes. It was rumored, and Singer believed it, that Karoz had even breached The Box, the intelligence oversight group that was the most closely guarded secret in the British government. He tried to tell himself that if Karoz didn't trust him, it was probably merely the result of a highly developed sense of self-preservation.

At any rate, there was a certain amount of pride in being the middleman even if he had little of substance to pass on. It showed, despite the continuing criticism of Mossad, that Mossad had an astounding capability to put its fingers on essential information. And it was satisfying beyond measure that Weiss had come to him, was dependent on him and on the information Karoz fed him, even if it wasn't much, even if Karoz didn't quite trust him. Meir Karoz probably didn't trust anybody but Landau himself.

He was suddenly aware of Weiss beside him now, falling into step with him from out of nowhere, as if he had come alongside Singer and suddenly recognized him. Weiss nodded. Singer looked away, as if too much eye contact, even here on the street in Jerusalem, was not allowed between representatives of the services.

"Tell me again," Weiss said, "exactly what he said."
Singer repeated the conversation as best he could remember it. He had been debriefed before; he knew the importance of exact word recall, of tonations and emphases. When he had finished, he was reasonably certain he'd given Weiss a virtually exact representation of the latest conversation he'd had with Karoz.

"How did you understand the reference to the iceberg?" Weiss asked him.

"That he knew enough to know there was something dangerous, even if he didn't know everything yet."

"Yet? Did he indicate he would learn more?"

"Not this time. But he did in the first conversation."

"Which was yesterday morning."

"Yes. And then I called Shin Bet immediately because I knew—"

"Yes . . . yes. Did you have the impression that he had learned more in the interim?"

"Yes."

"Did he mention having talked with anyone? Any names?"

"I told you the whole conversation; he didn't mention

anyone's name. He didn't even say he'd talked with anyone. He just seemed more . . . certain."

"And that was exactly what time that he called?"

"Just after one o'clock. Five after, I believe, when I logged the call in. Of course they're two hours behind us in London."

"What made you think he was calling from London?"

Singer almost stopped dead still on the sidewalk; then, remembering where he was and whom he was with and that it would be less conspicuous if he kept on walking, he continued. "I just assumed," he said finally.

"Come along. Think. What made you think he was calling from London?"

"Well, he's based in London. Where else would he be calling from?"

"Is that how you people work? He's based in London, so where else would he be calling from?" Weiss shook his head in disgust.

Singer wracked his brains; there had to be some indication of where Karoz had called from. "The operator," he said at last. "When she told him to put the coins in, she had a British accent. And it was British money she was telling him."

"British. But not necessarily London."

"All right," Singer conceded, "Britain, then, at least."

"Or a place where they speak with British accents."

"It was pence she was talking about."

Weiss nodded, letting him have his little victory. "You have no particular reason to think he'll call back."

"He didn't say he would. He was trying to reach Landau, though."

"Where is Landau, really?"

Singer's head snapped around; he looked quizzically at Weiss. "I don't know."

They came to a street corner, but Weiss made no move to cross, even though they had the light. "Is he with the Prime Minister, do you think?"

"It would be my guess."

"And where is the Prime Minister?"

Singer stared, openmouthed. "I thought you knew."

Weiss smiled lazily. "I was just wondering if you did. It's time I got back." He nodded at Singer. "Time you did, too, I think." He turned and walked back in the direction from which they had come.

Yakov Singer started across the street, the last pedestrian just as the light was changing. He was lost in thought and barely noticed the light. He didn't at all see the white Fiat that roared around the corner from his left until it was too late.

Even after the Fiat struck him full force with the front of its left fender, it kept on going. Onlookers, trying to describe the car later, thought that the license plate might have been German, but it had happened so fast that no one could be sure.

LONDON

Meir Karoz leaned his left hand against the cool metal of the public telephone and waited as the line clicked and hummed and finally began ringing. One sentence was all he needed to speak, and that would make it impossible to trace the call. The moment the receiver at the other end was lifted, he began talking: "A woman has been murdered, apartment 401 of the block of flats at Maida Vale, just north of Bishop's Bridge." He hung up the receiver and touched his hand to his forehead, feeling the sweat. Poor Sophie; she never deserved that, nor to be a cadaver in some police van.

Then he fed a handful of coins into the phone, dialed another number, and waited impatiently while the cable and satellite links were completed.

"Yes," the voice at the other end said.

"I was expecting Yakov Singer," Karoz said.

"Singer is out just now. But he told me to expect your call. I am Abrams."

Karoz hesitated. But this was Mossad, after all. "He's been relaying messages from me to someone in Shin Bet. I presume you can do the same."

"Of course."

"Listen carefully. Tomorrow, a man named A. C. Mac-

Kinnon, British passport, will land in Cairo on an afternoon plane from Paris. He plans to single-handedly defend Bir el Khadim from a small attack force. He could use help. The security man with whom Singer was dealing will understand what I'm saying. Get this message to him in whatever way you can. It's urgent. And tell him, while you're at it, that Cockerel is to remain in seclusion."

"Is that all?"

"Is the Director available?"

"The Director is on holiday."

"Thank you." He hung up, looking at his watch. He could still make it to Hyde Park and the contact with Litvatov.

ZURICH, SWITZERLAND

Raymond Morse sat at a table beside a wide window of his seventh-floor suite in the Hotel Baur du Lac. From the window he could see the gardens below, still covered with snow, and the ice-bound lake beyond. The sky, a cloudless, pale blue, dropped beyond the mountains in the distance. Closer at hand, the man on the other side of the table sipped his coffee and then dabbed at his mouth with a snowy napkin. Wordlessly, Morse watched him, purposefully restraining himself from pouring more coffee. The Swiss made the best coffee in the world, there was no doubt of that, but before he indulged himself further, he would hear the man out.

Simon Keller set the porcelain cup on its saucer and in the same motion picked up the silver fork and cut another mouthful of the chocolate cherry torte. He closed his eyes, concentrating his attention on the flavors on his tongue. When he opened his eyes again, he smiled magnificently, showing his gold tooth. "Excellent," he said. "Absolutely excellent. A perfect choice, my friend."

Raymond Morse looked away, letting his gaze range fondly over the room. This one was decorated in mauve and gray. A tall, pearlescent vase, filled with spikes of iris, stood on the pale gray carpet next to the desk. The long windows afforded a spectacular view of the city and the mountains beyond, the city also looking gray under the pale sun. At this time of year Zurich breathed wealth, with skiers passing through between resorts, fur-wrapped women making hurried sorties to the nearby shops, and men shedding cashmere coats to meet in mahogany-lined boardrooms. He always enjoyed coming to Zurich.

Simon Keller leaned back in his chair, his vest stretching across an ample chest. "Yes," he said, nodding, "we had a slight scare, my friend, but it is all settled now."

Raymond Morse raised his eyebrows.

"Your partner with the guns . . ." Keller preferred not to use names, a stupid precaution, Morse thought, at the level on which they dealt, but he nodded and Keller continued. "Your partner with the guns left an unacceptable trace in California. The man contacted an associate in London. Presumably for help."

Morse leaned forward.

Keller cut himself another forkful of torte and then waited until he had fully enjoyed it to speak further. "The associate in London is Mossad, and he called his control in Jerusalem to warn the Israeli pigeon. Fortunately for us all, one of the principals from the Movement came into the loop and managed to deflect the warning."

Morse blinked once, thinking of the loose ends, trying to assess where the problems would be now.

"So the pigeon was not warned, and is, even now, at the shooting gallery."

"And the man in London?"

"He has been identified, and your partner with the guns was able to confirm the connection with the man in California. And"—he took another bite of torte, but this time, because the news he had to impart delighted him so, he didn't wait to chew it before continuing—"the London colleague phoned his headquarters again and asked for help in resisting the attackers. It seems that the California contact has even figured out the exact date of the attack."

"What are they doing about that?"

Simon Keller chuckled, a trace of chocolate-colored spittle running down the side of his chin. "The California contact will be one day late. Whatever his calculations, they were incorrect. He will be intercepted and, this time for certain, liquidated. Excuse me, but I think that is an old-fashioned term. You say now 'shopped,' I think. Or is it merely 'terminated'? I have such problems keeping current in these things." He chuckled to himself again. "And of course the Mossad one will have to be dealt with as well. He lives a rather precarious existence, so it will surprise no one if he . . . disappears."

Raymond Morse took a deep breath. "And that's it, then?"

"Quite well taken care of, I should say," Keller responded. "The Movement hadn't expected to have to lend a hand, but it turns out fortunate that they were able."

Morse frowned and looked out at the mountaintops. "The Movement knew from the start that this was a very delicate undertaking."

Keller nodded and took a sip of coffee. "And for that they are paying you all quite handsomely, I suspect." He looked around the room. "Quite handsomely."

Morse returned his gaze to the bulky man who sat opposite him. He had chosen his games well; he had never been involved in a deal that went sour and he was not interested in starting now. "For what they wanted, it will be most reasonable," he said. The end forever of talk about accommodation with the Palestinians; the fate of the occupied territories never again to be considered negotiable. The Old Man, who it was rumored was growing more moderate with age, replaced by younger, more militant leaders who would soon draw the wrath of even the most powerful supporters of a separate Palestine. As it turned out, there were indeed men who would pay quite handsomely for such assurances.

And now he wished this gross man would finish his sweet and go on his way. Raymond Morse was already thinking of the number that he wanted to call—and what he would ask for. A brunette this time, a young one. He had done his part, and now he was anxious for it all to be over. He was looking forward to going back to London and calling Pauline. He remembered the honey-colored hair and the fair British skin and the smell of asphodel. That one's name was Angela.

18

CAIRO, EGYPT

A. C. MacKinnon was the twentieth person off the plane, a position determined by long habit. The first man off any plane, and perhaps also the last, would be the most noticeable. One might wonder why anyone was in such a hurry, or why one was dawdling so. Customs officers were always more thorough with the first ones through the line. By the time they got past those first few, they had relaxed and conducted only cursory searches.

Even so, he had left the gun with Anne. He probably could have slipped it past Egyptian customs, broken apart, pieces lodged in unexpected hiding places. Once, when he had taken the identity of an independent oil consultant, he brought into Saudi Arabia two Sterlings knocked down and disguised as part of a surveyor's kit. But there had been little time for such cleverness this time around, and he couldn't risk getting hung up by customs on a gun-smuggling charge. He thought he knew where he might pick up a gun or two. And anyway, Karoz had contacts in Cairo who could get them everything they needed, and all they really needed was one good weapon apiece.

MacKinnon watched the customs agent working on the man ahead of him in line. He opened the man's passport, looked through it cursorily, then set it down and opened the man's attaché case. He lifted a couple of file folders, shoved a book over, peered into the flap on the lid, and then closed the case. He looked again briefly at the passport and then returned it, motioning the man on. MacKinnon watched the whole procedure with satisfaction; this customs search was bound to be only routine.

The customs officer now took MacKinnon's passport, hardly looking at MacKinnon as he did so. He glanced at it before laying it down. He unzipped MacKinnon's duffel, and then almost as an afterthought, he turned and called across the wide customs hall to a colleague. MacKinnon, who knew enough Arabic to get along, didn't catch the words. The man, who had been standing in casual conversation with two or three others, walked away now and disappeared through a closed door.

MacKinnon stiffened. There had been a time when he depended on some second sense to tell him when things were not quite right, and that sense was operating now. Yet the customs officer had returned his attention to the duffel bag in front of him. He was searching it quickly but thoroughly, and MacKinnon partially relaxed. The man would find nothing amiss because there was nothing amiss to find. It had been foolish to become alarmed; the two men were probably only arranging lunch together, or a coffee at some future break. There was nothing at all about MacKinnon that would attract anyone's attention.

The customs officer rezipped MacKinnon's bag and then picked up the passport and looked at it once again. He checked the picture against MacKinnon's face, then riffled through the entry and exit pages. With a professional smile he returned the passport. "Have a good visit," he said in English.

MacKinnon nodded and lifted his duffel. Nothing to it, after all.

He was almost to the exit when two uniformed men appeared at his sides. "This way, please, Mr. MacKinnon," one of them said, taking his elbow.

MacKinnon didn't even glance around. He knew that half a dozen uniformed and armed men would be ranged around the hall, waiting for him to make a move. They were going to be disappointed; he was not that big a fool.

The room they took him to was small, carpeted almost from one wall to another with an Oriental rug, still looking fine after what had probably been decades of use. MacKinnon had half-expected to see a man sitting behind a desk—that was the way these things usually began—but there was no desk, just a few upholstered chairs. There was also no window in the room. MacKinnon turned around to face his guards, but they were already backing out of the room, closing the door. He heard a lock click into place and then silence, not even the footsteps of the guards walking away. The door was solid oak, but even so he should have been able to hear the footsteps on the bare floor outside, unless the guards hadn't walked away.

MacKinnon set his duffel on the floor and walked slowly around the room, running his hands along the wall as he went. Then he lifted the rug and looked at the floor underneath. No windows, one door, locked and probably guarded. It was a pleasant enough looking room, but in fact it was no better than a prison cell. MacKinnon sat down in one of the chairs. He should have brought a gun in after all. It wouldn't have been any worse for him if they had found it, and if they hadn't, he'd be far ahead of where he was now. He thought of what was in his duffel, and then he stood and withdrew the belt from his pants.

It was more than an hour before the lock on the door clicked open. MacKinnon sat straighter. His belt was wrapped around the knuckles of his right hand, the buckle out, in such a way that he could either use it as it was or quickly pull it out with his left hand to form a garrote. They would expect him to try something, if at all, when they first opened the door; and because they would be expecting it, he was sitting calmly in the chair furthest from the door. *Proper timing won more battles than precipitous action*, Sergeant Major Hawk used to say.

The door opened and the two guards entered, one after the other. They were followed by two men in civilian clothes, suit coats unbuttoned, and with the darting eyes endemic to security men.

MacKinnon smiled to himself. Four against one, and the only weapon he had was a belt. He let his right hand drop slowly to his side, out of sight of the four men. He'd seen worse odds than these before, but what made him curious was that the security men were not Egyptians, nor even any kind of Middle Easterners. He would have bet money, in fact, that they were Americans.

The two guards stood beside the door, and one of the security men took only a couple of paces beyond it before hitching back his jacket in a move that was meant to convey readiness. "Please stand," he said.

The other security man, well over six feet in height and with short blond hair, stepped closer to MacKinnon. He grinned when he saw MacKinnon's right hand. "I don't think you'll be needing that," he said, relieving MacKinnon of the belt. As MacKinnon had guessed it would be, his accent was American. With quick, professional moves, he patted MacKinnon down, then stepped back and picked up the duffel bag. "Nor this, for the time being."

He took the duffel out of the room, followed by the two Egyptians.

A few moments later two more men walked into the room. The second one was obviously another security man, but it was the first one who caught MacKinnon's attention. He was smaller than MacKinnon by a good four inches, pudgy around the waist, with receding hair combed back from a deep widow's peak and thick round glasses on a round face. He looked exactly like the kind of boy they'd have called a "pigger" in MacKinnon's school days, the type they would have teased unmercifully. Under the circumstances it hardly surprised MacKinnon that this one also looked and dressed like an American.

"Mr. MacKinnon," the man said, stepping forward and extending his hand.

MacKinnon glanced at the two security men and then back at the man in front of him. The man's hand was still extended.

"Excuse me," the man said. "You're not an American, are you?"

"No, I'm not."

"The name is Howard Kammer; I should hardly expect you to recognize the face. I understand you've been in New Zealand for the last several years."

MacKinnon gazed at the man. "You're—"

"Yes," Kammer confirmed. "And it seems that each of us is connected with a very persuasive woman." He was grinning now.

MacKinnon smiled, too. *Annie.* "The best I'd hoped for here was to get a number where I could reach you. And then I'd expected to have to do some hard and fast talking just to get you to listen."

"They've done some of your hard and fast talking for you." He turned and motioned MacKinnon back to the chair and sat down himself with an audible sigh. "I was coming to Cairo anyway. It didn't involve much of a change in schedule. But I know precious little, and frankly I'm unconvinced, so you're still going to have to do that hard and fast talking."

MacKinnon sat down again. He'd been taking the measure of Howard Kammer since he entered the room, even before he knew who the man was. It was important, he'd always thought, to know exactly whom it was one was speaking with. Not what a person's name was or his job, but what kind of person he was. He was not yet sure of Kammer, and he was also not ready to trust the things he had heard and read about him in the last few days.

"I served almost all of my adult life in the British military, nearly all of that time in the SAS, the Special Air Service," he began. "That's the British equivalent of what you call special forces, although I use the word *equivalent* very advisedly. The SAS Regiment is the best in the world. Maybe only the Israeli Unit 269 is close. That's not chauvinism, that's fact. On the other hand, most of your special forces are a joke. You people don't fund them well, and even after all this time, you still haven't figured out how to organize them or how to use them effectively. As for my experience, you can check on that if you like."

Kammer nodded, and MacKinnon wondered if he'd already taken time to check.

"I was involved in a number of operations, and I did a fair amount of training. It seems I was quite good at that, the training." He shifted in his chair; he'd been sitting too long for his taste. "After I left the Regiment I went to New

Zealand, where I've been working on a sheep station for the last seven years. I worked sheep when I was a youngster, so it was a natural thing for me to do. I'll tell you something you may not know, Mr. Kammer. Sheep are incredibly stupid animals. They'll follow a lead sheep right off the edge of a cliff, if that's where he goes. Men, on the other hand, have to be trained for weeks to do such things."

Kammer tilted his head and frowned. "I would have thought you'd speak more highly of the men you've trained and led over the years."

"It's not the men I've trained that are the problem. It's the men who concoct the schemes and lead them against all their best interests that I misprize."

Though MacKinnon had paused, Kammer said nothing. His eyes were still on MacKinnon's. MacKinnon had come to the conclusion that those eyes were Kammer's best feature. From behind fat lenses they looked bigger than they must really be, and they held to a person in a way that MacKinnon had rarely seen. He had the feeling that Kammer was absorbing him, absorbing everything he said and a great deal that he was leaving unsaid. He had the feeling that Kammer was a very intelligent man.

"Excuse me," MacKinnon said, "but some of what I have to say is not for anyone else's ears." He didn't even look at the other men in the room.

Kammer glanced up at his security men and then looked back at MacKinnon. "They're used to hearing secrets. It's part of the job."

"But I'm not used to telling them in front of an audience."

Kammer stared at him for a few moments and then nodded for the men to leave.

When the door had closed behind them, MacKinnon went on: "I was hired to train what is called a surgical strike force, an assassination force, actually, to infiltrate by night a desert location and kill everyone there. The main target was to be Moammar Qaddafy, but to make sure we got him, we were to kill everyone present. My understanding was that it was probably funded by a number of countries—or maybe by just one country wealthy enough to spend a few million dollars on such a project. Such a country or countries would be able to see the benefits of eliminating the man but would have constraints of one kind or another against doing it themselves. It would not be the first time, I believe, that the United States government, for example, funded private parties to do what it couldn't constitutionally do itself. Am I not correct?"

Kammer nodded wordlessly.

"One assumes that when recruiting is going on in a country, and even more when training is taking place, the officials of that country at least countenance the project if not actually support it. That's the way such secret operations happen. When the training was done in the United States and when I discovered that most of the recruits were former American servicemen, I came to the logical conclusions. I believe now that that was the intent of the organizers—unless, of course, you are about to tell me that in fact in the highest reaches of your government an operation to eliminate Qaddafy actually has been put into operation."

"Your surmise is correct, Mr. MacKinnon. Such a plan has not even been discussed during this administration, I can assure you."

"And you would know if it had been?"

"I would. It might"—Kammer paused to clear his throat —"be done over my objections, but I would at least be aware of it."

MacKinnon was silent.

"I would know," Kammer repeated.

MacKinnon shifted in his chair. "Then who would you like to think that I trained sixteen men to kill, if not Qaddafy and his aides?" MacKinnon asked.

"I already know who you think."

"We searched the news stories to see if we could figure that out, Anne Rowen and I—did you talk with her, by chance?"

"I did." Kammer nodded.

"It was she who made the connection: you coming to the Middle East with what you believe is an important new

proposal and not scheduling a visit to the Prime Minister of
Israel. One would think that a little odd, certainly."

Kammer nodded but said nothing.

"And also, it seems, not with the President of Egypt, who
would be expected to support any moderate proposal and
would therefore ordinarily be consulted."

He paused, but Kammer still said nothing.

"The Prime Minister of Israel and the President of Egypt,
both unavailable to meet with the American Secretary of
State on what should be a matter of utmost importance. To
them both, I should think. What might they be doing that is
more important? And who might they be doing it with?"
MacKinnon shifted in his chair again. "Unfortunately, the
man who might really be able to help make peace in the
Middle East, the one man the majority of Palestinians would
trust, does not publish his daily schedule or his itinerary, so
it was not possible to locate him. And, unfortunately, you
had not attempted to meet with him."

"We are still being quite cautious—"

"Yes, and Israel refuses to meet with him, don't they?
They won't speak with representatives of the PLO, and
that's the rub. And that's also how some people want to
keep it, wouldn't you say? But let's back up a minute. In the
fall of 1977, Menachem Begin and Anwar Sadat met secretly
in the Sinai. At that time those two ironed out the beginning
of an accommodation between the two countries that was
publicly hinted at shortly afterward when Sadat made his
famous trip to Israel to address the Israeli Knesset. And
eventually there was Camp David. But first there was Bir el
Khadim, a meeting in a remote desert outpost between the
leaders of two countries that had been at each other's
throats for years. If another, similar meeting were held between two leaders—one of them this time being of even
more importance than the President of Egypt—where more
secret and more secure than the same place? Bir el Khadim."

Kammer was leaning forward, his eyes almost unblinking
behind the wide circles of his glasses.

"I was at Bir el Khadim the first time. Perhaps you didn't
know that." MacKinnon paused, but Kammer made no re-

action. "Each representative brought one aide. Each was also allowed to nominate a more or less neutral country that would provide security in the form of two military or special forces personnel. I was one of the Brits. I know Bir el Khadim. I also know that the mock-up of the camp Qaddafy was supposedly staying at—the mock-up that we used for training for five weeks in the California desert—could have been a double for the outpost at Bir el Khadim."

"Didn't the similarity strike you immediately?" Kammer asked. "Weren't you suspicious?"

"I should have been. Maybe I was. But, as I told you, one makes assumptions when one is hired for an out-op. That's an operation that's out of the bounds of normal operations. Recruiting and training in the States means U.S. support, or at least approval. That should have been a given."

Kammer leaned back in his chair. "What made you change your mind?"

"In the first place, I wasn't to go, which was odd, but at least not unheard-of. I accepted that as a quirk of the particular operation until the second thing happened. That was that they tried to kill me when the training was over." Kammer didn't react, and MacKinnon guessed that Annie had already told him that much. It flashed through his mind that Kammer might already have been told everything that MacKinnon had just said. It was a sign of the man's intelligence that he'd wanted to hear it again from a cleaner source. "That put a different light on things. When people begin tying up the ends, it means something. That was when I decided to find out what it meant."

Kammer nodded, and MacKinnon once again had the feeling that the man had already come to some conclusions of his own. "And what do you want of me?" Kammer asked.

"Two things. One: you may be the only person in the Middle East right now who can get through the very heavy security that's been thrown over this. No one is going to want to admit to what's going on. Maybe no one in Israel or Egypt even knows for sure. But somehow the people at Bir el Khadim have to be gotten out and gotten out fast. We don't have weeks on this; if we're lucky, we have one or two days. If we're not lucky, we have a matter of hours."

"How do you know the timing?"

"For security's sake, the strike was to take place in the dark of the moon. Get yourself an almanac if you don't believe me, Mr. Kammer. Tonight and the next two nights. That's it."

"And the other thing?"

"Help me get to Bir el Khadim."

"Why? If the conferees are gotten out, why would you need to go?"

"Were you ever in the military, Mr. Kammer?"

"No."

"A sergeant is responsible for his men, Mr. Kammer. I trained them. I built them into a unit that will act with precision and intelligence and a fierce will. What's more, I trained them so that they would follow their leader into hell. But I didn't train them to be betrayed by their leader, and that is just what's going to happen, whether the strike at Bir el Khadim is successful or whether you've managed to get everybody out before the strike force arrives. Either way, when Colonel Ken Glover decides that the time has come, my men are going to be killed. They're loose ends, too, you see."

Behind his glasses Kammer's eyes blinked once. "They'll follow this Glover, not you."

"That's correct."

"You'll be fighting them."

"That may be."

"You might be the one who's killing them. What's the difference?"

"If I do it right, I won't be killing them."

"One man against—what did you say?—sixteen?"

"I have to. They're my men."

"You're going to need some help. Maybe I—"

"I'm expecting some help—another man who was at Bir el Khadim and therefore who knows it, and who has as much reason as I to want to foil such a plan."

"Two against sixteen is still not very good odds."

MacKinnon grinned. "Don't forget who trained them. They may be a bloody fine fighting machine, but they're my fighting machine and that means I know them. You do your job, Mr. Kammer; you get those people out of there if you can, and you smooth the way for us to get in. After that, you leave the worrying to us. You're going to have enough to do as it is."

MacKinnon rose then, and Kammer slowly followed suit.

"You haven't told me who you think is behind this plan," Kammer said.

"That's for you people to sort out. That's politics and I'm a soldier; I don't know about politics."

Kammer took MacKinnon's hand and shook it hard. "Mr. MacKinnon, I suspect you know a great deal more than you let on. How are we going to get in touch with each other?"

AGHIOS GIORGIOS ISLAND, THE MEDITERRANEAN

Ken Glover stood at the summit of the headland, looking southeastward. The men had run four perimeters of the island this morning; even after all the travel, they were still in top shape.

The island was uninhabited and privately owned; it offered utmost security. Although its terrain was little more than stone and brush, it was still quite different from Bir el Khadim except for the inhospitable nature of both places. Geographically it was perfect. It hung below the southwest edge of Cyprus like a shy child not quite willing to venture out on its own. And that made it a virtual twin to Gavdo Island, which clung similarly to Crete.

Gavdo was where the men thought they were, barely two hundred miles from the Libyan coast. They had studied the maps Glover had shown them. Aghios Giorgios was where they really were, just slightly more than two hundred miles from the coast of the Sinai.

Travel to Aghios Giorgios had been uneventful, as had everything else related to the operation, Glover thought. Using four separate flights, the men had flown from San Diego to New York. Then, still using four different flights, they had traveled to Athens, all arriving within six hours of one another. Some of the men traveled in suits and carried attaché cases. The rest wore leisure clothes, as if on vacation. Diversified like that in both flights and clothing, they attracted no attention. At the Athens airport they had been picked up in two unmarked rented vans and transported over rain-slicked streets to Piraeus and the Limani Hotel, a quiet businessmen's hotel within view of the harbor.

After dark the men had slipped out of the hotel by ones and twos, dressed now in jeans and dark sweaters as if looking for a casual evening's entertainment. Though none of them took a direct route, within two hours all had managed to find the freighter *Anna Maria*, sailing under Panamanian registry. Once aboard the *Anna Maria*, they were directed to a series of cabins aft on the ship where they stayed for the next day and a half as the *Anna Maria* made its way slowly from Piraeus to Aghios Giorgios, stopping once at Paros to unload a shipment of refrigerators and once at Karpathos with tractor parts. Because none of the men had ever sailed the Aegean before, none of them realized that the trip to Gavdo should have taken less time; if they suspected it, the expenditure of time could always be explained by the need to sail out of the way in order to make the scheduled stops.

Tonight, with no moon to light the way, Glover would fly them in the Sikorsky to a site within eight miles of Bir el Khadim. He'd go in low, ducking the radar that scanned the whole Sinai coast. After they touched down, there would still be time to hike to the lying up position on the slopes of Gebel Megmar, overlooking Bir el Khadim, before first light. Then they would wait out the day, and tomorrow night they would make the strike they'd all been waiting and training for.

And they were ready, as he was. Mac had done it beautifully, including what had always been Mac's touch: Pavloving them in the end to eat out of Glover's hand, not his own. They were Glover's, not Mac's; by now they would go into hell itself for him.

And Raymond Morse had come through beautifully as well, making all the arrangements, everything coming together perfectly, whether transportation or a training site that so closely approximated the operation site that it was scary or this final staging site, which so closely mimicked Gavdo that the men thought they were four hundred miles farther west than they really were.

Even Kherman Shahabad, whom Glover had not trusted from the beginning, had managed it. When they had landed on Aghios Giorgios, the Sikorsky was already there, loaded with the Kalashniknovs, the Uzis, the grenade launchers—everything—and watched over by a pair of silent, beefy guards who said little but carried Kalashnikovs with them wherever they went. Shahabad himself had not shown up yet, though Glover still expected him. Only thirty miles off the coast of Cyprus; it would not be difficult for Shahabad to manage it.

In the meantime they had only to wait.

19

It was all falling apart. No matter what the contact in Zurich said, it was clear now that it was all falling apart.

Shimon Weiss stood at the window and looked absently out at the darkness that was enveloping the city. A break in the plan that had at first seemed easy to patch, then another break and another, and the patches were no longer holding. Though it should have been his job to keep the fissures from spreading, he knew now it had gone beyond his control. And his responsibility had been only for backup, in case some little detail went wrong. Now suddenly it was all going wrong.

Meir Karoz had called again, his call being delayed because it should have been handled by Singer, who was, at the moment of the call, lying dead in the street, having become too knowledgeable and therefore an unacceptable loose end. The normal quiet efficiency of Mossad had been interrupted, a momentary blip in the order of things. And then they had settled down, and someone had called Shin Bet and someone had asked the right questions, and finally, just over an hour after Karoz's call from London, there had been a quick coded message to Shimon Weiss's office. A. C. MacKinnon would be arriving in Cairo tomorrow afternoon and could use help.

Weiss had smiled to himself at the time. Too late, he had thought. Almost certainly too late. And then he had sat down to assess the damage. MacKinnon alive. Almost certain confirmation of that fact, finally. And that meant the links were still not broken, the trail not covered. They could cancel the operation; it was not too late. But the pigeons were already in Bir el Khadim, and MacKinnon had guessed —or had learned—that it was to be Bir el Khadim.

MacKinnon knew Glover and had seen the other two, whether or not he knew them by name or reputation. With MacKinnon alive no one could claim Palestinian involvement and make it stick. Neither PFLP nor any other dissident group would have hired a force to do their dirty work; they had Palestinians in camps all up and down the Bekaa Valley waiting for a chance to kill for a liberated Palestine. And go to Paradise as a reward for their faithfulness. No, the newspapers would tear at the story like a pride of hungry lions, ripping the careful deceptions apart and leaving the bones to bleach in the sun.

MacKinnon was a certainty; he'd have to be killed. And beyond that would depend on how much talking MacKinnon had already done. Meir Karoz for sure. Who else?

He had thought then, at midafternoon, that he had another day to plan it. He'd slammed his office door and stood before the map of Israel that covered half of one wall, thrust his fists deep into his pockets, and begun working it out. Damage control. At first he had worked on eliminating those who knew and going on with it. Then he'd thought briefly of aborting the strike, but leaking the meeting to the press, hoping that that would be almost as damaging. But in the beginning of the planning they had decided that a simple leak wouldn't be damaging enough. Avram Gershon would slide out of that as easily as he slid out of every other problem. Gershon, with his European suits, his effete manner, and his quick tongue, could talk his way out of a sheik's harem.

No, there was nothing for it but to go to Cairo this evening, be there when MacKinnon arrived tomorrow, and present MacKinnon with an offer of Shin Bet help. In that way he could go inside, assess the damage already done, and then make a decision. With any kind of luck, killing MacKinnon and perhaps one or two others would pull the thing back on track. It should have been Shahabad's job, but he was needed elsewhere. At this point in the game there was no other option.

He had turned away from the map, compartmentalizing already. He'd made a call to arrange transportation to Cairo for later this evening, then he'd made two more calls: one to the support desk for outside security of the Prime Minister, and another to his counterpart in Mossad. Then he put the whole business out of his mind for the next few hours while he attacked the paperwork that had been building on his desk.

At seven twelve a message was hand-delivered. A Mossad agent who worked at Cairo airport had reported that A. C. MacKinnon had arrived on a four-thirty flight from Paris and had been taken into custody immediately. He had been kept under guard for just over an hour before the American Secretary of State arrived and met in private with him. No one else had been in the room; there was no chance of learning what had transpired without talking with one of the two men involved.

Shimon Weiss stood abruptly behind his desk. He swore, walked briskly to the window, stared out into the gathering dark, and swore again. Then he cleared his mind. Almost two hours since that meeting. MacKinnon ahead of him. Someone— Karoz—passing on the wrong information. Intentional? He pounded the heel of his fist against the window jamb. Falling apart—unless he could pull it back together.

He looked at his watch. There was no point in trying to arrange faster transport to Cairo. He was set to leave in little more an hour anyway.

Shimon Weiss took the time for it. There was a host of things he might be doing, but he took the time because he felt the need. He walked between the carob trees of the Avenue of the Righteous. The low-ceilinged, bunkerlike building of Yad Vashem was closed at this time of night, but it didn't need to be open. In his mind's eye he saw the flame, flickering light and shadow against the rough lava rock behind it. He saw the names on the floor: Treblinka, Auschwitz, Belsen, Chelmno . . . on and on, twenty-one of the largest, of the worst. Including the name that he never looked at.

He saw again the line, moving slowly, inexorably, toward

the freight cars. A man, tall, slim, with round glasses that reflected the light. A woman, almost a head shorter, with a print dress and a wistful smile. A boy, almost ten, dark hair ruffled in the wind. A girl, six, in a dress of fabric that matched her mother's. The girl carried a doll; the mother carried an infant. And each person held one bag, all they were allowed. Suddenly a woman breaks through the ranks of the watching crowd. She has a blanket, which she shakes out and wraps around the shoulders of the mother. She kisses the mother on the cheek and just as quickly merges into the crowd and is lost. Because the mother now has a blanket around her shoulders, no one who might have been watching notices that she no longer holds the infant. He is gone. Three days later the woman, whose husband already flies with the Luftwaffe, will pack two suitcases, close her house, and go to live with her mother in Dortmund for the duration. She will take with her the infant, whom she will pass off to all but her mother as her own, and one picture of a neighbor family, a husband and a wife and a son and a daughter, taken the spring before at a backyard picnic, which she will one day give to the child.

Shimon Weiss chose a path that took him across the park and down the side of the hill. He was on chipped stone now, walking slowly past stone grave markers. He paused at a familiar one: Ari Herzl, blown out of his fighter at the age of twenty-seven in the Yom Kippur War. And, walking along the paths, another: Michael Cohen, a private, shot by a sniper in the territories. A new grave, not yet a year old.

He walked more briskly now, his time growing short. There, the grave of Netanyahu, who died at Entebbe. And all the thousands of other graves, lives proudly given. None of these thinking that their lives were more important than the State of Israel. It was a code he understood and believed and had held as he himself had gone under fire. It was a code they all understood, because Israel had been under siege from the day it was born.

He left the cemetery, hurrying now because he had lingered longer than he should have.

CAIRO, EGYPT

Meir Karoz stood in line, a copy of the *London Times* folded under his arm. His passport identified him as James Mc-Hugh Evanson, born in Liverpool, a resident of London. On his entry card he gave his occupation as home furnishings importer, the purpose of his visit as tourism. That would explain the heavy walking boots, the sand-colored pants and shirt, the webbed belt with canteen, compass, and other items the customs officer couldn't identify, all carried in a dun-colored backpack half-slung over Karoz's shoulder.

"You will go to Valley of Kings?" the customs official asked.

"Most definitely."

"You are prepared to walk in desert?"

Karoz smiled broadly. "I am always prepared to walk, my good man. Walking is food for the soul."

The man blinked and returned the passport. The English were a peculiar race. Six generations of English in Egypt, and still they were difficult to comprehend.

Karoz walked out of the terminal and waved for a taxi.

Twenty minutes later the Swissair flight from Jerusalem landed in Cairo, and Shimon Weiss, negotiating customs, walked through the same line as Meir Karoz had.

The taxi careened through the dark streets of Cairo, scattering a wake of pedestrians sent scurrying for safety. Meir Karoz sat in the middle of the backseat, hardly noticing. He still saw the scene in his mind's eye: Sophie, even more plain and more vulnerable in death than she had been in life, crumpled on the dingy floor of her own kitchen.

He kept seeing her like that, her eyes staring vacantly, seeing nothing. The first time he had killed a man, the dead face had haunted him for weeks afterward. The second time it had been less; the third even less. Finally a time came when the faces almost didn't haunt him at all.

But Sophie was different. He had seen friends and comrades killed before, but that again was another thing. Odd that it was MacKinnon again. He'd been young in Bir el

Khadim—barely twenty-seven then, though God knew he'd seen enough before that time to make age irrelevant.

Sophie was thirty years old—more than ten years younger than he—and for the last three years they had made a life for themselves. A peculiar kind of life if one looked at it dispassionately, but one that suited them. Or at least it had suited him. In the dim light of the bedroom her pale, yielding flesh would glow to ivory, like a Botticelli painting, and she would gather him into the folds of her body in movements at once erotic and nurturing. On other nights they had lain together in the same bed hardly aware of each other's presence. She had never asked for more than he had given, and he had never given what he might have.

The life doesn't suit itself to marriage. The words, spoken quietly into the night all those years ago, had found a home in his mind. *You're up and off without a word, and she spends her days and nights wondering where you are and when, if ever, you'll come back. And when you do, there's bound to be arguing and recriminations, and she'll end up locking you out of the bedroom, or you'll slam out of the flat and go down for a drink with the boys.* He had carried those words as if they were true, not so much because he had believed them but out of trust in the man who had given them. "It's as good as marriage anyway," Sophie used to say. And he would respond, "It's better." And she had believed it.

It had gotten her dead.

He wondered if marriage would have been worse.

He wondered if MacKinnon, after all these years, would still say the same things.

A. C. MacKinnon walked slowly onto the terrace at the side of the Mena House Hotel. A kilometer away, lights played on the Great Pyramid as the *Son et Lumière* show began. He heard but did not listen to the dull rumble of sound and the voice that began the presentation. Instead, his hands in his pockets, he stood for a moment facing eastward, away from the pyramids and the sounds and light of the production. Eastward, beyond the nighttime glow of Cairo's lights, toward the dark. Two hundred and thirty-three miles, by his best calculation.

Something—a second sense, a change in the breath of air, a new scent caught in the perfume of roses and oleanders— made him turn. Against the cast of distant colored lights he could see only the form of the man, shorter than he. Mac-Kinnon watched him come.

"They know," Karoz said without preamble. "You can count on it; they know."

"How much do they know?"

"They came to the flat and killed Sophie. She would have told them what she knew, which was that you had called and I left." He heard the soft expulsion of MacKinnon's breath behind his own words. He did not explain or defend Sophie. Nor did he explain the obvious—how they must have found her in the first place.

"God," MacKinnon said, but he wasn't thinking of God at all. He turned away and walked a few paces along a path of the terrace garden.

"I placed one more call, asking for help," Karoz said behind him. "I said you'd be coming to Cairo tomorrow afternoon. Thought I'd give you twenty-four hours at least."

"And see who you could flush?"

"That, too."

"That's a dodgy game you're trying to play."

"The whole fucking thing is dodgy," Karoz said. "What have you got for us?"

"I'm working on transportation, and I've managed a couple of handguns. I'm still counting on you for the power."

"It might have been compromised by now."

"It had bloody well better not have been!"

Karoz said nothing. He was still not going to defend Sophie. She hadn't known anything about what he was, and he had no right to expect her to have held back.

"You'll go tonight, now, right away."

Karoz nodded.

"I'll go with you."

Without further discussion Karoz turned and headed

toward the hotel. He made a call from the lobby while MacKinnon found a cab to take them back to the city.

They took the cab to Gezira Island, and from there they walked the rest of the way, crossing back on El Tahrir Bridge and then heading northeast along Talat Harb, past the square. On a side street they stopped at a stall offering *shwarma*, bought one apiece, and continued, munching on the spicy grilled meat. The air was mild, and the streets around them were still bustling with traffic, the sidewalks filled with young men and with couples walking arm in arm. Occasionally, in open doorways, long-robed men sat on stools and puffed on *narghiles* in silence.

Karoz turned again, this time into a darker side street. The wails of melancholy Egyptian music came from two coffeehouses, sitting side by side halfway down the block. Beyond, just out of the spill of light from the two establishments, was a white Fiat, parked at the curb. As they walked by, MacKinnon peered into the first lighted doorway, but all he could see were a half-dozen male figures sitting at tables half-obscured by a haze of smoke. The sounds of laughter and the crack of backgammon pieces and the tinny blare of recorded music reached toward the street, and then he had passed, and now he could see a man emerging from the driver's side of the Fiat.

MacKinnon stiffened and slowed, but Karoz continued, stepping into the street. Karoz met the man at the bumper of the car, and they stood in quiet conversation for a few moments. MacKinnon held back, keeping an eye on the street in both directions, and keeping an eye as well on the two doorways they had just passed.

Then the stranger unlocked the trunk of the car and unfolded a grease-stained blanket. MacKinnon took another step closer, his eyes still ranging the street. Meir Karoz was looking at the items that had been wrapped in the blanket, and MacKinnon moved forward and could now see the dull black of metal. He leaned closer. Two Uzis. He'd rather have an MP5 or a Sterling, but he'd take what he could get.

Karoz was talking to the other man again, and now that MacKinnon was closer he could tell they were speaking Hebrew. Karoz kept glancing at MacKinnon, and MacKinnon was now keeping not only both ends of the street but also the two men under surveillance. Suddenly the third man threw the blanket over the guns and slammed the trunk shut. MacKinnon's full attention was on him now, but the man's eyes had shifted to somewhere beyond MacKinnon's shoulder.

MacKinnon could hear now a change in sound coming from the nearest door, and he half-turned. Two men were exiting the coffeehouse. They turned right and took two steps toward the Fiat, and then it seemed to register with them that there were three men gathered around the trunk of the car. They looked at each other and, without exchanging a word, turned and walked in the opposite direction.

Karoz placed his hand on the trunk and said one sentence in Hebrew. The man responded with a single syllable, turned, and headed toward the driver's side again. Karoz motioned to MacKinnon and opened the door on the other side. MacKinnon got into the back, and Karoz sat in front. They drove quickly through streets that MacKinnon didn't recognize, though he could tell the direction was north and then northwest. The Fiat stopped finally beside an area empty of buildings that MacKinnon guessed, in the dark, to be a park of some kind. The driver got out, this time taking with him a duffel bag he'd pulled from under his seat. Karoz and MacKinnon followed. Again he opened the trunk, and without further conversation he broke the guns down, wrapped the pieces in the blanket, and then laid the whole thing carefully into the duffel. He handed the bag to Karoz, smiled briefly at MacKinnon, said a few more sentences to Karoz, and was gone.

MacKinnon watched the taillights of the Fiat growing smaller as the car moved away. "I hope you know where we are," he said.

As an answer Karoz turned left, and now MacKinnon could see the deeper darkness of the Nile not a hundred meters away. They walked toward the river, and Karoz said, "So far so good. We have the added power at least."

"At least."

"And we must not yet be completely compromised because he didn't try anything."

"Wasn't he one of yours?"

"Institute. Yes. But it had to have been the Institute that led whoever killed Sophie to the flat."

"Why the bloody hell did you get into the car with him, then?"

"I wouldn't have if you hadn't been along. But you have guns, you told me, so I thought—"

"I'm *getting* guns. I don't have any now."

"Not with you?"

"Not on me."

"Bloody fuck."

"Bloody fuck is right. One of us has been out of this business too long, Karoz."

20

CAIRO, EGYPT

The American Ambassador's residence was a pale square building three stories in height, set back from the street in a quiet neighborhood of Garden City, near the edge of the Nile and within walking distance of the Embassy. A high ornate fence surrounded the grounds, which were kept immaculately parklike with a broad grassy terrace surrounding a formal garden of roses, laurel, and camellias.

The man getting out of the taxi at the front gate was dressed in a dark suit and a red-and-blue rep tie. He could have been a high-level embassy official come to confer with the Ambassador. He spoke a few words with the guard at the gate and was nodded through. At the front door he spoke again to the guards stationed there and showed an Israeli identification. One of the guards stepped inside; within moments he returned, and the Israeli was ushered in.

Secretary of State Howard Kammer stood before the white-painted mantel of a fireplace where a gas fire burned relentlessly over fake logs. He believed in standing to receive guests, as if the gesture gave a formality and therefore an importance to the occasion. He often wondered if other men, risen to prominence by skill or luck, felt like interlopers, like trespassers in alien territory, as he did.

He heard the sharp smack of leather soles on the marble floor of the hall, and then the man entered the room; he was a head taller than Kammer, tanned and robust, with hair that was neither blond nor gray but something in-between.

Kammer held out his hand in greeting. "Colonel Weiss," he said.

Shimon Weiss stood stiffly as if at attention, nearly clicking his heels as he did so, and took Kammer's hand in a firm grip. "Mr. Secretary, it is most kind of you to see me at such short notice."

"Please," Kammer said, indicating a brocaded chair, "sit."

Weiss waited until Kammer was settled into a chair before he seated himself.

"What can I do for you?" Kammer asked.

"With your indulgence, I'll come right to the point." Kammer nodded as Weiss continued. "I have reason to think you may have been contacted recently by two men, one a British national and another an Israeli, about a matter of deepest concern, especially to the Israeli government."

"A British national and an Israeli," Kammer repeated. "What would make you think they would come to me? Why not to one of their own representatives?"

"Precisely. Because you could be a neutral party in this."

"More neutral than the American ambassador?"

"Certainly of higher rank. The aim would be to reach someone of the highest rank."

Kammer cleared his throat. "And what would be the purpose?"

Weiss glanced away, looking toward the open door, and then stood. "Would you mind if I closed the door?"

"There's really no need."

"I'd prefer it."

Kammer shrugged. "As you like."

Weiss strode to the door and closed it firmly. Kammer, uncomfortable sitting while the other man stood, rose and stepped closer to the fire.

"A planned attack on a most secret meeting place in the Sinai. They told you about it, I'm sure."

"I'm curious about how you would know such a thing," Kammer countered.

Weiss smiled slowly. "Because the Israeli is one of ours. Mossad, actually, but in this case the issue is the security of the Prime Minister, and that makes it Shin Bet business as well. Mossad and Shin Bet work together when necessary. When appropriate."

He walked closer, still smiling, and Kammer noticed now that there was something odd about his left eye.

"And in this case it happens to be both appropriate and necessary. Prime Minister Gershon's security happens to be my assigned responsibility."

"Then you've known about this meeting all along; and you must also know how to contact the place." The solution, Kammer was thinking, to the tricky problem he had yet to solve: how to warn the conferees of the imminent danger.

The corners of Weiss's mouth turned down. "Unfortunately not. Though he is my responsibility technically, the Prime Minister is partial to Mossad. Number One—the director of Mossad—reports directly to him. That fact has generally given prime ministers a special relationship to the Institute."

Kammer leaned an elbow on the mantel. He had come to realize that Weiss's left eye was glass. In an odd way the fact fascinated him, and he wondered how Weiss had gotten it. A military man: almost certainly in war, then. "And that means also that you have no way of contacting them?"

"No more than anyone else. Probably less than you, which is one of the reasons I've come here. I need your help, Mr. Secretary. The Prime Minister's life is my responsibility. I need to get him out of there. The attack could happen tonight, did they tell you that?"

Kammer nodded slowly. "And the other reason?"

Weiss seemed not to be listening. He was looking at his watch. "Five minutes after ten," he said. "Have they been able to arrange for a plane, or what?"

"You want to go with them," Kammer said.

"Of course I do. If we don't destroy that force, it'll just happen again. Another time, another place, another occasion."

"And I suppose you'd like to know who's behind it."

"It hardly matters, does it, when you have as many enemies as we do? Surely you can appreciate that."

"What is it you want of me?"

"Put me in contact with MacKinnon and Karoz."

"As a matter of fact I've already offered them my own security men, but the offer was turned down. It seems these two want to do it on their own."

"Are your security men soldiers? Do they know desert fighting?"

"No," Kammer conceded.

There was a knock at the door, and Kammer moved toward it, opening it just far enough to see one of his own security men there. He listened for just a moment and then turned to Weiss, smiling.

"Colonel Weiss," he said, "you're in luck. You can ask them yourself."

Weiss watched the men come into the room, interested in their reactions. He knew Karoz, and there was a flicker of recognition in Meir's eyes, but he said nothing. So MacKinnon's running it, Weiss thought. He would have expected it. It was MacKinnon's operation, after all. He didn't know MacKinnon except by reputation these last weeks. He looked older than Weiss had expected and somehow weary. Getting too much for him, Weiss thought. Training is one thing; going in yourself is quite another.

Kammer made the introductions in the manner of a man springing a marvelous surprise. Weiss wondered if MacKinnon thought the surprise was so wonderful. He'd seen no reaction at all in the man's blue eyes. If they were lighter in color, they might have been called icy. As it was, they somehow made Weiss think of the lens of a camera—impartially observing.

"We received your request for help, Meir," Weiss said. "As I understand it, time is of the essence."

"It is that," MacKinnon responded.

"I would like to think," Weiss went on, "that your warnings did some good. But this whole clandestine thing—I have no idea whether or not Gershon has gone there. He's somewhere in secrecy, of that I'm sure. But whether it's this or another place I haven't been able to determine. You'd think that Shin Bet would be party to such knowledge, or at the very least the man who's assigned to protect him would be informed." He was speaking directly to Karoz, and it was almost an accusation. "But he favors Mossad when it comes to deep cover. He's with your Landau, I'm almost positive of that. But where? God knows."

"Who sent you here?" MacKinnon asked.

"The messages were coming to me. It's my responsibility, after all. Through Meir's contact. I sent myself."

"Who else knows?" Karoz asked.

"I might ask you the same thing."

"Then it's up to us, isn't it," MacKinnon said. It wasn't a question. He turned to Kammer, who'd been hovering at the edge of the conversation. "The first thing—" He paused and glanced at Weiss, then back to Kammer. "Our contact in the States." Kammer nodded, not missing a beat. "That person's safety is jeopardized. I want protection. Immediately."

"I understand. Full protection. You'll have it."

"Now for the rest," MacKinnon said. "What have you been able to do?"

"I have a call in to the Egyptian Foreign Minister. There seems to be some problem locating him. The American Air Attaché is in contact with the Air Ministry."

"Will we get a helicopter?" Karoz asked.

"That's not definite yet."

"How far is it?" Weiss asked. "Can we drive it?"

"Two hundred and thirty-three miles," MacKinnon said. "Too far to drive."

"And make it tonight," MacKinnon said.

And that gives me time to call it off, Weiss thought. Or else it'll be over before we get there, which would also be acceptable. "Do you think they'll do it tonight?" he asked. "There's still a moon. Tomorrow night there'll be nothing."

"God help us," MacKinnon said. "We can hope for tomorrow night. If we don't get a copter soon, we might as well start out by car."

"There has to be some way to contact them," Kammer said. "They wouldn't go out there without that link."

"But what is it?" Karoz asked. "And who knows?"

He was looking at Weiss, but Weiss shook his head. "No one that I could find."

"And that's why we can't stand around waiting any longer," MacKinnon said.

"What else is there?" Weiss asked.

"We drive it."

"If it's tonight, we'll be too late," Weiss said.

"We drive it tonight," MacKinnon said. "We've got the car, haven't we?" he asked Kammer.

Kammer nodded.

"You'll need all the help you can get. I'm coming along," Weiss said.

MacKinnon gazed at him for a moment. "When were you last in battle?"

"When were you?"

MacKinnon suddenly grinned.

Touché, Weiss thought.

"Do you have any arms?" MacKinnon asked.

"I'll bet the Secretary's security men do."

MacKinnon turned slowly toward Kammer and then toward Karoz. "All right," he said without even looking at Weiss. "But you're going to have to hold your end."

"Don't worry about that."

It was a whole lot easier than Weiss had imagined it would be. He needed only two minutes to make the phone call, and the force would never be seen again. MacKinnon could spend the rest of his life wondering what it had been about, but everything would already have been covered. He was working it out in his mind even as they started down the hall. At Bir el Khadim he could dispose of MacKinnon and Karoz and give the story that they'd been attacked by the strike force, which had then taken off in their helicopter. Arabs—who would dispute it? Or he could wait it out with them until they concluded it had been a false alarm. Sometime in the future MacKinnon could be hit by a truck while crossing the street. Just in case. Maybe an accident for Karoz as well.

They were halfway down the hall now, Kammer accompanying them to the door. "I think," Weiss said, "that it would be a good idea, Mr. Secretary, if this whole thing were kept under wraps. I mean, permanently. As you can imagine, my Prime Minister is embarking on something that could cause serious problems politically for him if it were known. I'm sure he would appreciate your discretion."

"Naturally," Kammer said.

It would be accomplished then. At least the integrity of the operation would be preserved. And the anonymity. If they ever had another chance—pray God—they wouldn't have been blown.

21

CAIRO

MacKinnon paused, his hand on the brass door handle. "Mr. Secretary, would you call your Air Attaché once again? We need to know if they're going to get us a helicopter tonight or not."

"Certainly." Kammer dipped his head almost obsequiously and turned toward an anteroom.

"And don't forget the business in the States," MacKinnon called after him. Kammer nodded and hurried away.

"Meir," MacKinnon said, "bring the equipment around to the back. You'll see a vehicle there." Then his attention turned to Weiss. "Come with me. I need your help."

"I must make a telephone call. Check in with my office. Perhaps by now they've been able to raise a response at Bir el Khadim."

MacKinnon gazed at him for just a moment. "All right. But not just yet. Give me a hand first." He pulled the massive oak door open and stepped out. He nodded at the guards and headed briskly down the drive toward the street, aware of Weiss beside him.

At the street MacKinnon turned left, still walking fast. "What happened to your eye?"

"Six-Day War. Shrapnel."

"And that ended the soldiering. Tough luck. But evidently you stayed in."

"It ended that kind of soldiering. Yes, I stayed in. You don't necessarily need two eyes in Shin Bet; what you need is brains."

"I'm sure. Why didn't you just take your pension and find yourself a nice sunny apartment in Tel Aviv?" He had reached a cross street and turned right.

"Where are we going?"

"We've got a few things ditched around. You don't walk into the Embassy residence carrying the kind of firepower we're taking with us. So why did you stay in?"

Weiss cleared his throat. He was nearly the same height as MacKinnon, but heavier. "My whole family perished at Dachau. In the ovens."

MacKinnon didn't look at Weiss, as if it would be an intrusion, nor did he say anything. They were passing a massive house set close to the street. Light poured from its windows, and the sound of a string quartet wafted in the air around them.

"In their memory I fight," Weiss added finally. "Until breath leaves me, I'll fight. It's what I choose to give their memory."

"How did you survive?" MacKinnon's voice was quiet, barely heard above the violins.

"A neighbor. She raised me as her own. I don't know what she'd planned to tell her husband, but she was spared the lie. He never came home."

"One of the Righteous Ones." MacKinnon slowed at the corner for a passing taxi. He looked at Weiss, who nodded.

"But fucking few of them," Weiss said. "Not enough by half. If we had to leave it to others to protect us—"

"I'm a Scot," MacKinnon said. "Grew up in Liverpool," he added smoothly, as if it were true, "where the only thing worse than a Welshman is a Scot. You learn to fight your own battles, don't you?"

Weiss peered at him through the darkness, as if seeing him for the first time. "You learn not to trust anyone is what you learn. Everyone else has his own agenda."

MacKinnon nodded. "Just down here, beneath that shrubbery."

Weiss turned to look where MacKinnon pointed, and MacKinnon struck him full force on the neck with the edge of a stiffened hand. Weiss staggered, dazed and surprised. Before he had a chance to react, MacKinnon moved in and struck him again, this time at the back of the neck, hard, with the heels of both hands pressed together. Weiss went down, and MacKinnon was over him, straddling him, his thumbs forcing their way into twin pressure points at the sides of the neck.

Weiss flailed his arms and caught MacKinnon at the right ankle. MacKinnon tried to kick the hand away, but Weiss clung to it, his other hand now grabbing at MacKinnon's fingers, desperately pulling them back, trying to force them away from his neck. Now Weiss had both hands on MacKinnon's, pulling on them, tearing at their flesh with his fingernails.

MacKinnon kneed him in the kidneys. Despite Weiss's hands raking his flesh, he clung to the neck, feeling the pulsing between his fingers, sensing without even consciously thinking of it that Weiss was growing weaker.

Suddenly, with a massive surge, Weiss rose to his feet again, pushing MacKinnon's hands higher, weakening their grasp because they were now stretching above his own shoulder height. In a second desperate effort Weiss half-turned, his hands grabbing for MacKinnon's face, his fingers gouging MacKinnon's eyes. The movement, the turning, had further weakened MacKinnon's grip, and Weiss felt the renewal of blood to his head.

But MacKinnon's hands had fastened now onto Weiss's windpipe, digging into it. The full strength of MacKinnon seemed concentrated in those hands, driving powerful fingers into Weiss's neck, and Weiss again attempted to pry them away. This time, however, it was a frontal attack, MacKinnon's thumbs digging into Weiss's neck, the whole strength of the man bearing down on that one vulnerable spot.

Weiss raked his hands across MacKinnon's face twice, flailed in the air, grabbed at MacKinnon's thumbs, trying to force them back, but there was less and less air and his movements became more and more random, and his eyes bulged in realization that he was powerless against those hands, and his mouth opened for a scream, but there was only his tongue hanging out.

MacKinnon stepped back, letting the body fall, feeling older than he wanted to feel. For a moment he saw the sun shining on endless blue water and a man with hang-gliding gear stepping into the void and then the wind caught under bright red wings, and the man soared above the water, above the earth, above everything. MacKinnon shook his head then and the image left and he bent to pull the body closer under the shrubbery where passersby would be unlikely to see it.

MacKinnon found Meir Karoz at the back of the Embassy residence, leaning against the fender of a white Lincoln.

"Where's Weiss?" Karoz asked.

"What do you think?" MacKinnon asked in response. "Was he what you were trying to flush?"

Karoz shrugged. "Might have been."

"He has reason. Or at least . . . he thinks he has reason. I wasn't sure you wanted to be there. I hope you don't mind that I sent you back here while I did it."

Karoz stood straight. "Is he dead?"

"Not dead, but he's definitely disabled."

"Where is he?"

"Not far. We'll take him with us."

"Why? He'll be in the way."

"Because I don't want a question mark at my back."

"I don't want him along if that's what he is."

"Don't worry." MacKinnon grinned. "We'll keep him disabled. Who knows, maybe we can use him. What's the latest on the helicopter?"

"No word. Nothing yet."

"Then we go with the car. We'll borrow the Lincoln until we've liberated a Rover."

"A stolen car, MacKinnon, I don't know—"

MacKinnon clapped him on the back as the two walked toward the back door of the residence. "Don't tell me you're queasy on that one. By the time the Cairo police know it's missing, we'll be at Bir el Khadim."

Karoz stopped. "You said he has reason. What the hell is it?"

"Stand ground. Don't give an inch. Don't let one square centimeter of land go back to the ragheads. You've got whole parties in your little country that are predicated on that, don't you?"

"We don't kill our own for it, MacKinnon."

"You don't? Kill or be killed, isn't that the soldier's way? You've turned into a fucking nation of soldiers, my friend. What do you expect?"

Meir Karoz stared down at the body. The shoes and socks had been removed; the socks tied together now bound Weiss's ankles. A belt secured his wrists behind his back, and a second belt looped between the two bindings held his hands and feet tightly together. A handkerchief was bound around Weiss's mouth, and Karoz could almost guess that a second handkerchief was beneath, stuffed into the mouth. He glanced at MacKinnon and noticed his belt was missing. He wondered if MacKinnon's handkerchief was the one in Weiss's mouth and, perversely, if it was clean or dirty. Weiss stared, bleary-eyed, up at the two men. He's not come completely around yet, Karoz thought.

"Give me a hand," MacKinnon said. He bent down and lifted Weiss at the shoulders.

"You can't be serious about taking him," Karoz said.

MacKinnon dropped the shoulders and straightened. "We can't leave him, can we? Who can we trust him with?"

Karoz looked back down at the man on the ground, whose eyes had now fully focused. Then he leaned down and lifted the feet. Weiss struggled, kicking his feet as much as he could manage, making the task of carrying him as difficult as possible.

"Knock it off," MacKinnon said. "The alternative is we kill you."

Weiss tried a few muffled syllables through the handkerchief and then gave up. His body seemed almost relaxed as they carried him over to the Lincoln and stuffed him into the open trunk.

"You be a good scout and maybe you'll live to fight another day," MacKinnon said, looking down at him.

Karoz stared into Weiss's eyes and shook his head. "You

bastard. And you certainly didn't warn Cockerel, either, did you?"

Weiss glared back, but there was no sound from his muffled mouth. MacKinnon pulled the trunk lid closed, and then they got back into the car.

MacKinnon drove, leaving the quiet residential area, turning right onto the Corniche, heading north. Karoz, in the passenger seat, his head half-turned away, stared out at the traffic.

"You're having trouble with this," MacKinnon said.

"It's a wild story. From the start I thought it was a wild story," Karoz said. "I thought you were hallucinating. I thought you were hitting the sauce again. That's what I wanted to think anyway."

"You want out?"

"I'm here, aren't I? I thought it was fedayeen, PFLP, something like that. I wanted it to be them."

MacKinnon looked briefly at him. "You want out?" he asked again.

"It was Mossad I was calling, the usual contact. It had never been compromised before. It had to be someone inside, or someone who could get inside. It was too fast for anything else. He knew the code name, everything. Shit. Sophie." He took a deep breath and exhaled slowly. "Even then I didn't want to believe it."

"First thing you told me when you got here was that we might have been twitched."

Karoz nodded. "Yes, but I still didn't want to believe it." He looked toward the back, as if he could see into the trunk. "Shit, Shin Bet, the last line of defense. I wonder if he's the only one or if there's more."

MacKinnon shook his head and then pulled around a slow-moving truck. "We don't know for sure about him."

"Yes, we do. You do. And I do," Karoz said bitterly.

"A question mark, Meir. We can't afford a question mark at our backs, but that's what he is, no more."

"We're going the wrong way, you know that," Karoz said.

"Unfortunately. But the best place to steal a car is still an airport."

"You really mean to drive it."

MacKinnon didn't respond.

"You never really meant to get a helicopter, did you? Was that just smoke?"

MacKinnon nodded. "Part smoke. Keep people off balance, that's what I say."

"You sure it was SAS, MacKinnon? You sure it wasn't SIS instead?"

MacKinnon laughed softly. "You intelligence guys think you're the only ones with brains. Have you ever lain doggo on a barren hillside and psyched a shepherd's dog out of barking at you? Maybe even gotten peed on? Have you ever had to work out the deployment of terrorists in an embassy they've taken hostage?"

"When did you first suspect Weiss?"

"When I saw him. When did you? Same, wasn't it? Don't trust anyone, that's the way."

Karoz thought about Sophie again. "Makes for a fucking lonely life."

"Yes, it does, actually."

The airport was ahead of them now, and MacKinnon turned onto a secondary road. He circled around to the right and in five minutes was on the dark side of a car park for a rental agency. He pulled over to the side and slid out of the seat, leaving the keys in the ignition, the engine still running. "Meet me in the front," he said.

Then he was gone, around the back of the car, tapping twice on the top of the trunk as a kind of half joke, and by the time Meir Karoz had slid over and put the car in gear, MacKinnon was halfway up the chain-link fence.

22

EGYPT

The road between Cairo and Suez, while not as congested as the one to Ismailiya, is alive with traffic night and day. In daylight one can see precariously overloaded trucks and buses, decorated in fading colors and flowing Arabic appeals to Allah and festooned with plastic gew-gaws, as if such careful attention to the tools of their employment will bring not only success to the drivers but luck as well. In the dark these same trucks and buses lumber by with a roar and with the eerie glow of their headlights kept on dim in hopes of extending the life of the lamps.

They rode mostly in silence, MacKinnon at the wheel. In the pale gleam of oncoming trucks, he could see that Karoz's eyes were closed much of the time. Good sign. A man needed to catch his sleep when he could. From Suez, Karoz would drive until they reached Mitla Pass. Then it would be MacKinnon's turn to catch a few winks.

There are hills between Cairo and Suez, but mostly the road makes its way between them. Once beyond the city they were surrounded by dark, except for the trucks with which they shared the highway. Karoz's breathing had become deep and regular. Six hours, MacKinnon thought, seven at the outside. They should be in place before first light.

It was ten years since he'd been in desert like this. Ten years. The Delta Force attempt to rescue the American hostages had ended in a flash of fire and the stench of burnt flesh. He'd been in a sergeant's mess one day some months afterward, newly released and still wondering what to do with himself. He'd been half under, a partial bottle of whisky at his elbow, when Kenneth Glover slid into the chair beside him. He had known Glover from an excursion or two, but not particularly well. It was Glover who recruited him—that time, too—taking the bottle by the neck and telling him he could come but there wasn't going to be any booze.

His mind was still registering that the next day when he saw Meir Karoz again. They'd looked at each other, and then slow grins broke across their faces. For the chance to work with Meir again, he agreed to go off the bottle.

Three and a half years before that, in the fall of 1977, he'd been with Karoz in the Sinai, in a place called Bir el Khadim, where for two days in October, Anwar Sadat and Menachim Begin sat down together in utmost secrecy and worked out an agreement on how to proceed. By that time both men wanted to come to an accommodation, but both had been warned by their supporters not to proceed on their own. Nevertheless, they did it, each bringing one aide to Bir el Khadim. Sadat had brought a trusted deputy. Begin, perhaps considering where the meeting was to take place, brought Karoz, from Mossad. The rest of the security had been provided by special forces troops on special assignment, the country of origin to have been nominated by the two principals. The Israelis nominated American forces, and there were two Americans there, one of them being Glover. The Egyptians nominated the British, and two SAS men, MacKinnon and one other, joined the Americans.

The world never learned about that meeting. On the fifth of November, King Hussein warned Sadat against negotiating a Palestinian deal with the Israelis on his own, not knowing that Sadat had already met with Begin at Bir el Khadim. On November 9, Sadat announced to the Egyptian People's Assembly that he was ready to go to the Israeli Knesset itself to discuss Israeli withdrawal from the Sinai, and the whole world was astounded—the whole world, that is, except for fewer than ten men who had spent those two days at Bir el Khadim.

Nearly four years later, when Glover recruited MacKinnon for the excursion into Iran, MacKinnon had indeed been pleased with the chance to work with Karoz again. Karoz was not to go in, of course; that would have been too risky. But he was the coordinator, and that let MacKinnon and the others know who was behind it. No one ever said exactly who the people were that they were to rescue, but everyone could guess: Israeli informers caught inside Iran by the revolution, and probably in danger of being compromised. One thing you could say for the Israelis: they always took care of their own. And that was more than you could say for some others.

The operation had been half successful. Three men were in custody in a police jail in a town nobody had ever heard of in south central Iran. They got two out all right, but the third had been injured in a firefight at the jail, and even though they carried him along with them, he died in the helicopter even before it left Iranian air space. Better by far than what Delta Force had been able to do, but at least the Americans were eventually all released. One couldn't have hoped for such good fortune for Israeli operatives caught inside the Iranian revolution. Two out was probably still better than three in.

But it had been too close a call for all of them—the mad dash across the desert to the rendezvous with the helicopter and the ground fire catching them as they lifted off—and it was enough to make MacKinnon think again. Perhaps he was getting too old for this kind of thing. Perhaps he needed to get off the bottle and stay there. Perhaps he needed to regain something of what he had lost, though he hardly knew how to begin to find that, or even what it might be.

The one redeeming feature of it all was that he had done something with Karoz again. MacKinnon had admired a number of men in his life for one reason or another, but there had been precious few whom he had genuinely liked. Meir Karoz was one. If he had ever had a son, he would have wanted him to be like Meir. If he'd had a daughter that he'd raised himself and therefore had a right to have hopes for her life, he would have wanted her to marry a man like Karoz.

If. If a lot of things. If he'd known what he was doing in the first place. If the adrenaline and the time with the boys and the booze hadn't been so important. If he'd known then some of the things he knew now. He wondered about Meir's Sophie: what she was like and what she had been for him and what it was about her that Meir was keeping back, was not yet ready to talk about.

He wondered about Laurie: where she was, what she was doing, what she might be like. If he found her, what would he say to her? Did she even know that he existed? Why did he think after all this time that he had anything to say that she would want to hear?

He thought about a building that looked unlike any he had ever seen before, a building that looked more like a treehouse than a regular sort of building, and he wondered what things would have been like if everything had been different.

Then he put those thoughts out of his mind and concentrated on Bir el Khadim.

BIR EL KHADIM, THE SINAI

Avram Gershon stepped outside, into the dark. He heard a chair scrape, and then the door to the building closed softly. He glanced to his right; Landau stood there, silent, a half step to his rear. Gershon lit a cigarette.

"You haven't asked the obvious question," Gershon said.

Landau didn't respond.

"You don't approve, do you?" Gershon pressed.

"It's not my place to approve."

Gershon smiled. Nor mine to ask approval, he thought. "It's a correct answer," he said, "but no Israeli in his right mind is without opinion on this."

"I manage to keep my opinions to myself most of the time," Landau said.

"And other things as well, which is one reason I brought you. But I am going to tell you something. If you want to think it is self-justification, go ahead. Perhaps it is that. I prefer to think that I want at least one other person to really understand what this is all about. Once a nation, or even individuals for that matter, embark on a specific path, they usually persist in following it, even if it turns out to be wrong, until some kind of catastrophe occurs. Unfortunately, Israel is not a laboratory where, if one experiment fails, we can try another. The Middle East is too full of sophisticated weaponry—including chemical agents. We can't afford mistakes. We are incredibly strong for a small nation, but we *are* still a small nation. We cannot afford to alienate the whole world. We cannot afford to appear completely intransigent."

"They'll say you've sold out to the Arabs," Landau said.

"Of course they will. Saying that is their only recourse, because they can't survive as a political party if they admit the truth. It has to do with power, Isser. It's as simple as that."

Landau made a grunting sound and lit a cigarette.

"Some parties are finding themselves painted into a box. If they admit that Israel has to give up the occupied territories, they are acknowledging the erosion of the foundation on which their entire political agenda has been built."

"But the PLO is a terrorist organization."

He looked sharply at Landau. "You're too wise a man to believe that. There are terrorists there, yes. There are terrorists in Northern Ireland as well, both Catholic and Protestant, but not all Northern Irelanders are terrorists. To characterize the whole Palestinian community as terrorist is worse than simplistic—it is politically and morally wrong."

Isser Landau turned to face him. "But all parties agree that the way to lasting peace is through an open international congress, not through secret meetings. At least you could do that."

"Isser, you must know about the secret meetings that took place before Sadat and Begin made public overtures to each other. That's the way it's done. Each side must be assured of the areas the other considers negotiable and nonnegotiable, and that is more often done in secrecy than in public. Public pronouncements are for the purpose of assuring one's own side that one will not give away the whole store. But they are not to be taken seriously by the opponent. That's how politics works."

"You are a pessimist, Avram. You think we cannot hold ourselves together."

"No, I am here because I am pro-Israel and because I am an optimist. If power were more important to me than the State of Israel, or if I were a pessimist, I would have stayed home and rattled the sword. We are now into the third generation of Palestinians who have risen against their situation. They will not go away, no matter how much we wish it. They increase faster than we do. It is not a choice between good and bad; it is a choice between bad and worse. I am an optimist because I believe we can redeem this bad situation. The pessimists don't even see that."

Gershon felt more than saw Landau shrug. "So what good is it doing? Is it going the way you'd hoped?"

It was a rhetorical question. Things were not going particularly well. The Old Man alternated between two tactics: an unfocused dialogue that rambled on and covered nearly every conceivable issue, smothering his listeners in rhetoric, and a petulant taciturnity where every syllable dragged from him seemed a victory of verbosity.

"I don't know what the hell he's doing," Gershon said. "I don't know if he's come to deal or if this is some sort of evasive action."

"If he hasn't come to deal, why has he come at all?" Landau asked.

"I don't know."

The Old Man sat on the bed in his room, shoes off, feet up on the bed, his legs crossed in front of him, and reviewed again everything that had been said. He was a master of detail; no nuance, no lifted brow, escaped him.

One more day, he was thinking. One more day of this little game, and then we'll see what we've won. When one player holds nearly all the chips, when that one can deal from power and can even bring into play his powerful friends, then the other player must use what's left for him. Psychology. Balance. In another day, he figured, Gershon would begin screaming at him. *Have you come to deal or what?* And that was what he was waiting for, for Gershon to make the first move, for Gershon to admit that what they were here for was to make a deal. It was the only way he was going to get any kind of deal at all, and he had become convinced that the only way to survive was to deal. There were still those who clung to the dream so fiercely that they could see nothing else, but he'd moved beyond that. He had come to realize that it was possible to hold the dream and still accept the reality.

AGHIOS GIORGIOS ISLAND, THE MEDITERRANEAN

Kherman Shahabad arrived just before dark on a motor launch he'd hired out of Limassol. Kenneth Glover watched him walk up from the dock; the other men were inside, out of view as long as the launch was in the cove. Shahabad carried a tan canvas backpack slung over one shoulder.

"Cutting it short, weren't you?" Glover asked when Shahabad came within speaking distance.

Shahabad grunted a response and kept on walking, moving past Glover as if he weren't even there. Glover turned and followed him wordlessly. By the time they reached the building where the men were, the launch was out of sight beyond the eastern ridge of the cove.

"We leave at eleven thirty," Shahabad said before going inside, almost as if he were making the announcement, as if he thought that Glover didn't already know it.

"Yes."

"Everything's ready." Again, not even a question.

"Yes." Little shit, Glover thought.

Then, as if he had changed his mind, Shahabad turned away from the door and walked farther up the hill, toward the ridge beyond which the helicopter sat, hidden from view in a natural depression between three hillocks. Glover watched him go, not following. He was not going to play lapdog to that little fucker. If he wanted to make sure the helicopter was there and ready to go, let him. Glover had already been over it by daylight. He knew every inch of the craft. As the pilot it was not only his job, it was his life. Let the little fucker take a look if he wanted.

Glover shoved the door open and walked inside. The men were sitting on benches or on the floor and barely noticed when he came in. They were working their weapons over—

methodically breaking them down, checking them out, loading them. Glover knew what they were doing, and he joined them. When they had double-checked their own gear, they began on one another's, the comments circling the room: *How does it feel? Is that one working right? That grenade clip is loose.* It was the age-old way of soldiers, a way of getting the feel of combat again, of fine-tuning their minds for what lay ahead.

If Glover had thought of it, it might have crossed his mind that Shahabad was doing the same with the helicopter, that maybe, since he'd gotten it, he felt responsible for it. But Shahabad had escaped his conscious thought, as had everything else. Around the room the focus had turned to what lay ahead. Families were forgotten; the possibility of pain was disregarded; the hazard of death was ignored.

When the time came, Glover gave the signal. Their gear all ready, the men simply had to carry it up to the Sikorsky. Glover led the way under a cloudless sky and a crescent of moon so slim it was barely visible. Shahabad joined them from the shadows, having never come inside. What Glover had felt for him coming up the hill before was gone now, the task filling his mind.

They trudged up the hill in silence, sixteen men moving without speaking, and even though here there was no need for caution, their tread on the stony ground went nearly unheard. At Bir el Khadim, when they were trying, they would move over the ground like ghosts. It was one of the drills MacKinnon had stressed.

At the helicopter, Glover stood aside for the men to board, each stowing his gear. He caught Shahabad looking at the lighted digits of his watch and grinned into the night. On time, Shahabad, he thought. In a little more than two and a half hours they would be over the eastern Sinai: two o'clock in the morning, flying nap of the earth, too low for radar over unpopulated territory. Turning the dogleg southwest would take them to the LZ in just over an hour. That ought to give them a good three hours to walk the eight miles by first light. Enough time. Everything was going according to plan.

SINAI PENINSULA

MacKinnon had dozed fitfully; now he stared out at the glow of the headlamps on the road ahead.

They had checked the bindings on Weiss five kilometers before Suez and then thrown a blanket over him in case anyone got too close and too curious as they drove through the town. They left the blanket on afterward, figuring he could use the warmth, though Karoz wasn't all that solicitous.

As they neared Mitla Pass they didn't change drivers again. Karoz argued that beyond Nakhl there'd be no choice in the matter, so MacKinnon might as well rest now. The road wound below the high escarpments of the pass. Karoz drove in silence, his thoughts almost certainly on the Lion Brigade, on the Sinai Campaign, on the few who had fought to take and hold this place.

MacKinnon stared unseeing at the road and the nearly sheer walls of the pass. He wasn't crazy about driving the desert at night, but there was no option. If you want to keep your operation under wraps, you move at night. No choice. He was plotting once again in his mind the terrain at Bir el Khadim.

"I keep wondering who else," Karoz said abruptly.

"You may never know unless you can get him to talk," MacKinnon said, nodding his head toward the back of the Rover.

"I keep wondering about that, too, about how he's going to be handled. It's dicey, him being Shin Bet. Protective Security, my God."

"You planning to be there?"

Karoz shrugged.

"Despite what I told you," Karoz said, "I know that a reactionary group would probably not hesitate to kill an Israeli Prime Minister if they thought it was necessary."

"Does that surprise you?" MacKinnon asked. "Do you think you're different from other people?"

"Doesn't every nation think it's unique?"

"Maybe. But most of them aren't."

"But we are, as a matter of fact. We're incredibly small, a

speck on the globe when it comes to size. And yet we're a power, too. Militarily, look what we've done."

"You don't have to sell me, Meir."

Karoz hung his arm out the window, feeling the cool rush of air against it. "Even so, we spend our lives being unsure of our survival. Who else with a military like ours does that? Sometimes that makes our reactions slightly hysterical."

"As a matter of fact, you have a very good record of taking care of yourselves."

"Yes." Karoz nodded. "And that's why they would do this. If they firmly believed that Gershon or anyone else really threatened secure boundaries for Israel, they would not hesitate to kill him. And not just that, they would try to make the act look like the work of the PLO. And you know," he added almost proudly, "they'd carry it off."

"Not this time," MacKinnon said.

Karoz didn't respond.

MacKinnon turned to look at him for a long moment. "Should I ask you which side you're on?" he said finally.

"Whose do you think?"

MacKinnon let that lay for a while. A van with two sets of headlights, all on dim, passed in the opposite direction. There was very little traffic now, and they were making good time. He leaned his head out and gazed at the stars, Scorpius rising in the southeastern sky. "Tell me about Sophie," he said at last.

It took so long for Karoz to respond that MacKinnon might almost have thought he hadn't heard. "Not everyone's like you, MacKinnon," Karoz finally said.

"What is that supposed to mean?"

"A loner. Not interested in women."

"I had a wife once."

"Once? What happened to her?"

MacKinnon gazed at him. Nobody walked into my flat and put a bullet into her, he thought. "She left me," he said.

Karoz nodded, as if this confirmed what he'd already believed. "You told me, remember? 'Don't bring a woman into your life,' you said. 'Fuck all you want with the bar girls and whatnot, but don't make it permanent. One of you is bound to end up disappointed.' "

"When did I say that?"

"When else?"

"I was probably drunk."

"You weren't drunk."

"You didn't marry her because of that?" MacKinnon asked.

"It seemed like good advice at the time."

"You still lived with her. What's the difference?"

"Exactly," Karoz said.

"You should have married her. You should have gotten out of the business."

"You didn't do that."

"You should have," MacKinnon said.

Just over four hours after they left Cairo they reached Nakhl, a desert crossroads town with nothing to recommend it, especially at three o'clock in the morning. For the last fifty kilometers or so the road had been barely more than a track which disappeared now and then with the shifting sand. Here the desert was part sand, part rock and shale. MacKinnon knew, though he couldn't usually see them in the dark, that there would be occasional outcrops of larger rock. If any vegetation existed at all, it would be tough desert grass. Since Suez, the undulating landscape had become more and more inhospitable, the dry river wadis that crisscrossed the area more frequent. Occasionally they passed clusters of mud-brick walls at the side of the road, and behind them would be mud-brick houses, subsistence villages whose inhabitants managed to stay alive by running a few goats.

Three roads come into Nakhl, from the north, from the east, and the one from the west, from Suez. Driving south out of Nakhl there were two choices: one followed either the main bed of the al Arish wadi, which bent west and then south, or else a smaller one that almost exactly mirrored al Arish, going first southeast and then turning south. Bir el Khadim lay almost equidistant between the two, thirty miles or so as the crow flies from Nakhl.

MacKinnon chose the more easterly wadi, the smaller one. There were good reasons not to take it. A larger one would allow more maneuverability. They could more easily find firmer ground, and they would be able to drive faster. On the other hand, there was a mountain between al Arish and Bir el Khadim. It was well placed for taking a bearing, but there was no point in climbing over it or walking around it if they didn't have to. Despite its disadvantages, then, the smaller wadi had in its favor that they could save precious time by not having to walk so far, as long as they could avoid blundering into soft sand, or skidding through the unstable surface of a bed of flint, or breaking the surface of the occasional salt flats.

Once into the wadi, MacKinnon stopped the Rover, got out, and walked its width and a dozen meters down its length, getting the feel of it under his feet. Desert driving at night was always easier if one knew the ground surface. That surface translated itself through the tires and the steering wheel into the hands of the driver. It had been years since he had done it, but MacKinnon felt confident; it was like sailing a boat, he thought: once you knew how, you never forgot.

While MacKinnon tested the ground, Karoz walked around to the back of the Rover and took out a spray can of blue paint that he had brought from London. He sprayed the headlights with it, slowly changing their pale shine to an eerie blue glow.

At the sound of MacKinnon's steps returning to the Rover, he turned. "It's going to make it harder to see," Karoz said.

"It is," MacKinnon said, stepping back into the Rover. It was also going to make them harder to be seen.

He turned the key and started the engine. There was some solid ground out there. They would be going uphill, but from the north the incline was fairly gradual. On the good stretches they ought to be able to do thirty miles an hour. On the bad stretches they could probably go faster if they were walking. He hoped not to reach too many bad stretches.

As he drove now, he concentrated fully on the dim spill of

light ahead, watching for the purplish cast of softer sand, feeling through the steering wheel the changes in the crust beneath the wheels. Most of all he looked for the almost pink-white cast of the occasional salt flats, the most treacherous friend of desert driving. Friend because if the salt crust is solid, one can race across the surface as fast as the vehicle will go; treacherous because if one breaks through the crust, it's the end of the trip, with the vehicle mired helplessly up to its axle.

They didn't speak now, both concentrating on the way ahead. The surface was mostly firm, and they were making good time. MacKinnon took a quick glance at the stars, figuring the orientation. One hundred seventy degrees, he thought. The wadi meandered some, but it hung a relatively straight southerly line.

His ears picked up the strain of the engine, and his foot on the accelerator felt the tug. He angled slightly left to take the hill more easily, then angled back right when he came near the rock walls at the wadi's edge. The motor was well tuned, and he grinned to himself. No problem in taking a hill.

Suddenly the bottom fell out. There was nothing in the faint spill of light and MacKinnon braced himself, knowing what that must mean. The wadi dropped unexpectedly in an almost straight decline of soft sand. He headed the wheels directly at the bottom, or what he could see of the bottom, but the back wheels slid right and the front wheels, despite his best efforts, began skidding left. He turned the wheel, fighting it, steering into the slide, gained control again, and then slowly maneuvered the Rover back into a straight down position. This time he was able to hold it until they reached the bottom, where they slid hard to the left again before the wheels caught and he was able to pull it back to the straight. Karoz looked at him across the dark front seat. "God almighty," he said.

"Bloody fun when you make it," MacKinnon responded. "A broken neck if you don't."

But it had been a warning, and he took it. He slowed down, proceeding with more caution. As the time slid by, he became more and more aware of the Tih Plateau into which he drove, of the feel and the winds and the occasional scents of it. He knew, even in the dark, what it was like: walls of rock in various shapes, bare and stony wastelands, extensive sheets of gravel and flint. Even the Bedouins called it "the great and terrible wilderness."

On better occasions one might hope to see signs of other human beings in this formidable place, but this time that possibility became a grave concern. There was a good chance that somewhere around them Glover and his men were also making their way toward Bir el Khadim.

23

BIR EL KHADIM, THE SINAI

Dawn was a pale violet promise in the eastern sky behind them. Three hundred meters to the southwest and perhaps a hundred meters below the high ground on which they lay, a light burned in one of the buildings. MacKinnon wondered. Someone up all night? An early riser? A cook making breakfast? Someone afraid of the dark—keeping a light on all night to scare away . . . what?

Meir Karoz was within touching distance, but MacKinnon left him alone. The man was probably still sleeping; he could sleep through anything, MacKinnon had found. MacKinnon himself had been that way once, but no longer, not this time at least.

His gaze moved away, to the west, and again took in Leo, just to the left of the dark mass of the seven-hundred-and-fifty-meter Gebel Megmar. Back at Covington Station, of course, he'd be seeing Capricorn these days. He wondered how Phil was managing. He hadn't even said good-bye to Jesse, who'd been away at school. He'd left him a note, but knowing Jesse, that wouldn't have been enough. Funny what one thought of. Barbecued ribs, the best he'd ever eaten. Licking his fingers afterward. Laughing.

He touched the scrim netting that would shield them when daylight came, a trick so old he was almost unaware he did it, something to bring him back to where he was: lying up on high ground, waiting.

Karoz's contact had supplied the netting along with the guns. It would have been even better if he'd also supplied camouflage tabs, but beggars couldn't be choosers. When you put together an operation on the fly, you make do with what you have. Before, sometimes, he'd had to make do with a great deal less than this.

At least in this case he knew whom he was dealing with and how many there were. He knew as well as anyone could what they had been trained for and how they were planning to do it. He knew almost as a certainty that they'd be on the slopes of Gebel Megmar, five hundred meters away, almost directly west, on the other side of the plateau below, and probably at least fifty meters higher than his own position.

Though there had been no way to make sure how they would get there, MacKinnon was sure that Gebel Megmar was their lying-up place. They would have come in the night, as he and Karoz did, and they would spend today in reconnaissance. At dusk, their east-facing slope already in shadow behind them, they would begin the slow, cautious, downward move, as he had shown them. With the brown-and-gray hessian cloth camouflage tabs on their fatigues, they would be close to invisible. Anyone looking at the mountainside from the compound would see only the dark, shadowy face of Gebel Megmar, surrounded by the lighter sky of evening. They would be able to move with impunity until they were on the lower slopes, only three hundred meters away, well within range. After nightfall they would move in even closer, silently, cautiously, with the slow rolling gait he had taught them—no gravel crunching underfoot, no sounds at all to be heard by the sentries.

And he and Meir would be here to watch, to see if it was going to be tonight or tomorrow night. He had debated his own best placement as he pored over the maps, recalling the terrain of Bir el Khadim. There were advantages both ways, but in the end he chose what he assumed would be the opposite slope. In that way there'd be no accidental running into the strike force in the dark, and it would be a prime location for observing their movements. He and Meir could lie up here, could make last-minute adjustments, could move down closer to the men at nightfall. It made sense.

If they hadn't come last night, they would come tonight. This morning would be the time to determine if they were already there. The sun in their faces as it moved slowly across their hillside—picking out every shadow, every undulation of surface, every rock and bed of scree—that would be the time to find them. He might not have the advantage of camouflage tabs, but he did have the advantage that he wasn't moving anywhere, didn't have to get into position. All he had to do was watch.

Kherman Shahabad woke, saw the rose-colored band in the eastern sky, and closed his eyes again. He already had reservations for the Cairo Concorde where, on request, they would put silk sheets on the bed. Holding that thought in his mind, he fell back asleep.

Fifty meters to the south on the same hillside, Kenneth Glover watched the dawn arrive, first rose with desert dust, then golden orange as the sun climbed, and finally brilliant, piercing white, painting the rock and desert crust before them a hard, pale gray.

He was twenty-four hours away from a million dollars. Not the easiest twenty-four hours he could think of, but probably not the worst he had ever spent, either.

Less than ten meters from Glover, crouched behind his own scrim netting, Archie Lawrence watched the compound to the southeast. He had served with the Regiment in the Middle East before, and he was used to terrain like this— barren, deadlooking. Vast tracts of rock and gravel and hard-packed whitened earth. After duty in such places, England always seemed like a close green garden.

Beside Lawrence lay the dull metal tube of a rocket-propelled grenade launcher. The only former SAS trooper in the group, he had thought at first, with a dry, self-deprecating humor, that he'd been chosen as the token Brit. Even MacKinnon, under whom he'd gone through training all those years ago, had barely acknowledged his presence at Coacantico Base. He'd been surprised when he was tapped as one of the launcher operators. Not that he wasn't as good at it as any of the others—better, in fact, he thought—but the Yanks always cared for their own, and Christ knew MacKinnon had never shown him any favors.

Egyptian President Hussein Bakr had been up all night, writing and rewriting a statement he planned to read at the beginning of this day's session. He had not gone this far, brought off what might have seemed the impossible, just to have it dissolve in rhetoric and intransigence. Without blaming the Old Man, without appearing to take sides at all, it was imperative that he bring this meeting onto the track. It was expecting too much to think that such a meeting would ever take place again. If it failed this time, and so far it was beginning to look like a monstrous failure, there would be no hope at all.

He glanced back down at the text he'd written, scratched out a word, and substituted two others. His eyes could barely focus. More than anything, he'd like to be able to sleep, but there would be other nights for sleep, and it was now already light. Today, if things weren't turned around, they might as well go home and start fueling up the tanks.

It was almost nine in the morning when Meir Karoz saw the helicopters. MacKinnon had the glasses and was making a systematic sweep of the flanks of Gebel Megmar, just as he'd been doing for the last two hours. The sun behind him, he could use binoculars with impunity, another reason to be on this hillside instead of the other. Left to right, he covered a three-foot swath each time—a path the height of a man crouching. He'd found two men lying up; one was peering around a rock, the other had turned on his side and was relieving himself. He'd failed with that one—Kozlewski, it looked like. You can piss all night, he had told them, but in the daytime you hold it or else you'll have to piss in your own nest. Shit, the sun not up three hours and already the guy couldn't hold it.

Karoz spoke softly: "Ten o'clock, just to the left of the peak. Looks like two Commandos in front." MacKinnon moved the glasses, caught the peak in his line of sight, and moved them slowly left.

"Two Sea King Commandos in front, two Gazelles behind," he confirmed. "Coming out of Cairo, I'd say."

"The cavalry arrives?"

MacKinnon slowly lowered the glasses and looked at the specks the helicopters had become. "Maybe." He couldn't

hear them yet, and because they were behind the men on
the mountainside opposite, they wouldn't have seen them.
He put the glasses to his eyes again and returned to his
surveillance. The men across the way wouldn't hear the copters until they were almost on them, until they came beating
over the high ridge of Gebel Megmar. It was the way of the
world in war, especially this kind of fighting. Something
always goes wrong; like Weiss tied up back there in the
Rover, something always intrudes.

Expect the unexpected, John Hawk used to say. He'd seen
troopers make all the right moves only to discover that the
targets had pulled out three days before. He'd seen a subma-
rine slip into port with its own torpedo wedged into its con.
So maybe Kammer had finally gotten through, and the helicopters were taking the conferees out. Or maybe it was some
other bloody thing. At least he could make hay from it,
knowing ahead what the men on the hill opposite had yet to
learn. If the helicopters weren't a part of their plan, he could
hope for a reaction of some sort. Some of the men might
spook, scurrying for deeper cover; at least a few of them
would look. It would be the best time to catch them out.

The helicopters came over a ridge of Megmar, their rotors
beating a fierce rhythm. With his glasses, MacKinnon
scanned the hillside. Nothing stirred. He moved them down
to where he had seen Kozlewski. The man lay still as death
against the ground, his face turned away. If MacKinnon
hadn't seen him before, hadn't known where he was, there
was no way he could have discovered him now, the outline
of his body masked by the camouflage tabs, no movement at
all from him.

"Bloody good discipline," MacKinnon said softly.

Karoz, still watching the copters, said, "One would almost
think you were proud of them."

"One would almost," MacKinnon responded.

"Egyptian air force," Karoz said. "Will your boys realize
that?"

MacKinnon took the glasses from his eyes. The copters
were coming in from the southwest, still too far away to see
the insignia yet without binoculars. "They won't have

glasses," he said. "Glover will, but not the rest. They have all the firepower they could want, but he won't have trusted what they might see with binocs. When the copters come closer, maybe then they'll see . . ."

The two Commandos were holding back now, maintaining altitude and surveillance while the Gazelles came in to land. MacKinnon put the glasses on the lead copter, only two hundred yards away now and at almost the same height, as it moved in to land. He could see the pilot at the controls, the insignia on his helmet. "Egyptians, inside and out," he confirmed. Then he caught another face and he held his breath in astonishment. Blond hair and a suit. Bloody God, a suit even at Bir el Khadim?

He swung the glasses toward the second Gazelle, coming in close behind. Surely not. Surely not. But there he was, high forehead with that widow's peak, eyes peering eagerly from behind the glasses. Not in the copilot's seat at least, but there, in the jump seat just behind the pilot, leaning forward between the two seats as if he couldn't wait. There, for God's sake. *Fucking goddamn there!*

MacKinnon pulled the field glasses away from his eyes. "Howard Kammer's in the second Gazelle," he said as if he couldn't believe it still. Above the two that were landing, the Commandos hovered. Security, he thought. What the hell kind of security did they think they were buying for him?

"He's got guts," Karoz said.

"He's got no brains is what he's got." But he remembered his own words to Kammer: *You may be the only person in the Middle East who can get through* . . . The man did have guts.

"All it's going to take is one sniper shot. Whatever you have on the hill over there can get well within range."

MacKinnon nodded. The Gazelles, throwing up twin dust storms, were landing within sixty feet of each other. Above, the Commandos made cautious circles against the pale blue of the sky. They want to get them all, he was thinking, leave no trace. They'll wait. He tried to imagine what Glover was thinking now, how he'd do it now. Had the men seen what he and Meir had, that the planes were Egyptian? Would they hesitate at that? Would any of them begin to wonder?

Two men in uniform and two in suits had climbed down from the first helicopter, the two in suits moving immediately toward the second chopper, which was still settling to the ground. MacKinnon put his glasses up again. Kammer was the first off, his descent shielded by the two men from the first helicopter. He was immediately followed by two more men in suits, machine guns at the ready, and the four ringed him so that he was no longer visible even at this height, the men each a head taller than Kammer and holding him in a tight ring.

"Fucking bloody job that is," Karoz remarked.

"Keep your eye on them," MacKinnon said, turning his attention to the hillside opposite. Kozlewski had turned his head and was watching now. "What are you thinking, boy?" MacKinnon whispered softly. He found the rock behind which he had seen another, but saw nothing now. He ranged the hill with his glasses and picked up movement, finally, behind an outcrop of rock. He couldn't tell what was happening or even how many were there, only that there was activity where just minutes before there had been none. What are you going to do now, Glover, he wondered. Have our boys figured out what you've led them to?

Kenneth Glover sat behind a screen of scrim netting, rubbing the knuckles of his right hand against his teeth. They know, he thought. It's been compromised somehow. He forced himself to look at his watch and to relax. We've got all day, he told himself. Maybe it's just one of the participants coming in a little late. If it was something else, if they had been compromised somehow, Shahabad would surely have been warned. They had men as far inside as could possibly be, he knew that, though he had no idea who or where those men were. They'd had an open radio right up until they left the helicopter, but nothing had come through. It's something else entirely, he told himself, a little blip. From where he sat, cradling his knees against his chest, he couldn't see Shahabad. You little shit, he thought. I get out of this and I'll never deal with the likes of you again. He grinned to himself then, despite his churning stomach. As a matter of fact, he realized, I won't even have to.

"Launchers ready." He spoke into his throat mike. Three launchers, four helos—enough. If they move out, we take them. A direct on a helicopter is as good as a hit on a building. Better, in some ways.

Glover looked to his left and down the hill fifteen feet, where Seipke sat behind an outcrop of rock. Thomasson had joined him there, and Seipke had begun fitting the tube onto the launcher even before receiving the radioed message. Good man, Glover thought, think on your feet. The thought of MacKinnon flashed through his mind. A well-trained force; MacKinnon had done the job. "One more for the Gipper," Glover whispered, his throat mike not picking up the sound. "At least make the old boy proud of you—wherever he is."

As far back as he could manage in the shallow cave, Shahabad crouched as still as a stone, his eyes taking in the scene below, his mind working on what it must mean. Egyptian helicopters, men in business suits. Someone apparently being guarded. Who was it? Why hadn't he heard from the contact within Shin Bet after the first flutter of warning? He didn't like it, and he didn't like sitting on this hillside exposed to anyone who had the intelligence to look. It wasn't the way he usually operated, out in the open, in broad daylight like this. Too dangerous. He'd put that kind of thing away when he left Beirut. He wouldn't have come along at all if he hadn't had to make sure about Glover and the men. He didn't like this kind of job at all—too many fingers in the pot, too many chances for things to go wrong. If it hadn't been for the money, for the incredible price he was being paid, he would never have agreed to do it.

"They're taking mighty long in there," Karoz whispered. It was nearly forty minutes since the helicopters had landed. "Does Kammer like to hear himself talk?"

"Not that I noticed, but I hear the Old Man does."

"Get on with it," Karoz said softly. "Get your butts out of there."

MacKinnon's eyes held the hillside now, every rock and crevice had become familiar. There was movement to the left, and he followed it: a man, barely visible as it was, becoming invisible before his eyes—head, shoulders, trunk disappearing. Crawling behind scrim netting. Movement always meant something. Without taking his eyes from the hillside, without looking back at the helicopters, he knew what it must mean. The scrim netting there: one. The outcrop of rock to the right: two. And somewhere else: the third.

Above, the two Commandos hovered, their rotors beating the heat-laden air as it rose from the flat ground below. Without looking at them MacKinnon knew what they were doing, and he wondered what, if anything, they had spotted. He had few options now—an unexpected turn of events for him as well. There was no way to communicate with the compound below or the men on the opposite hill without drawing fire from somewhere. He turned that over in his mind.

"There's movement," Karoz whispered, and now MacKinnon heard the distinctive, accelerating *thwack* of rotors starting up.

MacKinnon shifted his gaze. At first there was nothing from the compound, and then, as if in concert, two tightly formed groups of half a dozen men each appeared at exactly the same moment from two of the buildings. Without any pause at all, they half-ran to the two helicopters.

With his left hand MacKinnon touched Karoz's arm and then pointed to the hill opposite. "That outcropping of rock, two-thirds of the way down from the peak at about four o'clock: one launcher is there." He moved his hand left. "Twenty meters to the left and seven meters higher on the hillside is another, masked by scrim. There'll be a third. I don't know where, but watch for it." He lifted the drape of the netting and slipped outside.

"They won't fire at you," Karoz said.

MacKinnon flashed him a grin. "We'll see how well trained they are."

He moved slowly away, trying not to draw attention to the place where he'd left Karoz. When he was fifteen meters away, he began picking up speed, running down the side of the ridge toward the flatter ground below and, beyond it, the rise of Gebel Megmar.

To his left, at the compound, the men were nearly all into the copters, and the first one was starting its lift-off. From the opposite hill, nothing happened. He looked toward it, then tried a shout. Still nothing. He pressed the trigger of his Uzi for a single burst. Again, nothing. "Who ever trained you bleeding snake-eaters?" he shouted across at the hillside. But there was no immediate response from there.

One of the two Commandos that had been hovering overhead moved in closer for a better look and a clearer aim.

Karoz kept his eyes on the hillside, MacKinnon only a movement in his peripheral vision. The outcrop of rock: nothing. The other place—what had MacKinnon seen there anyway? Also nothing. And one more. Where?

He heard MacKinnon's shout, and there was no movement from across the way. He heard the blast of the Uzi, and still nothing. And then MacKinnon's words floated up to him, and despite himself, he smiled.

Gordon Seipke wedged himself against the rock, one knee on the ground in the classic firing position. He hadn't taken his eyes from the helicopters since they had landed except when he was assembling the launcher. Glover's voice came over the receiver in his ear. "Seipke, number one Gazelle is yours. Let's see how good you really are." He shouldered the launcher now, sighting down its tube, his eyes holding the rotor assembly of the first Gazelle. A hit on the rotor would knock the thing out of the sky. Maybe the pilot would be good enough to bring it down anyway, though with a direct hit it was hard to imagine how. On the other hand, a hit in the cabin would explode everything inside to kingdom come. He adjusted his aim downward; then, accounting for trajectory at three hundred meters, adjusted it back up again. No wind, no drift to account for. He was ready.

He heard the shout and thought it came from his own hillside; then, on second thought, that it came from the copters below. When he heard the burst of fire, he realized that it came from the opposite side of the tableland. "Who the hell—" he started to ask. Then he heard the voice, and for a moment he thought he was back at Coacantico, but still he didn't move.

Behind him, Thomasson was crouched beside the store of grenades. "If I didn't know better," Thomasson whispered, "I would have thought it was the Bastard."

"Okay, Lawrence," Glover's voice came through. "Any little shit can hit a building. Let's see what you can do with a moving target. The first Commando that comes this way is yours." Glover's voice was quiet and firm. They think they're getting out of this, Archie Lawrence thought. They don't even know we're here.

All war is deception. Lawrence knew the truth of that. A. C. MacKinnon had drilled that into their heads at Hereford nearly fifteen years ago, and he hadn't been on an operation where deception wasn't a deciding factor. The scrim netting now was a constant reminder. He could see everything—the compound, the helicopters, the broad sweep of the tableland, the ridge on the other side—but no one in any of those places could see him. Deception. A quiet hillside, the middle slopes of a mountain named Megmar, barren, treeless. Deadly.

At first he saw just the movement, someone running down the ridge opposite, too far away at four hundred meters for the naked eye to tell for sure who it was, except that the man carried what looked at this distance like a weapon. Instinctively Lawrence's hand reached for the launcher.

The man shouted something, but it echoed across the way and bounced from the surrounding stones and rock in a way that made the words unintelligible. Then, still running forward, he let out a burst of fire. "Bloody fool," Lawrence said, and almost as the words came out, there was a faint awareness. Something. Something about the man.

The man was still running forward and he shouted again, and this time Archie Lawrence caught the words: "*Who ever trained you bleeding snake-eaters?*" Archie Lawrence's eyes were as big as pies, and the awareness was no longer faint. Hereford. The forty-kilometer-killer, as they used to call it, weighed down by full gear and forced to run part of the way. And that's what MacKinnon used to shout at those who thought they couldn't make it, who had given up. Taunting them. Daring them to prove him wrong.

Lawrence shook his head. MacKinnon shouldn't be here now, shouldn't be running across that flat, unprotected three hundred meters of space, running toward the men he had trained, running toward them shouting and shooting so that the lead Commando was bearing down on him now, was already sending out machine-gun fire, bearing down, searching for the range. And behind everything was the sound of Glover's voice from the radio: "*Fire! Fire!*"

And then Lawrence saw the helicopter as if for the first time, and the realization of what he was seeing turned him cold. Arabic writing, and he'd thought Libyan. But the insignia on the side was a three-striped rectangle: red, white, and black. Not green. *Not green.* What the hell was that, red, white, and black? Whatever it was, he knew what it wasn't: not green, not Libyan. He realized now that he'd known that all along. Deception. *Goddamn it*, he thought, standing, shoving the scrim netting aside, *deception*.

Below and in front of him MacKinnon was running faster now, and Lawrence could see a dark splotch on the arm of his uniform and he knew what it was. There was only one way that any of this made any sense. He shouldered the launcher, not even listening to Glover's voice with a new command. He sighted on the copter, hearing the sharp sounds of stones and crusty earth grind underfoot as someone rushed toward him. Take your time, take your time, he thought, the sound of the voice in his mind not his own but MacKinnon's, who'd drilled that into him and every other trooper he had ever trained. The footsteps almost to him now, he pressed gently against the trigger mechanism and before he even knew if the grenade had found its target he was hit from behind, knocked down, and as he was falling he heard the explosion and at first he thought it was himself hitting rock, but when he looked the Commando was shattering before his eyes. And MacKinnon was still running toward him, a second dark splotch blossoming on his pant leg.

Meir Karoz ran down the side of the ridge, a good hundred meters behind MacKinnon, the debris of the helicopter falling in front of him. His Uzi was on his hip, and he sprayed over MacKinnon's head toward the hillside opposite as he ran. He'd never expect to kill anyone that way, especially at this range, but he might at least buy MacKinnon some time, some space in which to find safety.

Gordon Seipke peered over the edge of the rock, watching in awful transfixion. The man running toward them; the Commando bearing down; the sudden movement of Archie Lawrence, fifteen meters away, coming out from hiding, raising the launcher to his shoulder and aiming it at the wrong target, not at the man running toward them, the man Seipke now recognized; Glover running down the edge of the hill, his feet sending avalanches of stones with each step, the end of their concealment, knocking Lawrence down with one fierce blow; the almost simultaneous flash at the end of the launcher's tube. And then Seipke registered the insignia on the side of the Commando just before it exploded. Still, none of it made any sense until Glover cradled his Kalashnikov, and then suddenly he knew who the enemy really was. But by then it was too late for him—the launcher in his hands. To destroy Glover would wipe out Lawrence as well. And then the sound burst from beside him, Thomasson cutting Glover down where he stood with the awesome stopping power of a Kalashnikov AK47.

The second Commando dove in, laying a swath of firepower before it was even close to the target. Then, as if yanked by a

string, it wheeled right and tore off in the direction from
which it had come.

MacKinnon, on the ground with his leg hurting like hell,
watched it go, gaining on the two Gazelles as it went, heading south, away from the ground forces, leaving them to
fight it out between themselves. I owe you one, Kammer,
MacKinnon thought, and then his eyes turned toward the
hillside and the intermittent sounds of small-arms fire.

Not all the men had seen the insignia on the Commandos,
and not all who had seen it had registered its meaning.
There was shouting across the hillside and talking into the
throat mikes they all wore, a confusion of static and voices
that served more to confound than to illuminate. The
targets gone now, mostly it was yelling.

With Glover down, Archie Lawrence threw his launcher
to the ground and careened down the hillside toward Mac-
Kinnon, half-sliding on the scree beneath his feet. He didn't
know the man who was running toward them from the
other side, but it was clear he'd been with the Bastard.

MacKinnon grinned at him as he approached. "You the
one who took that copter out?" he called.

"I did."

"Good shooting, and thanks. But they were the good
guys. Where's Glover?"

Lawrence pointed.

"You didn't do that as well?"

Lawrence shook his head. "Thomasson. We were closest
to the action; I guess we saw first what it was."

"That was you behind the scrim."

Lawrence didn't respond because it wasn't a question.
MacKinnon always knew, it seemed.

"Who were they really?" Lawrence asked.

"People you probably wouldn't have wanted to kill."

"How did they fool you?"

"Same way they did you. We wanted to believe it, didn't
we? One more time, a big pile of money, get rid of somebody we all had reason to despise."

"What were they going to do with us after?" Lawrence asked.

"Help me up."

Karoz, who was standing beside MacKinnon by now, bent to give him a hand.

"What were they going to do with us?" Lawrence repeated.

Karoz stared at him, thinking how young Lawrence looked, though he couldn't have been too much younger than Karoz himself. "What do you think?" Karoz asked.

"They let you go," Lawrence said to MacKinnon, ignoring Karoz.

"They tried for me twice," MacKinnon said softly.

"Who? Not Glover."

"The other. Shahabad."

Lawrence automatically turned back toward the hillside, and his eyes caught Thomasson at the entrance to the shallow cave. "He's gone!" Thomasson yelled down to them.

"Shahabad?" MacKinnon asked.

"He's cut out," Lawrence said, "running scared, I'd say. We'd have drawn and quartered him if he'd stayed."

"A man like that cuts his losses," Karoz said. "He'll live to fight another day."

MacKinnon's eyes ranged the hillside now, seeing the men come together in threes and fours. "It's not over till it's over," he said. "He still has us at his back. We know who he is. He can't let it go at that."

"How could he kill us all?" Lawrence asked.

"Lots of ways," MacKinnon said, thinking of one.

And Annie, too, he thought.

24

BIR EL KHADIM, THE SINAI

The scene played before Kherman Shahabad like the out-door cinemas he used to sneak into as a child. Paint-chipped wooden chairs on hard-packed earth, scratched and spotted images projected on a white-washed concrete wall, sound tracks dissolving into static, worn-out film breaking in mid-scene. In the dark, when the movie had started, he would climb over the wall or sneak in from the front when the ticket taker was engrossed in the action. Mostly they were Egyptian or Turkish or Indian films, the Turkish and Indian ones subtitled in Arabic. Determined heroes cut wide swaths through masses of enemies, enticing women beckoned men to enchantments more insinuated than shown, black-hearted scoundrels led the hero into unimaginable dangers. The hero always prevailed.

He had watched MacKinnon running forward and he'd brought his Skorpion to his shoulder, waiting for MacKin-non to come within range. The first hit had been his: Mac-Kinnon's left arm, not six inches from the heart—a good hit considering that MacKinnon was running on ragged ground, but it wasn't good enough. He had heard Glover's command then, on the radio transceiver he carried, and he'd waited with a sense of irony: MacKinnon's own men killing him. But the shot had gone wide or, more likely, had been meant for the Commando in the first place. He had caught MacKinnon once again in his sights, this time wait-ing more patiently for a killing shot. Then suddenly the second Commando had roared down, passing right in front of the cave entrance where he stood. He'd seen the look of surprise on the gunner's face and the barrel of the machine gun swinging toward him. He had ducked back behind rock, the scene lost to view, and then he'd heard the staccato beat of the gun from the Commando. Moments afterward the sound dimmed, and then the explosion came.

When he crept forward, everything had changed. Glover was sprawled facedown, and a couple of the men were racing to MacKinnon who also had fallen midway between the ridge and the mountain. The rest of the men looked stunned, still wondering what had gone wrong. Shahabad didn't wonder; he knew. He slipped out of the cave and climbed upward while the others were moving down. In the distance the Gazelles were beating away with the single remaining Commando catching up behind.

From experience, Shahabad knew that a person could count himself lucky if half of the situations as complicated as this worked as planned. No one could imagine, much less account for, all the variables, and that was why men like himself took a considerable portion of their pay up front. Failure is an orphan, someone had told him once, and that was the first and last time he'd been left holding an empty bag. No one paid for a dead horse. He had delivered the weapons to the men and the men to the site, and in addition he'd prepared for their final disposition; but if the whole thing had gone wrong, that wasn't his responsibility, that was Glover's. Glover, who was lying dead or dying in his own blood, shot down by his own men.

Wait until Raymond Morse heard that. It had been MacKinnon that Morse had worried about. He should have been thinking about Glover. He should have been thinking about the logistics of the whole deal, of what might happen if the men discovered what it really was. If he was going to worry about MacKinnon at all, he should have worried that the man might turn out to be smarter than they had counted on.

Shahabad had reached a ridge, which fell away to the southwest. Flattening himself so he wouldn't be outlined against the sky, he turned and surveyed the scene. Two men had climbed up to the cave where he had been and found him gone. They began scanning the hillside for him but were guessing he had gone northwest. Slowly he slid himself downward, the crest of the ridge now between him and his pursuers. Let them go to hell, he thought, and grinned to himself because he had already provided the means to accomplish that. Those men were nothing to him one way or the other. Even if he stayed around to make sure they were finished off, he wouldn't get the rest of his money now; with the primary targets safe, the principals would consider the operation a failure.

It wasn't his fault, he told himself; he had done all he'd contracted to do. He ran diagonally across a bed of scree, lost his footing, and slid. He picked himself up and kept on running, putting as much distance as possible between himself and what was happening on the other side of the ridge. He wondered if they would come after him. He wondered if they even cared about him now that it was all over and in a shambles anyway.

He found a rock crevice and wedged himself inside to catch his breath. There was no sign of pursuit. It looked as if they didn't give a damn about him. Or he about them.

Except that wasn't quite true. None of it was quite true. It had gone wrong because of MacKinnon. He probably could hide that from the principals, but he still knew it to be the truth. It had gone wrong because of MacKinnon, and MacKinnon had been his responsibility. It was not a matter of money anymore, because whatever he did would not bring the targets together again at Bir el Khadim for a second chance. It was something more basic than money. It was pride.

Four miles to the southwest, in a smaller wadi that branched off from Wadi al Arish, was the all-terrain vehicle that had been left for him. His own contact would have brought it, someone completely separate from this operation, and therefore the vehicle almost certainly was safe, though he never completely trusted anyone. He had arranged for his own transportation because a return trip in the Sikorsky had always been out of the question.

He scanned the ridge once more and then decided to wait where he was until dark. Even though he couldn't see them outlined at the ridge, they could still be up there, watching for him to come out of hiding. He had all the time in the world and only one more target to reach. And he knew, even if all else failed, who could lead him to MacKinnon.

MacKinnon was on the ground again, and one of the men—Holden, a former Ranger—was packing his leg. A bullet had torn through the flesh and just nicked the bone. There was an appreciable amount of blood but, considering the possibilities, not much damage. He had asked Lawrence if by chance he was a medic—a one-in-four chance for a former trooper—but Lawrence had shook his head and trotted off. He came back with Holden, who didn't have any equipment but seemed to know what he was doing. MacKinnon wondered if any of the men had noticed beforehand that there were no medical supplies and if they'd registered what that should mean. He tried another one on Lawrence: "Were you explosives by any chance?"

"No, sir, sorry. I was signals."

MacKinnon winced as Holden bound the wound. They had taken Glover's shirt and torn it into strips, figuring he'd have no further use for it. One other, Ruiz, had been hit by fire from the Commando, his femur shattered. Now there was the problem of getting them all back. "What about you?" MacKinnon asked Karoz.

"Not likely. Nor is it likely anyway that we've got a pilot. Or is that another of your hidden skills?" Karoz asked.

"Unfortunately not." MacKinnon waved him away. "See what you can find."

Lawrence looked from one to the other and then trotted after Karoz.

Holden rocked back on his heels and admired his handiwork. Then his eyes moved to MacKinnon's, his freckled face crinkling into folds as he squinted against the sun. "You think they meant to kill us all."

"You heard me say who was really in that compound?" MacKinnon asked. "What do you think?"

"How would they have done it?"

"How would you do it, Holden?"

Holden moved from a crouch to sitting position, his legs flexed, his arms folded over his knees. "They wouldn't want the bodies found," he mused. "They wouldn't want the attackers identified. They probably meant it to look as if we were Arabs, the guns we had and all."

"Indeed," MacKinnon said.

"So they'd have to get us out of here. The copter, of course."

MacKinnon said nothing.

"They could take us back to the staging area. An isolated island. They could have shot us all there, but you seem to think it's a bomb."

MacKinnon turned to him. "I think a bomb is not out of the question."

"Rigged, then, to go off over the sea," Holden went on. "Are there sharks in the Med? We'd drown or get eaten? No, they couldn't count on that, could they? It would have to be something else—get us out of here but not back safely. A bomb set to go off when we were landing, then. Wired to the altimeter so that we'd have to hit altitude and come back down before it'd go off." He stopped, as if he were picturing that.

"Could have been something like that."

"Would have had to be a really low altitude because we flew nap of the earth over the coast to come in under radar."

"Or a timer of some sort," MacKinnon suggested.

Holden nodded. "A timer then, set to click in after we reached altitude, and when the time was up, to click in for a landing. Pretty complicated—" He stopped, realizing finally. "Glover, too, wouldn't it have been?"

"It's the thing you fear, isn't it?" MacKinnon said. "An ambush, but you never expect your own commanding officers, do you?"

"But he would have gone with us."

"Indeed. I don't imagine he was expecting that."

"Who would have done it then? That guy, that Shahabad?"

"Did he have the chance?" MacKinnon asked.

Holden leaned his forehead on his arms, thinking. "I don't remember," he said finally. Then he turned back to

MacKinnon. "Did Archie Lawrence tell you what Glover's last command was?"

MacKinnon shook his head.

"It was, 'Don't shoot, Lawrence. Hold your fire.' "

MacKinnon looked away.

"Lawrence was supposed to fire on the Commando that was coming after you. Then Glover told him not to. I heard him over my radio."

"Indeed," MacKinnon said. Lawrence had thought he was the token Brit. Not that simple, MacKinnon thought. Out of courtesy, Glover would have had to ask for names of good men, and it would have looked strange if there weren't any Brits at all. But Glover wouldn't have wanted a force full of troopers. They don't teach you to think for yourself in the other services; even Mossad trained its men to follow orders without question, no matter what. Lawrence thought it was because he was the closest, but it wasn't that simple. No bloody thing was that simple.

"How far to the plane?" MacKinnon asked at last.

"A good eight miles, I'd say. D'you think they can disarm it?"

Twice as far as to the Rover. Someone had better get back to the Rover and see how Weiss was doing. It was just about noon, and the sweat was running down MacKinnon's back. In another hour their shirts would be soaked, even sitting still. But someone was going to have to get word back.

"Do you think they can disarm it?" Holden asked again.

Karoz and Lawrence were walking toward them with two others. "What do you think of Shahabad, Holden?" MacKinnon asked.

Holden looked at him quizzically. He had asked the question twice and still MacKinnon hadn't answered it. "I don't know. He never said two words."

"Would you ride in anything he'd had his hands on? Even if you did disarm the bomb you found?"

Holden let out a long breath. "I guess maybe I wouldn't."

"I bloody well know I wouldn't," MacKinnon said. "There are more ways to bugger a helo than planting a bomb. Whether they find one there or not isn't going to mean shit. I can throw the man farther than I'd trust him."

They watched the men approach. "I found two for the bomb squad," Karoz called when he was ten meters away. "I'll take Lawrence, too, since he's signals."

"Go pick up the Rover on your way," MacKinnon said. "Check out your Weiss, see if he's still breathing."

Karoz nodded.

"Don't try to make the copter workable. If Shahabad's been at it, you'll be lucky to make the radio work without killing yourselves. Get us some transport we can trust."

The men started away, but MacKinnon's voice stopped them.

"Lawrence, how's your Close Quarter Battle?"

"I took a first in training, sir, and I've kept it up. I was at Prince's Gate."

"Good," MacKinnon replied. "Karoz, get in touch with our friend Kammer. Give him my regards first."

"I thought I would."

"And tell him that I think it would be a good idea if somebody gave me some sort of recognition for the service I've rendered."

"I understand."

"Good. Then you and he can work it out."

Karoz started to walk away but stopped at MacKinnon's voice. "One more thing, Meir. Tell him to keep the security on our contact."

Karoz nodded.

MacKinnon watched him walk away, wishing he could walk away, too, wishing it were over. Then he turned. He would not think of that. Yet.

NICOSIA, CYPRUS

Originally he had planned to drive all the way to Cairo, but as things turned out, he changed his plans. The most important element always: Never lock yourself into a plan. Glover should have known that. Glover shouldn't have let himself get shafted by some stupidity like that. If it hadn't messed everything up, he would almost have thought it was what

Glover deserved, but the way it was, it ruined more than just Glover. He had thought from the start that the man was a stupidity. Too much ego, too sure that he was right, typical military mind as far as that was concerned. Glover hadn't been his idea; he'd been Morse's. If Morse had been smart, he would have hired someone less like Glover and more like MacKinnon.

Because Cairo was out of the question, he drove south to Ofira, where he talked his way onto a plane bound for Tabuk. That one was full of oil field workers who had been on holiday, scuba diving at Sharm el Sheikh. They were a motley crew from half the countries of Europe and the Middle East, even some Americans. No one particularly noticed one more passenger. From Tabuk he found an air freight plane to Amman, and from Amman he took a regularly scheduled flight to Nicosia, arriving in the early morning hours.

The Nicosia Olympus wasn't as good as the Cairo Concorde would have been, but it was good enough for the present. He showered and ate in his room, then showered again. When he woke the sun was already low in the west. He called room service and ordered a plate of fruit and a bowl of rice pudding. And *Al Ahram*. If there was going to be anything anywhere, it would be in *Al Ahram*. He showered and wrapped himself in a clean towel.

When the waiter came with the food, Shahabad gave him a hundred dollars to run out and buy a change of clothes, keep the tip. Then he settled down in a chair and tried a spoon of rice pudding. Not bad, perhaps a shade thin.

His eyes caught on a headline on the front page, and he slowly opened the paper fully, reading quickly as he did so. Nothing. Nothing. He kept on reading, a slow smile spreading across his face, his tense body, after all the hours of travel, even after the sleep, finally relaxing. Nothing to link him. Just an ambiguous story about an attempt on the lives of the American Secretary of State and President Bakr of Egypt. Unclear where. Unclear how. The American Secretary of State. He hadn't even known that one was there. But there was nothing about the others. Nothing about any kind of plot. Nothing at all about someone named Kherman Shahabad.

And then he reached the last paragraph. In honor of the bravery of the man who had foiled the assassination attempt, the President had invited him to Washington for a White House reception in his honor. In another day or two, Mr. A. C. MacKinnon would be flying back to Washington with Secretary of State Kammer.

Almost without thinking, Shahabad reached for a banana and leaned back in the chair, smiling. There was a seventy-five percent chance it was a trap—he had come to respect MacKinnon enough to expect that by now—but there were still ways he could do it.

25

CAIRO, EGYPT

A. C. MacKinnon walked back to the exit door of the commandeered El-Al plane. He glanced once more down the aisle toward the front, where all he could see was the back of Shimon Weiss's head. The man was no longer trussed like a porker going to market; he now wore handcuffs and legcuffs, and for further precaution, was tied into his seat. He'd had a meal and seemed little the worse for wear after having spent most of a day bound and gagged in the Rover. MacKinnon stepped out onto the platform of the rollaway ramp, and Meir Karoz followed.

"He won't talk," MacKinnon said in a low voice.

Karoz nodded.

"Whatever you're hoping to get out of him, he's not going to tell you who else is in. He'd rather die first."

"Granted," Karoz said. "But we'll hold him anyway. And we'll work him over if for no other reason than to make it look good and maybe to throw a scare into someone. Sooner or later somebody will ask a question. Someone will indicate an interest. It may be a very oblique interest, but it'll surface somehow."

"You hope," MacKinnon said.

"He had to get where he was with help. They would not have just waited around for a lucky break. Someone put him in Shin Bet and made sure of his rise there."

MacKinnon's eyebrows raised.

"The population of all of Israel is four-and-a-half-million, MacKinnon. It's a small country, after all, and everybody of importance lives or works either in Tel Aviv or Jerusalem. Half the jobs, especially the high government ones, are gotten by *protekzia*, by connections, or the help of an influential protector—a horse. How did Weiss get where he was?

Who is his horse? That's what we'll be looking for. And quite likely someone will become very worried about what we're finding out."

"I wouldn't have thought you would publicize this," MacKinnon said.

"Of course we won't, but there will be ways of finding out, and when Weiss disappears, someone will be looking to see what happened. After all, they've invested considerable money in this."

"One has to hand it to your people," MacKinnon said. "You manage to keep a great many of your secrets hidden."

"We have no choice. Given our size and situation, we have to appear invulnerable. Everyone understands that, even the press."

"How soon will you be back in London?"

"Twenty-four hours."

"Good. I'm counting on you." They shook hands, and MacKinnon walked down the steps to the tarmac.

WASHINGTON, D. C.

He had never been to Washington before. New York, yes. Once he had delivered a Czech-made Skorpion fitted with silencer and night scope to a man who talked like an American but acted and dressed like a German. He hadn't known what it was about, but the thirty thousand dollars was deposited in his Zurich account within twenty-four hours. And of course he'd been to California.

The 747 came down through soup at Dulles, first mist and then full-fledged rain hitting the side windows. Even at ground level visibility was less than fifty feet, fog dimming the runway lights, the airport buildings glowing ghostly before them. They were lucky to be able to land at all.

He stood in the shortest customs line. In other situations he might have chosen the longest line: a harried agent was always more careless. But this time his documents were impeccable, and he was bringing in nothing of import. The time to worry was not now; the time to worry was when he set it up. And did it.

Bo Sullivan and Gordon Seipke sat in the windowless

room staring in silence at the monitors, one and then another and then another, their eyes moving slowly back and forth across the range of displays.

"Him," Sullivan said.

Seipke turned and looked toward the monitor that Sullivan was pointing at. He frowned, stood, stepped closer. "Might be," he said.

"It is." Sullivan joined him before the monitor. "He's a cool bastard, isn't he?"

"Well?" asked the third man in the room.

Seipke narrowed his eyes and watched the man on the monitor. The customs agent, his back to the hidden camera, was opening the man's briefcase. The man looked up, his eyes sweeping the hall, then looked down again. "Yeah," Seipke said, "it's him."

The third man in the room stepped to the monitor and pressed a button beneath the screen. Sullivan could see a light come on below the counter, where the customs agent could see it but out of the view of the man on the other side of the counter. Sullivan watched the customs man's back for a reaction but saw nothing. "He didn't see it," he said.

"He saw it," the third man said.

"He's not doing anything," Sullivan said. On the screen the customs agent snapped the briefcase closed and shoved it across the counter to its owner. Then he took the man's passport, opened it to the proper page, and stamped an entry stamp on it. "He didn't see it," Sullivan repeated.

"Shit," Seipke said. "MacKinnon was right on the button. Came into Dulles cool as a cucumber. I would've thought he'd have driven in from Canada."

"What difference does it make?" Sullivan asked. "The way this city is blanketed, they would've fingered him anyway, eventually."

The man under discussion had walked out of the monitor's range now, and Seipke was talking into a hand-held radio. A second customs agent had come into view on the monitor, and he touched the first lightly on the back. The first agent turned and walked away. One minute later he came into the windowless room. "Gary Brouillard, textile manufacturer, of Brussels, Belgium," he said as he entered.

The man who had pressed the button under the monitor turned to Sullivan. "You're sure it's him?"

"I'm sure," Sullivan said. "He stole my watch when he thought I wasn't looking. He's one sneaky bastard. He thought I didn't know who took it. He stayed in the background and thought nobody would ever notice him, but I noticed. I watched him, the son of a bitch."

"Okay, then," the man said. "Is there anything else we need to be doing?"

"I guess not," Seipke said. "We've passed him off; he's not ours to worry about anymore."

"You ever get your watch back?" the customs officer asked.

"No," Sullivan said. "But I'll tell you this: if anybody can match that guy, it's you. That was one smooth play."

The customs officer grinned. "That's what I'm paid for."

"And not enough by far, I'll bet," Sullivan said.

"True."

Sullivan and Seipke walked out of the room, leaving the other two inside. "Works pretty smooth when you have the Secretary of State greasing the wheels, doesn't it?" Seipke said.

Sullivan grinned. "I wonder what the little bastard'll say when he finds that out."

He took a taxi into the city, asking the driver for the name of a hotel near the White House and near a Metro line as well. The cab driver delivered him to the Sheraton-Carlton, less than half a mile from the White House and only two blocks from a Metro station. He walked in the rain up 15th Street to Pennsylvania Avenue and then along the high black iron fence, wondering where they were putting MacKinnon up. Not here for sure; it wasn't going to be that big an honor. Probably in some hotel somewhere. His hair soaked, he hunched himself down further into his jacket and turned back. First thing in the morning he'd call the White House and get the President's schedule for the day. He hoped it was going to be soon.

He walked a block north to H Street and then turned east, hurrying the two blocks to the bus station. The mist had turned to rain again, and he didn't have an umbrella.

Inside the station he turned right. At the third public telephone he lifted the receiver with his right hand while feeling under the shelf beneath the phone with his left. Pulling away the tape, he withdrew the key that had been left there. Then he replaced the receiver and walked away from the phone.

He found the baggage locker that corresponded to the number engraved on the key and opened it. Inside was a briefcase similar to the one he had left back at the hotel, similar to the ones he always used. He pulled it out of the locker and turned, leaving the key in the lock.

He walked into the restroom and glanced around—it was empty. He stepped into a stall, latching the door behind him. Then he opened the briefcase. Inside was a Heckler & Koch MP5 and a Czech-made CZ-75. He left the MP5 in place and took out the CZ-75, a 9mm automatic pistol, black with a knurled plastic grip. He checked the gun over carefully, then loaded a magazine and racked one into the chamber. There were three more magazines for the gun in the briefcase, and he put those into his jacket pockets. He shoved the gun into his belt and walked out of the lavatory.

He walked swiftly back toward his hotel. The rain stopped when he was halfway there.

At the hotel he waited around until he was the only passenger going up in the elevator. He didn't like being enclosed in an elevator with strangers. There were certain precautions he took as a matter of course.

He never walked into a strange hotel room unprepared. He never allowed anyone at his back. In the future he would only work solo; the best assurance that a job would go right was to run it oneself from start to finish.

He'd left a piece of lint just at the top of the doorknob. If anyone had disturbed the knob, the lint would have fallen. It was still in place. He fit the key into the lock and opened the door. He had left the lights on, and he took a quick survey of the room. It was 11 P.M. in Washington, six in the morning Eastern Mediterranean time—he had a right to feel tired. He pulled down the bedspread and stood for a moment looking at the sheet. Then he turned toward the bathroom.

A. C. MacKinnon stood leaning against the doorjamb of the bathroom, his arms folded loosely across his chest. Shahabad didn't even think, didn't ask how MacKinnon had known or how he'd gotten in or anything else because the reaction was automatic. He pulled the gun from his belt and pointed it at MacKinnon's chest.

At the same moment Shahabad heard the click behind him and knew immediately what it was. He didn't turn around; his finger pressed against the trigger.

In the split second it took Shahabad to react, three bullets spit from Lawrence's gun and tore into the back of Shahabad's head. MacKinnon watched him fall, then stepped over and toed the weapon from Shahabad's limp hand. "I don't wonder that you took a first," MacKinnon said, "but I do question why they let you through. You're supposed to aim for the torso, not the head."

"Torso to disable, head to kill," Lawrence responded. "You didn't want me taking any chances, did you?"

"Bloody hell," MacKinnon said, looking down at the body. "I told Kammer we'd take him alive."

Lawrence's eyes widened. "You didn't tell me that."

MacKinnon looked at him. "Bloody hell. Didn't I?" Then he walked over to the phone and dialed a number. A woman's voice answered. "Mrs. Kammer, is your husband home?"

"No," she said. "He's out. It's Mr. MacKinnon, isn't it? May I take a message?"

"You may. Tell him he can have the package picked up any time he likes. I'm sorry, but it's a little more damaged than we'd counted on. On the other hand, it makes it so there's no hurry. And tell him good work, thanks, and good-bye. I'll be trying to make the midnight flight to London."

"I'm sure he thanks you as well, Mr. MacKinnon."

"Good-bye, then."

"Good-bye."

MacKinnon turned from the phone. "And now for the other end of the worm," he said to Lawrence.

LONDON, ENGLAND

MacKinnon dialed the number, and when the voice answered, he spoke: "Did you get the information?"

"Lowell Hotel, Suite B. The place has only two suites, both on the same floor. The other suite is unoccupied. I have the layout of the suite and the other stuff for you."

"Our friend has expensive tastes, doesn't he?"

"Who is he?"

"The money man. The real link, if there is one, between Weiss and Bir el Khadim."

"I want in on this one then."

"No, Meir. I'll give him to you on a platter, but you'd better let Lawrence and me take him."

"You didn't have such a low opinion of me when you needed my help at Bir el Khadim."

"You weren't emotionally involved then. You are now. You know what that means as well as I do."

"You'll have to come to me to get the stuff."

MacKinnon sighed. "How is it going?" he asked.

"I made it back for the funeral. It was yesterday. I'd never met her mother before, did I tell you that?"

"No, you didn't."

"She was awkward about us living together, so I never met her. I'd met her sister, though. She's the one who told me about the funeral."

"You know why you can't come along."

Silence.

"Meir. Please."

"Mark."

"Mark, then. Don't they teach you anything in that outfit of yours? You haven't forgotten about Operation Suzanne, have you? And what about your hit team's thirteenth kill?

Both went wrong because somebody thought he knew better than to follow procedure. Not this time. Not with me."

"Shimon Weiss is dead."

MacKinnon stood silently for a moment, digesting the news. "Repeat that," he said finally.

"You heard me. Weiss is dead. Poison. He took it himself. He was thoroughly searched, inside and out, and all his clothes exchanged for others before they locked him up. Someone had to have slipped it in for him to take. Even his food was prepared under observation."

"You people have a problem there."

"Don't I know. And what about your man?"

"Same. Dead. That one wouldn't have talked either."

"Yes. So now it's down to Morse, isn't it? That's part of the reason I'm going along. I could have done it before you even got here. You wouldn't even have the stuff if it weren't for me."

"But you didn't, which shows how smart you are. You may be trained in arms, Meir—Mark—but you probably don't have much experience in Close Quarter Battle. In that respect you're never going to measure up to the man I already have with me. We'll be by." MacKinnon hung up the phone.

"Does he have them?" Lawrence asked.

"He does, but he wants to come along."

"That's no good."

"I told him that, but we're going to have to tell him again in person before he'll give us the guns."

Lawrence shook his head. "Two Brits in London, and we have to get our arms from a bloody Israeli."

"Don't complain. Their airline smuggled them in for us, after all. I'll bet we couldn't get British Airways to do the same."

Meir Karoz dialed the number from a phone in the lobby, and out of the corner of his eye he could see the receptionist answering the phone. "This is Kenneth Glover," Karoz said. "I was to meet Mr. Raymond Morse ten minutes ago, but he hasn't appeared. He hasn't by any chance left a message for me, has he?"

He could see the receptionist flipping quickly through a message box. Then she looked at the board behind her. Then the response: "I'm sorry. I don't find any message for a Kenneth Glover. Would you like me to ring Mr. Morse's room?"

"Please. The fellow's probably overslept again. Late night again last night, I think," Karoz said, forcing a chuckle.

MacKinnon heard the phone ring six times before it was answered. His ear against the door, he heard the muffled sound of Morse's voice as the man answered the phone. *A call from Mr. Kenneth Glover*, they'd be telling him, but MacKinnon didn't wait to wonder what Morse would do then. He held the sound-suppressed Uzi submachine pistol against the lock and riddled the door with it.

At the same moment Archie Lawrence shot off the chain lock, and the door fell open. Morse was halfway to the briefcase in the corner, the towel he'd wrapped around himself already starting to fall away. There was a pale-haired girl in the bathroom doorway, nude, too terrified even to scream.

MacKinnon cut Morse down at the legs before he reached the briefcase, and the girl wheeled around, slamming the bathroom door closed. She had found her voice and was sobbing and screaming at the same time. MacKinnon thought of saying something to her through the door to let her know they weren't going to kill her, but he figured she was crying so loud she wouldn't hear anyway, so he just walked over and picked up the briefcase. Lawrence was standing over Morse, daring the man to make a move. Blood ran steadily from Morse's mangled legs. In the bathroom the girl was sobbing.

Karoz came running into the room and stopped when he saw Morse on the floor. "You didn't kill him?" he asked.

"Not this one," Lawrence said.

MacKinnon walked toward him, holding the briefcase. "He's all yours, but let the girl go."

Karoz stared at MacKinnon as if he hadn't heard him.

"You all right, Meir?" MacKinnon asked.

Karoz nodded.

"Let it go," MacKinnon said, taking him by the arm. "Let someone else extract what he knows. Get rid of him and get out of this business."

Karoz shook off MacKinnon's arm and, walking closer to Morse, gave him a perverse kick. To his credit Morse didn't scream, though it must have hurt like hell. MacKinnon watched a moment and then nodded at Lawrence.

They walked out of the room, propping the door closed behind them. The girl was still in the bathroom, sobbing. The other suite empty, there was no one on the floor to have noticed. They walked to the elevator and took it to the ground floor. By the time the elevator doors opened, MacKinnon had searched the briefcase. Sixteen thousand pounds and a safe deposit key. Raymond Morse was a methodical man. The bank would be a Swiss one, and MacKinnon figured it would be close by.

"How's he going to get that guy out of there?" Lawrence asked.

"The place is probably crawling with Mossad already," MacKinnon responded. "They're very good at that kind of thing."

He handed the briefcase to Lawrence. "If you can get the money out of the bank, split it among the troopers. Whatever is in there is probably less than they deserve. Keep what's in the case as a bonus for yourself. It's little enough."

"Got any suggestions about how I get it out?"

"Trooper style," MacKinnon said, smiling. "No flash, no dash, just inventiveness and guts. Sneak it out or brazen it out, whichever works."

Lawrence grinned.

"Buy yourself a shop with what's in the case. Find a girl and settle down."

Lawrence opened the briefcase and peered inside. "How about a stop for a bitter? I'm buying. I seem to remember that was your drink."

"*Was*," MacKinnon said. "I don't drink these days."

"One won't hurt anything. I think we deserve it."

MacKinnon opened his mouth to respond but then thought better of it and just nodded. "All right," he said, and they turned into the nearest pub, finding it dark after the daylight outside.

They stood together at the bar, and Lawrence ordered a bitter apiece. Just noon, MacKinnon thought, cradling the mug in his hands. There was a time when he'd have thought that was some kind of victory, not having a drink before noon. There was another time, longer ago, when he'd have thought that such a situation called for a double to catch up. He stared at the liquid now.

"They had to make it look right, didn't they," Lawrence said. "That's why we had all those East bloc weapons."

"And all of them with clear traces back to known terrorist suppliers, I'm sure."

"And the Uzis? From that Israeli settlement that got wiped out, do you think?"

MacKinnon nodded. "Clever move, that. A little frosting —as if terrorists were trying to make it look like Israelis did it."

"You think they'd wipe out a whole settlement for that?" Lawrence asked.

"Haven't you heard what they call people like that? Gypsies. Few loyalties and fewer scruples. Worse than real gypsies, probably. They carry out the job, whatever it is."

"Even killing their own?"

"They'd have hired that done, as they hired us."

Lawrence was silent for a while, thinking about that. MacKinnon looked around the place; it was mostly filled with barrister types.

"What will you do—go back to New Zealand?" Lawrence asked, wiping the back of his hand across his mouth.

"I don't know."

"It'll seem pretty tame after this, won't it?"

MacKinnon thought of the dogs bounding up the hills, of the smell of spring grass crushed underfoot. He thought of a little house where, when the windows were open and the wind was blowing right, you could smell the sea. A salt wind. "It's another kind of life entirely," he said.

"You sort of like it, though, don't you?" Lawrence had turned to him, and their eyes met in a brief moment of understanding.

Then MacKinnon shoved the mug away, still full, and stepped back from the bar. He took Lawrence's hand and shook it briefly and then, leaving the man to finish his drink, he walked back out into the sunshine.

LA JOLLA, CALIFORNIA

She opened the door and hesitated, her gray-green eyes growing wider. Then her face broke into a smile, and he realized suddenly that he had never seen her smile like that before. Maybe he had never seen her actually smile at all, except that cautious, reserved expression she'd used that had told him she was pleased, but afraid at the same time. There was no fear at all in this smile, and it made her face shine. All by itself, it was worth coming back for.

He hadn't known what he would say or do when he saw her again, but he needn't have worried. She did it for him. She reached her arms out and pulled him close. "I was afraid you—" The rest of her words were only muffled sounds against his chest.

His arms wrapped around her, and they stood for a long time like that, as if it was the first time either of them had held another close. He kissed her hair, and the scent of it rose to him.

Then she leaned her head back and scanned his face, looking at the bruises and murmuring words he didn't hear. He kissed her lips gently; then he kissed them harder.

Her hands were at the shoulders of his jacket, trying to pull it off, and he shoved the door closed behind them and, with her help, shrugged out of his jacket, his bandaged arm aching, but it didn't matter.

He held her face in his hands, trying to read her eyes, but there were tears in them now. She pulled him close again and hungrily kissed his lips, his chin, his neck.

Suddenly their hands were everywhere, touching, unbuttoning, caressing, with a desperate need to make up for all the time they had lost. She led him into the bedroom, or he led her, and as they went he drew the blouse from her shoulders and she unfastened his pants. She pulled him down on the bed with her, her hands roaming his body, her lips kissing and murmuring over the old and new scars. He lay back and closed his eyes, marveling at the way her touch made him feel, whispering her name over and over. And she was there for him.

Afterward, she made him tea, strong, the way he liked it. He sat at her table in his skivvies and watched as she worked. She wore only a robe, and as she moved he caught glimpses of her long slim legs and the cleft of her breasts. He wondered if she knew how to cook mutton, or if she'd be willing to learn.

He looked at the pattern of the tablecloth beneath his hands. "Do you think—after all these years—she'd want to see me?" he asked.

"Why don't you try her?" she responded.

He nodded, not looking up from the flowered tablecloth.

"She'd be a fool not to," she added after a while.

"My mother was a romantic," he said slowly, "and when she chose what she considered suitable names for her children, my father let her have her way. And so she named her first child after a Scots clan she'd read about in a book and after a river she'd never at that time even seen." He traced his forefinger along the edges of a tulip. "What she didn't know was that it was a failed clan she'd named him after, and a river that is more muck than water by the time it reaches the sea."

"Allardyce Clyde," she said softly.

His hand paused on the edge of the tulip, and then continued its trace. From the living room the clock ticked into the silence. Finally he spoke. "How long have you known?" After a moment he looked up at her.

"For a while," was all she said. And then her face broke into that wide smile that made him know again that it was right to have come back.